*This book is affectionately dedicated to*

**GWEN** *and* **ED RIGG**

*whose kind understanding and warm friendship*

*have gone far beyond the call of duty*

*of ordinary inlaws!*

## AUTHOR'S NOTE

*Some of the anti-submarine warfare techniques and equipment described in this work have been deliberately obscured. This has been done because the author has had access to certain confidential naval information imparted to him in his capacity of marine researcher and has no wish to betray such trust or embarrass his associates.*
*This in no way impairs the validity of the story, which in essence and spirit remains a potentially true one for as long as we live under the present circumstances.*

MARK R. RASCOVICH

# PART ONE

## THE WAR

# 1.

The loudspeaker outside the stateroom door squealed with a discordant facsimile of a bosun's pipe, a sound which was immediately followed by an incongruous hacking and wheezing. It alerted all hands of the U.S.S. *Tiburon Bay* to the fact that their second officer was trying to clear his infected sinuses before delivering an important message over the ship's PA system.

"Now hear this—now hear this! The smoking lamp is out—the smoking lamp is out." It was very like him to put this emphasis on a routine regulation before anything else. If he had to call out "Abandon ship!" he would precede it with "The smoking lamp is out!" The unhappy second officer was not only addicted to colds, but suffered from a phobia about fire, both qualities making him singularly unsuited for service aboard a fleet tanker on cold war duty in arctic waters. "The smoking lamp is out," his voice repeated. "Pumping crews, man your stations for refueling DDL 113 approaching our starboard side. Line handlers and riggers to wear immersion suits. Personnel scheduled for transfer report to highline station on forward main deck. That is all."

Lieutenant Commander Chester Porter listened with his bulky body braced against a sluggish roll of the ship, then zipped up the flap of his blue Valpack bag. "That means we've got less than twenty minutes," he said to Ben Munceford, who was lying in the top bunk of their steel cubicle. "Captain Finlander is awfully sensitive about the *Bedford's* record for the fastest refueling at sea of any destroyer in the navy."

Munceford was nursing a shot of bourbon in a soggy paper cup and continued to drag on a cigarette in spite of the second officer's insistent announcement; he showed very little concern over Porter's implied suggestion that he immediately prepare himself for the impending transfer to the *Bedford*. He had not even dressed and was lying there in a suit of thermal underwear which was unzipped to his navel, the toes of his naked feet playing with the electrical conduits which snaked across the ceiling above his bunk. Munceford had been napping away the forenoon to make up for a late session of cards in the PO mess during the previous night. "I'll wait till you're clear, Doc," he drawled. "No use getting in each other's way."

"I thought you wanted some pictures of this operation," Porter said as he squirmed into a heavy sweater.

Munceford glanced toward the gray opaque eye which was the single porthole of their cabin. "Not enough light out there."

"About as much as you'll get in these high latitudes. In November there's only six hours of daylight here—less when we get farther north."

"That's okay, Doc. I'm more of a reporter than a cameraman anyway. How about one for the road before we head into the great unknown?"

Porter finished pulling on a hooded windbreaker and eyed the bottle which Munceford had produced from under his pillow. "No, thanks, Ben," he answered with a stiff smile. "By the way, I should warn you that the *Bedford* is not run as informally as the *Tiburon Bay*. Even as a guest of the navy, you'll be expected to only drink liquor when it is prescribed by me against shock or snakebite."

Munceford was a rawboned southerner with an incredibly boyish face for his thirty-six years, and when he was piqued, it could take on a childishly petulant expression—as it now did for an instant. "I can take it or leave it," he said, scowling from the surgeon to the bottle.

"The *Bedford* is a go-go ship operated by a bunch of trade-school boys," Porter told him. "Captain Finlander is a cinch to make admiral on the next list."

"Okay, Doc. I'm not going to hold him back," Munceford exclaimed with a laugh. He swung his legs over the edge of the bunk, jumped down, flipped the clamps of the porthole, opened it and tossed the half-full bottle of bourbon into the sea. Then he turned and jokingly saluted the lieutenant commander. "Sir, I beg to report that the U.S.S. *Tiburon Bay* is now bone dry, according to regulations, and that all danger of contaminating the U.S.S. *Bedford* has been removed."

Porter's round red face rippled through a series of expressions of surprise, amusement and anger. "Jesus, Munceford! Don't you even know the rules about dumping floating garbage overboard?" he asked, half laughing, half snarling.

The injured childish look flashed back. "Are we at war, for Christ sakes, Doc?"

"Out here we play it that way. Especially when Finlander is in command."

"This Finlander must be some jonah! You've got me hating him already."

"Oh? I was hoping you'd be an objective sort of correspondent," the surgeon said acidly, then reacted to the sound of bells from deep in the ship's engine room. The vibration of the turning screws dropped to a lower register. "You'd better snap it up. We'll be transferred right after the mail and fresh milk." He picked up his Valpack, opened the door and squeezed himself into the passageway.

After the lieutenant commander had gone, Munceford was left with a frustrated and uneasy feeling. He was suddenly quite certain that he would not get along well with the *Bedford* and her captain, that this whole assignment was jinxed from its start. For a moment he toyed with the idea of aborting it and returning to port on the *Tiburon Bay* with a couple of hundred feet of film and tape describing life on a navy tanker. But, of course, that would put him in a bad light with the PRO he had badgered into accrediting him an official navy correspondent. And then there was Nancy's lawyer waiting for him on the stateside docks. Jinxed or not, he had to go on. With a shrug he opened up the porthole again to toss out his cigarette.

A waft of raw, damp air struck his face, ice cold compared to the stuffy warmth of the cabin. But he held the glass open and continued to peer out because something had caught his attention on the misty periphery of the lazy swells. There were wisps of sea smoke drifting off their undulating surfaces and, far out there, a low bank of fog lay like a translucent gray wall between the gray sea and gray sky. Out of that fog, Munceford suddenly noticed the shadow of a vessel's superstructure materializing like a ghost ship. For an awesome minute she appeared to be floating on air, her hull only slowly solidifying, hesitating to touch the sea. The tall foremast with its lacework of halyards and aerials remained for a long time the only part crisply etched against the diffused horizon, a rotating antenna of a search radar making a strange pulsating effect as it turned. Gradually the shadowy shape transformed itself into the classical lines of a destroyer slicing along at flank speed, plunging and rolling with a weird kind of slow motion as she thrust ahead, a pale grin of a bow wave curling from her stem. Crystals glinted with baleful winks out of the ice which sheathed her foredecks and turrets. But even as she merged into sharp focus, she retained a mysterious aura of mist which clung to her as if she had torn loose some shreds out of the fog and wrapped herself in them. On the curve of her bow, between the rise and fall of flying spume, the white number 113 became clearly visible— DDL 113, the U.S.S. *Bedford.*

Ben Munceford stared wide-eyed, shuddering from the cold which was stabbing at his bare chest, and from the sight of the *Bedford.* He suddenly crossed himself as if he were beholding some kind of evil specter. It was a peculiarly senseless thing to do and it made him angrily slam shut the porthole, turning the destroyer into a shapeless blur behind the film of moisture on the glass. Why had he crossed himself like that? He was neither superstitious nor Catholic. Why did the uneasy feeling which had been gnawing at his insides ever since leaving Portsmouth suddenly turn into outright foreboding? He, who prided himself on being a cheerfully cynical person, should not suffer such notions! He looked at himself in the mirror above the tiny washbowl and wondered what was getting under that skin he fancied to be so thick. "Is it Porter turning stuffed shirt all of a sudden?" he asked his reflection. "Or that character Finlander everybody's bowing to the east over? Or maybe Nancy's still bugging me!"

The thought of Nancy aggravated his irritation as he began to dress. If anything wrong was to happen on this trip, it would really be her fault, because he had undertaken it to escape her silken whining in that coffin of a studio apartment in Greenwich Village. Like the other Nancys before her, she had first seduced him with a voluptuous body, then repulsed him with a barren, selfish mind which was nothing but a ganglion of short-circuited female nerves. Like some kind of bull animal, his life with women seemed fated to follow a pattern of courtship, rutting and desertion. "Why can't you get a regular job at home?" they would all eventually scream at him. "Because then I'd be stuck with both you and the job," he would answer. "At least give me money for a divorce!" "With your legs and tits, you'll always find yourself another pigeon if you don't wait too long." "A wife's got some rights! *I'm going to see a lawyer!*" "That's why I'm leaving. By-by, honey!" Well, the other Nancys had got their divorces without his having to spend a nickel. This one would too, he hopefully told himself as he stamped his feet into a pair of old fleece-lined air-force boots. But just to make sure, he would leave the *Bedford* in Reykjavik, beg a ride on a MATS plane to London, peddle his story to one of the American television outfits there, get paid and be off on some other interesting overseas assignment. No Nancy would ever catch up with *him!* Never!

There was a knock on the cabin door and a young seaman who bulked monstrously large in his arctics looked in. "The second officer's steaming because you ain't at the highline station, Mr. Munceford. The *Bedford*'s bearing down on us right now, you know."

Munceford grinned and patted him on the shoulder with the familiarity he liked to show enlisted men. "It's okay, sailor. Tell Mr. Boomer to keep his shirt on. I'll be there in a couple of minutes."

"But you ain't even got your gear together," the boy exclaimed with a certain admiration. "Can I help you with any of it?"

"I travel light," Munceford told him and yanked his duffel bag out of a locker. It had hardly been unpacked during the four days since they had left Portsmouth, and all he had to do was to shove in his toilet kit and some dirty socks.

"What about your camera 'n' stuff?" the seaman asked, helping him to knot the bag and nodding toward the large aluminum case under the desk. "Want me to deliver it to the cargo sling?"

"I'll carry that myself, thanks. Might want to run off a few feet of film on the way over."

"Mr. Boomer won't allow it, sir," the boy told him. "All baggage gotta go across in a sling on account of we once lost an ensign who went in the drink and was dragged under by some personal gear he'd strapped to himself."

Munceford swung out the case by its leather shoulder strap and plonked it on the lower bunk. He opened it up and the sailor stared with fascination at the jumble of equipment which was jammed into it. At first glance it gave an impression of the wealth of film, tape, cameras and recording gear which a professional TV feature reporter would be expected to carry with him on a navy assignment, but this was an illusion created by the disorder. The single movie camera was an old sixteen-millimeter Bell and Howell, the miniature battery-operated recorder a cheap Japanese make; many boxes of film and tape were pushed down among filter cases, lens shades and a tangle of microphone cords, yet really not enough to satisfy any professional doing the kind of job Munceford was.

"Gee!" the sailor exclaimed, genuinely impressed. "You sure got some fancy stuff there, sir."

"I only bring old equipment on a story like this," Munceford answered with studied indifference. "Salt air raises hell with cameras and recorders. All this will be written off and thrown away after the job's over."

The sailor's eyes popped. "Christ! I'd like to be around when you start throwing it. Must be a thousand bucks' worth."

Munceford smiled and left the exclamation answered by an effective silence. He had actually bought everything in the case from a New York discount store for a little over two hundred dollars—having borrowed half the cash from a friend who was a technical director for NBC and charged the rest to something which the salesman called Instant-Credit. When he yanked out the camera, there was a general collapse of knick-knacks within the case and its contents suddenly did not look at all impressive. He quickly shut the lid, locked it, then looped the strap over the sailor's shoulder. "I'm much obliged to you," he told him. "Tell Mr. Boomer that I'll be along shortly."

The boy left with the duffel bag and camera case, gingerly wiggling through the narrow door as if he were carrying a load of fresh eggs.

Munceford heard the engine-room bells' muffled clang and felt the beat of the *Tiburon Bay*'s engines increase from their idling rumble. The *Bedford*'s siren let out a blast which reached his ears as a distant wail. He looked around the bare cabin with his lips pressed together and a frown on his face as if hesitating to leave it. But then he began to move with some urgency, pulling on the quasi-military fleece-lined windbreaker which had become the envy of every young sailor aboard. It was made of brown, green, yellow and pink camouflage twill. On the shoulder of the left sleeve blazed the patch of the Strategic Air Command, on the right a patch of the 82nd Airborne Division; on the left breast a submarine insignia was pinned above a combat infantryman's badge; on the right was stitched a leather strip with the word CORRESPONDENT embossed in gold letters upon it. The cap which he carefully adjusted at a rakish angle on his head was of the type worn by soldiers in arctic climates, with a fur lining and large earflaps that neatly snapped together across the crown. Pinned to it was the silver insignia of a paratrooper.

After taking a last look at himself in the mirror, Ben Munceford picked up his camera and hurriedly left the cabin.

# 2.

Captain Larsen of the U.S.S. *Tiburon Bay* was a Commander, U.S.N.R., who had been recalled to duty from his highly paid civilian job as skipper of a tanker belonging to Standard Oil. Because that company had generously continued paying him half of his regular salary, he was actually making as much as he had become accustomed to and was therefore not as disgruntled as most of the reservists under his command. Mr. Boomer, for instance, he suspected of deliberately nurturing one cold after another in order to be returned for medical reasons to inactive status and thence go back to his fancy marina in Fort Lauderdale. And Mr. Carmichael, the assistant engineering officer, did nothing but worry about a plumbing business in plush Westchester County of New York, from which he had been cruelly torn during a construction boom which flourished regardless of the cold war. Well, only out here did the cold war take on any real meaning. The thermometer attached to the wheelhouse registered eleven degrees below freezing.

As the *Bedford* emerged out of the fog which reduced the surrounding vastness of this frigid ocean to a couple of square miles of visible bleakness, Captain Larsen drew a sigh of envy. There was the real professional navy! The destroyer itself he did not care about so much—even modern ones like the *Bedford* were terrible riding and Larsen had reached the age where he preferred comfort to excitement. What he envied was Captain Finlander's staff of officers, who were one-hundred-per-cent Annapolis graduates, probably *all* with a rating of superior (or better); his enlisted crew were all career men, many of the chiefs being on their third six-year hitch. Even a bucket like the *Tiburon Bay* could be efficiently run with a gang like that! He watched the *Bedford* through his binoculars for a moment, then called toward the wheelhouse: "Log visual contact with DDL 113 at 1350 hours. Captain will take the conn at this time."

The executive officer was standing next to him, his eyes glued to his binoculars, watching the destroyer intently. Lieutenant (J.G.) Laurin Wilburforce also envied the *Bedford*, but for purely romantic reasons. "Jesus! She's gorgeous!" he muttered, as if he were speaking about a beautiful woman who was far above the class of a plain clod like himself. He was indeed an undistinguished-looking young man, but at least he was an Annapolis graduate, the only one aboard the *Tiburon Bay,* and, because of this, was exec in spite of holding a lower rank than several officers under him. Captain Larsen suspected that Wilburforce either had been the lowest in his graduating class (1957) or had somehow managed to sully his record subsequently. He was a dully efficient young officer, but why else would he be exiled to an old fleet oiler manned by reservists, children and exiled thirty-year men? "Will somebody back there acknowledge the captain's orders?" Wilburforce irritably called to the wheelhouse.

Barnwell, the quartermaster, appeared briefly in the door. "Visual contact at 1350 hours and captain taking over conn, both logged, sir." He quickly vanished back into the warm inside.

Wilburforce had not taken his eyes away from the binoculars which he kept trained on the *Bedford*. "Jesus! She must be doing forty knots!" he gasped in admiration.

Captain Larsen grunted and pulled his head deeper into his parka. "Come to zero-four-zero degrees," he called to the helmsman, then strode to the shelter of the starboard wing, from where he continued to watch the *Bedford*. A blinker light was winking from the destroyer's bridge and he was able to read the challenge: COLDSNAP.

The light on the *Tiburon Bay*'s signal bridge clattered out the countersign, slowly and with some hesitation (another reservist going through halfhearted motions): H-O-A—R——F-R-R-R—O-S-T. Larsen glanced up at the signal bridge with patient suffering, then back at the *Bedford* just in time to see her rap out:

WILL EXECUTE HIGHSPEED BUNKERING AND TRANSFER. HEAD 070 AND MAKE 15 KNOTS.

The *Tiburon Bay*'s signalman hesitated and, instead of acknowledging, asked for a repeat. The *Bedford* expressed her irritation over this inefficiency by repeating the message even faster. Captain Larsen left the shelter and headed for the wheelhouse; before entering it, he looked up to the signal bridge and called with an even voice: "I got the message even if you didn't. Simply acknowledge!"

Two boyish faces peered down at him, glowing with crimson embarrassment in the hoods of their parkas.

Stepping into the wheelhouse, he ordered the helmsman to change course to 070, rang up full ahead on the telegraph, then called the engine room on the telephone: "Give me exactly two-forty revolutions on both screws if that won't shake your engines loose from their beds," he said with a flat inflection.

Mr. Carmichael was at the other end of the line, some four hundred feet aft and a hundred feet below. "Aye, aye, two-forty revs, Captain," he answered. "Request permission to blow my tubes."

"Are you mad?"

"No, sir."

"Request denied."

Captain Larsen shook his head and hung up the instrument. He gave the seaman second-class at the helm a searching glance, trying to remember whether or not he too was an incompetent reservist. High-speed re-fueling at sea required a sure hand at the wheel, as the 18,000-ton tanker could severely damage the 3,400-ton destroyer if the two came together. Both the helmsman and his relief looked like children—neither of them could be much over twenty, too young to be reservists. Too young for solid experience. But the boy at the wheel had a confident look in his blue eyes, which he kept glued to the gyro-repeater, and Larsen decided to take his chances on him. "Are your kidneys and bowels cleared for a long session, son?"

The blue eyes flicked up for a second and there was laughter in them. "Sure thing, Captain."

"Okay. When 113 pulls alongside, I don't want to see you as much as blink in her direction. Let us fall away one degree and you'll get fed to Finlander in small pieces." He softened the terrible threat with a flash of a grin, then said to the relief: "You stand exactly two feet behind and one foot to the right of the wheel, ready to instantly take over in case your buddy has a seizure—understand?"

"Yes, sir," the other man answered with a nervous smile.

Captain Larsen returned to the starboard wing of the bridge, stopping next to the executive officer, who was bawling out the signalman. Three decks below he could hear half-choked nasal noises which were those of Mr. Boomer bawling out the pumping crew. From somewhere around the port side of the bridge superstructure he heard the curdling profanity of CPO Grisling, who was bawling out men preparing the highline gear (Grisling was an old pro who would be aboard a carrier if it were not for his unfortunate drinking habits in port). A half-mile astern, the *Bedford* cut through the *Tiburon Bay*'s wake, made a blast on her siren and heeled over in a turn to bring her alongside. She still had a bone in her teeth and it was obvious that Finlander was going to make a hot approach. "I hope the bastard overshoots us," Larsen muttered. He noticed a bulky figure coming up the companionway from the boat deck, and the gold-braided visor peeking out from beneath the hood identified Lieutenant Commander Porter.

"Request permission to come on the bridge, sir," the surgeon said with a snappy salute.

Captain Larsen returned it in a more casual fashion. "No use trying to hide up here, Commander," he told him. "Finlander has come to get you and I've got to hoist you over to him, dead or alive."

Porter laughed politely. "I've come to thank you for a very nice trip, sir, and to pick up the dispatches for DDL 113."

Larsen interrupted his executive officer's lecture to the unhappy sig-nalman. "Mr. Wilburforce, will you go and fetch Finlander's secrets out of our safe, turn them over to Commander Porter and obtain a receipt from him for same. Thank you." While waiting for the documents to be fetched from the chartroom, the captain kept a wary eye on the *Bedford* while engaging in gruff small talk with the surgeon. "I'm glad you enjoyed your days on this dear old oiler, Commander. I'd hoped you would take care of some of our sniffles and piles while you were aboard, but then I realize you've been steeling yourself for your forthcoming ordeal." Noticing a small wiggle in the wake of his ship, he raised his voice to a shout. "Steady up, helmsman! You're outmaneuvering that destroyer!" Lowering his voice back to Porter: "How's your shipmate, the glamorous war correspondent, getting on? Hiding in the lazaret, maybe?"

"He's playing it cool, sir." The surgeon laughed with a doubtful headshake. "I left him in his underwear, still sacked out. He spent half the night playing cards in the enlisted mess, you know."

"Oh. He's a champion of the common man, eh? I suppose he will expose the snobbery which exists between fo'c'sle and quarterdeck aboard the *Bedford*. Finlander will appreciate that." Even as he spoke, he spotted Ben Munceford's jarring camouflage jacket and fur cap coming down the catwalk which bridged the long main deck between the superstructures of the tanker. The captain's normally crinkled eyes narrowed to pained slits. "Yes, Finlander is going to *love* that character," he added, more to himself than to the other officer.

Wilburforce came out of the wheelhouse and handed Porter a large plastic envelope, sealed and with conspicuous lead weights attached to its corners. The surgeon signed the receipt, shook hands with both the exec and the captain, saluted them and left the bridge.

"Have the B flag hoisted, Mr. Wilburforce," Larsen quietly ordered, noting that the *Bedford* was now only a hundred yards astern and still closing fast. The destroyer sheered off a few points to port and white foam erupted around her fantails as her eighty thousand horsepower kicked into reverse to break her speed.

"Jesus! He handles her like a god-damned Chris-Craft!" the executive officer exclaimed with breathless admiration.

Larsen grunted. He estimated that Finlander was not going to overshoot after all and crossed through the wheelhouse to take up his position in the shelter of the port wing.

The tanker plodded ahead, her bow rising and falling with an easy, solid motion through the long, low swells which she was now meeting head on. Mr. Boomer was still shouting at his pumping detail, which cursed with impersonal passion as it struggled with ice-crusted valves, hoses and lines. Grisling's more seasoned profanities blistered the cold air around the highline station. As the booms swung outboard with the whips supporting the hoses, they dropped showers of icicles on the crew below. More cursing. On the shelter deck of the after superstructure, one of the cooks braved the cold in his bare whites, leaned over the rail and pointed a camera at the *Bedford*.

The destroyer had spilled most of her excess speed and was inching up alongside, some hundred feet off the *Tiburon Bay*. Her rolling and pitching were quicker and more nervous than those of the tanker, but her conning was exact and sure. From close quarters, much of the graceful effect of the *Bedford*'s lines was lost. Her hull was marred in several places where the undercoating had bled through to form ugly red sores on the gray plates; ice had scarred a lot of the superstructure, which was made of aluminum and shone a dull burnished color where the paint had worn off. She showed all the attrition of hard service in the arctic, yet still gave an impression of enormous power and efficiency. There was an eager rumble from her engine rooms and blowers, almost a living animal-like sound. A few hooded faces peered over the windscreen of the bridge, but otherwise she seemed strangely deserted. Only six men huddled together on the weather deck, grotesque shapes in their arctics and life jackets.

"Ship ready in every respect for bunkering DDL 113," Mr. Wilburforce informed his captain.

Larsen glanced over the bridge to make a quick check that everybody was occupying his assigned station—the exec standing by the annunciator, a talker next to him with his telephone plugged into the jack, the chief quartermaster now in charge of signals, the chief boatswain's mate keeping his eyes peeled over the windscreen and Ensign Fisher, the JOOD, standing in the wheelhouse with a jaundiced eye on the gyrocompass. All was in order, but the captain suddenly bristled as a lanky figure in a fur cap and an outlandish camouflage jacket popped up the companionway.

"Hi, Skipper! Mind if I get a few shots from up here?" Munceford cheerfully asked, brandishing his camera.

"Yes, I do, Mr. Munceford. I'd hate to have you miss your appointment with Captain Finlander, so please report immediately to Chief Grisling at the highline station. Good-by and good luck. . . . Mr. Wilburforce! Hoist the red flag and let's get going."

Ben Munceford stood there for a moment with a pouting smile frozen on his face and an unspoken objection on his lips, but everybody had turned away from him and there was nothing he could do but retreat from the bridge.

The *Bedford* had drawn slightly ahead of the *Tiburon Bay* and was hanging there, still a hundred feet off, jockeying slightly until her speed exactly matched the tanker's fifteen knots. The wash of the two vessels met between them and chopped into irregular patterns. The blinker on the destroyer flashed: EXECUTE.

"Acknowledge affirmative!"

The lamp on the tanker's bridge clattered briefly—this time without hesitation.

The *Bedford* veered inward and dropped back slightly. Suddenly the oily sea between them turned into a churning millrace as the two hulls closed together, eighty . . . seventy . . . sixty . . . fifty . . . and finally only forty feet apart. The destroyer took a roll, and for an instant the revolving radar antenna on her mainmast threatened to hit the tanker's bridge; then she steadied and began maintaining exact station. Messenger lines snaked across from the *Tiburon Bay*'s main deck. The seamen on the *Bedford* moved with precision to pick them up and start hauling over the fuel and highline gear.

"Log commencement of refueling operations as of now!"

Two minutes later the talker reported to Captain Larsen that telephone connections were established with the *Bedford*'s bridge. There were no greetings or small talk exchanged between commanders, only a brief, routine discussion between the respective executive officers. "They wish to immediately send over the officer Commander Porter is replacing, sir," Wilburforce informed his captain.

"Must be damned eager to get rid of him. Tell them okay."

The exec spoke a single affirmative into the mouthpiece, then listened for thirty seconds with a frown. "They want us to know, sir," he told Larsen, "that a half-full bottle of whisky was spotted in our wake about three miles back."

The captain did not take his eyes off the men on the *Bedford*'s main deck who were just completing the connection of the fuel hoses. "Apologize," he said, "and compliment them on their very sharp lookout."

# 3.

On the main deck Lieutenant Commander Porter sat down on a ventilator and waited in acute discomfort for his transfer. He had been helped into the cumbersome rubberized immersion suit which enclosed him from his head to the soles of his feet in its stiff folds, only his face protruding through the opening of the hood and pinched by the tight drawstring. A few feet away a couple of young seamen were making a hilarious game out of prying Ben Munceford into a similar outfit. The surgeon deliberately ignored the clowning and followed with his eyes four sacks of mail wobbling across the highline toward the plunging destroyer-leader.

"Christ! This thing's cutting my balls off!" Munceford squealed with mock agony as one of the men heaved on the zipper.

The sailors brayed in ribald delight. "Better than freezing them off in case you get dunked," one of them explained.

Chief Grisling increased his steady flow of profanity to a torrent which included instructions to the man on the outhaul of the highline to keep an even strain. Farther down the deck, Mr. Boomer's haranguing of the pumping crew was temporarily curtailed by a fit of sneezing. The supply officer, an overage Lieutenant J.G. who looked frozen blue in spite of his enormously thick clothing, nagged at the commissary detail as they stacked stores according to the order of transfer. The pumps clattered. Winches ground their gears. The sea between the two ships hissed and beat against the steel plates of their hulls.

Although he kept his eyes on the *Bedford,* the noise of men and machinery penetrated through the thick rubber hood covering Lieutenant Commander Porter's ears and he became impatient to leave the bedlam of this fleet oiler which Captain Larsen ran like a slovenly tramp steamer. Well, Larsen was nothing but a merchant skipper, really, so what could one expect? You could tell he was used to insolent union crews from the way he handled his men; in fact, he seemed to run the *Tiburon Bay* as unnavylike as possible. The surgeon looked forward to escaping across that trench of rushing water to the smooth discipline and secure service traditions of the *Bedford,* but he regretted that Ben Munceford would be joining him. There was another tramp, an immature and unstable one at that, who made light of discipline and tradition, who made sport of breaking regulations. How could the Navy Department grant such a man the privileges of a correspondent? How could any reputable broadcasting company trust such a judgment? Either he had some special talents which had not shown themselves as yet, or the man was a skilled bluffer and finagler—in any case, a very unpleasant character.

The surgeon sighed heavily and wiggled against the oppressive weight of the immersion suit. He noticed that the mail sacks had reached their destination and were being efficiently manhandled aboard the destroyer. His turn would come soon now and he wondered what awaited him over there. Even though he looked forward to service aboard one of the navy's latest crack ships, there had been several unsettling things which presaged developments of possibly unpleasant nature for him. The cold war had intensified lately and for the first time since the Korean truce Porter sensed that it had a good chance of becoming a hot one. He knew from bitter experience that nothing upset the comfortable routine of his navy life more than real *war.* When the Korean one came along, for instance, he had had to give up his research in forensic medicine at Bethesda to sew up mangled marines on a hospital ship plying between Pusan and Nagasaki. If war came again, it could trap him for the duration on this destroyer—a far different matter from a two- or three-month temporary assignment.

Chief Grisling was suddenly directing his obscenities at the seamen forty feet away on the opposite end of the highline. The *Bedford* should, according to established procedure, send over their own outgoing mail sacks, then receive perishable stores. But now there was a delay. Grisling hung on a stanchion and leaned far out over the side, his leathery face screwed into a gargoyle expression as he tried to make out what was happening. His outrage became nearly apoplectic when he saw that they were switching the rig for personnel transfer instead of mail and stores. His talker, who was connected by telephone to both his own and the *Bedford*'s bridges, confirmed the change of arrangement. Grisling hurled his clipboard with the schedule of transfer across the deck, then bawled at a seaman to retrieve it for him.

Porter knew that the man about to come across would be Lieutenant Barney Hirschfeld, another reason for his vague uneasiness about this cruise. He was replacing Hirschfeld, who had been the *Bedford*'s surgeon since her commissioning ten months ago. This sudden relieving of a medical officer in mid-ocean was very unusual in peacetime operations and had caused Porter some inconvenience when he was ordered to replace him on a couple of days' notice. The whole affair had strange and mysterious overtones. If Hirschfeld had become ill, Porter would have heard about it, so it had to be something else. Something else which Estelle Hirschfeld obviously knew about—otherwise why had she actually *cursed* the *Bedford* in a painful scene in the Officers' Club? Of course, Estelle tended to be emotional and high-strung, not at all a good steady navy wife like his own Martha. But to curse her husband's ship in public . . . Horrible!

Watching Lieutenant Hirschfeld start his journey to the *Tiburon Bay*, Porter decided he certainly was not sick. He was sitting perfectly upright in the bosun's chair, balancing himself with ease as it swung out over the millrace between the ships and twisting his head around to keep staring back at the *Bedford*'s bridge.

"Hell! That looks too dangerous for me!" Munceford clowned and pretended to take flight. A pair of laughing seamen grabbed him. He broke away from them, suddenly remembered the camera in his hand and began shooting some pictures of the transfer.

Porter got up off the ventilator and shuffled over to where Hirschfeld would touch the deck.

"Stand clear, goddammit . . . *sir,*" Grisling bellowed.

Porter gritted his teeth and shuffled two steps backward.

The destroyer took a long, lazy roll to starboard, slackening the highline so that Hirschfeld was momentarily almost touching the waves and enveloped in spray. Thirty seconds later he was standing on the *Tiburon Bay*'s deck with salt water running in streams off his immersion suit.

"Hello, Barney," Porter greeted him.

Hirschfeld peeled back the rubber hood covering his head and stared at the surgeon with tired eyes which did not seem to recognize him at first. Then he said: "Oh . . . hello, Chester."

They were both in the way of a sudden frenzy of activity, so Porter took Hirschfeld's arm, trying to lead him aside for a few words. But

Chief Grisling yelled: "All right, Commander, as long as the schedule's all screwed up, we'll take you next."

"Take Mr. Munceford ahead of me, Chief," the surgeon snapped.

But Munceford had suddenly decided that he needed some forgotten accessory out of his camera case so he could take pictures on the way over. The case was in a cargo sling far down the deck. Grisling had a fit over this new delay.

"How are you, Barney?" Porter asked the younger officer, trying to ignore the fracas around them.

"Fine, thanks," Hirschfeld replied, starting to peel himself out of his immersion suit.

"Your wife has been worrying about you and . . . so have I."

"How is Estelle?" Hirschfeld asked, evading the implied question.

"Like I say, worried. Maybe something you wrote upset her."

Hirschfeld's dark, troubled face became furrowed by a frown. "What are you pumping me for, Chester? You've obviously gone over everything with Estelle."

"Listen, I only ran into her at the club last week. Mentioned I had orders to replace you. She began laughing hysterically, then called your ship some pretty bad names for a lady. After I calmed her down, she shut up like a clam and finally ran off. That's all I know, so help me, Barney."

Hirschfeld stared at him, not with the shock which Porter had expected, but thoughtfully and perhaps even with a trace of a smile. His mouth opened to speak, but before any words could come out, the bullhorn on the *Bedford*'s bridge rattled across with a loud commanding voice, urgent, impatient and with a steely quality, as though it belonged to the ship itself:

"Belay the socializing, please! Commander Porter will come over to me immediately. Also do not send our guest until stores are transferred."

Grisling had just dragged Ben Munceford away from a packed cargo sling, where he had failed to get at his camera case, and was about to buckle him into the bosun's chair. Upon hearing the order from the *Bedford*, the old chief boatswain's mate became so overwrought that he could only make a supplicant gesture toward the *Tiburon Bay*'s bridge, then roughly yanked Munceford clear of the highline gear.

Hirschfeld reacted to the voice from the *Bedford* with a fearful start and glanced uneasily toward the bridge of the destroyer. "Finlander is watching us," he whispered hoarsely.

Porter noticed that one of the faces showing above the windscreen was partially obscured by the lenses of a pair of large binoculars aimed right at them. Instinctively lowering his voice, he hurriedly exclaimed: "For God's sake, Barney! What's been happening to you on that ship?"

Hirschfeld refused a direct answer, but quickly and ominously injected: "Just keep your eye on Finlander, that's all."

Chief Grisling was calling Porter's name, but the surgeon had been rooted to the spot by the inflection of Hirschfeld's words. "What do you mean, keep an eye on Finlander?" he demanded, suddenly severe and formal. "You say that as if you were suggesting he has been acting irrationally."

The young medical officer shook his head and laughed bitterly. "Oh, no! You're not going to pin that one on me! He's no Captain Queeg of the *Caine* who's about to have a mutiny. No, sir. If anything, he's the *only* sane one on that blighted can. Him and the German. He's driving everybody else . . ." Hirschfeld stopped abruptly as Chief Grisling stepped up and saluted with a seething politeness.

"Pardon me, sirs, but DDL 113 is most anxiously awaiting the commander's transfer!" His lips continued moving after the audible part of his request was completed, silently mouthing through some of his favorite epithets.

Lieutenant Barney Hirschfeld kicked his feet clear of the soaking immersion suit, said: "Gook luck, Chester," in a low voice and hurriedly retreated down the cluttered deck. Shaken and confused, Lieutenant Commander Porter allowed himself to be led by Chief Grisling to the bosun's chair. The straps closed tightly over his thighs and a moment later he swung clear of the *Tiburon Bay*. As the block creaked on the wire overhead and the tanker fell away, his eyes sought to pick out a last glimpse of the surgeon-lieutenant among the crowd of men lining the rail, but the only one he could clearly recognize was Munceford squinting horribly at him through the viewfinder of his camera. Twenty feet beneath him, black water raged, and spume stung his face with icy needles.

# 4.

Larsen followed with his eyes the progress of the awkward shape dangling like a weird marionette from the highline. He knew it was Lieutenant Commander Porter and found himself sadistically wishing that the two ships would roll together, dunking the starchy surgeon in the freezing Atlantic. The wish startled him a little because Porter was a good officer and a gentleman of adequate intelligence and humor; probably a dedicated doctor too. Perhaps it was that he took the gentleman part somewhat too seriously; or the dedication to it all. But this was no reason to wish him the victim of a cruel prank, so perhaps the real truth was that he resented the professional navy which this man represented. Resented it and envied it, both. It seemed like a hundred years since he had applied for a regular commission, when the last war was over, and been turned down because he had gone to sea instead of to college. That still rankled in the back of his mind, even though he earned as much as an admiral in his job with Standard Oil and commanded far bigger and better tankers than this one. Being a Commander, U.S.N.R., was not really bad in itself. Still . . . if he had made it back in 1946, he would certainly have been Captain, U.S.N., by now . . . like Finlander.

Larsen's eyes flicked from the highline to the destroyer's bridge, which was so much lower than his own that he could look down into it. The figure in a pure white duffel coat, hunched over the bulwark and watching the operation with a casual sort of alertness, had to be Captain Finlander. The profile was hidden by the upturned collar and when he glanced up at the *Tiburon Bay*'s bridge, the face was shadowed by what appeared to be a long-billed fisherman's cap. Only Finlander would be permitted such eccentricity of dress. In fact, there was something eccentric about such a high-ranking officer being captain of a mere destroyer instead of a missile cruiser or super-carrier—as Larsen would have preferred for himself. But they said that Finlander badgered his superiors into keeping him at sea on the cans, that he loved them with a passion, that he was a superlative seaman who became intransigent and morose on routine shoreside assignments. No doubt a fine seaman was necessary to command a ship in these arctic waters, and perhaps a full captain was necessary because it was such a critical area in the cold war—but a man like that had to be somewhat mad, or childishly romantic, to deliberately seek such an assignment. College or no college, Larsen would have made a less flamboyant, more flexible Captain, U.S.N.

Lieutenant Commander Porter made it over to the *Bedford* without being dunked and was received by a crew fewer and far more silent in their work than those aboard the *Tiburon Bay*. With smooth efficiency they had the outgoing mail sacks on their way within a minute. Captain Larsen cocked his hooded head away from the biting breeze, watched them for a moment, then checked the fuel hoses swaying from their whips and saddles—"the teats of your fat sea cow," Munceford had cracked about them yesterday when they refueled the *Fritiof Nansen* off Cape Farewell. Well—the *Tiburon Bay was* a plodding sea cow, maybe, but the glamorous destroyers could not operate so long and so far from their bases without her. If she failed to show up and nurse them on schedule, they would have to limp home on two boilers, leaving the northeast approaches to the American continent open to probes by Soviet submarines and spy trawlers. So it actually all depended as much on a lowly sea cow and her Commander, U.S.N.R., as it did on ships like the *Bedford* and her Captain, U.S.N. Finlander might make admiral in due time, while Larsen never could surmount his reserve rank. But he did stand in line to become Vice-President in Charge of Marine Operations for Standard Oil eventually . . . and *that* job paid $25,000 per annum, plus bonuses, which in turn would put *both* his sons through M.I.T. with plenty to spare. Then the navy would beg him to have them accept regular commissions—something he would be most cagey about!

"Sir—Lieutenant Hirschfeld is logged aboard and wishes to speak to the captain."

Larsen turned from watching the refueling operation to glance over his shoulder at his executive officer and a man standing next to him wearing nothing but a thin windbreaker and an ordinary cap as protection against the raw cold of the bridge. He was a dark, brooding-looking young man with a hooked nose and heavy black eyebrows arched over it. Handsome in a Jewish way, but the lines around his eyes and mouth suggested a permanently troubled personality.

"You some kind of fresh-air fiend, Lieutenant?" Larsen asked him, then turned his head away from a salute, not out of rudeness, but because he had to keep his eyes on the fueling of the *Bedford*.

"My heavy gear will be over shortly, sir," Hirschfeld answered. "Can't wear too much padding under an immersion suit."

Larsen grunted.

"Sir, I am sorry to disturb you at this time," Hirschfeld continued, "but Captain Finlander ordered me to report to you immediately."

Larsen looked toward the *Bedford*'s bridge and noticed that the figure in the white duffel had a pair of binoculars aimed right at them; at that short distance he could no doubt almost read their lips. "Why, Lieutenant?" he asked.

Hirschfeld spoke as if it were an entirely routine matter, without urgency or emotion. "I am to report, sir, that for the past five days I have been relieved of my duties as surgeon of the U.S.S. *Bedford* and confined to quarters. Captain Finlander requests that this status be continued for me aboard the *Tiburon Bay* and that I have nothing but necessary official contacts with officers and men under your command until I am put ashore at Portsmouth."

Larsen turned around and stared at him. "You are under arrest?"

"Confined to quarters pending a board of inquiry, sir."

"Inquiry into what, Mr. Hirschfeld?"

"Captain Finlander has ordered me not to discuss the case, which he has placed under maximum security, sir."

Captain Larsen looked back at the *Bedford*'s bridge and saw the glint of binocular lenses still trained on them. "Take the conn, Mr. Wilburforce!" he snapped to his executive officer, then pushed his way past the two men to go over to the telephone talker. "Get me the captain of the *Bedford*, please."

The young quartermaster spoke into his instrument and after a moment informed Larsen: "Sir, the executive officer says that Captain Finlander is busy and unable to talk to you at this time."

Larsen's customary grunt became an angry snarl. "Give me that phone, son!" He pulled the headset off the man's head and stuffed one cup inside his hood to press it against his ear. "This is Captain Larsen speaking," he said into the microphone. "I am also extremely busy at the moment and, I do believe, engaged in the same mission as Captain Finlander. But I trust my exec enough so I can speak on the phone for a minute or two without expecting to founder. I hope Captain Finlander has matters well enough in hand to do likewise."

The voice on the other end of the line was not in the least fazed by this cutting sarcasm. It remained evenly courteous. "Good afternoon, Captain Larsen. This is Commander Allison, executive officer, speaking. If you wait one moment, I will check again with Captain Finlander."

Larsen could still see the *Bedford*'s bridge by standing on tiptoe and could pick out her exec as he poked his head out of the wheelhouse and evidently called to the shape in the white duffel. There was no visible reaction from the latter. A few seconds later the courteous voice came back: "I am sorry, Captain Larsen, but Captain Finlander regrets he is unable to speak to you unless it is an urgent tactical or navigational matter. However, *I* suppose you are actually calling about Lieutenant Hirschfeld, sir?"

Even to an easygoing reserve officer, this was a gross breach of naval etiquette, and if it had not been for his long indoctrination in rudeness aboard unionized merchant ships, Larsen would probably have lost his temper completely. But sardonic humor was his principal and most deadly weapon. "Well, yes, Commander," he answered in a chatty tone. "I am given to understand that the man has committed a crime. Of course, the *Tiburon Bay* is perfectly accustomed to acting as a convict ship for the destroyer fleet, but our chief executioner's mate becomes confused if he is not given a bill of particulars to govern the treatment of individual criminals in his custody."

The voice from the *Bedford* remained unfazed. "I see your point, Captain Larsen. The case is really not as sinister as Lieutenant Hirschfeld's attitude might indicate. You may still treat him as an officer and gentleman, sir."

"Ah! Then he's only committed a misdemeanor. Perhaps a little mischief our medical officers are likely to get into, like supplementing their income by engaging in illegal operations, or pushing narcotics in the ward room, or watering the skipper's supply of medicinal brandy?"

"Well—it's not exactly a joking matter either, Captain," the commander told him, a certain annoyance creeping into his tone.

"I'm only an unsubtle tanker captain, Commander. If it is neither a sinister nor a joking matter, you leave me dangling in confusion."

Commander Allison's voice was suddenly coldly official. "The matter involves medical practice rather than naval discipline, Captain Larsen. As such, it is beyond the concern of officers of the line and therefore should not be a matter of discussion between us. I believe Lieutenant Hirschfeld himself agrees with this. Certainly it is the wish of Captain Finlander that it be treated in that way, and I respectfully submit that you comply with his judgment in the case."

"O-oh! I see! That clears it all up for me," Larsen exclaimed, making a wry grimace. "My compliments to Captain Finlander and my thanks to you, Commander. Out." He pulled the earphone out from under his hood and thrust the instrument back to the talker. Turning around, he found himself facing the young surgeon, who had evidently been standing directly behind him throughout the conversation. The captain looked searchingly into the tense face, then smiled. "As far as I'm concerned, you are welcome aboard this ship, Mr. Hirschfeld. If you choose to confine yourself to your cabin and not socialize with my officers, that's your business and we'll presume you have good reasons. Either way, we'll give you the benefit of doubt. In the meanwhile, there's coffee in the chartroom, so why don't you go in there and thaw out?"

A trace of a grateful smile passed over Hirschfeld's lips. "Thank you, sir." He started to move toward the wheelhouse, but hesitated momentarily and said: "It is only fair for me to warn you, Captain, that I'm going to resign from the navy as soon as I get back Stateside."

Wilburforce heard him and stared at him as if he were mad, but Captain Larsen only nodded and took the conn back from his executive officer.

The *Tiburon Bay* and the *Bedford* plowed on at a steady fifteen knots, the big ship heaving with a cumbersome motion as she rose and fell with the swells, the smaller one stamping her forefoot with a nervous, coltish action. The breeze ruffling the surface of those swells was less than Force 1, a mere zephyr wafting down from the north which made the slightly warmer ocean steam with patches of sea smoke. Low banks of fog still compressed the horizon, which had lost its shimmering pearl-gray color and become darker as the short arctic day faded into a gloomy twilight. A ragged patch in the overcast glowed a mysterious amber color for a few moments as it caught the devious rays of a sun setting beyond the pall of scud to the southwest.

Oil flowed from the *Tiburon Bay*'s vast tanks into the bunkers of the *Bedford,* throbbing through the hoses at a rate of better than two tons per minute. The highline swung containers of fresh dairy produce across to the destroyer in hundred-gallon and hundred-pound lots—milk, eggs, butter and ice cream, all less than a week away from Rhode Island farms. Back and forth over the wild trench of water hurtling between the two ships the sling traveled, conveying forty twelve-pound rib roasts, seventy crates of vegetables, twenty-eight hams, a hundred pounds of pork sausage, two hundred and eight pounds of coffee, a bundle of magazines, fifteen full-length feature movies, a case full of fragile transistors and radio tubes, the replacement armature for a burned-out auxiliary generator, seventeen cases of toilet paper, two hundred and forty pounds of soap, two ten-gallon cans of cola syrup, a case of chewing gum, Lieutenant Commander Porter's Valpack, Munceford's duffel bag and camera case. . . . Finally, there was Munceford himself, jerking across with his camera stiffly pressed to his face as he registered a wildly swaying scene of his transfer through spray-splattered optics.

It was at this moment that Captain Larsen was jolted by the muffled clanging of the *Bedford*'s General Quarters alarm, the sound suddenly penetrating the intervening forty feet of hissing sea. Even as the significance of it was penetrating his brain, the bullhorn on the destroyer's bridge blared at him:

"Now hear this, *Tiburon Bay!* We have detected a high-frequency radar emission upon us. Break off operation at once! Break off operation at once!"

Larsen tensed, called back over his shoulder to the talker: "Notify all stations to stand by for break-off!" He glanced at the *Bedford*'s bridge and saw that the white duffel coat had vanished from its position in the wing, then he focused his attention on Ben Munceford, who was dangling from the highline midway between the two ships. The bosun's chair hesitated and stopped; the figure in it looked up from the viewfinder of the camera, the face glowing a startling pink in the hood of the immersion suit as it twisted sideways and upward, staring back questioningly at the tanker's bridge. The line suddenly slackened, and for a second or two Munceford's feet cut a foaming wake in the water rushing beneath him; then the line cracked tight again, catapulting him into violent gyrations which came within a hair of looping the whole rig and jamming it midway. A small object detached itself from the struggling black figure, arcing gracefully through the air before splashing into the sea; it was Munceford's camera on its way to oblivion, a hundred fathoms down. Some howls rose from the *Tiburon Bay*'s main deck, topped by Chief Grisling's profane invocations to the devil.

"Steady up, helmsman!" Captain Larsen roared at the wheelhouse. "Steady up or you'll break the highline and put a man in the screws!"

Mr. Wilburforce screamed "Jesus!" and rushed into the wheelhouse.

By some miracle the highline held, the bosun's chair settled down from its wild swaying and suddenly began moving again toward the *Bedford*. It seemed that the sagging shape encased in black rubber had hardly touched the destroyer's deck before that end of the rig was cast off and allowed to fall clear. Almost simultaneously the fuel hoses were knocked out of the quick-release fittings, their ends splashing into the waves, where they writhed like serpents. The destroyer was clear, pulling ahead and veering away with a rising whine of her turbines, all within a little over a minute since the GQ alarm.

"Tell all stations to retrieve and secure gear as quickly as possible," Captain Larsen told the talker. "I want an immediate report from Mr. Boomer on the amount of bunkers transferred as of break-off." He went into the wheelhouse and interrupted his executive officer's lecture to the helmsman on steering techniques. "You may take the conn, Mr. Wilburforce. Continue on zero-seven-zero for the time being. Might as well slow down until we get the hoses and lines back aboard."

"The *Bedford* is calling on the TBS, sir," the chief quartermaster announced.

Larsen unzipped his parka and flipped back the hood as he walked into the navigation office. When he took off his cap and threw it on top of the chart table, pure white locks of hair fell over his forehead and they made his face suddenly look much older. The TBS radio was attached to the bulkhead next to the LORAN and the chief quartermaster handed him the mike. As he took it, he noticed Lieutenant Hirschfeld slumped in a chair, nursing a mug of coffee.

"Hoarfrost to Coldsnap. Captain speaking."

The voice which came back to him had a strange crackling quality caused by the scrambler which protected the TBS circuit from enemy ears, but he immediately recognized it as belonging to the *Bedford*'s executive officer. "Coldsnap to Hoarfrost. We are proceeding to investigate emission. You will leave area immediately and execute maneuver Able Fox before resuming mission to rendezvous and feed Polarbear. Maintain radio silence. Acknowledge and repeat."

Captain Larsen confirmed the order, hung up the receiver and switched the set to stand-by. After calling the new course to Lieutenant Wilburforce, he went to the big Thermos and poured himself a cup of coffee, which he wolfed down scalding hot. Hirschfeld had watched him silently while he talked to the *Bedford* and now their eyes met and locked in what became such a long stare that something had to be said.

"Well, Mr. Hirschfeld . . . looks like your Captain Finlander is tearing off on another of his wild war games."

"They are not games, Captain."

"Takes them pretty seriously, eh?"

"Very."

"I've never met him personally. Refueled him twice before, but never met him. But I hear he's a remarkable officer. A real genius at antisubmarine warfare."

"Are you asking me to tell you about Finlander, Captain?" Hirschfeld asked him, cocking one of his sensitive black eyebrows.

Larsen shrugged. "Everybody's curious about Finlander, aren't they?"

"Yes, he's a remarkable officer," the young surgeon told him in his flat, unemotional voice. "Yes, he's a genius at anti-submarine warfare. And because the cold war is not a real war, he's like Captain Ahab sailing his *Pequod* through a closed season on whales." He contemplated the dregs in his empty cup, dropped his tone to a whisper and added: "But Ahab finally met up with his Moby Dick, didn't he?"

Captain Larsen looked perplexed for a moment, grunted and walked out of the navigation office, thoughtfully crossing the darkening wheel-house to one of the windows. The *Bedford* was a blur dissolving into the distant murk, leaving only a ghostly white furrow to linger on the swells.

# 5.

Two seamen had grabbed Ben Munceford as he swung aboard the *Bedford,* roughly manhandled him off the highline and steered him out of the way, leaving him clinging to a stanchion while staring in shock toward the spot, already far astern, where his camera had fallen from his hands. Now there would be nothing to show for his trip, no film for any TV news directors to buy and no pay to alleviate the relentless creeping deficit in his finances—not even fare back to the United States! He felt like screaming at these men that they were a bunch of incom-petent asses, but only one paid brief attention to him.

"Welcome aboard, Mr. Munceford," a huge young officer greeted him in passing. "I'm Ensign Ralston, JOOD." His gloved paw shot out and gave Munceford's hand a hearty pump. "Sorry you got roughed up. Couldn't be helped. We've got a GQ on and you'll have to be shunted below for a while. Steward's Mate Collins will take you to your cabin." Without awaiting any reaction, he rushed off to supervise the hurried stowing of stores which were still piled on the destroyer's deck.

"I'll be a son of a bitch!" Munceford spat out between clenched teeth, staring accusingly at the enormous steel flanks of the *Tiburon Bay,* falling away from the *Bedford* with the disconnected hoses and highline dragging in her wash. He could still hear Chief Grisling's fading curses and see Captain Larsen casually leaning over the port wing of his bridge. "God-damned clumsy bastards!" Unheeding his fury, the tanker majestically steamed on while he felt the deck beneath him heave and tilt as the destroyer pulled ahead and sheered away.

"Excuse me, sir, but we've got to clear the deck fast," a man said to him, gripping his arm. The face framed by the hood was that of a hand-some Negro. "If you'll step this way, I'll get you out of your suit, then show you to your quarters."

"I'd like to speak to the captain," Munceford fumed, resisting the tug.

The steward's mate merely shook his head and began applying firmer pressure. Munceford had a last glimpse of the crew working in swift silence as they grappled with the tangle of gear and piles of containers, then was shunted over the high combing of a door and plunged into the darkness of the *Bedford*'s interior. His eyes adjusted themselves to the dim red glow of blackout lights in a passageway. The hand gripping his arm shoved him under one of them and began unfastening his immersion suit.

"You know they lost me my camera," Munceford exclaimed bitterly.

"That's rough, sir," the Negro steward sympathized, "but they shouldn't have sent you across with anything loose in your hands. Against regulations." With a firm, quick skill he peeled the rubber folds downward and, for a second, stared in surprise at the gaudy camouflage jacket beneath them.

"That *Tiburon Bay*'s a screwed-up bucket," Munceford told him, angrily kicking his feet clear of the immersion suit. The steward's mate picked it up without answering, threw it on top of another one which was lying in a puddle on the deck, then said: "Follow me, please."

On amazingly silent feet the Negro ran down the passageway, turned a corner, stopped and pressed Munceford against a bulkhead to allow a group of shadowy figures to run past them. There followed the sound of watertight doors clanging shut from somewhere below, but he plunged down a hatch and companionway, padded along another long corridor, turned another corner, opened a door and pulled aside a curtain to reveal an even smaller cabin than the one Munceford had occupied on the tanker. "This is it, sir," he said. "Top bunk. Starboard locker. Your gear will be brought down after GQ. Now I must go to my battle station." Without any further formalities the steward's mate vanished down the passageway. A few seconds later another watertight door was heard to close with a solid metallic thump.

At first Munceford thought that there would be nobody else occupying the cubicle, it was so sterile and neat. But he noticed a toothbrush stuck in the bracket above the washbowl, and a pipe lay in the ashtray on the tiny desk. He looked around the bulkheads for a porthole, but there was none; a hissing airduct provided the only ventilation. The cabin swayed and pitched with a strangely detached motion, making him feel that he was imprisoned in a sealed tin box which had been cast upon the sea. With a sudden sense of claustrophobia and loneliness, he sat down on the immaculate lower bunk, listening to the urgent whine of the turbines, the only sound to break the oppressive silence. The foreboding which had come over him when he first saw the *Bedford* appear out of the fog returned and changed his anger over the lost camera to a gnawing depression. Where was his cabin mate? Where was *anybody* in this empty, throbbing ship?

Munceford considered leaving the cabin, but decided he would become hopelessly lost in the labyrinth of dark passages and only run up against closed watertight doors, so he lay back on the bunk to rest his muscles wrenched by the wild ride across the highline. Feeling something hard pressing through the thin pillow, he reached under it and pulled out a small photographic portfolio made of luxurious morocco leather. Flipping it open, he found himself looking into the face of a gaunt, elderly woman with a benign smile; across the tweedy slope of her bosom was a stiffly penned inscription: *To Peter, with Love from Mumsy.*

"Christ! *A Mumsy's boy,* yet!" Munceford exclaimed aloud.

But the frame was the kind with four panels folded accordion fashion and while the two middle sections were empty, the last one contained a photograph of a girl. Such a beautiful girl that she instantly aroused Munceford's old animal instincts and made him forget all his troubles of the moment as he stared at her in fascination. She could have been a natural blond or a redhead, her glossy soft hair very stylish, yet with just the right touch of casualness. The eyebrows were delicate without being weak and the widely separated eyes beneath them had to be either blue or green—there was a wonderfully humorous twinkle in them. Her nose was very fine and ever so slightly turned up. Her full, sensuous lips were drawn into a wistful little smile which created a delicious dimple on her left cheek. The long, aristocratic neck blended into a magnificent pair of bare shoulders and there was a slight suggestion of freckles on her chest where it met the curves of her breasts. These had to be enormously exciting . . . but the photographer had left them to the imagination. In the white space where they should have been, there was scrawled in a boldly impudent hand: *All of me for Pete's sake—Adoring, Shebeona!*

Shebeona! What a name! Ben Munceford pursed his lips to let out a soft whistle, but no sound crossed them. Here was a woman to take your breath away! Those eyes held wisdom, mischief, understanding and fun. But, above all, here was real beauty, earthy and divine all at once. Not of the crude shallow kind of his discarded Nancys! Her voice had to be vibrantly soft, not wheedling or whining or shrill. Yes—here indeed was a woman! If he ever met her, he knew he would be lost. Perhaps even now, while only holding her picture in his hands, he had become lost to her spell. What kind of man was it who possessed her? Did he really possess her? What sort of chap was this Pete to whom she had so humorously and ardently inscribed this photograph? Was she his wife? Fiancée? Or just a girl friend? How intimate was their relationship?

Munceford suddenly became conscious of the fact that he had no right to stare at Shebeona like this, or to lie with her in this bunk. Reluctantly he closed the folds of the portfolio and tucked it back under the pillow. Then he abruptly got up and guiltily brushed aside the curtain to peer into the passageway outside the cabin. It was dark and empty and smelled faintly of fresh paint. He could hear no sound beyond the moaning from the engine rooms. Directly opposite, there was a closed door marked with the numeral 5 and he impulsively stepped over and knocked on it. There was no answer.

"This is a hell of a way to see life on a destroyer," he mumbled bitterly to himself and returned inside his own cabin. The ship heeled and shuddered as she sliced through a big swell. He lost his balance and clumsily flopped back into the lower bunk, but did not bother to get up again. Penetrating through the steel of many bulkheads, the sound of rushing water faintly reached Munceford's ears as the *Bedford* rose up and shook off the spray enveloping her. He lay back on the pillow, feeling the hardness of the frame under it; presently he sneaked another look at Shebeona.

# 6.

When the GQ alarm sounded, Lieutenant Commander Chester Porter had only been aboard the *Bedford* for some forty minutes. He had just completed a telephone conversation with Commander Allison, the executive officer, in which it was decided to postpone a courtesy call to the bridge until after all his gear and some replacement medical stores had arrived and he could report himself ready in every respect to assume his duties as ship's surgeon. The call to battle stations had precipitated matters and startled him a bit, but he was an experienced officer who did not allow small confusions to get the better of him; even though not familiar with this particular vessel, he had served on destroyers before and knew their ways in general. While aboard the *Tiburon Bay,* he had conscientiously plowed through the Qualification Course for this latest class of DDL, something not actually required of a medical officer. However, Lieutenant Commander Porter was a meticulous and precise man who prided himself in always doing a little more for the navy than it required of him. Thus, when the call to General Quarters was so unexpectedly thrust upon him, he promptly sought his post in surgery, where he was gratified to find that a chief pharmacist's mate and two corpsmen had the situation well under control. Whatever had been Lieutenant Hirschfeld's transgressions, they obviously did not include failure to train his medical staff properly.

Porter made certain that the compact surgery was ready to receive casualties, checked sick bay, whose six bunks were fortunately empty, then stepped into the small receiving office and sat down at the desk. The chief pharmacist's mate, who looked more like a bright intern than a sailor, followed him in and reported: "We have two corpsmen stationed on the boat deck and two in the engine room, all ready with first-aid kits. Pharmacist's Mate Engstrom with a party of litter carriers are in the seamen's mess. Chief Steward's Mate Lang and Smythe are organizing an auxiliary dressing station in the wardroom. All according to SOP, sir."

"Good. Looks like you have this department running smoothly. What is your name?"

"McKinley, sir. You will find the complete roster and watch schedule on that clipboard there. The medical log is in the top drawer of the desk. Here is the key to the narcotics locker. It is unlocked during GQ."

The surgeon took the key and carefully clipped it into the ring attached to his belt. "Are morphine ampoules included in the first-aid kits even during practice GQ, McKinley?"

"Yes, sir. You will find that almost all our GQ's are *actual* GQ's."

"Oh? How often does Captain Finlander pull them?"

"Whenever there is a contact, sir. They happen three or four times a week."

"Real intensive training, eh? I suppose we bring in simulated casualties too?"

The pharmacist's mate's high forehead wrinkled in momentary perplexity, as if he were having trouble making the new surgeon understand the situation. Then he smiled. "There's darn little *simulated* stuff aboard the *Bedford,* sir. Everything's for real—except actual bloodletting."

"Well, I am surprised Mr. Hirschfeld hasn't ordered litter-carrying drills. I'll take that up with the captain."

"Yes, sir. In the meanwhile, may I suggest you report the medical department ready at battle stations. I had not had time to do that when you came in, Commander."

"Oh, God! And here we are gabbing away!"

McKinley pushed a telephone in front of the surgeon and depressed a button marked BRIDGE. A talker identified himself with a businesslike tone and accepted the report. When Porter hung up, hoping that Finlander would be impressed that he had taken hold so quickly, the chief pharmacist's mate had left and could be seen checking the sterilizers in the surgery. Porter began to get up to join him, but a long roll of the ship pressed him into his chair and he decided that it would be best if he stayed out of the way for the time being. Until he had familiarized himself with things, procedural matters of the department could be run by McKinley, who seemed very competent. So he remained at the desk and engaged himself in the safe activity of examining some of the paperwork which it contained.

The medical log showed that the *Bedford*'s crew were unusually healthy. In leafing through it, the surgeon found very few entries during the twenty-one days the ship had been on patrol. A cook had been treated for grease burns. A seaman first-class had had his throat swabbed for laryngitis. A radar operator had suffered from a stye. A machinist's mate had spent one day in sick bay with suspected appendicitis, which had turned out to be acute indigestion. All of these cases were certified returned to duty in Lieutenant Hirschfeld's precise handwriting. The only thing which caught Porter's eye and struck him as being slightly strange was the fact that a page had been neatly cut out of the log, leaving a blank strip of paper between November 28—six days ago—and November 29. There were actually no missing entries, but as logs are not supposed to be in any way altered or defaced, the surgeon wondered about it briefly. Then he decided that it might have been a matter of accidental damage or spilling of some staining liquid. He leafed through to the present date and signed himself in as medical officer in charge, relieving Lieutenant Hirschfeld.

He next flipped through the hospital inventory forms which were neatly stapled together in a folder, then glanced through the NAVPUB-MED file, which appeared complete and very up to date. Finally he opened the deep file drawers which contained the individual medical records of every man aboard the *Bedford*. They were inside 324 in-dexed folders and he leafed through a couple of them at random before, on a sudden whim, he deliberately picked out Captain Finlander's. It was empty.

"Chief McKinley!"

McKinley came to the door of the office and braced himself against the roll of the ship. "Yes, Commander."

"Where is Captain Finlander's Form 28?"

The pharmacist's mate appeared to flinch slightly and he hesitated a moment before answering. "Two or three days ago Mr. Hirschfeld took it up to the captain's cabin, sir. He did not bring it back."

"Any reason?"

"Well . . . not that I know of, sir."

"Any reason why I shouldn't ask to have it back?"

McKinley's forehead wrinkled. "No, sir . . . not unless it has some-thing to do with the troubles between Mr. Hirschfeld and the captain. . . . That's just a guess on my part," he quickly added.

Porter thought for a moment, staring down at the empty folder. It was not customary to discuss such things with enlisted men, but the medical department was somewhat privileged, so he decided to ask the question preying on his mind. "What was the nature of those troubles, McKinley?"

"I don't know, sir."

"Not even any scuttlebutt?"

McKinley hesitated a fraction before saying: "Everybody likes Cap-tain Finlander. Everybody liked Lieutenant Hirschfeld too, but . . ."

"But what?"

"But he sometimes had some queer medical ideas, sir."

This shocked the surgeon, who was perhaps more jealous of the sanctity of the medical than of the naval profession. "That's not exactly for a pharmacist's mate to judge," he snapped.

"Sorry, sir. You asked me my opinion."

"Well, yes, and you're entitled to it. But I'm saying I don't think it's a *qualified* opinion, that's all." He paused to let the man's very evident discomfiture sink in, then asked: "How long have you been in the navy, McKinley?"

"Ever since I flunked out of pre-med at Duke, three years ago last June."

Porter could not tell whether there was a genuine meekness or subtle arrogance in that answer. Was he confirming his incompetence or rubbing in the fact that he had, at least for a time, attended one of the finest medical colleges of the U.S.A.? Certainly it was evident that this was no ordinary enlisted man who had barely made it through high school in the lower third of his class. Even to qualify for Duke pre-med, a B+ average was necessary. Porter suddenly felt himself on the defensive with this subordinate, and before he could stop himself from saying anything so revealing, he exclaimed: "You should know better than to make irresponsible statements about a medical officer."

The wrinkles on McKinley's forehead rippled and vanished into an expression of blank resignation. "I am sorry, sir," he said, leaving no doubt that he certainly was very unhappy about the whole discussion. However, it did not have to be continued, because at this moment the *Bedford*'s engines suddenly dropped their high whining song to a throbbing whisper. The deceleration which followed was so pronounced that the pharmacist had to grip the bulkhead to stay on his feet and the surgeon, who was seated facing aft, almost fell over backward. Without bothering with the customary bosun's whistle, the PA system came to life with a crackling voice:

"Now hear this! Rig for silent ship! Rig for silent ship!"

Porter suspected the tactical purpose of what was going on, but, jumping at a good reason to break the tension between himself and McKinley, exclaimed with cheerful annoyance: "Now what the hell is happening?"

"Nothing to worry about, sir," the chief pharmacist told him. "We're going to try a maximum-effect sonar sweep of the area. When under way at high speed, the ambient noises tend to blanket our own sound gear."

"Ah! Of course. Well, go ahead and carry on with your duties. I'll handle Captain Finlander's Form 28 myself."

As the *Bedford* wallowed in the swells with bare steerage way and only a murmur from her turbines, the surgeon spent his time memorizing the roster of the medical department, checking through the narcotics locker and inspecting the instruments in the surgery. Finally the engines picked up their normal tone and the *Bedford* modified her sloppy rolling as she steadied on a course at standard cruising speed. A few minutes later the PA announced securing from General Quarters but with the retaining of all battle stations on stand-by—exactly as on a vessel patrolling under real wartime conditions. The telephone in the receiving office rang and Lieutenant Commander Porter was invited to come up on the bridge. Before leaving, he opened the file drawer of the desk, considering whether or not to bring the empty folder with him. But he decided to take up *that* matter later.

# 7.

Ben Munceford heard the recall from GQ and sat up on the lower bunk, where he had been lying for the past hour. He smoothed out some of the wrinkles and made sure the pillow was in place over Shebeona, then sat there, disgruntled and impatient, listening for any sounds which might indicate human activity. He heard the thumping of running feet, but from the deck above, and they quickly faded. The lonely isolation persisted. Then suddenly the curtain was thrust aside and he found himself looking up at a tall young man in a navy-blue duffel coat of unfamiliar cut. The insignia on his cap was also strange to Munceford, who did not recognize it until he heard the British accent.

"Hello—you must be the reporter! Or should I say correspondent?" The handsomely serious face broke into a quick smile.

Munceford half rose to his feet and accepted the handshake. "I'm Ben Munceford."

"Glad to meet you." His eyes took in the camouflage jacket carelessly draped over the chair, but he registered no special reaction. "I'm Peter Packer."

The funny name startled Munceford. "I guess you're with the British navy. How come?"

"Oh, this is a regular Noah's Ark with all sorts of breeds of animals aboard." He laughed and looked over his bunk, which had not been returned to its former state of perfection. "Would you prefer the lower berth, Munceford? All the same to me."

"No, thanks. I'm okay in the upper. But I'd sure as hell like to get out of this cell and look around."

Packer shook himself out of his duffel. He was wearing a white turtleneck sweater under it. "You've been stuck here all through GQ, I gather. What a bore!"

"That's not the half of it. Lost my camera from the highline."

"Oh, dear! Bad day all around, eh?"

Munceford winced at the "oh, dear."

Packer smiled pleasantly and opened his locker to hang up his coat. Everything in it was stowed with neat precision. "The ECM lads sniffed the emission of a strange radar while we were refueling," he explained. "The Russians watch us even as we watch them, you know. Only it isn't fair, because this is *our* part of the playing field. Not that *we* don't sneak over into theirs occasionally, of course." He moved to the washbowl and began to lather his hands vigorously. "But that doesn't mean we don't react with proper indignation when we catch them over here. So we get lots of jolly GQ's and chase each other all over the ocean. A nuisance, but keeps us on our toes."

"I'm surprised I wasn't just cut loose and dropped in the drink, like my camera," Munceford observed sourly.

The British officer finished splashing water on his face and answered through the folds of a towel: "Oh, Captain Finlander was watching you, all right. I distinctly heard him say: 'Let's get that man across if we can. He may give us some good publicity.' He's got a marvelous dry wit, old Finlander!" Packer laughed at the recollection.

Munceford's churlish expression did not change as he contemplated the English officer. "So what did all this eager-beaver stuff accomplish?" he asked. "Did you find one of those Red trawlers lurking around making like it was fishing?"

"No. The emission was most likely from a sub which submerged long before we got within range." He was back at his locker, taking from it a jacket with one and a half gold stripes on its sleeves and crowns embossed on the gold buttons. There was not a wrinkle in it. "We're over a deep trench here with some currents which cause temperature layering. Makes sonar unreliable. A sub can hang deep, undetected. The Russians haven't got any nuclear units that we know about, but they can go down a thousand feet or better, which is pretty safe in these waters."

"In other words, they screw us."

Packer turned and his face was deadly earnest. "Never fear, Munceford. You can tell your readers that in naval matters we're giving the Russians a bad inferiority complex."

"I haven't got readers. I'm in television and radio."

"Ah. Sounds more exciting. I like the telly."

"What exactly is your reason for being here?"

"Communication liaison with NATO. And, of course, spying for the Admiralty on your latest type of destroyer."

The curtain whipped aside and the door was suddenly filled by the hulking shape of Ensign Ralston, the officer who had briefly greeted, then deserted Munceford when he was first dumped aboard the *Bedford*. "Damn right he's a spy!" he loudly exclaimed. "But we're perfectly safe because the Limey navy can't afford expensive toys like this any more. . . . You all squared away, Mr. Munceford?"

Munceford looked hopefully at this magnificent American animal who must have been a tackle on the Annapolis football team as well as in the top third of his class—which could hardly have graduated more than a year ago. He was scowling with ferocious affection at the English officer and, before Munceford could answer his question, said: "I gather you've become acquainted with *Left'nant* Peter Packer of Her Majesty's Royal Navy." He pronounced the name *Peterpacker*, all run together with emphasis on the *p*'s. "He's not only a very funny chap, but has a very funny name too. The ship's company gets knocked out every time it's called over the PA."

Lieutenant Packer was calmly looking himself over in the tiny mirror. "That's all right, chaps," he said. "I have a couple of middle initials in reserve for the day when I make flag rank. Admiral Sir P. L. M. Packer sounds dignified enough."

"The day you make admiral, Pete, your navy will be down to one ceremonial barge."

"Rowed by Yankee ensigns!" Packer quickly injected.

The two officers laughed at each other and Munceford emerged out of his grouch to join in the mirth. "I've got to remember to tape some of you guys' dialogue," he told them.

"Any time," the ensign agreed. "But I want you to understand that I write all of Peterpacker's funny lines for him. . . . Keee-rist! What's *this?*" He stepped into the cabin and picked up Munceford's camouflage jacket off the chair, holding it between thumb and forefinger as if it were not entirely sanitary, and eying the profusion of badges and patches with amazement. Spotting the fur cap, he picked it up too, examined it and, removing his own, put it on his close-cropped blond head. "Keee-rist!" he exclaimed again, staring at himself in the mirror. "What is it?"

Packer shrugged. "Anybody can see it's the official uniform of an American war correspondent."

Munceford was used to taking some kidding about his dress and really enjoyed the attention he derived from it. He had even once worn it up to the production offices of CBS News, a very conforming and dignified place of business. But he seldom had received the hilarious reaction which Ensign Ralston now gave him.

"It's pure crazy!" he boomed in delight, draping the jacket across his own enormous chest. "Crazy as hell! Gee, welcome aboard, Mr. Munceford, and join the club. We're *all* crazy aboard the *Bedford,* you know. So certified by our former medical officer. So you'll fit in perfectly. Here! Put this outfit on, please! I've got to see you in it."

Munceford laughed and obliged him, creating a terrible jam in the tiny cabin as he stood up in it together with the giant ensign and tall lieutenant. When he had the jacket on, Ralston transferred the cap to his head, then stepped back and examined him with more curiosity than hilarity.

"You cruise on a pigboat?" he asked, indicating the submariner's insignia.

"Only for a week out of Key West," Munceford admitted. "Just an ordinary diesel rig. I'm bucking for an assignment on a nuke, though."

"And you've jumped with the paratroops too?" Ralston asked, pointing at the patch of the 82nd Airborne Division.

"Yes—I followed a pair of recruits through jump school and took the course myself to get the feel of what they went through."

Ralston's rugged face showed genuine admiration. "You really believe in living your stories, don't you."

The conversation was interrupted by the arrival of Steward's Mate Collins, who was bringing in Munceford's camera case and duffel bag. The squeeze in the cabin became intolerable and Ralston took Munceford by the arm, dragging him out into the passageway. "I actually came down to escort you to the bridge and meet our skipper. He'll love that outfit of yours. Come on, Mr. Munceford."

"Call me Ben," Munceford told him, now feeling almost completely cheered up. Maybe he could scrounge a camera from somebody aboard. This ensign was all right and the Englishman was not really too bad. But, remembering Lieutenant Commander Porter's ominous hints about the captain, he asked: "What is this Finlander like?" as he followed Ralston down the narrow passageway.

The ensign made a circle with his thumb and forefinger, but did not answer. They went through a watertight door and up a companionway to the next deck. Then another long, cramped passage lit only by the red blackout lights. The low ceiling was crammed with pipes and conduits, the gray metal walls sporadically broken by closed doors. They had not met a single man anywhere, so far.

"Where the heck are the three-hundred-odd people who are supposed to be on this ship?" Munceford asked.

Ralston's rolling gait, which balanced perfectly with the motions of the destroyer, did not falter in its steady progress. "On stand-by battle stations," he answered softly over his shoulder. "Or at work. Or sacked out." His former boyishly boisterous manner seemed to have turned completely businesslike.

The ensign turned a corner and suddenly vanished upward. Munceford blinked, then noticed a ladder leading vertically up a shaft containing the same red glow as the passageways; Ralston's silhouette was springing catlike up the steel rungs. Moving slower and more cautiously, he followed. The ladder passed a small recess, or landing, containing a closed metal door on which was stenciled the word RESTRICTED in large red letters; above it a small blue bulb burned with a faint light. "What's in there?" Munceford asked.

"CIC," Ralston's answer came down, barely audible as he continued climbing up the shaft. They were obviously going to some place on a higher level, but Munceford had lost all sense of direction and was completely confused. The shaft ended in an open hatch and he shot past the last rungs without touching them as the ensign reached down and boosted him up with an iron grip on his arm.

He found himself deposited in a large area which was not even lit by the red blackout lights. It was almost totally dark, much colder, and he immediately sensed that it was occupied by a number of men. As his eyes adjusted themselves, he made out their shadowy shapes and noticed the silhouette of one which stood out more clearly against a pale green glow emanating from what he recognized to be a binnacle and gyrocompass. So this had to be the wheelhouse and although it was only a few minutes past four, it was already shrouded by a black night. Except for a faint pinging sound which Munceford identified as sonar, and the soft moaning of the wind sweeping the bridge outside, a complete silence prevailed. The effect was eery and tense.

Munceford took a couple of cautious steps, then stopped because the grip on his arm was gone and he lost Ensign Ralston among the other shadowy figures. As he stood there, the door to the port wing of the bridge opened and for a brief moment the wheelhouse was filled with the sound of sea and the ice-cold draft of salt air; then the door rolled shut on silent runners. A low voice said: "Cover is ten-ten again, sir. No sight possible." There followed a subdued conversation in which Munceford could not catch a single word. Somebody passed very close to him and as he turned his head to follow their movement, he noticed a radar scanner, its sweeper revolving with a cold phosphorescent fire. Behind him there were the green and red and amber pinpricks of some kind of control panel.

Beyond the helmsman, the glass of windows glistened faintly and Munceford was taking a tentative step in their direction when the strong grip on his arm returned and he found himself led off in the opposite direction. A curtain was swept aside and he suddenly found himself in the same soft red light which seemed to prevail throughout most of the ship. Ensign Ralston had him in tow again and was introducing him to an officer bent over a chart.

"Sir, this is our guest, Mr. Ben Munceford."

"How are you, Captain?"

The officer shook his head. "I'm not the captain. I'm the exec, Commander Allison. Captain Finlander apologizes for delaying in meeting you, but he and Commander Porter went down to his cabin on some business. He will see you a little later. In the meanwhile, I hope to make you feel at home."

Munceford felt a stab of guilty uneasiness over the fact that Porter was getting to Finlander before him. He fumbled the handshake with

Commander Allison, who was a short, robust man with a big nose. "Have you ever been out with the navy before, Mr. Munceford?" the executive officer asked him.

Munceford hesitated before answering, hoping that Ralston would inject something to the effect that he was an experienced military correspondent who had dived in submarines, jumped with paratroops and flown with the Strategic Air Command. But now that he was on the bridge, the ensign's transformation was complete. His demeanor and silence were rock-like and Munceford's hesitation became a suspicion of uncertainty. "Yes," he finally said. "Submarines, and also on a short DE cruise with a reserve unit. DE's are kind of like destroyers, so I'm not completely lost here."

"I see," Commander Allison said. His eyes were suddenly glued to the camouflage jacket and Munceford became aware that it glowed with a hideous hodge-podge effect in the red light. For the first time he felt embarrassed over it. "Well, DE's are somewhat similar, of course," the exec agreed, as if he actually resented the comparison. "But this DDL is damned near as big as a cruiser. However, the main thing to remember is that we are not on a reservists' cruise, Mr. Munceford. We are an active part of NATO defenses and operate our ship virtually under wartime conditions. And *that* reminds me—may I see your credentials, please?"

The abrupt request took Munceford completely by surprise. He fumbled inside his jacket and brought out the creased envelope which contained the orders from the Navy Department attaching "Munceford, Benjamin J., Civilian Correspondent," to DDL 113 for a period of two weeks, handing it to the commander. Then he fished his wallet out of his back pocket, picked about among the few bills and many dog-eared membership cards for his War Department correspondent's ID. Finding the plastic square, he gave it to the exec with the same resentful feeling he had often felt when handing his driver's license to a tough cop.

"Thank you." Commander Allison briefly checked the orders and the ID, then gave the latter to the ensign. "Mr. Ralston, will you please note in the log that Mr. Munceford's credentials have been checked and enter the serial number of this ID." He flashed a thin smile at Munceford. "Like I say, we operate under virtual wartime conditions. There's a lot of highly classified equipment on this ship."

"And what would you have done if my credentials hadn't been in order? Thrown me overboard, Commander?"

The smile remained, but the executive officer obviously did not think this question funny. "We would confine you to quarters while the matter was being checked through with COMFLANT," he answered dryly and turned his attention to the chart from which he had been diverted when Munceford was brought before him. "Maybe you are interested in the *Bedford*'s current position and our projected patrol for the next week. This is where we are." He pointed with a stubby finger to an X penciled over a course line. "Approximately at the southwest entrance to the Denmark Strait. From here we will patrol through it toward the general vicinity of Jan Mayen Island—here." The stubby finger jabbed a tiny speck in the vastness of the Arctic Ocean to the northeast of Iceland. "The course line shown here is nice and straight, but it probably won't work out that way in practice. Radar and sonar contacts have to be investigated. Ice conditions and weather can get awfully bad, pushing us off course. How are your sea legs, by the way?" He stole another doubtful glance at Munceford's jacket when he asked the question.

"I can make out, Commander. Do you expect we will run into Russian subs?"

"Some."

"How about their trawlers?"

"Some of those too."

"I'm getting the impression that they are far more active than has been let on at home. Is that so, Commander?"

Allison's answer came clipped and definite. "I will let Captain Finlander brief you on the tactical situation, Mr. Munceford. He will have to decide what to tell you and what not to tell you. Frankly, I am surprised that you are here at all. This area is far too critical to make a TV show out of it." He pronounced TV as if it were a dirty word.

"You mean you want to fight yourselves a sort of private cold war out here?" Munceford acidly asked. From this moment on, he knew they would dislike each other. The commander did not answer him. Ensign Ralston returned to the chart table and handed the ID card back to the executive officer, who in turn passed it on to Munceford. For a moment there was a painful silence while the camouflage jacket received another strongly disapproving scrutiny.

"It gets pretty cold in these latitudes," Allison finally said. "Mr. Ralston, will you see that Mr. Munceford is issued some regulation arctics out of our slop chest, please."

"Oh, don't trouble yourselves," Munceford protested. "This is my regular working outfit and it keeps me plenty warm enough." But as he said this, Ralston snapped out: "Yes, sir," to the commander.

"Now, if you'll excuse me, I've got some duties to perform," Allison politely but firmly announced.

Munceford found himself started on the long return journey through the *Bedford*'s intricate interior maze of passages, once again following behind the ensign's broad back. On the way down the shaft from the bridge, he ventured to observe: "The commander is an abrupt cuss, isn't he?"

"He's okay by us," Ralston answered shortly.

They went the rest of the way in silence. When they reached the cabin they found Lieutenant Packer seated at the desk, writing in a black note-book. Pipe-tobacco smoke hung in a blue mist around his head.

"All right, Pete!" Ralston boomed out with a startling return of his former hearty manner, which he evidently reserved entirely for this area. "Quit scribbling complaints about us to your Admiralty and take charge of entertaining our guest. I think he needs a drink."

"A drink?" Munceford exclaimed with hopeful surprise.

Packer put down his pen. "Don't expect too much," he drawled. "This navy isn't trusted with the real stuff. You have a choice of a whisky sour without whisky or a Bloody Mary without blood. What did you think of our old man?"

"Didn't meet him," Munceford answered, then added with a wry grimace: "But I met a Commander Allison. He could charm the balls off a brass monkey." He immediately sensed a frosting of the two officers' demeanor, but did not care. His ugly mood had returned and his boyish face showed it.

"And what do you think of the ship as a whole?" Packer asked evenly. "Any interesting snap judgments there too?"

Ralston snickered.

"The corridors are clean and all the doors neatly closed, as far as I could see—which wasn't much, on account of the peculiar indirect light-ing."

"That's so our eyes can quickly become adjusted to total darkness if we have to go on deck," Packer explained. "Kind of gloomy at first, but you'll get used to it. Let me take you to the wardroom and I'll show you some of the gayer side of life on the Bedford." He knocked the ashes out of his pipe and got up from the desk.

"The wardroom is warm and cozy," Ralston pointedly told Munce-ford. "You won't need your jacket in there." Before hurriedly leaving ahead of them, he gave it a last amused glance. "It's sensational, Ben! It knocked out Commander Allison! . . . See you later."

As Munceford took it off, he swore to himself he would wear his jacket as much as he damned well liked and to hell with Allison.

# 8.

The Bedford's wardroom was not exactly gay, but it turned out to be at least cheerful in décor and almost spacious. One bulkhead was covered by blue drapes with green and gold palm trees which created an incongruously frivolous departure from the austere warship's atmosphere

and the cold, dark sea she was traversing. The opposite bulkhead gave
the impression of having been paneled with walnut, but it was actually
a very clever kind of plastic coating which created this illusion. The
proper naval touch was provided by a framed reproduction of the *Bon-
homme Richard* engaging the *Serapis*. There were two long tables, one
of which was being set for the evening meal by a steward in a spotless
white jacket; he was dropping stainless steel cutlery into the individual
compartments of a mahogany rolling-guard fitted over the tablecloth.
The surrounding chairs were functionally comfortable and padded with
a blue vinyl which matched the drapes; a small settee was covered with
the same material and next to it was a stand full of very battered magazines. A sideboard held a steaming silver Thermos of coffee and two
jugs, one containing a red, the other a yellow liquid.

Two lieutenants (J.G.) were seated at the empty table, poring over a
large sheet of paper filled with complex electrical diagrams and were so
immersed in a deep discussion when Munceford and Packer entered that
they did not even look up. But the Englishman went right over to them
and started the introductions.

"Gentlemen, I want you to meet Mr. Munceford, the TV reporter
who is going to be with us for a week or so. Ben, this is Lieutenants
Krindlemeyer and Spitzer, the electronic wizards of the old *Bedford*."

The two officers bobbed to their feet with vacantly surprised expressions. Although one was dark and the other light-complected, they somehow looked identical and both stared myopically at Munceford through
identical spectacles. "Where did you come from?" Spitzer asked as he
shook hands.

"Do you only know what goes on in the sky and under the sea?"
Lieutenant Packer asked. "Aren't you aware there was an eighteen-
thousand-ton tanker alongside of us this afternoon?"

"Oh, that! Sure. We picked up the *Tiburon Bay* on the QB-two-R
when she was fifty-eight miles off."

"Yes," Krindlemeyer confirmed. "And detected her emissions at over
eighty. Do you know at what range she picked *us* up on her radar, Mr.
Munceford?"

"No. I was sacked out."

"These ECM chaps live on a pink cloud all of their own," Packer
explained, steering Munceford away from them and toward the sideboard. There he introduced him to the steward, whose name was Martin and who regarded him with considerable curiosity.

"Are you going to put us on TV, Mr. Munceford?" he asked.

"Sure am," he answered, not really knowing *how* without a camera.

"Us ordinary guys too?" the steward asked with a sly glance at the
officers.

Packer screwed his face into a grimace which was supposed to express a lampoon of British stuffiness. "Well, of course, Martin. This is the democratic American navy, isn't it? Absolutely anything goes."

"I wasn't knocking the system, sir," Martin answered softly and with a twinkle of amusement. He glanced toward Krindlemeyer and Spitzer, who had resumed droning at each other over the diagrams. "It's all the fancy education around here that gets an ordinary mortal down. There was a time when you'd pick up some good dirty jokes in a destroyer's wardroom."

Both Packer and Munceford chuckled.

"By the way, sir, you got some letters," the steward announced in a normal voice and handed Packer four of them from a tray on the sideboard which was stacked with mail.

"Oh, thanks, Martin!" the Englishman casually exclaimed and shoved them into his coat pocket, but not so quickly that he did not take time for a hasty glance over the handwriting on the envelopes. Three of them were in Mumsy's precise penmanship; only one was addressed with Shebeona's bold scrawl. This gave Munceford a peculiar sense of gratification when he noticed it. He did not want that beautiful creature to be a puritanically faithful navy wife or sweetheart whose letters caught up with her sailor boy in carload lots. The near indifference of the recipient was also encouraging. "What's your poison, Ben?" Packer was asking. "The whisky sours are spiked with lemon extract. The Bloody Mary's with tabasco sauce and the stuff Martin puts in his hair."

The steward chuckled as he left through the pantry door.

"I'm a whisky drinker, myself," Munceford answered without much enthusiasm over the prospects of an ersatz. "Are you a married man, Pete?"

"Not bloody likely on my salary. Are you?"

"Just getting rid of my third."

"Gad! You must have something to do with the population explosion we hear so much about."

"Hell, no! I'm a pillar to the birth-control industry." This changed his companion's grin to a frown of mild shock.

Lieutenant Packer mixed the drinks by simply dropping an ice cube in each glass and pouring the juices over them, but he did it with a flare and conviction which indicated a determination to kid himself as well as Munceford. Even when he sipped the concoction, Munceford was not entirely sure that it was *nothing* but fruit juice. "Almost fools you," he admitted as they sat down at the opposite end of the table from the oblivious Krindlemeyer and Spitzer.

"What do you mean *almost?*" the Englishman laughed. "Twenty or thirty of these and you'd be in sick bay."

Munceford noticed that he was subconsciously fondling the pocket containing the letters. He wanted to ask whether he was engaged, but instead inquired: "Is it a fact that there isn't a drop of hard stuff aboard? Not even up here in the Arctic Ocean?"

"Surgeon has some. If it were old Hirschfeld, I'd say you might stand a chance, but I don't know about the new chap. I may throw a fit in a day or two and try him."

"I bunked with Commander Porter on the *Tiburon Bay*. He's pretty strait-laced. If Hirschfeld was so cooperative, why did you get rid of him?"

Packer reacted with a sudden frown and an icy: "What do you mean by that?"

"Well . . . nothing in particular. I only thought—"

"Lieutenant Hirschfeld is a closed subject," the Englishman interrupted with surprising vehemence. "Forget it."

Munceford blinked, sighed, stared down into his glass and wished to God in Heaven it would miraculously change into one-hundred-proof bourbon. If ever he had needed a real drink, it was now. He thought of the bottle he had tossed out of the porthole of the *Tiburon Bay* just to needle Porter, now lost forever on a dark, empty sea a hundred miles astern. Perhaps it would drift ashore on the Greenland coast where some Eskimo would pick it up and get roaring drunk. He wished he were that Eskimo right now. He wished he were anywhere but on this destroyer.

Lieutenant Packer sensed that he might have inadvertently betrayed a secret which was not suspected, that he had unfairly been rude to Munceford, and suddenly became very flustered about it. He glanced up the table toward Krindlemeyer and Spitzer, who remained preoccupied with their own electronic problems, then toward the pantry door, which was swinging silently back and forth on its hinges as the *Bedford* breasted the swells. "I'm sorry, Ben," he said with an earnest whisper. "I know it was accidental, but don't ask any questions about Hirschfeld on this ship. He's a devil of a sore subject. Had a big row with the skipper."

"Is Finlander so hard to get along with?" Munceford asked without bothering to lower his voice.

"Captain Finlander is one of the finest officers I have ever known," Packer answered, also raising his voice to a normal level and with a certain defiance in it. "And that includes my own Royal Navy, which is going some, believe me."

"Well, okay."

There had been no reaction from Krindlemeyer and Spitzer, who could have heard the last remarks. Martin came in, distributed some ketchup bottles in slots of the dinner table's rolling-guard and left. Munceford sipped his fruit juice and noticed that Packer's right hand was still nervously resting on the pocket containing the letters. "Look, Pete," he said. "You don't have to entertain me. Go ahead and read your letters."

"Oh, they can wait."

"Hell, go ahead! You haven't heard from Shebeona for weeks!"

Packer's jaw dropped open. "How do you know her name?" he stammered.

Munceford felt himself flushing a bright scarlet. He bit his lips, rocked back in his chair, then pounded his fist on the table and exclaimed: "Oh, damn!"

Spitzer looked up from his electronic diagrams, but from the expression on his face it was hard to tell whether he had been startled by the profanity or was staring into space at some imaginary blackboard filled with phantom equations.

"How do you know her name?" the Englishman demanded again, this time with a sharp insistence.

"Pete . . . I lay down on your bunk this afternoon. I felt the frame under the pillow. So I looked. So shoot me. So I'm sorry!"

"I'd damned well think you would be. That sort of thing isn't done, really. Very bad manners." His voice was very low, very even and very angry.

"I said I'm sorry, Pete. Now go ahead and read your letters."

"Thanks. I think I will." Lieutenant Packer got up from his seat opposite Munceford, moved to another chair at the center of the table, twisted his back to him and in a moment was a thousand miles away as he opened the first letter with restrained agitation and began to read. It was from Shebeona and only filled half the page.

Munceford drained his insipid drink and, after finally tearing his eyes away from the letter, stared smugly at the palm trees on the drapes, which swayed with a peculiar realism as the roll of the *Bedford* rippled the material. The steward padded in on silent feet, deposited some butter dishes on the dinner table and left. The turbines hummed softly and their vibration set up a momentary resonance in a cup full of coffee spoons on the sideboard, making them buzz with a thin metallic sound. The murmur of Krindlemeyer's and Spitzer's whispered conversation suddenly seemed almost loud and Munceford could not help overhearing it.

"You've got to remember that when you interrupt an inductive circuit, switches will create arcs," one of them was saying, his nose almost touching the sheet of diagrams. "That would give you peaks and craters in the contacts."

"Right, but I think this is a matter of contact bounce," the other answered. "There's a sequential repeater on that circuit with a rate of ten milliseconds. The operating time is considerably longer than the bounce, and that's what produces the noise in the system."

"And, Jesus, we can't allow any noise on this ship," Munceford muttered between clenched teeth. He got up and took his empty glass to the sideboard, where he debated with himself whether to switch over to the pitcher containing the red juice. The yellow had left an unpleasant sour-sweet taste in his mouth. He was standing there contemplating the problem with a morose indifference when Lieutenant Commander Porter entered the wardroom and saw him.

"Hello, Ben. Having withdrawal pains?" he quipped with a sadistic smirk.

"You tell me, Doc," Munceford shot back. "I've been seeing blondes and palm trees, and it hurts right *here*." He patted his rump.

"I prescribe a bland diet and plenty of fresh ocean air," Porter answered, reaching for the red jug. "The captain has asked me to tell you he will see you in his cabin now."

"God! And here I am reeking of fruit juice! Oh, well—I might as well have *everybody* aboard on my tail. Where do I go?"

"Turn left outside this door, stagger twenty feet along the passageway and knock on the door marked CAPTAIN," the surgeon directed him dryly, then turned toward the other officers and loudly introduced himself: "Hello, gentlemen. I am Commander Porter, your new medical officer."

Lieutenant Peter Packer looked up with a start and jumped to his feet, quickly shoving his letters into a pocket. As Munceford left the wardroom, he saw Krindlemeyer and Spitzer rise and briefly come out of their technical trance with the same vaguely amazed expression they had shown when they met him.

# 9.

Captain Erik J. Finlander was a man of medium build but with an unusually large head—or perhaps it was the very heavy jaw and pronounced brows which made it appear that way. Or maybe the thin neck with the very prominent arteries, one of which was crossed by the scar of what must once have been a nearly fatal wound. His hair was cropped short and the color and texture of a steel brush; the eyebrows were the same and joined together over the bridge of a nose which had been broken a long time ago. His eyes were the greenish-gray of the North Atlantic, set deep under heavy lids and among many little wrinkles etched by a combination of humor, temper and driving winds. He was ugly. He was also handsome. And when he smiled, all the hardness in his face vanished—except in the eyes, which merely mellowed from a cold gleam to a mischievous twinkle.

"Very glad to meet you at last, Mr. Munceford," he exclaimed in a voice which had a quiet, husky quality. "I wanted us to get together much sooner, but this has been kind of a busy day."

"That's okay, Captain. Quite okay," Munceford answered, wondering whether or not this was the sort of looking man he had expected.

"I also want to apologize for the shaking up you got on the highline," Finlander told him, still keeping a strong grip on his hand. "Was that an expensive camera you lost?"

"About five hundred, new," Munceford lied, managing to sound casual.

Captain Finlander winced and transferred his grip to Munceford's elbow, steering him into the middle of his cabin. It was not as large as Munceford had expected, but a luxurious touch was provided by the same plastic "paneling" used in the wardroom, and by a bulkhead-to-bulkhead carpet of deep red color. Munceford was surprised to find another man standing at the desk and his first impression was that he was a civilian. He wore a black leather jacket without any insignia, and his trousers were tucked into a pair of non-regulation black rubber boots. When he looked up from the papers he was examining, the face was either that of a young sixty- or old forty-year-old; it was heavily lined, hard and somewhat melancholy.

"I'd like you to meet Commodore Wolfgang Schrepke of the DBM," Finlander said. When he saw Munceford's blank expression, he smiled and added: "That's the Deutches Bundes Marine—West German Navy to you."

"How do you do?" Schrepke said, giving him a quick, hard handshake. He spoke with a harsh German accent.

"The commodore and I have a matter to discuss for a minute or two," Finlander apologized pleasantly. "In the meanwhile, have yourself a drink and sit down." He pointed toward a chest on which stood a tray with two pitchers—one containing red, the other gold-colored fluid.

This time Munceford picked the Bloody Mary and sat down in a chair to wait. He felt himself hopefully impressed by Finlander, but confused by the presence of the German. The rank of commodore he associated with yacht clubs and had a vague recollection that it had been discontinued in the American navy since World War II. But he remembered it was just below admiral—more rank than Finlander! Yet the man looked like a chief bosun of a freighter. After his low conversation with the captain was ended—it was about something they called low-frequency returns—he put on a battered naval officer's cap with gold on the visor, excused himself with a polite military formality and stalked out of the cabin.

Finlander put the papers away in a drawer of his desk and came over to pour himself a drink. He seemed to be closely appraising Munceford and also reading his puzzled thoughts. "Commodore Schrepke is an anti-submarine warfare expert with NATO naval forces," he explained after the door had shut behind the German. "You have heard of him, of course? No? Well, during the war he was one of Dönitz's ace U-boat commanders. Sank over two hundred thousand tons of Allied shipping. It's funny how things turn out, but we find it's probable that I depth-charged him while escorting a convoy to Murmansk. Now here we are sixteen years later, serving together *against* the Russians."

"That *is* a story," Munceford said, really impressed.

"Yes, but I don't know that it should be publicized. A lot of our Congressmen and their constituents are sensitive about foreigners serving on our ships, especially Germans. Sometimes I don't think we are at all ready for the NATO concept. Yet we've *got* to make it work. Frankly, I myself still have an ingrained dislike of all U-boat crews, a hangover from my younger days when I fought them with more passion than science. But now I control my feelings, get along with men like Schrepke and try to do a strictly professional job." He raised his drink of tomato juice, his eyes boring into Munceford over the rim of the glass. "Cheers! . . . Well, now . . . back to the matter of the lost camera. I suppose, like all press people, you've got cases full of assorted replacements, so you'll be able to carry on."

"As a matter of fact, no," Munceford answered, then found himself lying to Finlander in spite of an uneasy feeling that the man could see right through him. "I accidentally smashed my spare aboard the *Tiburon Bay*. Didn't even bother to bring it with me to the *Bedford*."

"Then, to put it exactly, you are in a fix," Finlander exclaimed, his bristling eyebrows curving into a Mephisto expression.

"Can't shoot any movies. But I have a tape recorder, which means I can produce something for radio, at least."

Captain Finlander had been about to sit down, but now he went back to the desk, dialed a number on the telephone and ordered whoever answered: "Send Yeoman Pinelli to the captain's quarters at once, please." Almost the instant he hung up, the ship's PA system could be heard paging that individual. As Finlander came back to sit down, he said: "The destroyer service is nothing if not versatile, so we'll probably be able to put you back in business, Munceford. In the meanwhile, give me your first impressions of my ship."

Munceford remembered what Commander Allison had said about the *Bedford* and assumed it would be pleasing to her captain. "She's damn near as big as a cruiser. Much more impressive than the little DE I once did a story on."

"My first command was a DE during World War II," Finlander informed him. "I built a reputation as a U-boat killer, you know, and did it with that type of ship, one of the best classes ever designed. So don't be overly impressed by size, which in itself means little. For instance, not far from where we are steaming right now lies the sunken remains of the largest battle cruiser ever built, the H.M.S. *Hood*. A single hit from the *Bismarck* blew her to pieces in 1942 during the first minute of the hour she and her two-thousand-man crew were supposed to justify their existence. Incidentally, and to speak of strange coincidences which seem to devil the *Bedford,* a son of one of the *Hood*'s officers is aboard this ship—Lieutenant P. L. M. Packer of the Royal Navy."

"I'll be damned!" Munceford exclaimed. "Why, I'm sharing a cabin with him. Seems like a—"

"Yes, yes . . . he's a good boy," Finlander interrupted him with a certain impatience. "The Packers have been in the British navy since they stopped the Armada. Between then and the *Bismarck* action, not a single one has ever found a dry grave for himself—something which would worry me if I were superstitious. Well, anyway, the point I was trying to make before getting sidetracked was that the most impressive thing about the *Bedford* is not her size, but the sophistication of her weaponry, which gives her the contradictory characteristics of specialization and flexibility. She's an engineering marvel and a scientific miracle; she is also a cranky and complex bitch at times, which means she can still make an old destroyer man feel at home. All right—what's your impression of her crew?"

Munceford decided to try to be candid. "The few I've met are kind of puzzling characters. I'm mostly impressed by their absence and silence."

Captain Finlander laughed softly. "Well, for one thing, we have automation to eliminate much of the manpower which used to be necessary to operate a ship of this size. For another, we are hunters—*stalking* kind of hunters—who track by ear a foe who is also intently listening for *us.* To be quiet and stealthy becomes second nature under the circumstances; I deliberately instill this in my men. The fact that we are fighting a nebulous cold war without decisively obtainable tactical objectives has a lot to do with creating some puzzling characters among us. Take myself, for instance. . . ." He leaned forward in his chair, thrusting his face toward Munceford, who found himself staring back almost as though hypnotized.

"As captain, I must key all my men to an intense fighting pitch and keep them keyed that way through hundreds of boring sweeps through an ocean most of them can't even see, only feel through bruised and wrenched muscles. Then, if we get a contact, I must key them to an even finer pitch so they hang on, close up and drive in for a kill they know will end in nothing but the dull mockery of an anti-climax. The same man who extracted every last measure of their skills, who numbed their minds to the fact that this is nothing but a sadistic game, must belay all their efforts with a few bellicose words over the ship's PA. 'Well done, men! You've given those Commies down there an inkling of what it is like to die in a submarine. Now stand down from General Quarters. The movie in enlisted mess tonight will be Liz Taylor in *Butterfield 8.*' . . . The truth really is that the Commie submariners have learned more from the operation than we have and will be twice as hard to pin down next time. But we've got to oblige them with this training, and that's the sort of thing which strains the minds of officers and thinking men on destroyers in this cold-war zone—understand?"

Munceford was not sure that he did, although Finlander was eloquent to the point of being spellbinding. "I get the idea that there's a lot more Russian submarine activity here than is generally realized."

"It's a free ocean," the captain answered with a bitter chuckle. "Technically, they can come and go as they please, cold war or no cold war. So can we. Contrary to certain scuttlebutt, we aren't out to spy on each other's missile ranges or atomic tests. That kind of work can be done cheaper and easier by one man in a U-2 type of aircraft. It is DEW-line and NORAD emissions Soviet subs are recording and checking out to help them penetrate our defenses when the time comes. I also suspect scouting and ranging of submarine missile-firing positions. These are objectives worth tremendous risks. They are worth killing over."

"You *actually* attack them?"

Those wiry eyebrows arranged themselves into a sly expression. "Do you mean officially?"

"I mean . . . does anybody get hurt, Captain Finlander?"

"Fear hurts. Unrelenting tension becomes a physical pain. Uncertainty and frustration can turn into a crippling agony. But I suppose that to you, actual killing is the ultimate hurt, so I can truthfully answer: *no,* nobody has been hurt—so far." His eyes left Munceford's face for a moment, flicking to the gyro-repeater and clock attached to the bulkhead above his desk. "Where is Pinelli?" he asked with sudden irritation. "It's been four minutes since I called him."

Munceford was trying to correlate in his mind the implications of what Finlander had told him. "Jesus! I may be on to a real hot story for a change!" he exclaimed. "What's going on out here will come as a hell of a shock to a lot of people."

Finlander's eyes snapped into him. "I'm giving you background material, *not* a story, Munceford. This is not a piece of political taffy to be pulled and fingered by pundits and politicians, like they are doing with Berlin and Laos. Those items have at least a certain sticky elasticity. *This* is the hard-core, *war* part of the cold war. Here we clash in the privacy of a black, empty ocean with no audience but our own conscience; both parties want to keep it that way because the stakes are such that no compromise is possible. If you doubt me, then ask yourself what the United States has left if its DEW-line and NORAD systems are cracked. What have the Soviets got if they never crack them? So both parties need secrecy to protect their freedom of maneuvering against each other. So don't expect to run wild with your story."

Munceford hunched down in his chair. "You feel, like Commander Allison, that I shouldn't be here, Captain?" he countered defensively.

Finlander laughed, but with a cold light in his eyes. "Did Buck hurt your feelings already?" he asked. "Well, you've got to understand that an exec who is privy to too many of his captain's darkest secrets becomes tense and cautious with strangers. His responsibilities make him more conscious of simple, tactical requirements than subtleties of strategy. And, believe it or not, Munceford, your being aboard is a matter of strategy."

Munceford blinked. "What?"

"Take my word for it and leave it at that. Go anywhere you like on my ship except in the CIC, where I'd want you escorted. Please be careful on deck and only move out there when the crew are around. You'll find that we've got a lot in common with the subs in that we travel buttoned up most of the time. Too cold outside, for one thing; too rough, for another." He reacted to a knock on the door, glanced at the clock and shouted: "Enter!"

A yeoman came in, saluted and remained stiffly at attention as he announced himself: "Yeoman Pinelli reporting to the captain as ordered, sir." He was much out of breath.

"Good evening, Pinelli," the captain greeted him with a pleasant gruffness. "What took you so long? Were you up in the crow's-nest?"

"In the shower, sir."

"In that case, you did well," Finlander told him, bringing relief to his worried face. "I'm sorry to break into your off-watch period, Pinelli, but it seems Mr. Munceford has already managed to lose or break all his movie cameras. Do we have any we can spare?"

"We have three, sir. Two Model Seventy-H's and an Arri."

Finlander turned to Munceford. "Seems you have a choice. Which would you like?"

"The Seventy-H is fine," Munceford told him. He would have preferred an Arri, which was a two-thousand-dollar camera, but he was afraid he would show his ignorance by being unable to operate it.

"All right, Pinelli, let him have one of those. And I want you to assist Mr. Munceford in every way you can. Maybe you will learn something from him." With a very subtle gleam of malice, he informed Munceford: "Yeoman Pinelli is the *Bedford*'s official photographer, but he only gets pictures of ASROC launchings, the inside of boilers, hedgehog patterns and dull things like that. I hope you'll be patient with him."

Munceford instantly knew that this ordinary-looking sailor was probably a very skilled professional photographer. This put him on his guard because he was a rather sloppy one himself and sensitive about it. But he said: "I'm sure we'll get along fine and I'll be glad to show him any tricks I know." The yeoman gave him a somewhat baleful look, and after the captain had dismissed him, Munceford observed: "You certainly have a variety of talents aboard."

Finlander nodded his big head. "Time was when a destroyer could be run by nothing but a gang of ham-fisted sailors with their guts in gimbals.

Today, men like that would be about as effective as a crew of Vikings plucked out of the tenth century."

"Still takes guts, I bet," Munceford injected.

"Sure, sure! Listen to me. I can't give you much more time." Captain Finlander seemed bent upon delivering a monologue, speaking with a quiet intensity which discouraged the conversational form. "Something less than forty per cent of my complement are seamen in the strict sense of the term. The rest could staff the science department of a medium-sized college. Take your pick of subjects! Thermodynamics, microwave analysis, submarine ultrasonics, computer circuitry, guidance systems, dielectric telemetry, doppler and inertial navigation systems, meteorology, physical oceanography—I have specialists in all these fields." His face darkened and he added beneath his breath, more to himself than to Munceford: "I even had a psychiatrist to muddle in all that brain-power."

Munceford almost asked him if he were referring to Lieutenant Hirschfeld, but remembered Packer's warning in the nick of time and said nothing. Finlander continued:

"We carry a million dollars' worth of education on a ship like this, and have to fight for every nickel of it. For the first time in history, the navy has to contend with press gangs from colleges and industry who are out to pick off our people for their own classrooms and labs. Instead of plying them with booze in water-front dives, they lure them into fancy hotel suites and cajole them with promises of wealth, status and fringe benefits. They get Annapolis men to resign their commissions after the navy has put them through M.I.T. post-graduate courses; they secretly sign up enlisted technicians with a year still to go on their hitches. We can't afford to lose these men, especially since they are three times as hard to train for the navy as for any civilian job, where all they've got to do is to sit on their rumps with a slide rule or computer. *We've* got to make halfway decent seamen and fighters out of them, too. It's very hard to find men with all three qualifications: fighter, seaman and scientist. For instance, after our last patrol I had to ship home a genius on sonar gear, simply because he could not stop vomiting all over the Combat Information Center when the going got rough—which it inevitably does up here. Then I had a guidance-systems man with an IQ of one-sixty-three who got to brooding about warheads and started infecting his division with pacifistic ideas. He had to go too. If I can't keep a fighting spirit in this ship, or keep her scientific gear operating at peak efficiency, or keep her steaming through anything this ocean can throw at me—then, for any one of those reasons, I might as well open her seacocks and scuttle her. Are you beginning to grasp some of the problems, Munceford?"

Munceford wagged his head in a noncommittal motion. "Sort of—but how do you keep going with all those troubles, Captain?"

"The book recommends to instill pride of service and a strong sense of duty," Finlander answered him with a wrinkling of his nose. "It also says to give the men frequent current-affairs talks so they know what it's all about. That sort of thing doesn't even stem the tears of a reservist crying to return to his junior vice-presidency. A professional needs something far more concrete to dedicate him. The brutal truth is that nothing will do it as well as a *real* enemy challenging him to a fight. And that's where I hold an advantage over commanders in other cold-war areas. We're not here to make faces at Commies over a wall; we're not in a base area indoctrinating simple-minded natives into the complex savagery of modern guerrilla tactics; we're not sitting in an air-conditioned Florida blockhouse trying to shoot a bigger hole in the moon, weather permitting. Here we *hunt* Russians. Here we have our enemy and, more than accepting his challenge, go after him without any inhibitions of containment policies or technical inferiorities. We miss the kill, but have become addicted to the chase, and I admit that I shamelessly use its exhilaration to inspire my crew." He stopped and stared thoughtfully at Munceford through half-closed eyes which seemed to smolder beneath the heavy lids. "Are you shocked?" he asked.

"Well, surprised, sir," Munceford answered and winced a little over finding himself "sirring" Finlander. He had always made it a point to address *all* officers on an equal basis. "And I wonder if this won't provoke a real attack one day; if somebody won't lose their temper and pull a trigger."

"Oh, you mean that old saw about somebody accidentally starting a war?" the captain countered with a contemptuous flick of his head. "We're not amateurs on either side, acting impetuously or subject to fits of temper. Nor do we have any red telephone or a bunch of keys which serially unlock the firing switches. But the whole business is so inherently calculated and technical that it is naturally kept under control at all times."

"And really only a game, after all," Munceford said with an unconvinced laugh. "Maybe the Commies get a kick out of bitching you too." He immediately sensed that he had said the wrong thing.

Finlander's eyes narrowed and the scar on his throat began to pulse visibly, betraying an inner pressure. But his voice remained even. "Bitching me?" he repeated. "I don't know what has been whispered to you about that. I make no secret over being concerned over *one* Russian sub. But bitching implies unrequited frustration." He paused with lips pressed together into a thin, hard line, and Munceford waited breathlessly, suspecting he had inadvertently touched a sore point which was about to be revealed. He was not expecting what came next.

"Have you read *Moby Dick?*" the captain asked.

"Uh . . . well, I saw the movie. All about whaling and . . ." He received such a coldly contemptuous look that it stopped him in mid-sentence.

"It's not *all* about whaling. Well, never mind." He twisted impatiently in his chair and suddenly seemed quite uninterested in continuing the discussion. When a knock on the cabin door broke the painful silence between them, it was with relief that he shouted: "Enter!"

It was Commodore Schrepke, and behind him a steward was carrying a tray full of food. Finlander got up and exclaimed: "Dinnertime already? Good. I'm starved. But first have yourself a quick drink, Commodore."

Munceford thought that he was about to be invited to have dinner in the captain's cabin, but as the steward passed him to put the tray down on the desk, he saw it only contained service for two. Finlander quickly dispelled any remaining notions that he had been accepted on such intimate terms. "If you'll forgive me, Munceford," he told him, "the commodore and I will dine alone together in order to go over the day's operations. I'm sure you'll find some interesting company in the wardroom."

Munceford got up. "Yeah—okay. Thanks for your time, Captain."

"Quite all right. We will talk some more after you get settled." He turned to Schrepke, who was pouring himself some juice. "You should tell Mr. Munceford some of your U-boat experiences, Commodore. It would help him understand the over-all picture of ASW operations."

Schrepke glanced at Munceford and it was as if he decided then and there that he wanted no part of him. "There are several books on the subject," he said with a forbidding politeness. "My own experiences are of no interest to the American press, thank you." As he spoke, he took a small silver hip flask from his pocket and blatantly proceeded to spike his drink with its contents. Munceford stared in amazement at this flagrant violation of American navy regulations, then shifted his eyes to Captain Finlander, expecting a blistering reaction from him. The heavy eyebrows were drawn together in an ominous line and the scar on the throat pulsed a dull red; but he said nothing.

Schrepke raised his glass, exclaimed *"Prosit,"* drained the drink with a grimace indicating a pleasurable pain, looked right through Munceford and caught the expression on Finlander's face. "I presume, Captain, that Lieutenant Hirschfeld's medical prescriptions are still valid even though he himself has been removed from his practice aboard your ship." There was an unmistakable note of irony in his voice.

The steward fumbled a plate, barely managing a noisy retrieve against the edge of the desk.

Captain Finlander glared at the German, then wheeled away from him without answering. He grasped Munceford by the arm and ushered him toward the door. "You will find that submariners who've been overly hunted develop permanent instabilities in their nervous systems," he said so loudly that it was obviously intended as a direct jab at Schrepke. "So killing them isn't always necessary. . . . I will see you tomorrow. Good night."

The cabin door slammed shut and Munceford found himself alone in the dim red glow of the passageway. He stood there for a moment, listening, half expecting to hear an explosion inside the captain's cabin. None came. So he shuffled off in the direction of the wardroom, bracing himself against the bulkheads as he tried to balance his movements with those of the destroyer.

Munceford found eight officers in the wardroom who were already halfway through their supper. Lieutenant Peter Packer was the only familiar face and he made the introductions so quickly that the names hardly impressed themselves on his memory: "Ensign Lissholm . . . Commander Franklin . . . Lieutenants Harwell . . . Petersen . . . Goodfellow . . . Brubeck . . . Samuels . . ."

None did more than nod or mumble a barely comprehensible word of welcome through a mouthful of roast beef and mashed potatoes. There was a minor confusion on one side of the table as everybody had to squeeze down in order to make room for him. Nobody tried to engage him in conversation, but neither did they talk among themselves; most of them were occupied with reading mail delivered by the *Tiburon Bay* while eating at the same time. Steward Martin put down a plate in front of Munceford which was heaped with meat and vegetables, all washed in a miniature surf of gravy activated by the roll of the *Bedford*. The lieutenant next to him automatically passed salt, pepper and a sticky bottle of Worcestershire. The commander giggled softly over something amusing in his letter. The ensign squeezed up the last of his gravy with a piece of bread, then sat back and began picking his teeth, one hand shielding the other according to best Annapolis etiquette. He watched as Munceford tried to separate a piece of fat from a piece of lean, and finally asked with offhand interest: "Was the chow good on the *Tiburon Bay?*"

"What? . . . Oh, sure. Pretty fair."

"113 serves steak or roast beef three times a week."

"Fine. I was on a sub for a while and they served all the steak we could eat."

The ensign said: "They need it," and terminated that conversation by turning his attention upon a dish of chocolate ice cream which the steward put before him. Nobody asked Munceford about his experiences on a sub, and for a moment he was tempted to announce loudly that when they did not eat steak, submariners lived on prairie oysters. But instead he filled his mouth with food, masticating as silently as the rest, his thoughts going back to his session with Captain Finlander. He had not really made up his mind whether he liked the captain or not; he was a strange, yet compelling personality. But at least he *talked*. At least he seemed to care about Munceford being present on the *Bedford*. What was it he had said? ". . . *believe it or not, Munceford, your being aboard is a matter of strategy*." What had he meant by that? Some sinister implication behind it, as there was behind some other things he had said?

After a while Lieutenant Packer announced to nobody in particular that he had to attend to some decoding and left without having given his cabin mate a glance or a word since the cursory introductions; he was evidently still sore over the incident with Shebeona's photograph. One by one, the other officers finished their meals, folded up their letters and departed too. The commander was the last one to leave, and before passing out the door, he stopped a moment and looked back at Munceford. "Which broadcasting company did you say you work for?" he asked.

"I'm free-lance."

The commander frowned. "But you're on a definite assignment, aren't you?"

"Well . . . NBC has expressed a lot of interest."

"Uh-huh. Good night."

Munceford found himself alone in the wardroom with a dish of melting ice cream and a cup of tepid coffee, the commander's question having channeled his thoughts into fresh worries. An assistant director of NBC's news department *had* expressed interest, but with certain reservations. The story had to show some fresh action scenes from a destroyer on arctic patrol, it had to give a clear insight into the operational problems, it had to contain human interest and drama. Otherwise, the best he could hope for was the sale of stock footage at the going rate of $1.25 per foot—perhaps $250 as against $5,000 for a feature. How could he meet those requirements if Captain Finlander insisted upon the secrecy of the operation? How could he get human interest and drama if men like Commodore Schrepke were evasive and uncooperative? How Nancy would laugh if she could see him in this predicament! Yet Finlander obviously wanted *some* kind of story. What? Well, he'd have to stay on the good side of that man, no matter how difficult and strange he turned out to be.

Munceford drained his cup and left the wardroom to pick his way through the empty passageways toward his cabin, which he found only after making several wrong turns. Packer was not there and the cubicle was as lonely and oppressive as ever. Neatly laid out on his bunk were a regulation navy arctic parka and, on top of it, a shiny new Model 70-H camera, complete with three lenses in its turret. Munceford stared for a moment at this evidence of the *Bedford*'s enormous efficiency, but without any particular admiration or gratitude. He listened tensely to the silence beyond the whine of the turbines and hiss of the ventilator, then turned his attention to Packer's bunk, which was once again immaculate in taut perfection. Leaning down, he surreptitiously slipped his hand beneath the pillow, cautiously probing under it with his fingers. There was nothing there. Shebeona had been removed to safety by her jealous lover and Munceford found himself thwarted in this innocent game of cuckoldry. He had hoped to go to bed with her exquisite beauty refreshed in his mind's eye, but instead there would only be Finlander, whose face remained indelibly burned into it.

# 10.

The heavy overcast cleared during the night, and by 0500, when the cooks sleepily manned their galley, the *Bedford* was steaming over a glass-calm ocean which mirrored a fantastic dome of starlit space. There was no moon, but northern lights rippled across the heavens with curtains of cold blue fire which cast their luminescence over the ship, sharply etching her on a silent course twixt abyss and infinity. Her tall mast described lazy circles around the constellation of Corona Borealis; the stars also touched the sea around her and broke into sprays of dancing diamonds in her wake. On the bridge the quartermaster of the watch came out of the wheelhouse to check the thermometer for his hourly weather entry in the log; it stood at two degrees above zero. He also checked from a respectful distance the figure crouching by the windscreen, the same figure which had been there the hour before, in exactly the same position, not facing up and outward like a man entranced by the arctic night, but staring downward at the black waters sweeping by the hull beneath him. Black leather glistened with a faint sheen where it was stretched tight over broad, hunched shoulders. In these dark hours before dawn Commodore Wolfgang Schrepke could always be found here, unless the bridge was so swept by freezing spume as to become untenable even for him. No duty called him here; no officer of his rank stood a regular watch. He came only for his own troubled reasons to find a brooding solitude with the sea, to stare into it like an insomniac contemplating a cemetery which holds too many of his departed kin.

At 0600 reveille was piped through the ship's PA and men began stirring inside her. Deep down in her lower vitals, where the biting cold of the Arctic Ocean was replaced by a humid heat radiating from roaring boilers, Fireman Second Class Bert Meggs checked dials and made a minor adjustment to the steam manifolds to compensate for the hot-water requirements of shipmates taking their morning showers. In the galley the first couple of hundred pancakes were coming off the griddles to be stacked by messmen in the steam tables; fumes containing the tingling aroma of frying bacon were sucked into the ventilators and wafted into the freezing outside air, where they rose on a following breeze and stimulated the nostrils of Seaman Willy Kolinsky, crowded high up in the crow's-nest. He shifted his cramped position and pressed himself harder against the heater coil which kept the *Bedford*'s masthead lookout from freezing to death in his lonely perch. Above him the radar antenna whirred softly as it turned, sweeping the night with its sensory microwaves. The northern lights had faded, but no trace of dawn had as yet replaced their glow, and the night enveloped the ship, darker than ever. Ensign Ralston emerged from the wheelhouse with a sextant and unerringly sought out Regulus among the sparkling myriads above; Commodore Schrepke finally moved away from his isolation in the wing and stepped up behind the young officer, watching him for a moment as he took his three-star sight. Then the German retreated to his cabin and Ralston went into the navigation office to calculate his position and check it against the observation made a half-hour earlier by Lieutenant Harwell.

The watch changed at 0745 and only then was there a faint lightening on the eastern horizon which began washing out the stars hanging low in that quadrant of the sky. The thermometer on the bridge now registered exactly zero degrees, and because of this extreme cold there was no muster or inspection on deck this morning. Only a detail of gunners showed up to traverse the turrets and launchers in order to make certain they had not become frozen in their tracks during the night. In the chartroom Commander Allison sipped coffee with the OOD while listening on the monitoring circuit of the communicator system as the weapons-control officer checked all his stations from the CIC. Captain Finlander finished a spartan breakfast in the isolation of his cabin, put on his white duffel coat and the long-billed fisherman's cap with its tiny silver eagle and went up on the bridge to watch the dawning. From there he descended into the tense twilight world of the CIC and silently joined Lieutenant Spitzer's vigil behind the sonar operators, listening with them to the hollow pings and watching the sterile green glow of the PPI scopes in their consoles. After a while he shifted his position to the main search-radar scanner and saw the sweeper activate incandescent rows of blobs to the west—the return from mountain ranges on the Greenland coast thirty miles away. Up in the crow's-nest a new lookout, Seaman First Class Robert W. Jones, also spotted those mountains, but as a jagged white line appearing with startling suddenness on the horizon where snowy peaks were kindled by the first streak of dawn and reflected back its light. Jones picked up the phone and dutifully reported his sighting to the bridge, seventy feet below him. In the Communications Center three radio operators sat at their sets listening to a cacophony of jumbled Morse signals, their trained ears separating the vital from the trivial; near them Lieutenant Peter Packer, R.N., turned a receiver to the commercial ship-to-shore RT frequency and suddenly found himself listening to a voice speaking English with a thick north-country accent. He listened with a wistful sentimentality as the man talked about a poor catch of codfish he was bringing back to Grimsby. In his cabin Ben Munceford woke up, found himself as alone as ever, rolled out of his bunk and wondered if he were too late for breakfast.

At 0921 the sun at last cracked the rim of the sea to the east and reluctantly rose out of it, a pale burnished disk without the slightest trace of warming red. For a long time some of the larger stars successfully defied it to extinguish their light. In the crow's-nest Seaman Jones adjusted his binoculars and carefully studied the horizon ahead of the *Bedford*. He had caught some flashes out there, something like weak blinker signals, but he quickly identified the source and telephoned the bridge to report drifting ice ahead. It gave him great satisfaction to do this because he knew that neither radar nor sonar had been able to detect this hazard in spite of all their intricate technological gobbledy-gook—a good pair of eyes was still needed. In the wheelhouse Captain Finlander discussed the report with the OOD, Lieutenant Harwell.

"That will be floe ice drifting down from north of us," the captain said. "With this light wind, it's certain to be scattered."

"Shall I change course four or five degrees right, sir?"

Finlander frowned. "If our mission was merely to steam along like a passenger liner, that would be an excellent idea." He waited for some reaction which did not come quick enough to suit him. "What *is* our mission, Mr. Harwell?"

"To patrol for Russian submarine activity, sir."

"And if you were a Russian submarine commander operating under these sea conditions, what would you do, Mr. Harwell?"

"I would use the ice to screen my movements, sir."

"Correct. As a matter of fact, don't you think you might move closer to the Greenland coast so as to confuse any tracking destroyer's radar and sonar sweeps?"

"Yes, sir."

"Then act accordingly, Mr. Harwell."

"You mean move closer to the coast, sir?"

"I suggest at least ten miles closer. I also suggest a series of maximum-effect sonar sweeps."

"Every fifteen minutes, sir?"

Finlander sighed like a teacher priming a difficult student. "Why every fifteen minutes? To help the Russian set his schedule accordingly for silent running? Come on, Mr. Harwell! Try being a little unpredictable about it." Finlander flashed him a condescending grin, pulled up the collar of his white duffel coat and went out on the bridge. Lieutenant Harwell ordered the helmsman to bring the *Bedford* to a new heading which put the distant line of snow-capped mountains right over her bow. Ten minutes later he alerted the ship for a maximum-effect sonar sweep and signaled the engine room to stop engines. While the destroyer coasted silently over the lightly ruffled swells, Lieutenant Spitzer and his sonarmen intently listened and watched their PPI screens. But the surrounding deep remained as silent as it is legendarily supposed to be.

Inside the crow's-nest a twenty-year-old seaman second-class nicknamed Squarehead (John Thorbjornsen was his improbable real name) had relieved Jones, who climbed halfway down the tube-like inside of the mainmast, there to steal a quick smoke. (This was the *only* safe place on the *Bedford* to steal a smoke on watch.) Squarehead felt the faint vibration of the engines fade out and took the opportunity to rest the objectives of his binoculars against the glass of the windshield, thus steadying them for a minute examination of the horizon. As he peered, his body remained relaxed, his jaws masticating rhythmically on a wad of gum. His sharp young eyes, made tenfold more efficient by the powerful lenses, picked out crevasses and faults in the glaciers of the Greenland mountains and noticed the shimmering line of ice beneath them; the ice looked as though it hugged the coast, but he knew it stretched out several miles beyond. Shifting the binoculars slightly, he picked another piece of the horizon for careful scrutiny. Then another. Then the jaws suddenly stopped and went slack. His body did not visibly tense, but he held his breath for about ten seconds, took his eyes from the binoculars and blinked them a couple of times before looking again. His pupils contracted to black pinpoints against the brilliant glare of the morning sunlight on the sea. He was watching a pair of skua gulls persistently circling a spot nearly two miles away. But his interest was not that of a birdwatcher. Rather he was trying to make out what interested *them*. Finally he communicated his suspicions to Seaman Jones, perched in the shaft below him.

"I think I got something."

"What?"

"Garbage."

Jones quickly tamped out his cigarette in the palm of his gloved hand and slipped the butt into a pocket of his parka so as to leave no evidence of his misdemeanor. Then he sprang up the rungs and squeezed himself into the crow's-nest with Squarehead. "Where away?" he asked.

Space was so cramped that there was no longer room to wield the binoculars. "Zero-two-zero—about two miles. Not sure, though."

"Well, okay. Report any sighting even if you're not sure. Besides, you know how the skipper loves garbage."

Squarehead nodded and reached for the telephone.

# 11.

In sick bay Lieutenant Commander Chester Porter had attended his first full-fledged muster of his department—which consisted of only *two* permanently assigned men, Chief Pharmacist's Mate McKinley and Pharmacist Engstrom, a lanky boy with rimless glasses. However, under battle conditions eight stewards and commissary men were assigned as corpsmen and litter carriers, and it was up to him to have them trained in these, their secondary duties. This morning they all squeezed into the empty sick bay, and when Porter looked them over, he felt this was not much of a command for an officer of his rank; but he balmed his pride with the thought that, technically at least, he was chief medical officer of the 1st Destroyer Division, NATONAV 1—which meant that the medical departments of two other destroyers, patrolling somewhere within the fifteen-thousand-square-mile area, came under his nominal control.

McKinley introduced each man to the surgeon, who then made a short speech in which he omitted the customary flattering references to his predecessor. He expressed satisfaction over the condition of the department, but stated his intentions of running some litter-carrying drills in the immediate future. After the men were dismissed from muster, one of them requested a word with him. It was Collins, the Negro steward. Porter asked him to step inside the receiving office.

"Sir, after my hitch is up, I intend to qualify for medical school," Collins told him with a respectful but firm directness. "Lieutenant Hirschfeld has been tutoring me in pre-med subjects during off-duty time. I am wondering if the commander would kindly do the same."

The surgeon was taken by surprise. "Well, now . . . ah, that's very commendable," he fumbled and shot a questioning glance at McKinley, who was standing in the door. He expected his chief pharmacist to correct the word "tutoring," which implied an unusual personal attention from an officer. But McKinley did not intervene. "Ah . . . how old are you, Collins?"

"Twenty-four, sir." He looked much older.

"You realize it takes eight years of college and medical school to make a doctor?" Collins obviously knew this, so he went on to ask: "How much education have you had?"

"I graduated from high school with an A average, sir," Collins answered without a trace of cockiness or even pride in his voice.

"Well, now . . . that's fine. Very fine. But pre-med studies in addition to your other duties?"

"I intend to return to the navy after I obtain my degree, sir," Collins told him, then added: "I would very much appreciate the commander's help."

Lieutenant Commander Porter felt a twinge of old prejudices welling up inside of him as he pictured this handsome Negro as a medical officer in the navy. He knew it was a terrible fault, but deep down he firmly believed that Negroes should be stewards and nothing more. That was what he had been brought up to believe; that was what had been accepted in the navy during nearly half of his career in it. He was ashamed of this attitude, but his only way of reacting to it was to be scrupulously, painfully, insincerely fair. "Naturally, I will try to help you every way I can, Collins," he said, looking down at the steel top of his desk. "But you must give me time to settle into my new job. Then I'd like to go over the work you did with Lieutenant Hirschfeld and see what can be done."

Collins said: "Thank you very much, Commander," saluted and left to clean up the officers' toilets.

After he was gone, McKinley added to the surgeon's discomfiture. "That man has a superior rating throughout, sir. I hope you can find time to work with him."

"I didn't say I wouldn't," the surgeon snapped defensively; then a look of malice came into his eyes. "How much do *you* help him, McKinley? Didn't you tell me you've had pre-med at Duke? Wouldn't that qualify *you* to tutor him?"

McKinley smiled and shook his head. "He's far beyond where I left off, sir. On neurocellular structures right now, I believe." He excused himself to attend to some duties in the surgery.

Porter decided he would talk to Captain Finlander about Collins—which would naturally lead to a discussion of Lieutenant Hirschfeld and thence to the matter of the captain's missing Form 28. He and Finlander had had a pleasant meeting yesterday afternoon during which he had been much impressed by that officer's lucid description of the *Bedford*'s operational problems, but there had been no opportunity to deal specifically with those of the medical department. As captains should be, Finlander was only concerned with the over-all picture, not details. However, the surgeon had analyzed him as a man who missed nothing, a man one could talk to and be understood by. Whatever Hirschfeld had implied about him—he was wrong.

The surgeon was about to reach for the telephone and call Finlander to ask for an appointment at his convenience when Pharmacist Engstrom came to the door and announced: "Commodore Schrepke requests to see the commander, sir." The German officer was behind him and politely waited for Porter to invite him into the office—which he instantly did while respectfully standing up.

Schrepke said, "Good morning, Commander. I will only take a few minutes of your time," then shot a look at the pharmacist which made him close the door to give them complete privacy.

"I hope you are not feeling sick, sir," the surgeon said, trying to avoid looking too pointedly at the German's strangely un-naval dress. The black leather jacket would be more in keeping for a motorcyclist, but he vaguely remembered that U-boat crews used to wear something like that during the last war.

"I feel very good, thank you," Schrepke told him. "I am here because your captain informs me a prescription given by the former medical officer should be renewed by yourself."

"Oh? Just one moment, sir." Porter opened the file drawer and the German patiently waited while he searched for his Form 28. But there was none in the folder, only a plain sheet on which were typed the man's name, serial number, blood type and a notation: *foreign officer —Form 28 waived.* In the lower left corner, in Lieutenant Hirschfeld's handwriting, was written: *Medication provided by subject officer may be taken at his own discretion.* This brought a perplexed frown to the surgeon's face. Here was another strange irregularity in the *Bedford's* medical records! "I am afraid Lieutenant Hirschfeld neglected to either note the prescription or the nature of the condition it is supposed to treat," he said to Schrepke.

"That is all right, Commander. The doctor and I had an understanding."

He said it as if this were the most natural thing, yet there was something in his guttural tone which put Porter on his guard. "What was the medicine?" he asked.

"Schnapps."

"Schnapps, sir!"

"Yes—schnapps." Commodore Schrepke suddenly produced his little silver hip flask and put it down on the desk in front of the astounded surgeon.

Lieutenant Commander Porter stared at the flask, then slowly picked it up and turned it over in his hands. It was quite old, had several buckles in it and some engraving which had almost been worn off. Beneath a crest, which he recognized as that of the Nazi navy, he made out an inscription in German script, but of this he could only read: *U-797.* Opening the cap, he sniffed a strong whiff of what smelled like pure alcohol. "B-but, sir . . . this isn't really medicine."

"It is the only kind I have ever taken in my life."

"Yes, but—"

"You carry brandy in your medical supplies, do you not, Commander?"

"Yes, of course, but you see—"

"Well, I carry schnapps in mine," Schrepke snapped, beginning to show signs of irritation.

As the surgeon tried to collect his thoughts to decide whether to overlook the whole thing or act according to strict navy regulations, he heard the PA announce a maximum-effect sonar sweep and felt the turbines slow down to a murmur. "I don't know, Commodore," he said. "Perhaps I had better check this out with Captain Finlander. B-but you say *he* suggested you see me about it?"

Schrepke reached out and retrieved the flask, putting it back in his pocket. "It really makes no difference to me what you do, Commander," he said. "I have nothing to hide, only prefer everything on record and in order so as to cause no embarrassments. But it does not really matter. I am sorry I troubled you."

He started to leave and Porter jumped up out of his chair, very flustered. "Please, Commodore. You must understand my position in this. If only you could explain . . . well, I mean, why do you *have* to have schnapps?"

Schrepke's face wrinkled in deliberately exaggerated thought, an expression which made his hard features almost comical for a moment. "I don't really know, Commander." He shrugged. "I have had three schnapps a day since I joined the navy in 1931. One in the morning, one at noon and one at night. I have had them that way ashore, on the ocean, under the ocean, and your English allies were even so kind as to let me have them when I was their prisoner of war. *Why* I must have schnapps, I can't really explain. But if you are worried that I am an alcoholic . . ."

"Good God, *no,* sir!"

"Then perhaps you and your navy will indulge an old sailor, yes?" He did not await any answer and excused himself with a quick explanation that he was due to join the captain on the bridge.

After he had gone, Lieutenant Commander Porter sat staring at the folder until he became aware that McKinley was standing in the door, looking in at him. "What do you know about *this* lack of records, Chief?" the surgeon asked, holding up the sheet of paper.

McKinley evidently knew enough about it so he did not have to study it. "Commodore Schrepke is kind of a special case, sir."

"Damn right! No proper forms. Motorcyclist jacket. Carries his booze on his hip. I'll say he's special! A full admiral couldn't get away with that in our navy. Why the hell should he? But I suppose Lieutenant Hirschfeld concocted some obscure justification."

McKinley shrugged. "Only that the commodore is very senior and has never been able to get over his experiences in the war. If a few shots a day make him feel better, well, that's legitimate medication."

"Hell, McKinley! Our submarine boys had some shaking experiences too, you know."

"Yes, sir. But Commodore Schrepke was sunk twice and is the only commander in history who ever got all his men out of a wrecked sub lying over a hundred feet deep. Some of them burst their lungs on the way up, but he kept the survivors together until they were rescued ten hours later. The second time he was sunk, a British can blew him to the surface the day before the war was over. Only he and one sailor got clear, but when the Limeys tried to pick him up, he fought them off and attempted to swim away and drown himself. They caught him and put him in a POW camp, where he stayed for a year while they tried to decide whether or not he was a war criminal. He had too many Nazi medals, besides having sent down nearly one hundred of our ships. But once he towed survivors in lifeboats for a couple of hundred miles just to make sure they had a fighting chance, and not even our boys ever took risks like that. So they let him go, and he went home to Germany to try and find his wife and kids. His home was in the Russian zone, and he was there just long enough to find out his family had all been killed. Then the Russians picked him up. They had captured a number of the latest U-boats in half-finished condition and needed experts to help put them together and operate them. So he spent the next two years at forced labor in Russian yards until he managed to escape. He and another German officer *sailed* across the Baltic in an open boat during the dead of winter; the other man froze to death within sight of the Swedish coast, but he made it. The Russians claimed he had not only sabotaged some of their submarines, but also killed a guard while escaping, so they raised so much hell that the Swedes were about to agree to extradite him. He escaped again, perhaps while the Swedes looked the other way, and finally reached West Germany. When the German navy was reactivated, they gave him back his commission and, because he knows all about Russian subs, he was put in charge of ASW work. The sonar boys tell me Commodore Schrepke is so sharp he can listen to a signal or analyze its trace and tell you what type of sub it is, what kind of engines it has and whether it's been out long enough to have barnacles growing on its hull." The chief pharmacist grinned at his own exaggeration, then added very seriously: "He is a strange duck, but, kraut or no kraut, he's also one hell of a fine naval officer."

The surgeon said nothing for a moment, looking down at that nearly blank piece of paper which was all the official record he had of this man Schrepke. "How do you know all this?" he finally asked.

"Captain Finlander spread the word just before the commodore joined us last month, sir. He himself never talks about his past that I know of. . . . Do you want me to enter his visit this morning in the medical log, sir?"

"Hell, no! Not until I talk to Finlander about him," Porter answered testily. "But I'll tell you one thing, Chief. I'm going to go through *all* these records with a fine-tooth comb. I don't want any more surprises."

He opened the file drawer all the way and lifted out a fistful of Form 28's.

McKinley laughed. "You've already stumbled on the only two cases that aren't kosher, Commander," he said and withdrew.

Undeterred, the surgeon plunged into his self-imposed paperwork. But he had difficulty in concentrating, not only because his mind kept slipping back to dwell on Commodore Schrepke, the captain's missing Form 28, Hirschfeld's mysterious dismissal and the strange lingering of his presence aboard, but also because the *Bedford* seemed to be going through some strange maneuvers. The maximum sweep had been terminated and her engines were all ahead standard, yet he could feel her weave on a constantly changing course. The sea was still flat calm with only a slight trace of oily swells, but as she turned, she would heel slightly and the motion would change in a disconcerting manner. He wished the receiving office had a porthole so he could see the ocean. He wished he had some patients from other departments so he could pick up some scuttlebutt from them. And as he thought this, it struck him that it was also peculiar that so few of the *Bedford*'s crew ever reported for sick call. All the other ships he had served on which had over three hundred crew would produce at least a half-dozen minor cases a day, including the inevitable hypochondriacs and malingerers. But not on the *Bedford*. As he checked the forms, he hoped he would find somebody who was overdue for a regular physical examination. By the time he had gone through five or six and found nothing out of order or unusual, he gave up the project and decided to write a letter to his wife. Lieutenant Commander Chester Porter wrote at least one page a day to his wife when he was at sea, posting off a ten- to fifteen-page epistle whenever he reached port or connected with a supply ship.

*Dearest Martha:—Well, I made it to the* Bedford *and am just settling down aboard her . . . or trying my best to. During the transfer I met Barney Hirschfeld for a moment and think he's in a real mess of some kind, although I'm not quite sure what. Better not say anything to Estelle about it for the time being. Had a long talk with Captain Finlander and think he is*

He was sitting there, tapping his front teeth with the pen while wondering whether he *really* wanted to write that Finlander was "a fine officer who will be a pleasure to serve under" when he heard the noise of some men entering the surgery. Patients? He decided he did not want to write Martha any definite opinions quite yet, tore up the sheet of paper and threw it in the wastebasket. Then he got up and went to find out what was happening.

Two seamen had come into the surgery and Porter could tell at a glance that they were perfectly healthy. But he was astounded to find them emptying the contents of a bucket into the sink while Chief Pharmacist McKinley was watching with eager anticipation. The contents of the bucket were unmistakably garbage.

"What in hell are you doing?" Porter exploded.

The two seamen came to attention. McKinley smiled. "Seems we've picked up some goodies, Commander," he said pleasantly.

"What's this garbage doing in my surgery?" the surgeon bellowed, certain that he was being made the butt of some kind of insubordinate prank. This belief was heightened by the smugly amused expressions on the faces of the seamen.

"It's all part of our total ASW program, sir," McKinley told him. As Porter glowered into the sink at what appeared to be some moldy cheese rinds, potato peelings, vegetable scraps and half-dissolved bread crusts, the chief pharmacist went to a cabinet and brought out a microscope case. "Captain Finlander says hunting submarines is sometimes like hunting animals," he explained while setting up the instrument. "You can tell a lot by their droppings. For instance, from this garbage we might be able to tell the nationality of the ship it came from, how long since they threw it overboard and, from that, whether it was a Russian sub still within our immediate area."

The surgeon was now almost speechless. "You mean to tell me I'm expected to do some kind of pathological work on this vile stuff?" he stammered.

"Oh, no, sir," McKinley shot back. "That's a smelly job only for enlisted men." The two seamen laughed quite openly, then shrank back and hurriedly left the surgery with their bucket as Porter wheeled on them. The chief pharmacist sobered and worriedly looked at his superior. "I'm sorry, sir. I guess I should have forewarned you about this. But, no kidding, it's SOP for us to pick up any floating refuse and go over it pretty thoroughly. Two weeks ago we tracked a sub—the one we call Moby Dick because he bugs hell out of the skipper—and lost all sonar contact. But then we picked up two loads of his garbage and knew he was still in the area. Red cabbage with lots of black pepper is a dead giveaway of Russian ships. If its got traces of hydrogenated fats—butter, you know, sir—it's pretty certain it comes from submariners because, like our own, they get the fanciest rations. Trawlers cook in vegetable oils mostly; the Norwegian ones in fish oils. The state of decomposition of the cells tells us how long it's been soaking in salt water. Really pretty simple and sometimes effective."

"I'll be a son of a bitch!" the surgeon exclaimed, again staring at the filthy mess in the gleaming sink.

"Don't worry about it, sir. I'll take care of the whole thing. Excuse me." McKinley respectfully pushed the lieutenant commander away from the sink and, with a pair of forceps, gingerly transferred some soggy potato peelings to an enamel tray. "Potatoes are real dandy for determining how fresh the droppings are," he explained and began preparing the specimen for microscopic study and doing it with all the starry-eyed eagerness of a young scientist on the track of a cure for cancer.

# 12.

Ben Munceford had been too late for breakfast. The wardroom was deserted when he arrived there a little after eight-thirty, the officers having scattered to their respective duties and the stewards having reported to meet the new surgeon. But there were a Thermos full of coffee and a plate of very good doughnuts on the sideboard, so he was able to stem his hunger, although the lingering smell of bacon and eggs left him with a frustrated yearning. When he finished ten minutes later, he found himself still alone and set out in search of some activity, having in mind to find the shaft which led to the wheelhouse and bridge. He quickly became lost in the passageways and wound up going through a door which opened upon the main deck. Starlight still shone through a pale dawn and the cold bit savagely at his ears. He quickly retreated inside and eventually found his way back to his cabin, withdrawing into it in a very disgruntled state of mind. The next twenty minutes he spent examining and loading the movie camera which had been loaned to him. Then he tried on the regulation arctic parka; it fitted him well, but he decided to wear his own camouflage jacket this morning just to flaunt his independence at the surly executive officer. He was putting it on, preparing himself for another lone reconnaissance through the *Bedford,* when there was a knock and Yeoman Pinelli came through the curtain.

"Good morning, sir. I'm sorry I'm late, sir," he said, addressing Munceford with the same formality he would show toward an officer.

"Late for what, sailor?" Munceford asked.

"The captain asked me to assist you, sir," Pinelli reminded him. He spotted the camera lying on the desk and picked it up, handling it with the familiar ease of a professional photographer. "Is this satisfactory, sir? Are the lenses what you want?"

"They'll do, thanks."

Pinelli noticed the empty film box. "You've loaded it with *that,* sir?" he asked with a frown. "I'd advise a faster emulsion. The light is very poor and the few daylight hours are usually socked in anyway. We use a Tri-X type of film and push its ASA rating to four hundred at least. Have you got plenty of that kind, sir?"

"No."

"I'll let you have some. How about a Solarpack for night and interior shots?"

"Didn't think I'd need one. Besides, I was told to travel as light as possible." He saw the shocked expression on the yeoman's dark Italian face as he stared down at the jumble of photographic knickknacks in the case which was open at the side of the desk. Reaching out with his foot, he kicked the lid closed. "Look, sailor. I don't want to put you to a lot of trouble over gear and stuff. All I need is to have somebody show me around the ship so I won't keep getting lost. That's all."

"The captain told me to assist you, sir," Pinelli doggedly insisted. He was now looking at Munceford's jacket, and the strain of keeping control of his facial muscles made them do strange things. "If you will follow me, I'll take you to the darkroom and get you straightened out . . . ah, I mean fixed up, sir. By the way, it's thirty-two degrees below freezing outside."

"I've got thermal long-johns and a sweater on under this," Munceford snapped. "So let's get going, okay?"

Another long trek through the *Bedford*'s gently heaving, red-lit, deserted passageways. Then Pinelli opened a door and motioned Munceford inside a darkroom which immediately impressed him as a marvel of technical and organizational efficiency. Developing tanks and contact printers; a sixteen-millimeter automatic motion-picture film processor; a sink with thermostat and circulator; compartmented shelves holding trays, chemicals, print papers and a better assortment of film than most camera stores ashore could offer; a filing cabinet and a desk; a felt-lined, glass-topped case full of lenses, each neatly snapped into a holder and with its optics protected by rubber caps; another case held graphics, miniature and movie cameras. All of this was compressed into an air-conditioned space measuring no more than eight by twelve feet; every inch had been carefully designed for maximum utility. As the yeoman reloaded his camera for him with more suitable film, Munceford looked around and realized that nobody on this ship would be impressed with his own skills and equipment. "How much has all this set back the poor taxpayers?" he ungraciously asked.

"I don't know, sir. I didn't buy it myself." Pinelli matched Munceford's tone with a snidely polite one of his own.

"From the looks of it, you'd think that getting pictures of the enemy was the main business of the *Bedford*."

"Well, we do that too, sir," Pinelli told him. "There's a teloptic Mark VII mounted on a turret topside which can get a recognizable shot of the officers on the bridge of a ship two miles away. It can be tracked automatically by radar, just like the guns and rocket launchers. But mostly we shoot for technical records, like the captain told you, sir." He handed him back the camera, which he had loaded three times as fast as Munceford could have done it. "There! Figure ASA four hundred on this emulsion if you are shooting for TV negative. Now I'll rig you a Solar-pack light." He went to one of the equipment cases and unlocked it with a key out of a large bunch he carried on a brass ring.

Munceford's jealous resentment of this sailor's obvious technical superiority was overcome by a curiosity over his background. "Listen, stop sirring me. I'm no officer, you know. What's your first name?"

"Vincente, sir."

"Mine's Ben."

No answer.

"All right, be formal if you like. How come you know so much about photography? Is that part of navy training these days?"

"The navy has had an official photographic section since March of 1922, sir," Pinelli dryly informed him as he checked the battery of the Solarpack. "I was an apprentice in the photo labs of Time Inc., but decided the navy could give me the all-round experience I need in the profession, so I signed up for a four-year hitch. When I muster out, I'll have my old job back with a promotion."

"Doing it the long, hard way, eh?"

"Is there any other worth a damn, sir?" the yeoman asked, then hung the Solarpack by its strap over Munceford's shoulder. "Where do you want to start shooting?"

Munceford made a wry grin. "So let's do it that long, hard way you admire so much, Vincente. Bottom up, from the engine room?"

Yeoman Pinelli shook his head and shrugged. "Okay, but it looks like one of those rare days when we will have some sun. You won't have too many opportunities to work on deck, and if you want my advice, I suggest you take advantage of them."

"All right—on deck, then."

Pinelli wiggled into his parka and selected a camera of his own to take with him. "The captain wants some pictures of you working, sir," he explained. "I guess it's for the PRO at COMFLANT. Hope it's all right with you."

Munceford would normally have welcomed his picture being taken for a Fleet Headquarters, but somehow he had a feeling that Pinelli considered himself to have been assigned to cover the activities of a freak. "What the captain wants, the captain gets." He shrugged with resentful indifference and followed the yeoman out of the darkroom. They emerged into the cold morning sunlight of the foredeck just in time to witness the garbage operation.

Munceford blinked and squinted his eyes to get them adjusted to the sudden brilliant light shimmering from sea and sky. To his surprise, he found that the *Bedford* had almost stopped. A couple of hundred yards away, slabs of drifting pan ice were bobbing on the glassy swells, their polished surfaces catching the sun rays and throwing them back at the ship in blinding flashes. A pair of skua gulls circled the bow with plaintive calls, protesting the *Bedford*'s stealthy approach to the raft of garbage which had, until a few minutes ago, been their rightful treasure trove. Some hooded heads were peering over the windscreen of the bridge, watching a pair of seamen wielding a dip net at the end of a twenty-foot aluminum pole. They swung it over the side and leaned far across the lifelines, moving carefully and goblin-like in their heavy arctic clothing.

"What in hell's going on here?" Munceford asked.

"We call it the cherry-picking detail," Yeoman Pinelli answered. "Actually collecting refuse to check if it originates from a Russian sub." When Munceford eagerly began to move toward the scene of action, simultaneously trying to yank his exposure meter out of a pocket, he followed him, calling out: "Shoot it at F-twenty-two, sir. It's awfully bright."

"You and your damned fast emulsions!" Munceford grumbled, then shouted at the two seamen with the dip net: "Hey, you guys! Hold it a second! I want to line up a shot of this!"

The two men turned their heads and stared with startled surprise at the approaching figure in the garish camouflage jacket, then were jolted back to their job by a bellow from the bridge: "Wake up, down there! If I have to make another approach, it'll be your hides!"

Munceford had still not quite grasped what was happening, but sensed it was something unusual and should be recorded on film. As he frantically wound up the camera, he began to run to reach a position close enough for a good shot. He was still running while bending into an awkward crouch and raising the viewfinder to his eye when he sailed out over a sheet of pure ice sheathing part of the foredeck. Suddenly he was entirely horizontal and suspended in mid-air for a flailing instant before landing flat on his back with a dull thump; the camera hit with a more brittle sound and went skidding off in the opposite direction, shedding several bright little component parts as it did so. As the wind was knocked out of him, it blasted across his lips in the form of a single coarse four-letter epithet which rang loudly over the still arctic sea and was clearly heard by the masthead lookouts leaning out of their crow's-nest, one hundred and ten feet above. It was also heard on the bridge, of course, where more heads popped over the windscreen, including one in a long-billed fisherman's cap. The only two men who could not afford to look at the strange sight were the seamen manipulating the dip net; they had just plunged it into the raft of unsavory flotsam now heaved upward on the long pole and swung it back in over the deck with its meshed sack bulging with dripping garbage. Munceford sat up and was splattered by an ice-cold sobering little shower as it passed over his head. He heard a sharp *che-click* of a camera shutter, then Yeoman Pinelli reached him and yanked him to his feet, exclaiming:

"Jesus, sir! Be careful! There's lots of ice on deck!" He did not linger to waste any sympathy on the correspondent, but turned his attention to the far more important movie camera. Retrieving it and its dislodged pieces out of the scupper, he tenderly began to examine them.

Munceford clamped his mouth down over more bitter profanity which was starting to well up out of him and felt his face burn in spite of the freezing cold. Somehow he managed to make a sound which was like a laugh. "That was a damned fool thing to do! I hope the camera isn't busted."

"I'll have to check it out," Pinelli sourly answered. He aimed it at the two seamen who were busy emptying the contents of the net into a bucket and shot a few feet of film. "Sounds all right, but . . ." He shook his head doubtfully, then reacted to the captain's voice calling down to him from the bridge:

"Pinelli! Will you take a secure grip on Mr. Munceford and escort him up here, please!"

# 13.

"What kind of clumsy loudmouths are being issued War Department press cards these days?" Commander Allison asked the captain with disgust. They were on the bridge, looking down on the foredeck.

Finlander smiled. "Munceford's no Ernie Pyle, but I think he's just what we want. What they call a hack in his profession. He won't come up with anything much, yet our records will show a card-holding correspondent has covered the operation, proving everything has to be above board and run as safely as any friendly little cold war should. Right?" He gave his executive officer a sly wink and turned to the OOD, who was standing behind them. "All right, Mr. Harwell, resume your base course, but try to stay clear of the ice."

They all went into the wheelhouse, where Lieutenant Harwell rang up ALL AHEAD STANDARD on the annunciator and gave the helmsman a heading which would continue taking the *Bedford* northward along the Greenland coast. Ensign Bascomb, a lanky meteorological officer on loan from the Naval Air Service, came in from his morning observations and took personal credit for the fine weather. Chief Quartermaster Rickmers, a leathery veteran of eighteen years of destroyer duty, cynically predicted snow by afternoon. The talker, a redheaded seaman attached by a headset and cord to the master communication panel, announced: "Masthead lookout reports a whale spouting; bearing zero-five-zero, estimate one mile range."

Captain Finlander glanced through a window in that direction and was able to catch a vanishing puff of vapor rising above a swirl on a distant swell. His wiry eyebrows cocked themselves in a mischievous line and he nudged Commander Allison with his elbow. "Ask the CIC if they have anything to report. Ask it sort of casual-like without tipping them off about that whale."

The executive officer went to the communication panel and picked up the phone; after a minute's conversation he hung up and informed the captain: "Mr. Spitzer reports all readouts negative . . . except one whale which they picked up twenty minutes ago, now bearing zero-five-eight at two-zero-five-zero yards, making six knots on a northeasterly heading, sir. By the way, Queffle is on the MTS."

Finlander made a gesture of mock anger over having been deprived of catching the *Bedford*'s underwater-detection experts flatfooted, then he laughed. "Very good! Nothing much gets by our boy Queffle. . . . Mr. Harwell! Compliment the masthead lookouts on their alertness and accurate range estimation. *No!* Belay that! I'll do it myself and make those boys' day for them. Who are they?"

"Jones and Thorbjornsen, seamen second, sir."

The captain telephoned the crow's-nest and expressed his pleasure to the lookouts in a few tersely complimentary words. When he hung up and turned around, he found himself facing Yeoman Pinelli and Ben Munceford. He did not react at all to the camouflage jacket with its odd collection of insignia and only made an oblique hint at having seen the pratfall on the foredeck. "Good morning, Mr. Munceford. Good morning, Pinelli. Have we suffered another camera casualty this morning?"

Pinelli was still carrying the instrument and gave it a quick, confirming examination. "No, sir—only a bent sunshade and chipped paint."

"Anything chipped or bent on *you,* Munceford?" Finlander inquired.

"I've got a pretty hard ass, Captain," Munceford answered, managing a laugh to cover his embarrassment. The bravado did not go over at all, bringing a wrinkling of Commander Allison's nose and a hardening glint in Finlander's crinkly eyes.

"All right, Pinelli, you are relieved of your escort duties for the time being. I will take Mr. Munceford in tow myself." He waited while the yeoman reluctantly returned the camera to the correspondent, acknowledged his salute, then took Munceford by the arm and steered him into a corner of the wheelhouse. When he spoke, he dropped his voice somewhat, but not so low that he could not be heard by the half-dozen men in there. "Are you really a naturally coarse man," he asked, "or do you pretend to be because you think it makes you fit in with what you fancy to be a rough bunch of sailors?"

Munceford's face arranged itself into a defensive pout."I hadn't given it any thought, Captain. I—"

"Don't be offended, Munceford, and don't think I am a prude," Finlander told him, speaking like a stern but just father. "A normal amount of mild swearing is all right, but I do not permit within my hearing the kind of profane words which are vulgar vernaculars of copulation and certain bodily excretions. It's not because they shock my sensitive nature. I have forgotten more hard language than most men on this bridge will ever learn. But the kind of expletive which came off the foredeck a few minutes ago is offensive to me because it indicates a loss of self-control— and *that* is something I cannot tolerate on my ship. If it takes thought and concentration to keep from senselessly cursing through a trying situation, so much the better. Thought and concentration are the crux of this operation. Self-control is essential to it."

An unwilling apology began curling off Munceford's lips. "I'm sorry I offended you, but—"

Finlander's severity switched back to a gruff good humor with a bewildering suddenness, the bristling brows relaxing from their rigid line, the scar on his throat fading from an ugly red. "Very good, Munceford! This is, after all, part of the necessary background material for your story about us, so don't take it too personally. Have you found any good picture material yet?"

"Well, I was going to shoot some of the garbage collecting, but . . ."

The captain waved a hand to indicate that he disapproved of that subject matter. He looked around for his executive officer and called him over. "Buck! It's such an unusually fine day that I think we should organize a ball game on the fantail later this morning when the light is best for photography. Would you speak to Mr. Ralston about it, please." Turning back to Munceford, he said: "Now, *that* should interest the TV viewers, don't you agree? A volleyball game on a destroyer cruising near the arctic circle in the dead of winter! The kind of thing which shows the high morale of our forces, right? If the boys can play ball, they've got the situation well in hand, right?"

If Munceford had not been so angry over the lecture on profanity, he might have detected a subtly ironic overtone in the captain's voice and noticed a sly glint in the deep-set eyes. But now he became even angrier because Finlander was turning out to fancy himself an amateur movie director—one of his pet hates. "I guess there must be a couple of million feet of film of servicemen playing volleyball all over the world, Captain," he told him.

"Precisely!" Finlander exclaimed, seemingly too pleased with himself to take notice of the disgusted tone. "And we'll show the *Bedford* has one of the best teams. Now, let me see. What else can we line up for you, Munceford? . . . Ah, yes! *Whales!* Of course! Whales and volleyball. Don't you think that would make a terrific combination for television?" This time he did not wait for an answer. He hurried over to the communications panel, pushed a button and spoke into the microphone: "CIC, this is the captain speaking. Do you still have a readout on that whale?" An affirmative answer came out of the speaker, including the range and bearing of the animal. "Very good, Mr. Spitzer. Lock on and close. Mr. Munceford would like some pictures of it and you can show him how good you are at sonar tracking at the same time. The bridge will yield the conn to CIC now." He turned from the intercom and looked toward Lieutenant Harwell. "Did you get that, OOD?"

"Yes, sir. I'm yielding the conn to CIC for sonar tracking exercise. Steering now on automatic remote control."

Munceford thought that he detected suppressed laughter in Harwell's voice and suddenly became aware that everybody in the wheelhouse seemed to be holding himself in check with some difficulty. Chief Quartermaster Rickmers had turned his back on him and his shoulders appeared to be shaking convulsively; the helmsman made a weird coughing noise. All the others were deliberately averting their faces from him. Was Finlander making him the butt of a joke after having dressed him down a few moments ago? "Look here," he loudly protested. "I like to shoot film off the cuff and candid-like, getting things the way they happen naturally. There's no need to trouble with a lot of set-ups on my account, see."

Finlander came over and took him by the arm, leading him toward the door to the open bridge. "I believe in *making* things happen," he retorted. "Besides, it is no trouble at all. We certainly must uphold the navy's tradition of being cooperative with the press!" As they moved out of the wheelhouse, Munceford came within a fraction of digging his heels in and resisting the captain's pull, but something warned him to be careful and he reluctantly allowed himself to be guided to the forward windscreen. "The whale will soon appear close ahead of us," Finlander told him, selecting a position and pointing him in the right direction. "All you've got to do is to have your camera ready, keep alert and wait." With that he hurried back into the wheelhouse, leaving Munceford alone there, staring at the empty sea.

He did not really believe that any whale would appear at all and strongly suspected that he was being made the victim of an elaborate practical joke—like sending a "boot" on a mission to procure feathers for a crow's-nest. But it was not the prospect of such a joke which disturbed him so much; in spite of his self-esteem, he had steeled himself to take a certain amount of ribbing. It was being publicly dressed down for his language and then told *how* to shoot his story which rankled; the icy breeze sweeping over the bridge could not cool his burning resentment over this. To make matters worse, for the first time in his stormy career he felt that he was at the mercy of an absolute authority without any possibility of telling him to go to hell and then quitting forthwith—his preferred technique for coping with such a situation.

Whales and volleyball! Did Finlander really think he would be pleased with such material for his story? Was he going to interfere like this throughout the assignment? Munceford had experienced self-appointed movie directors before, the kind who wanted to produce the whole show as well as star in it. He had had some rough dealings with such people, including some important ones like a U.S. Senator, a Mormon bishop and a captain of industry who considered himself as unassailable as any captain of the navy. A distorted camera angle, a quote edited out of context—these were formidable weapons in the hands of a disgruntled television correspondent. Of course, the aggrieved subjects could and did retaliate, which had something to do with why Ben Munceford only found himself on assignments which were too inconvenient or risky for the more established reporters to cover. Like crawling out on a fortieth-floor ledge to interview a prospective suicide, or making a delayed-drop parachute jump with the paramedics for the sake of a few feet of spectacular film. News directors could occasionally use such a man to liven up the routine work of the precociously dignified, status-conscious "commentator-analysts" who had lately taken over the field. Not too often and always on speculation with no prior commitment, of course—all of which suited Ben Munceford fine. No boss, no strings, no pussy-footing home office, everything strictly on a take-it-or-leave-it and go-to-hell basis. But could he make it work here on the *Bedford?*

His eyes caught a fleeting glimpse of a swirl ahead of the ship. He left the spot Finlander had assigned him and walked out to the wing of the bridge where a lookout was stationed. "Say, sailor!" Munceford said to him. "Is there really a whale somewhere out there?"

The seaman neither turned nor took his eyes off the quadrant of ocean he had been assigned to watch. "Excuse me, sir," he answered. "Lookouts are only permitted to speak to the OOD while on duty."

"Oops! My mistake!" Munceford snapped. He was about to needle the man with a sarcastic remark about the dedication of the *Bedford's* crew when he heard a loud whooshing sound. He turned toward it just in time to see a large whale broach and spout no more than fifty yards ahead of the bow. The animal was badly frightened by this ship which was suddenly pursuing it and filling the protecting deep with an uproar of electronic signals; its huge fluke rose high with a cascade of spray, then vanished through the vortex of a creamy whirlpool. Munceford was jolted out of his paralyzed surprise when the lookout softly, and mockingly, exclaimed: "Thar' she blows!"

"I'll be damned!" Munceford yelled and belatedly raised his camera to shoot some useless footage of the fading ripples left by the sounding whale. He became aware that Captain Finlander and Commander Allison had come to the door of the wheelhouse and were watching him.

"You've got to be quicker than that!" the captain disparagingly shouted.

Fuming, Munceford returned to his original position at the windscreen, propped his camera over the edge of it and waited for another opportunity with his finger on the trigger. All right! If this ship spent the taxpayers' money chasing after whales, then, by God, he would see to it that they at least got a movie out of it! Volleyball and whales! Finlander's cold war! But would they believe it?

# 14.

On this morning there was another young man aboard the *Bedford* suffering from a disturbed state of mind, the same kind of disturbance occasioned by a vacillation between anger and that peculiar kind of fear generated by injured pride; but, unlike Ben Munceford, there was no question of any lack of discipline or self-control, these qualities having been indelibly impressed upon his character throughout a spartan boyhood spent in English public school and naval college. Lieutenant P. L. M. Packer, R.N., knew how to submerge his personal troubles and at least give the outward appearance of the classically jaunty and efficient British naval officer. The human nervous system can stand only so much suppression for a given amount of time before it starts to cripple itself, but Packer's training helped him to contain or delay this effect; he was also helped by the motto on his family crest—not one of those inscribed in the dead foreign language of Latin, but consisting of a single succinct English word: *Endure.* Simple, forthright and sometimes tremendously difficult to live up to. So difficult, in fact, that all male Packers seemed destined to die in the attempt. It was this family curse which was preying upon his mind this morning, not because of his own physical fear of it, but because of Shebeona's evident decision that she was not prepared to accept the motto as her own, especially if it meant to *Endure* a widow's weeds.

Lieutenant Packer had completed the coding and decoding of routine signals which constituted the *Bedford*'s daily contact with NATONAV 1, of transmitting the weather report, of monitoring the traffic to other scattered units of their flotilla spread so thinly over this vast ocean, of estimating the schedule of even skimpier air patrols by intercepting and deciphering position reports on the NATOAVIAN frequency. All business to do with NATO signals was his responsibility, but since this was only a small part of the Communications Center work, it took only a couple of hours of his time each day. Everything else was handled by Lieutenant Andrew S. Beeker and his smoothly efficient staff of radio specialists, which meant that Packer had much time left over in which to brood about the navy he loved and his beloved who hated it.

"Anything exciting I can help you with?" Packer asked Beeker, poking his head inside the EDA room, which housed the high-frequency direction finder (HUFF-DUFF) and multiplex emission sensors (MESS-PLEX).

"No, thanks, Pete. Take five." Lieutenant Beeker almost always declined any help from Packer, who suspected he carried a latent germ of anglophobia in his pragmatic heart. In spite of his youth and low rank, Lieutenant Andrew S. Beeker was one of the foremost radio-communications experts in the United States Navy, the author of an official text with the formidable title: *Theory and Practice of Emissions Detection and Analyses in Naval Tactics*. He had been born twenty-eight years ago in a slum section of Chicago, escaping by only one day from having been foreign-born, a status which would have made his Annapolis appointment virtually unattainable in spite of his extraordinary aptitudes. His parents were refugees from the Russian Revolution who had taken nearly ten years to make it from Kiev to Chicago, via Istanbul, Marseilles, Lisbon, Havana and Toronto. They had baptized him Andrei Simeonovitch Beikerman—a name which was changed in the nick of time so that he was able to enter the Naval Academy as Midshipman Andrew S. Beeker. A few friends called him Andy, but mostly he was known as The Beek—in spite of the fact that he had a rather thick, blunt Slavic nose. The Beek could receive seventy words per minute of Russian Morse and that was one of the principal reasons for his presence aboard the *Bedford;* that, and the fact that he could instantly recognize a Russian transmission, often identify the ship (or submarine) it originated from and pinpoint its location within a square mile with his HUFF-DUFF. The Beek would undoubtedly be a full commander within the next ten years, but that would be as far as he would go; he was, after all, nothing but a technically brilliant Russian Jew and the navy had already had its unnerving experience with one of those who reached flag rank. To Lieutenant Packer, however, Beeker was simply an American midwesterner reared a thousand miles from blue water and in a city whose mayor had once threatened to punch King George V in the nose.

"I'd be glad to pick through the red frequencies for you," the Englishman offered with a kind of defeated enthusiasm. He knew The Beek would only say again:

"No, thanks, Pete. Take five."

So Packer went back to his desk in the main radio room, sat down and listened absently to the twittering Morse signals which came off the monitoring circuits, stared dully at the backs of the operators guarding their sets and finally, reluctantly, took Shebeona's letter out of his pocket and read it for the fifteenth time since it had arrived yesterday.

*Peter, darling! It was wonderful to get your letters at last, but again I had to wait too long for them. Of course it isn't your fault—I know there are no post boxes in that beastly ocean of yours. It's simply that the waiting and the worrying becomes too unbearable for me and the fulfillments too elusively fleeting. I have felt the same lines eating into my face which I have seen in your mother's and know their roots are deep in a lonely heart, far beyond the aid of cold creams and pancake makeups. Alas, my poor Peter, my love is not turning out as unselfish as hers and therefore is not worthy of you.*

*Alan Sternway has asked me to marry him and I have accepted. I am awfully fond of Alan—that's all. But he will always be there and, anyway, I am told that one's first love is only good for tender memories. These I will have of you for as long as I live. Devotedly—Shebeona.*

Packer had to smooth out many wrinkles in the faintly scented pink stationery in order to read those words; last night he had angrily crumpled up the letter and almost ruined it. Now those wrinkles made him think of the lines in his mother's face which Shebeona spoke about. It was unthinkable to him that her beauty would ever be marred by such things, yet his mother must once have been almost as beautiful. There was that wedding picture he had found in the attic to prove it; in spite of the ghastly fashions of the mid-thirties, it showed a lovely girl all aglow next to a young naval officer who looked extraordinarily like himself. Seven years remained before widowhood. Seven years which for her contained only thirty days each of fulfilled love, all the rest being the long wait while her husband's ship cruised from one distant station to the next, moving inexorably toward that fatal rendezvous with the long rifles of the *Bismarck*. When the Battle of the Denmark Strait took place, Peter was less than five years old; the only man he could remember from early childhood was the one who came to tell of his father's death. He had never really known his father, and now he wondered how well his mother had known him. And his grandmother, who had lost her husband in the Battle of Jutland—how well had she known *him?* Even in the long period of peace which followed the Napoleonic Wars the naval Packers had managed to get themselves killed at sea: Sir John had survived Trafalgar only to be killed in a skirmish with an American slaver, and Sir Winston had foundered in the ice of the Antarctica he had been sent to explore. . . . Could he really blame Shebeona?

His gloomy thoughts were interrupted by The Beek, who came out of the EDA room and called an order to his chief radio technician: "Benton! Patch in a tape and record the transmission on three-point-nine megacycles while I take a HUFF-DUFF on it!"

Lieutenant Packer quickly put away Shebeona's letter and jumped up to reach the bank of recorders ahead of Chief Benton. "You got something hot?" he called to Beeker.

"I think it's a bogey—that so-called research ship *Novo Sibirsk* which always seems to indicate the presence of Moby Dick. The transmission is about three hundred miles off." He quickly vanished back inside the EDA room.

"I'll take care of the recording, sir," Chief Benton told the English officer, respectfully but firmly nudging him aside.

Packer watched him for a moment, then slumped back into his chair and began to shuffle absently through the file copies of the morning's dispatches. He did not bring out the letter again, but his mind could not tear itself away from it. What would his mother say about the broken engagement? She always looked forward so much to the weekends when Shebeona would drive out to the old house in Surrey and keep her company for a few hours—the two waiting women, the old widowed one and the young engaged one who had so much of that kind of waiting ahead of her. There would be no more visits now, because Shebeona would, of course, be with Alan Sternway.

Peter's anger boiled up as he thought of Alan Sternway and it almost broke the blank surface expression on his face. The Sternways had once been a distinguished service family too, but Alan believed that the dissolution of the British Empire had relieved him from any obligation to conform to tradition. Instead of going into the navy, he had joined the merchant marine, and instead of going to sea, he sold tickets in block lots to other Englishmen who were also severing their ties with history and emigrating out of the country. Alan's ships did not even fly the Red Duster, but were refurbished tubs under Panamanian registry, owned by Italians who fronted for Greek-American financiers. Old Admiral Sir Percival Sternway would be tossing restlessly in his grave over his son's doings, but all Alan tossed was money. Enough money for a flat in Mayfair, an American Thunderbird, vacations on Capri—*and Shebeona!* Damn her! If there were lines eating into her beautiful face, they were those of dissolution of character, of failure to *Endure,* not the attrition of abiding with her heart's true love. To reject him and marry a man like Alan Sternway was as bad as . . . as bad as marrying a man like Ben Munceford! Well—*he* had been attracted to her, hadn't he! Maybe that was her type, after all!

"Sir, I have an action signal from Narwhale!" one of the radiomen announced, yanking a sheet out of his typewriter and sailing it over onto Packer's desk. Narwhale was the code name of the Norwegian destroyer *Fritiof Nansen,* and when the NATO communicator ran her message through the decoder, he found that she too had picked up the Russian transmission on 3.9 megacycles and was drawing the *Bedford*'s attention to it.

"Do they think we are asleep?" Lieutenant Beeker dryly asked when he read the signal.

"Rather trying to show us *they* aren't," Packer answered. "Shall we call the bridge about this, Beek?"

"No. Let's wait a moment and give Captain Finlander a nice complete package of information." During the next couple of minutes Beeker listened to the tape recording which Chief Benton had made of the transmission, then checked it against a master recording of sample transmissions he had compiled of all the known Russian vessels frequenting the area. Only his trained ear could pick up subtle differences and likenesses, and finally he announced with absolute certainty: "It's the *Novo Sibirsk*, all right. Now we had better keep our ears glued to their submarine frequencies for Moby Dick." He sat down and quickly typed out the information on a message sheet, including the exact position as determined by his HUFF-DUFF bearing, clipped the signal from Narwhale to it and called for a messenger.

"Wait—let me take it to the bridge, Beek," Packer pleaded, then impulsively explained: "I want to ask to speak to the captain, anyway."

The Beek looked a little suspicious. "You do? Why?"

"It's a personal matter. I need his permission to send a telegram to . . . er, ah, home." He suddenly felt himself blushing as the American officer scrutinized him with a puzzled curiosity.

"That's only permitted in emergencies, you know, Pete. Did you have bad news in the mail yesterday?"

"You might say so," Packer answered, making a desperate attempt to sound casual about it.

"Nobody's died, have they?"

"Yes—I suppose *I* have a little." He said it with a shrug and a bitter little laugh. Then, with a sudden switch to complete indifference, he reversed himself and exclaimed: "Never mind. I'll catch the skipper this evening if I still feel like getting in touch with home."

He started to return to his desk, but Beeker stopped him, shoved the papers into his hand and swung him around toward the door as if suddenly anxious to get rid of any kind of problem which was beyond the scope of radio technology. As Packer left, he settled down to make a translation of the intercepted Russian transmission.

Outside the Communications Center the sun had climbed higher into the clear sky and begun to counter the terrible cold left by the long winter night; given more time, its rays might have driven the temperature upward to somewhere close to mere freezing, but another night was due only three hours past high noon and the thermometer would soon start another downward plunge. In the meanwhile the Arctic Ocean had lost the dazzling shimmer of dawn and taken on the spectacular deep blue color it wears on its rare fine days. The slick parts where a flat calm prevailed were like undulating sheets of polished steel; other parts ruffled by cat's-paws of icy zephyrs changed their hue to a gunmetal patina which spread, contracted, vanished and reappeared on the slopes of the restlessly quiescent swells. On the eastern horizon, sea and sky met in a sharp unbroken line, but to the west the frosted pinnacles and crags of Greenland's mountains stood out with a startling clarity which made them seem much closer than they actually were. Between them and the ship, remnants of an icefield drifted in strangely orderly columns, like flattened snowmen floating down an invisible stream within the sea. The *Bedford's* wake curved away from their course, cutting a softer emerald swath through the hard blue of the surface.

Lieutenant Packer stopped on his mission to the bridge to allow his eyes to take all this in and his mind to savor the remoteness of it from the troubles assailing him from faraway England. It made Shebeona and Alan Sternway and their trite little love triangle seem utterly unreal and unimportant. This ship and this bleak but protecting sea were all that mattered and all that was real for him, as it had been for all the Packers before him. No! He would send no pleading message. Certainly not! Let *them* have each other and let *him* have this. But, God, it was so cold! And lonely!

A quickening of the pulse from the engine room, together with a slight heeling of the deck as the *Bedford* tightened her turn, brought Packer out of his brooding. The ship was being put through some kind of seemingly erratic maneuver, but undoubtedly it had a calculated purpose which had to do with the frequent ASW exercises which Captain Finlander devised to keep the CIC in a constant state of alertness. Remembering the papers fluttering in his gloved hand, Packer hurried to the bridge, where he reported to Commander Allison inside the wheelhouse:

"Sir, I have a radio-intelligence report for the captain."

Finlander was only ten feet away, but with his ear close to the sonar monitor's speaker, listening intently as CIC kept relentlessly on top of the hapless whale. Packer was hoping he would notice him and step over to circumvent the through-channel procedure, but his attention was completely absorbed in the persistent *ping-ying . . . ping-ying.* Allison took the report and checked through it to determine whether it warranted immediately disturbing the captain—which he decided it did. Holding it up in front of Finlander's face, he silently put one finger against the significant words: *"Novo Sibirsk"*—and had the report snatched out of his hand. When the captain finished reading it, there was the fire of excitement smoldering in his eyes. "Excellent! This may mean the hunt is on. Let's start a tactical plot and do some figuring, Buck." Beckoning his executive officer to follow him into the chartroom, he hurried off without ever noticing Packer—who felt a pang of frustration. Well, the captain would be too busy for a while to bother about anybody's personal problems. And, anyway, hadn't he decided not to send a message to Shebeona . . . not immediately, at least?

"What's the big deal, Pete?" Lieutenant Harwell had sidled up alongside him to find out what was so important it had been brought up by the NATO liaison officer instead of by ordinary messenger.

"The Beek sniffed out Moby Dick's mother—that's all."

"That's all!" Harwell let out a meaningful whistle, then slapped his hands together. "That's all, he says! So let's cut out this horsing around and get going! What's holding the skipper back?"

"Maybe the fact that the emission originated from somewhere three hundred miles northeast. It's my guess H.M.S. *Obdurate* is in a better position to do something about it." Even as he spoke, he heard the scuttlebutt start its whispering course through the wheelhouse and knew that in a matter of minutes it would permeate the entire ship.

Harwell made a disparaging snort which was only part joking. "We'll never give up Moby Dick to any Limey can, boy!" he exclaimed. "Not as long as the *Bedford* is in the same ocean."

Packer flashed a grin and needled him back. "Yes—and maybe that's why nobody ever catches him."

Harwell recoiled with a horrified expression. "Jesus, Peterpacker!" he whispered with an uneasy glance toward the curtained entrance to the chartroom. "What's happened to make you no longer want to go on living? Only a desperate character would say anything like that on this bridge!"

He was joking, of course, but the Englishman nodded seriously. "You don't know *how* desperate, Dick." With a wry grimace he turned and went out onto the open bridge. He had decided to take his time about returning to the Communications Center. Maybe Captain Finlander would quickly break off whatever exercise was taking place, lay a course toward the *Novo Sibirsk,* then come out here to restlessly join the lookouts in watching the sea. Maybe engage him in conversation. A conversation which could lead up to the subject of home. A casual request for permission to send a personal telegram. But supposing he wanted to know the *nature* of the telegram—that would be perfectly within a commanding officer's right, of course. Could he think up something innocuous which would still convey his anguish to Shebeona? He noticed that, besides the lookout, the only other person on this side of the bridge was Ben Munceford, who was leaning over the windscreen, clutching his camera and staring at the sea beyond the bow.

"Hello, Ben," he greeted him, placing himself next to him. "You look like you expected a chorus line of mermaids to pop out of the sea."

Munceford looked up with a start. "Well, well!" he exclaimed with a pouting smile. "It's the jealous English lover boy. How're you today? Still mad at me?"

"All right, Ben—I guess I deserve that," Packer answered after gritting his teeth together for an instant. "I'm sorry I acted so badly last night."

"Well, okay, Pete! Like I told you, I had no business with your girl's photograph."

For a moment they both silently watched the sea. Then the English officer asked: "You found her very attractive, didn't you?"

"Damned handsome broad. I'm not going to stick my neck out with you by saying any more than that. Say, where is that silly whale? It's been fifteen or twenty minutes since it was up last."

"Oh, is that what we're doing? The old Ahab stuff. If it's a humpback whale, which it probably is, it's good for about a thirty-minute dive. Much less if badly scared. . . . She's about to be married, you know."

"Yeah, I got that message. To you."

"No. Not to me. To somebody else." Packer horrified himself as much over actually putting the calamity into words as over *whom* he was saying them to. He made it much worse by adding: "So, you see, it doesn't really matter to me whether you are interested in her or not."

Ben Munceford looked at him sharply, his freckled face wrenching itself into sardonic surprise. "Say! Don't tell me that was a Dear John letter you got yesterday. The old kiss-off?" He spoke so loudly that the lookout in the wing might have heard it. The Englishman's face remained inscrutable, his eyes still on the coldly sunlit sea, so it was not his reaction which made Munceford abruptly switch his manner to one of genuine concern. It was the fact that he suddenly realized this was the only person aboard the *Bedford* who was trying to act like an ordinary mortal human being with him. "Listen, Pete!" he said in a much lower and more sympathetic voice. "Don't let them get you down! All women are emotionally unstable opportunists. I ought to know—I'm just shedding my third wife, so I've learned in the school of hard knocks, believe you me. Like if you love cats, you're going to get yourself clawed from time to time. It hurts, but it heals. So don't let it get you down."

Packer nodded, but toward the sea. "There is your whale," he said.

"Damn! Skunked again!" Munceford exclaimed and fumbled with his camera. However, this time the whale did not immediately sound. The long frantic chase had so exhausted it that it wallowed on the surface, painfully spouting vapor through its blowhole, a weirdly scalloped flipper waving listlessly in the air as it half rolled, showing a pale, fluted belly. There was something pathetic about its floundering effort to get out of the way of the *Bedford*'s sharp prow, and only in the nick of time did the fluke make a churning stroke to propel its hulk clear of the slicing column of steel bearing down upon it. With his camera still grinding away and his eye glued to the viewfinder, Munceford raced to the edge of the bridge, photographing an unsteady but dramatic sequence as the huge, half-submerged blimp of a beast was buffeted by the wash of the passing ship. He did not stop shooting until it had fallen astern and floundered in the foaming wake which stretched in a pale blue, crazily looping serpentine track across the sea behind them. Then he looked up with a grin of satisfaction which almost immediately changed into a frown. "Say!" he said to Packer, who had followed him across the bridge, "couldn't you call this cruelty to a dumb animal? I don't know if I like it being done on my account."

Before the Englishman could answer him, Lieutenants Spitzer and Krindlemeyer came out of the wheelhouse and stared astern through binoculars at a swirl where the whale was attempting to sound. They both looked very pleased and Spitzer gleefully exclaimed: "Boy! Human and system control were all go on that run! We got a perfect trace too. Those hypersonic pulses drove him crazy!"

Munceford heard him quite clearly and although he did not fully understand what he was talking about, it somehow further offended one of his few sensitivities—an almost maudlin love of animals. "How would *you* like to be chased with hypersonic whatnots anyway—eh?" He lifted the movie camera, pointed it at the two officers and shot a quick sequence of their faces as they gaped at him in confused amazement. It must have been a very unflattering shot.

Lieutenant Peter Packer was suddenly amused by the incident and became full of suppressed laughter. "Look here, Ben, old boy," he said after Krindlemeyer and Spitzer had slunk back into the wheelhouse, "if you think they were chasing that whale for *your* benefit, forget it. Destroyermen and submariners hate whales because they bugger up their sonar systems with false echoes. I dare say more depth charges have been wasted on whales than on real targets, and it's still damned hard to tell the difference, even with our latest models. So, you see, partly out of spite and partly for necessary practice, Finlander frequently allows the CIC to make runs on them like this."

"Are you saying they can't tell the difference between a whale and a submarine even with all the high-priced brains and equipment on this ship?" Munceford asked with a sneer. "That's great! And I think maybe it's news."

Packer's amusement turned to alarm. "I didn't say that, so don't quote me on it," he answered, keeping his eyes on the wheelhouse door. "What I do say is that it is sometimes difficult. Every creature in the sea, from whale to plankton, makes a noise of some kind and can give a return echo on sonar. It is a matter of gaining experience in making proper identification, of learning thousands of separate sounds and characteristic echoes, often picking them out of the confusion. The deep isn't always silent and still. It can be as uproarious as an Italian street riot. And, speaking of underwater sounds, here's the *Bedford*'s special magician at sorting them out!"

Munceford followed his gaze and saw what appeared to be an ordinary seaman come out of the wheelhouse and step to the after bulwark of the bridge to scan the sea astern of the ship, evidently searching for a sign of the whale which had finally managed to dive out of sight. He was a very young, very skinny boy, bareheaded except for a pair of earphones clamped to his head, the oversized cups bulging out, but above his ears, and with the connecting cord dangling around his knees. He was wearing an unzipped windbreaker which bore no insignia of his rating, and, instead of the usual heavy boots worn in this climate, he had a pair of ordinary navy oxfords on his feet. In one hand he clutched a black notebook, in the other a ballpoint pen. After squinting at the empty sea for a moment, he made an almost effeminate gesture of annoyance, looked about the bridge and, spotting Lieutenant Packer, trotted toward him with a peculiar skipping gait.

"Mr. Packer!" He hailed the officer without any formality at all and with a voice which still contained a strident note of puberty. "Did you make out what kind of whale that was?"

"A humpback, I believe."

"Are you sure, sir? Did you get a good look?"

"Quite sure, Queffle," Packer insisted with a kind of patient indulgence.

"Darn it!" the boy exclaimed with the petulance of an innocent child. "I wish they'd assign a marine biologist to this ship. I suggested one, you know—but no! I get an oceanographer instead. Now, what earthly help is an oceanographer in cataloguing ambient noises of animal origin, I ask you?"

"I am sure Lieutenant Burger is doing his very best," Packer told him acidly.

"Oh, yes, sir. I didn't mean anything personal, of course. And, actually, I am quite sure it *was* a humpback. My own readout on the MTS indicated it, you see. So let's record it as such." He began scribbling in the notebook, his long, bony fingers, already an unhealthy purplish crimson from the cold, curling around the pen in a painful, double-jointed grip.

When he had completed his notes, Packer got around to introducing Munceford to him: "Ben, this is Sonarman Second Class Merlin Queffle, our ace sonar operator. It is rumored that Captain Finlander ran roughshod over a dozen destroyer and submarine skippers in order to obtain the services of this lad. Unfortunately, he is perfectly aware of his own importance and treats his ordinary mortal shipmates in a most cavalier fashion . . . up to and including the executive officer."

Queffle took the sarcasm with a guileless smile which revealed his front teeth to be very large and very crooked. "Oh, get off it, sir," he exclaimed with a high-pitched giggle, then turned to Munceford and extended a slender hand toward him. "You must be the television man who joined us yesterday. Glad to meet you. Gee, that's a sharp jacket you're wearing. I like it!"

Ben Munceford had been staring at and listening to this strange young sailor with an openly amazed disbelief. Now he was a little slow in grasping the offered handshake, and when he did, it felt somewhat like grasping a bunch of wilted asparagus. "How are you, Kwivvle?"

"*Queffle,* sir," the sonarman corrected him. "Merlin P. Queffle. It's French . . . Breton, really. A lot of my friends call me the Breton Kid."

"And some call him Merlin the Magician," Packer injected.

"Oh, get off it, sir. . . ."

"Because he has ESP," the English officer persisted in explaining to Munceford. "A formidable secret weapon in submarine tracking."

"ESP? What the hell is that?"

"Extrasensory Perception," Queffle brightly told him, with neither humility nor bombast. "The idea is that I'm supposed to be able to *sense* whether or not a subsurface sound is of man-made origin. Well, the long fancy name is all right, I suppose, and I do kind of enjoy the ring of it. But I prefer to think I'm simply in tune with the sea and what goes on down there. I'm from a long line of Grand Bank fishermen and captains, although you'd never guess it to look at me." He jokingly sucked in his cheeks to exaggerate their gauntness, then flashed a buck-toothed smile. "My mother played violin with the Boston Symphony before she married my father, and I suppose I inherited my sensitive ears from her. Anyway, the combination seems to make me pretty hot on the sonar and—" He would have rambled on about himself in an unabated torrent had he not been rudely interrupted by an angry voice calling his name from the wheelhouse door.

"Queffle! What the devil are you doing out there without cap and gloves?" It was the OOD, Lieutenant Harwell, and he came rushing toward them with a belligerent annoyance which at first boded ill for the sonarman, but then somehow quickly and mysteriously abated. The dressing down which followed was not only mild but almost pleading. "Do you realize what the temperature is out here, Queffle? Twelve degrees! For God's sake, boy! What do you think the captain would do to me if you caught a cold in your ears during my watch? Besides, it's against regulations to enter the bridge without proper dress, you know. Please go back inside at once. *Please!*"

Queffle had watched the OOD's approach and listened to his words without any special alarm; now he looked around and sniffed the brisk slipstream sweeping the bridge, his nostrils and lips parting slightly and giving him an extraordinary rabbit-like appearance. "It really is quite cold, isn't it?" he agreed, then excused himself and ambled off toward the wheelhouse door.

"Damn it, Pete! You should know better than to let him stand out here like that," Harwell rebuked Lieutenant Packer. "Don't you remember there was hell to pay when Queffle got infected sinuses last month?"

The Englishman laughed, but somewhat cautiously. "Sorry, but, frankly, I'm awfully inhibited about how to handle your precious Merlin. Delicate, precocious children always have thrown me, actually."

"Now, don't give me that, Pete," Harwell angrily retorted. "Merlin Queffle is an enlisted sailor in the United States Navy and should be treated like one."

"Then why don't you?" Packer instantly countered, the humor gone from his eyes, leaving them coldly serious.

Lieutenant Harwell became terribly flustered as well as angry. "B-because . . . uh . . . because, you know damn well why! Although I see no reason for him to come up here in the first place. I'm going to speak to Spitzer about that. With two million dollars' worth of sonar gear aboard this ship, I can't understand why we've got to pamper a primad—" He abruptly stopped himself in midsentence as Commander Allison stepped out on the bridge and came toward them.

"I hate to break up your gossiping in the sun," he dryly announced to Harwell, "but we seem to have a tactical situation shaping up and there are a few details to be taken care of by the OOD—which is you, is it not, Mr. Harwell? Fine! First bring the ship to sixty-five degrees and increase her speed to eighteen knots. Then please send your JOOD to find Commodore Schrepke, present the captain's compliments and ask him to come to the bridge. Also notify Lieutenants Spitzer, Beeker and Burger to report to the captain's day cabin in exactly five minutes. That will do to start with."

Harwell said: "Aye, aye, sir," then could not contain himself from asking: "Are we on to Moby Dick, sir?"

"Maybe—maybe not. But you know the skipper. So get cracking and play it like we are!" He waited until Harwell had rushed back into the wheelhouse and called the new course to the helmsman, then he turned on Ben Munceford, gave his camouflage jacket an icy look and said: "Ensign Ralston is organizing a volleyball game on the fantail. I suggest you lay aft with your camera, Mr. Munceford."

"But I'd rather stick around here if there's going to be some kind of action, and—"

"The captain wants pictures of the volleyball." Allison cut off his protest with a slight, yet very threatening rise in his tone. "You must not keep the men waiting on deck in this temperature." Again he waited, this time while Munceford sulkily left the bridge. The executive officer's body was racked by a distasteful shudder inside his bulky parka and he said to Lieutenant Packer: "It must be rough on you, sharing a cabin with that man."

"He's not really so bad when you get to know him, sir," the Englishman answered with a certain hesitation. "I really suspect the brashness is a front."

"I hope you don't judge our American press by him," Allison growled. "I thought that type of reporter went out years ago, but evidently it has been reinstated by television."

"Don't worry, sir—we have that kind in England too." He coughed and cleared his throat, then blurted out: "I suppose the captain's awfully busy right now."

"Yes. . . . Something which I could help you with?"

Packer met the probing look in the commander's green eyes, and the indecision over whether to send a message to Shebeona became a jab of physical pain in his chest. He hoped it did not show in his face. "Oh, nothing important, sir. It can wait." He forced a smile, then covered his embarrassment with a sudden urgent exclamation: "Goodness! If Lieutenant Beeker is to report to the bridge, I must relieve him immediately at the Communications Center. Excuse me, sir."

He rushed off, leaving Commander Allison thoughtfully staring after him before turning his eyes to contemplate the distant, snow-crusted ramparts of Greenland's coast. The *Bedford* was picking up speed, and although the Arctic Ocean was still lying placid around her, she began to generate her own wind, which chilled the meager warmth of the sun. It gnawed with cold little fangs on his exposed face and he turned his back to it, looking aft toward the wake which had straightened out, unraveling itself from the twisting track of the whale hunt. He saw six men emerge onto the main deck, dressed in heavy sweatshirts and pants, and hurry toward the fantail, the last one in line hefting a ball as he ran.

# 15.

Standing alone on his bridge in a blackening, brooding mood, Erik Finlander watched this lovely day on the Arctic Ocean end with a breathtaking sunset. Even with his mind troubled by a tangled skein of plots and travails, he remained aware of every detail of it.

Some high cirrus clouds had come drifting across the clear sky, fashioned by stratospheric winds into delicate brush strokes of pearl white. In the land-bound west, fingers of mist had crept out of the fiords and closed around the coast, hiding in a silvery shroud all but the glacier crowns of the mountains and the glittering seaward edge of the icepack. Now, as the sun dipped, swelling into a red ball of fire, her shimmering disk hesitating and slightly flattening to the touch of the sawtooth escarpment of Greenland's frozen highlands, all things in the firmament, ocean and land became briefly kindled by the splendor of her departing glory. The clouds burst into flames. The soft surging swells were splattered by a froth of rubies. Even the austere warship, slicing along her hunter's course, shed for these moments her steely quality and turned into a ship of fire trailing a comet's tail of illuminated foam. Then the sun slipped behind the mountains with a startling suddenness, and from the darkening east the onrushing winter night cast its mantle to extinguish the afterglow. Red turned a dull gold, gradually tarnishing into a uniform bluish mauve which soon draped everything in a melancholy veil of deepening twilight. Only one thin thread of brilliance remained, a long, arrow-straight vapor trail stretching across the sky, headed by a tiny silver cross which was an aircraft flying so high it was still a speck in the eye of the sun.

Finlander was aware of the presence of the plane, but did not seem to pay it any particular attention. Through the small monitoring speaker which was attached to the bulwark beneath his elbow, he had been subconsciously listening to the reaction of the *Bedford* when her radar picked up the faint *pip* while it was still one hundred and forty miles away. The air-defense officer had immediately pulled an alert, the CIC starting to feed target information into the computers, which in turn digested and analyzed in a flash, then fed the results into the battery of TERRIER missiles poised in their launcher. Communications had issued a challenge which was quickly answered by the correct countersign, identifying the jet as an RB-47 on reconnaissance patrol out of Thule AFB. As a final precaution, Yeoman Pinelli had aimed his turreted Mark VII camera at the minute silver cross as it unraveled its wispy line to a point directly overhead, the huge lens gobbling up the intervening forty thousand feet, and in ten seconds producing a close-up on Polaroid film. The captain had heard those section commanders concerned report these procedures to the bridge and knew they were handling the matter properly without any necessity for his intervention. After a cursory glance upward, he dismissed the aircraft from his mind and turned his eyes from the sky to the sea which contained somewhere in its darkening vastness the real enemy occupying his thoughts.

Time was standing still for Finlander now, for the twilight periods before dawn and after sunset were ever the time of reconning for submariner and sub-hunter alike. The time to contest with each other for the ambush, to maneuver and countermaneuver for the weather gauge of darkness and light. Time to attack. Time to kill. Time to die. Time for captains to isolate themselves in taut watchfulness in conning tower or bridge. And that was where Erik Finlander would always be found during his every dawn and every sunset at sea since taking command of his first ship back in 1943. That was why time stood still, even retraced itself for him during these moments. Nothing had changed. It was always the same, whether on old four-stack cans or modern super-destroyers like the *Bedford,* whether in actual conflict or supposedly bloodless cold war where the intent to kill could not—or *should* not—be implemented. The sham of it only served to tense a captain like Finlander who had once tasted blood, his own as well as the enemy's.

The deep scar on his throat, now tingling with an accustomed pain as the icy wind probed the collar of his duffel, had been inflicted upon him in these same Greenland-Icelandic waters during that other peculiar cold war, the one which existed between Germany and the United States in the months before open warfare inevitably erupted. He had been exec on a recommissioned old four-piper, the U.S.S. *Benjamin Crocker,* engaged in what Washington called a "neutrality patrol"—a convenient subterfuge for aiding the hard-pressed British navy. The torpedo which came streaking out of the twilight (a twilight exactly like this one), ripping the old destroyer in two and sinking her in sixty seconds, had brought formal apologies from the Nazi government which in no way inhibited their informal gloating. It had also brought a Navy Cross to a young machinist's mate second class, Lauchlan S. MacKay, who supported in the freezing water a lieutenant (J.G.) and at the same time pinched closed the terrible wound in his throat, doing this for the better part of an hour before they were rescued. Ever since that awful sunset of eighteen years ago Erik Finlander had held on to a seething hatred of submarines through peace and war; he had likewise held on to that man Lauchlan S. MacKay, keeping him with him through a formidable roster of illustrious destroyers, including the *Bedford,* in whose engine room he was now the reigning chief.

Revenge had come to Captain Finlander, but too far away from the scene of treachery and defeat. He had sunk the U-784, the U-866 and the U-1020, but all in the Central Atlantic or Azores. His luck had not been as good on the Murmansk convoy routes, although he had participated in kills where the final fatal stick of depth charges was delivered by Canadian frigates; while given official credit for "assists," he did not count these himself. Thus he scoured this arctic sea today as if it still concealed the U-boat which had blooded him in the realities of submarine warfare, as if the same enemy commander lurked down there, ready to shrug off a "mistake" and pass on the responsibility for apologies to a cynical government, one still subject to the caprice of an absolute tyrant. Finlander's good sense told him, of course, that the chances were overwhelming that the U-boat which had sunk the *Benjamin Crocker* and killed one hundred and four of her crew, including two of his Annapolis classmates, had itself been eventually sunk during the course of that war—in the final tally, only one out of four German submarines had survived to be scrapped or impressed into the Soviet navy. Only a few U-boat commanders remained alive today, only one of these on active service, and that one relegated to an advisory capacity on Finlander's own ship. Commodore Schrepke, he was sure, would be ensconced in the opposite side of the *Bedford*'s bridge, driven by similar compulsions to the same lonely twilight vigil—the same, yet so different, his mind not only plagued by memories of terror and defeat in these waters, but by trepidation over his unnatural purpose aboard a former enemy's ship. A strange and subtly cruel fate, one which held an almost morbid fascination for Captain Finlander.

Being a man who could command a strong grip on reality, he also permitted himself certain flights of fancy, a kind of masochistic nurturing of old hurts and hatreds, of mulling over superstitions and omens, of deliberately playing these against his obsession. He believed, for instance, that the Denmark Strait had it in for him, that the presence here of the Russian submarine his men called Moby Dick boded old scores to be settled through a fated encounter threatened by an ill-starred past. Already they had twice met, and each time the submarine had mysteriously vanished, leaving his frustrated specialists helpless at the consoles of their miraculous electronic detection apparatus, but himself more stubbornly determined than ever. Like its legendary namesake, *this* Moby Dick only drove the pursuing captain to further tempt the very fate he suspected to be deviling his wake. Foolish superstition to occupy the mind of an intelligent naval officer? Perhaps for some, but Erik Finlander could afford such broodings and even turn them to his own advantage since they made him more flexible and more alert. They instilled in him a healthy skepticism about the complex scientific accouterments of his ship and their hold upon their technological servitors, making him depend at least equally upon the basic instincts of a human animal who had been both the hunter and the hunted. Never again would he stand and hesitate as he spied the split-second flash of sunset on the objective lens of a periscope, wondering because sonar was giving no return echo whether it was only the glint of a drifting bottle, glass fisherman's float or piece of ice, then realizing too late the fallibility of manmade instruments as torpedo wakes blossomed out of the dark waters a couple of seconds before the shattering explosion. One hundred and four shipmates had died because of too much trust in scientific gadgetry and too little in human instincts, his own blood barely stemmed from flowing out of his body by the convulsive grip of Chief MacKay's grimy thumb and forefinger. A far-off glinting little flash like . . .

"Lookout! Didn't you spot that reflection out there off the starboard bow?" Finlander shouted at the seaman huddled in the wing.

The boy gave a start and his head seemed to rise up out of the folds of his parka as if activated by a spring. "Y-yes, sir. I think . . . I might have seen a couple of winking sort of flashes, like . . . like off a bottle, or ice, or something like that, Captain, sir. . . ."

Finlander's gloved fist swung down beneath the combing of the bulwark and hit the red lever next to the speaker. The silence which had lulled the *Bedford* was torn apart by the raucous clang of her GQ alarm. Almost instantly the wheelhouse door thrust open and the OOD stuck his head out, eyes wide and questioning. "Possible visual contact, bearing three-zero-zero relative, one thousand yards," the captain called to him with a controlled urgency. "Execute Maneuver Able immediately, Mr. Collins . . . then relieve your starboard lookout!"

As the *Bedford* picked up speed and heeled in a turn toward the suspected enemy, the captain remained where he was, once again listening with a kind of alert detachment to his section commanders as their voices came through the speaker, reporting their respective battle stations closed up. He did not react to the somewhat irritated tone of Lieutenant Krindlemeyer as he announced from the CIC that all readouts on the detecting gear were negative; the ECM officers were never less than patronizing about "eyeball" contacts, often taking them as a direct affront to their instruments. Nor did he give more than a curt, perfunctory explanation of the GQ alarm to Commander Allison when he joined him and began sweeping the empty gloom ahead with his binoculars. But as the unfortunate seaman who had been lookout shuffled past him, Finlander's hand shot out and stopped him with a hard grip on his shoulder. "Do you know why I'm busting you off my bridge, sailor?" he asked in a voice which was both gentle and implacable.

It was too dark now to see the face inside the hood, but the answer told of the misery which was there. "Captain, sir . . . one *thinks* one sees all sorts of things out there that just ain't so," he protested, trying to express the suffering his responsibility entailed rather than make excuses for himself. "One don't like to sing out against the sonar and radar reading without being sure. One got to think it over. One—"

"All right, son!" his captain interrupted him. "If you had not seen those flashes, you would not be blamed. Our eyes can't catch everything in this kind of light. But you admitted to me you *did* see them, yet did nothing about it. It's not your duty to evaluate a sighting, only to report it. I don't want to see you up here again until you have so thoroughly familiarized yourself with the duties of a lookout that you instinctively react correctly. Now go below."

The sailor saluted stiffly, then sagged as he moved away, crushed by his failure. Finlander turned back to lean over the bridge bulwark and scan the sea. "I want you to ream out that kid's section commander, Buck," he gruffly told Allison. "He is a good boy and we owe him the proper indoctrination before making him responsible for the lives of his shipmates. I want it explained to him—and to *all* our lookouts—that sonar and radar also sometimes see things that are not there. Sometimes fail to see things that *are*. I want it understood by all hands that this ship depends first of all on her men, not her machines, which must always remain subservient to us. Even to an ordinary seaman. Understood?"

Out of the speaker came Krindlemeyer's plaintive voice reporting all readouts still negative. Allison said: "Yes, Captain," without taking his binoculars from his eyes.

The GQ turned out to be abortive. Within ten minutes the *Bedford* was secured from battle stations and once again returned to her north-ward base course, skirting the now invisible edge of the Greenland icepack. Commander Allison returned to the navigation office. A new lookout, doubly on his guard because of the calamity which had befallen his mate, took up his position in the starboard wing and probed the black emptiness of his assigned quadrant of ocean with fearfully alert young eyes. Commodore Schrepke came over from his isolation on the opposite side of the bridge and stood for a moment next to Captain Finlander, who was waiting out the last fading shimmer of afterglow staining the western horizon. "All Soviet periscopes are hooded to prevent reflec-tions," he quietly said in his fluently precise German-English. It was a statement of fact, not a reproach. Finlander barely nodded and remained silent. He owed explanations of his actions to nobody on this ship, not even to this, his technical superior in rank. Nor did he say anything when the commodore added before withdrawing in the dark: "But you did the right thing. Those hoods sometimes get knocked off."

The quartermaster of the watch came out to record the hourly tem-perature reading and exclaimed loudly over the thermometer's accelerat-ing plunge since sunset, then quickly retreated into the warmth of the wheelhouse. But the captain remained where he was, now alone on the bridge with the lookout, watching the first faint flare of northern lights darting among the stars, wondering if the commander of Moby Dick was watching them too and praying they would illuminate a safe passage into some secret fiord where he would plot a submarine missile launch against Thule . . . or Montreal . . . or New York. Inside the icepack he would be safe, safe until he sooner or later must come out and rendezvous with the *Novo Sibirsk;* then the chances would be good for a solid contact! Especially if this fine weather held without snow to hash up the radar and storm-scattered icefloes to bedevil sonar with false echoes. But fine weather never held for long in these waters, and the cirrus clouds, so beautiful with their filigree tracery aglow from the cold fires of the night sky, were precursors of another dismal blizzard. Finlander sighed, straightened up from his hunched position, stretched the freezing stiff-ness out of his arms, then went down to his cabin. There he found, pa-tiently waiting, Lieutenant P. L. M. Packer, R.N.

"Sir, I would appreciate a word with you regarding a private matter—if it is convenient, of course."

The bristly eyebrows gave a quick flicker of surprise, then settled back into a severe black line. The captain nodded and motioned the young English officer to follow him into his cabin. As he shook himself out of his white duffel coat, he said: "Sit down. I will be with you in a minute," and vanished inside his bathroom, where he proceeded to thaw out the numbing cold in his face by splashing it with hot water.

Packer perched himself uneasily on the edge of a chair and thought that he had picked a bad time to speak to the captain. He appeared in a forbidding mood. But when Finlander came back through the louvered door, he seemed also to have thawed his frosty manner somewhat. "Now, then, what can I do for the Royal Navy?" he inquired.

Packer suppressed his nervousness and smiled. "It's really something for plain Peter Packer, sir. Well . . . you see, I hear that you are permitting normal wireless traffic even though we are on a sweep after Moby Dick. In that case, I would very much like to get off a 'personal.' The truth is, I'm having some bother at home."

"Nothing serious, I hope?"

"I want to stop somebody close to me from doing something awfully foolish, sir."

The young officer sounded so coolly casual that Finlander had to peer intently into his eyes to see the trouble behind them. "I don't mean to pry, Mr. Packer," he told him, "but you will have to tell me more than that. Although we are officially operating under peacetime conditions which permit a certain number of 'personals' to be transmitted, war conditions are in fact imposed upon us." Having spoken as a captain, he dropped into a chair and tried to bridge the wide gap of age and rank with a softer tone. "Our friends and relations are constantly doing foolish things while we are at sea," he sighed. "That is one of the hazards of our profession."

"I realize that, sir. But this particular foolishness rather vitally affects me."

"A girl?"

"Yes, sir."

Finlander shook his head as if this was turning into an altogether too frivolous problem. "At your age the foolishness of girls assumes a major importance—I know that. But when you reach mine and look back on it, you'll realize it was all froth on the waves which rolled on regardless."

Packer's voice was suddenly not a bit casual. "I respectfully submit, Captain, that I am not your age, and to me, right at this moment, this is the most important thing in my life."

"More so than your navy career?" Finlander shot back.

"It is completely tied up with it, Captain."

"I see. Then I gather this is a matter of a broken engagement—right?"

"Yes, sir," Packer answered in a lowered voice.

"And another man?"

The Englishman's hesitation betrayed that this was so, even when he finally blurted out: "Shebeona is worried by my absence on long patrols and about . . . well, the rather uncertain future of it all."

Finlander nodded. "Absence and uncertainty must be faced by our womenfolk. Good navy wives are very hard to find. Yes, harder today in our indulgent soft society than in my own courting days. I never did find one myself, you know." His face twisted into a strange sort of pained grimace as he paused for a moment. "I cannot pretend to be an expert on women, Mr. Packer, but it seems to me that if this girl is so troubled by the prospects even now when she should be at her most ardent, you should pass her up as a bad risk."

"Captain, sir, I appreciate your advice on the matter," Packer answered with a chilly respect, "but I only wanted to trouble you for permission to transmit a personal message home. That is all."

Finlander silently contemplated him for a moment, then said: "Permission granted. You may inform Lieutenant Beeker I am allowing you to transmit ten words."

*"Ten* words, sir?"

"Ten words, Mr. Packer. Under the circumstances, I do not believe excessive loquaciousness on the subject would be fitting for either yourself or my ship."

With that the discussion ended, the English officer rising out of his chair, thanking the captain for his time and quickly taking his leave. Finlander remained seated for several minutes after he was gone, hands clasped under his chin, his brow furrowed by thought. Then he got up and moved to his desk, picked up the telephone and dialed the Communications Center. When Lieutenant Beeker answered, he told him: "Mr. Packer will shortly submit a 'personal' with my permission for its transmittal. Before you send it, I want you to phone me its contents for my personal clearance. This is a confidential matter and Lieutenant Packer is not to be embarrassed in any way whatsoever. . . . Thank you."

It was almost an hour later when The Beek called back and read to Captain Finlander a telegram containing exactly ten words over which Lieutenant P. L. M. Packer had agonized in the solitude of his cabin. With Shebeona's photograph before him, he had written and rewritten, racking his mind for the exactly *right* ten words, trying out dramatic ones, dryly witty ones, mildly sarcastic ones, even ones which were outright pleading. Then Ben Munceford had come bursting in and hoisted himself into the upper bunk, from where he launched a steady flow of griping about his assignment on the *Bedford,* at the same time surreptitiously eying Shebeona and the growing column of scratched-out ten-word lines with which his companion was filling the pad. Growing more and more agitated and self-conscious, Packer finally capitulated to forthright simplicity and hastily wrote on a fresh sheet:

I BEG YOU RECONSIDER AND AWAIT MY RETURN—LOVE, PETER.

After crumpling the others and stuffing them into his pocket, he hurriedly left for the Communications Center. As soon as he signed the transmittal order and departed, Lieutenant Beeker telephoned the captain.

Finlander listened to the message with his eyes closed, then left the line tense with a long painful silence as he thought back to long, long ago when *he* had begged a beautiful bitch whom he passionately, blindly loved. But she had married a wealthy stockbroker instead, then a banker, then an oil tycoon. If she had acceded to his begging, he would have wound up like them, a flaccid, shorebound source of alimony, fighting cholesterol and surtaxes. He had not thought about her for years, but now her face came back to him in a brief flash of remembrance, hazy in detail except for that selfish, sensuous half-smile her lips had always worn. An angry, impulsive and negative reaction almost expressed itself in words, but he managed to choke them back. "All right, Mr. Beeker," he said at last with something approaching sadness. "Let it go. Let it go if there's no priority traffic."

# PART TWO

# THE CHASE

# 1.

With a caprice typical of the arctic's weather system, the thermometer began climbing during the night and when a leaden dawn seeped through the thick overcast, it was twenty degrees warmer than it had been during the previous sunny day. But it did not *feel* at all warmer. Flurries of fine snow rode squalls of raw wind just strong enough to foam the tops of steep swells being funneled through the narrows separating Iceland and Greenland. The *Bedford* was angling across the seas with long, corkscrewing rolls, occasionally throwing bursts of spray over her long foredeck and adding to the weird surrealistic sculptures the freezing slush was creating on exposed parts of her superstructure. The gunners who came out to clear the traversing and elevation mechanisms cursed this savage thing which the meteorological officer euphemistically called a "warm front."

The glass-eyed aluminum capsule which was the crow's-nest on the mainmast flew through the air in lurching captive arcs which failed to disrupt the digestive processes of Squarehead Thorbjornsen's stomach. He had filled himself with fried eggs, ham and hash-brown potatoes before going on watch, washing it all down with two glasses of milk and a mug of double-sweetened coffee. His belly made sloshing sounds like a barrel full of fermenting pickles, but this did not bother him at all. What bothered him was the visibility beyond the rocking wiper blades. In the squalls it was less than a half-mile and when the scudding clouds dragged their dirty gray skirts to mast level, the bow itself vanished in a misty blur. The OOD had telephoned a warning about keeping a sharp lookout for drifting ice, but this was becoming extremely difficult, and that worried Squarehead, who had recently seen a movie about the sinking of the *Titanic*. Big icebergs were not common in the Denmark Strait during this time of the year, yet sometimes huge floes would be wrenched off the icepack and set adrift; they could be big enough to chew through the *Bedford*'s lightly built hull. "I sure hope radar is getting through this muck," he shouted down to Seaman Jones, resting in the shaft below him. "My own eyes sure as hell ain't!"

The OOD, Lieutenant Petersen, was also very much concerned with the possibility of heavy floes suddenly appearing ahead of his ship. But having alerted the "eyeball watch" to this, he himself had taken up station at the navigational radar in the wheelhouse, switched it to its most sensitive one-mile range and proceeded to follow the sweeper as though hypnotized. As it spun round and round the glowing tube, myriads of tiny sparks were kindled by the snow flurries to confuse the more solid echoes of ice. He would have liked to slow the *Bedford* down, but they were still some distance from the estimated position of the *Novo Sibirsk* and Finlander wanted to get a look at the Russian in daylight—for what that was worth in this dismal gloom.

The captain had stood his customary dawn watch in the starboard wing of the bridge, then, as if something of significance had been mysteriously communicated to him out there in the swirl of spume and snow, had ordered a change of course before retiring to his day cabin. A change of course which would take the *Bedford* across to the Icelandic side of the strait. He gave no reason, and, of course, nobody asked for one. Not even Commander Allison. Commodore Schrepke had come in from his solitary communion in the port wing a few minutes later, his black leather jacket a-shimmer with caked snow. He checked the gyro-compass, grunted and silently departed. The relief lookouts peeled back their hoods and steamed themselves on the heater coils in the back of the wheelhouse.

In the insulated twilight world of the CIC, Lieutenant Spitzer noticed that his tactical radar was becoming obscured by hash created by snow and the sharpness of the signal was turning fuzzy as freezing slush began coating the antenna revolving on the mainmast. He got up from his console at Master Control and adjusted the rheostat which shot more current into the heater elements in the antenna. Next he checked the echo-ranging signal, to which a sonarman was listening with a relaxed concentration as his body swayed with the roll of the ship. At eighteen knots the system was bothered by ambient sounds which made it crackle like a pocket radio being played in a thunderstorm, but this was an inherent limitation and the operators had been carefully trained to pick out a hard contact through the static. *One* might miss it, but there were three of them continuously on duty. And standing by there was Merlin Queffle, who had once, during a special demonstration for a Senate Naval Affairs Appropriations Subcommittee, homed in the *Bedford* on the bubbles from a frogman's breathing apparatus. To the delight of Captain Finlander and his grateful admiral, these political gentlemen had rushed back to Washington and restored to the budget thirty millions of dollars which had been lopped off by an economy-minded soldier-President. Ever since that occasion Merlin Queffle had been a privileged character aboard this ship. But Lieutenant Spitzer loathed the skinny, buck-toothed little enlisted technician who in blithe and brash ignorance could work miracles with fantastically complicated submarine-detection devices of whose engineering principles he only had the haziest understanding. Yet Spitzer could never implement his loathing because Queffle not only was the key to Finlander's very circumspect confidence in the department, but never gave any really concrete cause for a rebuke. He simply was a naturally abrasive, dedicated little bore.

"I feel like raising a hot contact today, sir," he cackled at Spitzer, his rodent tusks glowing a sickly green in the reflection of the PPI scope. "We're going to dish up Moby Dick on toast for the skipper real soon. I just feel it in my earbones, sir!" Queffle was constantly referring to his "earbones," being fully conscious of their enormous importance.

"Take care they don't swell up so they clog your whole head," Spitzer sourly answered him and, with Queffle's high-pitched laughter ringing in his own ears, fled through the hatch leading down to the CSP room, where Lieutenant Krindlemeyer presided alone over his robot faculty of mathematical wizards—the *Bedford*'s awesome battery of electronic computers. Down here all the intricate calculations relative to navigation, target analyses, even meteorological and oceanographic data of strategic nature were solved in a fraction of a second by a fabulous interlocking system of artificial brain cells which had a memory as well as a certain fundamental power of reasoning. There was also a perfectly ordinary electric coffee percolator which provided Krindlemeyer and Spitzer their only counter-regulationary vice, a potent brew of special java which they imbibed in the inviolate privacy of this inner scientific sanctum, like priests nipping sacramental wine in a sacristy. This they did now to the soothing accompaniment of the insect-like sounds of computer circuitry and the rustle of whirling spools of data tape. Even when their masters relaxed, these robot genies never did. But perhaps the privacy was not so complete after all, because sooner or later that damned intercom would inevitably break in with something like:

"Bridge to CSP! Stand by to process RAOB data. Balloon launch minus sixty seconds and holding."

On the narrow deck in the inadequate lee of the after stack, Ben Munceford was aiming his camera at Ensign Bascomb and two seamen who were struggling with the meteorological balloon, which was threatening to destroy itself as it whipped about in the wind. In a recklessly caustic mood, he had come up to the pilothouse after breakfast and, after making sure Finlander was not within earshot, loudly asked: "Volleyball, anyone?" The wisecrack brought no laughter, but Commander Allison had come out of the chartroom to inform him the captain wanted film of the meteorological officer at work to show TV viewers that "we also perform a vital peacetime service." Another dull subject! And one which would have to be shot in inadequate light with snow flying around to fog up the lenses. Why the hell couldn't Finlander and Allison let him handle this story in his own way? Yet, when Munceford found out that Ensign Bascomb was actually going to try to launch an instrument-carrying balloon in this weather, he became interested and did his best to line up some usable pictures of the operation.

The seamen clawed at the wildly buffeted gasbag, trying to hold it down while the met officer struggled to clear the coils of nylon cord which supported the radiosonde and radar target. Hands were made clumsy by thick, sopping gloves on which ice had formed in stiffly articulated globs. Eyes winced half-shut from the sting of flying brine. The slick deck canted dangerously with the ship's steep rolls. As the collar of his camouflage jacket beat against his frozen cheeks, Munceford braced himself with one arm hooked around a stanchion and squinted at the scene through his camera's viewfinder. Behind him, the ubiquitous Pinelli clung to a lifeline and wearily shouted into his ear: "F-one-point-five, sir!"

Suddenly a wild thrust of wind tore the balloon from the grip of the two seamen, shooting it off horizontally along the deck. The nylon cord snaked out of Bascomb's fumbling hands and snapped tight with a bow-string *twang* as the instrument package and target were yanked aloft. "Keep it from fouling!" the met officer bawled and in the next instant slipped and fell. "Munceford! Fend it off!" he screamed from his sprawled position.

Munceford was directly in the path of the box dangling from the cord and could easily have shoved it clear of the obstructions, but he kept grinding away with his camera instead. It was Pinelli who leaped forward in the nick of time and kept it from tangling. The big orange ball was momentarily sucked downward in the turbulence to leeward of the speeding destroyer, its cargo skipping the wave tops and making a series of white splashes in the gray walls of water. Then it shot upward and re-mained a bright blob astern for only a few seconds before fading into the scud. Munceford swung his camera around and shot a few additional feet of Bascomb as he lay on the deck, staring after the balloon with an expression of relieved misery. "Say! That was a good bit!" the cor-respondent exclaimed gleefully. "Let's do some more of that!"

Bascomb gave him a disgusted look. "You're a gutsy son of a bitch, Munceford, for a TV reporter . . . but mostly son of a bitch!" Then he gratefully said to Yeoman Pinelli: "Thanks for the hand, sailor! You saved that instrument package from smashing to hell."

In the Communications Center, Lieutenant Beeker briefly checked the telemetry signals coming from the balloon as it soared up unseen through the icy muck covering the ocean, then assigned Lieutenant Packer to monitoring the tape and feeding the data down to the CSP room. The Beek was anxious to keep the Englishman busy. He wanted no emotional upsets in his department, especially since he had been made the key figure in the hunt for Moby Dick. Using this vital job as an excuse to leave Packer abruptly to the routine RAOB duty, he quickly retreated to the EDA room, where the direction finders and emis-sion sensors had been on stand-by since 2300 hours of yesterday.

Twice during the night Beeker had been routed out of his cabin to monitor intercepted transmissions from the *Novo Sibirsk,* each time hav-ing to report to Finlander with a rough translation of what appeared to him to be pseudo-scientific oceanographic jibberish. At 0328 a frag-mentary signal, too brief for either taping or a HUFF-DUFF bearing, had been picked up on a frequency often used by Soviet submarines, and this had ended all chance for sleep. Ever since then he had been on continuous duty in the EDA room, waiting and listening in vain and fending off Finlander's frequent impatient calls. Evidently the captain too was spending a sleepless night, his mind uneasy and enervated by the suspected proximity of his enemy. An hour ago he had sent Lieutenant Burger, the *Bedford*'s oceanographic expert, to go over the translations of the *Novo Sibirsk* intercepts, and that officer was still seated next to The Beek, painstakingly plowing through the text, questioning this and that word or sentence for possible Russian double meaning, slang or colloquialism. Burger did not have a quick mind or much imagination and was redundantly thorough—a plodder, The Beek thought as he was diverted from concentrating on the sounds in his earphones to explain to him for the third time that he would be responsible for nothing but *literal* translations. And at that moment the same mysterious signal which they had heard during the night came crackling through in a short, staccato burst of Morse.

Chief Benton lunged for the HUFF-DUFF and Lieutenant Beeker jumped to pinpoint the frequency on the MESS-PLEX, but the signal lasted for less than five seconds. They waited for over five minutes, tensely poised to plot it if it was repeated. But it was not. Benton let fly the kind of four-letter expletive which Finlander had prohibited on the *Bedford*. The Beek slumped back into his chair, thought for a moment while rubbing the swarthy stubble on his jaw, then picked up the phone and called the captain. "We just intercepted another one, sir. Stronger than the last, but still too quick for a bearing."

"Well, could you read the signal?" Finlander's edgy voice demanded.

"No, sir. They put something like two five-letter groups through a scrambler." The Beek had thought he recognized two of those letters, but he was the kind of officer who hated to commit himself without being absolutely sure. Especially not with Finlander.

There followed a short, disappointed silence on the line, then: "I want you and Mr. Burger to report to my day cabin at once, please."

Captain Finlander was seated at his desk, the scar on his throat pulsing a stark red over the collar of a non-regulation sweater, his eyes cold glints beneath the heavy lids. The lines in his face were rigidly set like those of an angry, inanimate mask, but his voice had that soft, dispassionate quality which made his sarcasm all the more biting. "Our Soviet adversaries must know this ship carries one of the navy's top radio-intelligence officers aboard and are deliberately setting out to make a fool of him," he observed when Lieutenants Beeker and Burger presented themselves in the day cabin.

The Beek's face remained expressionless. "You may certainly count on them knowing we are in the area, sir," he answered. "And they must realize we are well equipped to intercept their signals."

"Are we?" Finlander countered.

"Neither of those intercepts lasted over five seconds," his communications officer patiently explained. "We need twenty seconds for the sensors to register a frequency and twelve seconds for the HUFF-DUFF to take a bearing with any kind of reliability factor, and—"

"I have acquainted myself with the technical capabilities of my ship's detection gear," Finlander interrupted him. "They are fascinating gadgets on the whole, Mr. Beeker. But they can't play a hunch. I have asked you up here to find out if you can excel them in this respect."

"I know you want me to suggest those signals came from Moby Dick, Captain, and indicate he is somewhere near us," The Beek answered, then adamantly added: "I regret I have no way of supporting such a premise."

Finlander gave a disgusted snort. "Can your mind only react to a given, measurable set of impulses, like your machines? Couldn't you just plain guess occasionally, Mr. Beeker? On whether or not this last signal was of Russian origin, for instance?"

The Beek's face flushed slightly, but he still resisted being drawn out. "Even that would be rash with only a couple of scrambled five-letter groups to go on, sir. I have ordered the suspected frequency continuously guarded by recorder, so if they come on again, perhaps . . ." He stopped, wavering under the piercing gaze, and after a painful hesitation suddenly blurted out: "Well . . . as a ball-park guess, Captain . . . I'd say they *were* Russian."

Finlander's black eyebrows cocked upward as he pounced. "Aha! Assuming so, it is also reasonable to assume they were intended for the *Novo Sibirsk*—right? Then why did she not acknowledge?"

Lieutenant Beeker fell into the trap. "It could be that the *Novo Sibirsk* would only query Moby Dick if she did *not* receive the signal. In other words, sir, silence constitutes an acknowledgment that the message was received according to a predetermined schedule."

The captain's face became animated by a quick, caustic grin of triumph. "My goodness, Mr. Beeker! You are given to playing purely human hunches after all! So don't look so sheepish about it, boy! That casts aspersions on my own judgment, because I happen to agree with your hunch." He turned from the discomfited communications officer and sharply scrutinized his oceanographic expert. "Well, Mr. Burger. Have you been able to make anything interesting out of the translations of the *Novo Sibirsk* intercepts?"

Lieutenant (J.G.) Kurt Burger cleared his throat with a series of hacking little coughs. "I have it all here, sir," he answered, holding out a neat file folder.

Finlander made no move to accept it. "Please don't shove paperwork in my face, Mr. Burger. Simply give me as shortwinded a verbal rundown as you can."

Another series of coughs rattled out of Burger's throat, betraying his nervousness. But he had decided to act in contrast to Lieutenant Beeker and come out with an opinion without being coaxed. "It seems quite clear that these transmissions are coded tactical intelligence reports disguised as oceanographic observations."

· "How do you arrive at that conclusion?" the captain inquired with a frown.

"They contain data supposedly gathered by Nansen bottle and bathythermograph, sir," Burger explained. "This is quite normal stuff for a research vessel, but it isn't normal to send back the information by radio to home base. It would simply be logged and held for evaluation at the end of the cruise. Then there is another, far more important discrepancy, sir." He paused for an exaggerated dramatic effect which merely made Finlander impatient. "The data contained in the transmissions is just enough at variance with the conditions up here to be highly suspect. Assuming the Soviets would not man a research vessel with incompetent oceanographers, it is a reasonable conclusion that their reports actually convey information of a completely different kind." His round face took on a self-satisfied expression which quickly returned to one of nervousness when the captain tartly asked:

"Such as what?"

"Well, sir . . . that is difficult to determine without thoroughly analyzing a whole series of such reports. It could be, ah . . . well, regarding submarine operations in this area, or possibly airborne telemetric analyses of our radar emissions, or even tactical hydrographic information." No longer sure of himself, Burger became fidgety and his eyes flicked from the captain to The Beek, who had been listening with a detached interest. "I'm not a cryptographer, you know, gentlemen," he added defensively.

"I am aware of your limitations, Mr. Burger," Finlander told him. "What I am wondering is whether the Commies would be stupid enough to send out obviously faked scientific data over the air."

"Yes, but . . . they would hardly expect to have their transmission monitored by a fully qualified oceanographer," Burger answered with a timidly smug tone.

The captain looked into the lieutenant's blue eyes, which were permanently bloodshot from too much reading, and wondered about the effectiveness of this strange new type of naval officer. Burger had graduated near the top of his class at Annapolis, been detached for postgraduate work at M.I.T., detached again to serve on the scientific staff of a Woods Hole Oceanographic Institution research ship, then assigned to the Office of Naval Research, from where he had been sent to the *Bedford* for the purpose of "determining the efficacy and practical usefulness of including an oceanographic specialist on the manning table of an ASW vessel under operational conditions"—or so the orders had read.

Maybe Bureau of Personnel simply didn't know what the hell to do with this overeducated genius! Finlander would personally have preferred to be given another all-round young line officer like Ensign Ralston, or if it had to be a narrowly specialized type, then another Merlin Queffle, who seemed to get more results out of the scientific apparatus aboard the ship than the scientists who were actually responsible for them. But Queffle had barely managed to graduate from high school, while this Burger had his Master's degree, so the captain had to be cautious about allowing himself to be influenced by his natural prejudices. "Thank you," he said to the oceanographer. "I'll think over your ideas, Mr. Burger."

After dismissing the two officers, Finlander went out into the navigation office, where he thoughtfully leaned over the chart table, his face darkly inscrutable. Commander Allison came up behind him, waited to be noticed and, when he was not, spoke up: "Anything new for the tactical plot, sir?"

"Yes," Finlander answered loudly and with a firm conviction. "Moby Dick is *here!*" he slammed his hand down on the chart with fingers spread wide, sweeping it along the Greenland coast from Scoresby Sound to Cape Hildebrandt.

Allison looked surprised. "You mean The Beek stuck his neck out on those signals?"

The hand on the chart rose in a contemptuous flourish. "The sticking out of necks remains the exclusive privilege of commanding officers, Buck. No hemming 'n' hawing. No equivocations. No academic procrastinations. One just weighs all the evidence, the solid and the nebulous, the educated guess and the pure hunch, then turns all the ifs, buts and maybes into a definite tactical proposition. *Moby Dick is here!*" The hand slammed down again. "Let's go nail him . . . after we intimidate his illegitimate mother, the *Novo Sibirsk.*"

Wheeling away from the chart table, Finlander swept through the blackout curtain into the wheelhouse, stalked up to a snowflecked window and peered out at the javelin-shaped bow as it streamed a plume of white spray. Beyond it, the massive slopes of the swells turned milky and blended into the leaden clouds which had dropped lower and become more turbulent as they were whipped along by the freshening nor'easter. Neither sea nor sky had a drop of color to relieve the oppressive, all-pervading sullen drabness which seeped through the clouded windows to fill the wheelhouse with gloom. It was eleven o'clock in the morning, yet as dark as if day were failing to shake off the grip of winter night. Finlander turned away from the depressing view, brushed past the OOD and moved over to the communications panel. "Quartermaster! I want to address ship's company, please."

After the piercing notes of the taped bosun's pipe faded on a melancholy minor key, Finlander's voice permeated every part of the *Bedford.*

"This is the captain speaking. I have every reason to believe that within the next twenty-four hours we shall close with our enemy. I am referring to the Russian submarine we call Moby Dick and I openly call him our enemy because he is intruding upon this part of the ocean with the objective of softening our defenses against the avowed Soviet purpose of burying us. While we are aware of our responsibility as part of NATO forces, we must primarily act as American sailors faced with a threat against our home shores. If any of you doubt this threat and are tempted to give the Russian leaders' protestations of peaceful intentions the benefit of doubt, then ask yourselves why his submarines prowl submerged through these waters attended by naval auxiliaries masquerading as innocent research vessels. Make no mistake about this! Their presence here is by nature of a clandestine operation preparatory to an eventual attack against our country. Any other interpretation is nothing but wishful thinking. But I am not going to deliver an orientation lecture on the evils of the Communist conspiracy, gentlemen. Suffice it to reaffirm that we are the professional complement of a United States warship—the *only* ship standing between our country's safety and that particular phase of Soviet aggression represented by the operation of Moby Dick and its charlatan consort, the *Novo Sibirsk*. I intend to show them that we are as ruthlessly determined upon thwarting their purpose as they are in committing it. I intend to hunt down Moby Dick, lock him in our sonar beams and hang on to him until he has no choice but to surface in our full view, then sneak home with no other truth to report than the certain prospects of defeat."

The captain paused to allow his words to sink home. When he resumed his speech, a slight—very slight—note of irony had crept into his tone.

"It was written about a hundred years ago that a certain Captain Ahab hunted a demon whale called Mocha Dick—or Moby Dick—and that he nailed a gold coin to the mizzenmast of his ship, promising this reward to the man who first spotted that whale and brought about a final reckoning with it. If I dealt in gold coin, or if you yourselves sought such, then none of us would be here, so I will make no such offer to the man who puts me on to our Moby Dick. All I will promise him is some slight favor over his shipmates when Christmas leaves are being allotted . . . and an emphatic 'well done' which I will put down in his record with my own hand. To ensure equal opportunity for all hands in gaining this sailor's reward, I am ordering my departmental commanders, including Engineering and Commissary, to rotate their men into stand-by tactical assignments with the regular sonar, radar and eyeball watches. I am convinced that this will be all the incentive you need to excel the already high standards of duty aboard this ship during the critical week ahead. Thank you."

Down in the receiving office of the ship's hospital, Lieutenant Commander Chester Porter listened to the captain's speech as it came through the speaker above his desk, a look of perplexed wonder on his face. When it was finished, he gave out a low whistle and said to Ensign Ralston: "My gosh! The skipper is a real tiger, isn't he! I suppose every man will jump at the chance for some extra leave and a commendation in his jacket."

Ralston had continued to stare at the speaker after it fell silent, a kind of luminous eagerness lingering in his eyes; now he came to with a start and shrugged his broad shoulders. "We all jump for Captain Finlander, regardless of any rewards, sir. And mark my words, the Commie commander of Moby Dick will rue the day he put to sea to cross this ship's course! . . . Now, sir, to get back to the matter of your litter-carrying drill. My objection can be overruled, of course, by Lieutenant Aherne or the exec. But I think you'll find them opposed to saddling the men with any work not directly connected with the operation at hand."

The surgeon frowned uncertainly at the ensign and experienced a resurgence of his frustrating feeling of being merely tolerated as a required item on the *Bedford*'s manning table. After breakfast he had dutifully presented himself in sick bay to await patients who never came. After sitting around uselessly for an hour, he had decided to pull a sanitation inspection of the galley. The cooks had appeared quite shocked, but were respectfully cooperative while showing him food lockers and refrigeration rooms which considerably exceeded regulations in their spotless cleanliness; that had turned out to be another hour wasted. Then, remembering that Lieutenant Hirschfeld had failed to carry out litter-carrying drills during GQ's, he had seized upon the idea of rectifying this situation at the very next alarm. For effective drills it would be necessary to arrange with other department commanders for simulated casualties, so he had optimistically set about organizing this. Picking Engineering as his first choice, he had descended into the engine room, where Commander Franklin had flatly refused his request. "Sorry, Doc! Can't spare any of my men just to play dead!" This had punctured his ardor somewhat, but he had stubbornly persisted and next accosted a more junior officer, Ensign Ralston, asking him, as assistant fire control, to allot him a couple of men out of relief crews. They should, after all, not be very busy during a GQ. But, to his surprise, Ralston had vigorously objected, even implying that the whole idea of litter-carrying drills was nonsensical. "Lieutenant Hirschfeld never went in for stuff like that, sir!" he had informed Porter and now was suggesting that his stand would be supported all along the chain of command—including the executive officer, who, of course, spoke for the captain.

"Seems to me Captain Finlander runs a real taut ship and would want all prescribed drill schedules complied with, Mr. Ralston," Porter protested in a plaintive voice.

The ensign smiled condescendingly. "You don't quite get the picture, Commander Porter. The captain is damned quick to throw away the book when it makes no sense to go by it. He's a stickler for operational performance, not for conformity with piddling sub-paragraphs appended to NAVREGs. He allows plenty of leeway in how you do a job, as long as you get it done *effectively*. Oh, sure . . . maybe some stuffed-shirt fleet inspector could pick on him for this minor infraction or that petty noncompliance, but you can bet your life we'd all make it our personal business to make any criticism of the *Bedford* sound utterly ridiculous."

Lieutenant Commander Porter was by no means accustomed to being talked down to in this way by an ensign, but he was only able to say: "My gosh! He certainly inspires a tremendous loyalty."

"And *performance*, sir," Ralston added, getting up from his chair and preparing to leave. "And don't worry! If litter drills were really necessary, he would be right on your tail, Commander—if you'll excuse me for being so blunt." He spoke pleasantly and continued in a lighthearted tone as he moved to the door. "Between you and me, there won't be any more old-fashioned battle casualties. If the *Bedford* were to take a hit, it would most likely be from a missile or torpedo containing at least a half-ton of amatol, if not actually a nuclear warhead. Our own supply of high explosives, rocket propellant and superheated steam would certainly go off regardless of all our automatic damage-control systems. The ship would blow to pieces. Maybe two or three freak survivors would find themselves in the water, but they'd be quickly incinerated by burning oil. Everything over in a matter of seconds. Total obliteration or total survival, that's the prospect, sir." Noticing the expression on the surgeon's face, he began to laugh outright—without actually meaning to be cruel, yet that was the effect. "Don't feel too bad about it, Commander. The odds are overwhelmingly in favor of total survival—*because of Captain Erik J. Finlander*. Now, if you'll pardon me, sir, I must prepare to go on watch." He left with a salute which was more a cheery wave.

Lieutenant Commander Porter sat there seething, but he was the kind of man whose temper never seemed to erupt at the right moment and therefore was always quite ineffective. When he finally shot out of his chair, rushed through surgery past a startled McKinley and burst into the passageway, Ensign Ralston was long since gone. He had intended to dress him down for not only being presumptuous and somewhat insolent but also quite illogical for a supposedly professionally trained navy man. Certainly warships had a tendency to blow up—but, on the other hand, plenty of them had remained afloat while being battered into hulks, then made it to port. "And the crew were damned grateful for a good medical department too!" he exclaimed aloud. "A medical department properly drilled in litter carrying!"

Ben Munceford came around a corner, stared at him and then up and down the deserted passageway. "What's up, Chester?" he asked with a puzzled expression on his freckled face. "Who are you talking to?"

The surgeon felt himself turning scarlet. "Nobody. . . . I mean . . .

I was asking if you'd be interested in acting as a simulated casualty in a litter-carrying drill?"

"Hell, no!" Munceford answered, then reacted as if Porter should be humored. "But I tell you what, Chester. Let me know when you get it organized and I'll take some pictures. It ought to go good with whales, volleyball, balloon flying and all the other shipboard activities of this cruise. Okay?"

"You go to the devil!" Porter snarled at him and stalked off in the direction of his cabin.

"A bunch of nuts!" Munceford muttered to himself after Porter was beyond hearing, then shrugged and headed for his own quarters.

When the surgeon stalked into his cabin he was surprised to find Steward's Mate Collins there, ostensibly to collect laundry, but actually rummaging through the small collection of medical volumes on the bookshelf above the bunk. "What are you doing with those?" Porter sharply asked the Negro.

Collins showed no trace of embarrassment. "I'm gathering up some books Lieutenant Hirschfeld left behind, sir," he explained. "He asked me to ship them to him together with some which he let me keep for my studies."

"I thought they all belonged to the ship's medical library," the surgeon told him irritably. "In any case, I'd like to check them against the department inventory."

Collins took this with better grace than the implication would warrant. "Yes, sir," he quietly agreed. He should have left the cabin with his laundry bag, but lingered and asked: "Has the commander settled down enough to consider my request of yesterday?"

"What request? . . . Oh, yes! You are the one who wants to become a doctor." Lieutenant Commander Porter barely checked himself from shouting "You don't know when you're well off!" Instead he dropped into the chair and, after gnawing on his knuckles for a moment, fixed Collins with a jaundiced eye and said: "Yes—I might help you with your studies when I have time. But I would expect you to do me an occasional favor in return. For instance, during the next GQ I've got something right up the alley for a man with your keen medical interests. . . ."

# 2.

The *Bedford* caught up with the *Novo Sibirsk* during the early afternoon when dusk was extinguishing the feeble daylight which had permeated the clouded Denmark Strait. Snow squalls had continued to follow one upon the other and the Russian suddenly materialized out of one of them, blossoming from a nebulous dark blotch into a solid, chunky little ship snorting along with spray bursting around her raked bow like vapor from a bucking workhorse. Thin smudges of diesel exhaust puffed out of her short stack, whose bright red band with the gold hammer-and-sickle insignia made a startling splash of color in the sullenly monotone seascape. There was less than a mile between the two vessels when the American destroyer sighted the Russian, who doggedly held his course as the warship bore down on him.

All of the "eyeball watch" on the *Bedford* sang out within seconds of one another, but without creating any surprise, as the officers on the bridge and in the CIC had been plotting the *Novo Sibirsk* position during the past two and a half hours. The Beck had picked up the emissions of the Russian's radar and, by computing their strength and bearing, had enabled Finlander to circle the perimeter of maximum-return echo and make his approach behind the shielding effects of the snow squalls and Iceland's mountainous coast. At least, that had been the tactical concept. Chances were, of course, that the Russians' detection equipment was as good as the Americans'. Yet, if they had known of the *Bedford*'s approach, they did not betray this fact by taking evasive actions. When the two ships were within three miles of each other, the CIC had reported a hard sonar contact which they plotted very close to the *Novo Sibirsk* and Captain Finlander had come near ordering battle stations in the brief hope of actually catching Moby Dick being serviced by its supply vessel. But Merlin Queffle's miraculous ears had quickly identified the contact as something much smaller than a submarine, and shortly thereafter Lieutenant Spitzer had obtained a trace of the echo which clearly indicated that the Russian was towing some kind of underwater object at the end of a long steel cable—probably a hydrographic device or biological trawl. Now, as the bridge watch focused their binoculars on the *Novo Sibirsk,* they could make out the cable streaming from a gallows frame on the forward welldeck.

"So chalk up another one for our boy Queffle," Captain Finlander exclaimed with a mirthless chuckle. "The Commies are putting on their usual innocent act!"

"Probably heard us coming and decided to try and look scientific," Commander Allison growled through the closed face flap of his arctic hood; his big nose stuck out beyond it and glowed with almost the same red as the Russian's stack.

The captain looked around his snow-swept bridge for his oceanographic expert and spotted him trying to crouch out of the way of the icy spume whipping over the windscreen. "Say, Mr. Burger! What kind of gear are they working? Anything you recognize as legitimate?"

Lieutenant Burger reluctantly exposed himself to the elements and poked his face over the side, his eyes squinting painfully through his binoculars, which quickly fogged up. "Can't tell, sir," he answered. "Not without knowing what's at the other end of that tow cable."

"Lot of use you are to me!" Finlander shouted back at him, but more jokingly than with real rancor. He suddenly seemed strangely elated and full of caustic good humor. When the CIC called up and warned of the rapidly closing range on a collision course, he said to the OOD: "I suppose it won't do to run her down, Mr. Petersen. Just intimidate her, that's all. And make sure Pinelli gets some good snapshots."

As Petersen rushed back to the pilothouse, he brushed past Commodore Schrepke, who was just stepping out on the bridge. The German officer unhurriedly strode up alongside Finlander and raised his huge Zeiss glasses for a long, careful scrutiny of the Russian.

"Can you pick out anything compromising about her, Commodore?" the captain asked.

Schrepke took his time before answering, then spoke in clipped sentences without taking the binoculars from his eyes. "She has much depth and beam for extra bunkers. There are large-capacity fuel valves on deck. Booms and winches are unusually heavy. The bow is reinforced against ice. Radar and wireless antennas indicate extensive communication and detection equipment. Her lines suggest East German construction, probably in the yards of Stettin."

"Ah! We are faced with proof of German enterprise wherever we go!" Finlander exclaimed dryly.

Schrepke gave him a quick, hard look, retorted: "We are what our friends and enemies have made us, Captain," and removed himself to an unoccupied part of the bridge, from where he continued to study the *Novo Sibirsk* apart from the other officers.

As the *Bedford* closed with the Russian and details of the other ship began emerging more clearly out of the diffusing snow flurries, Yeoman Pinelli crouched in the turret of his Mark VII camera, his right eye pressed hard against the rubber cup of its viewfinder. The cross-hairs were lined up on the *Novo Sibirsk*'s bridge and he found himself looking into the faces of a group of men who appeared to be staring right back at him; one of them aimed a Leica-type camera and they snapped each other's picture almost simultaneously. Pinelli smiled and activated the traversing mechanism of the gyro-stabilized turret, sweeping the howitzer-sized lens over the alleged research vessel and shooting close-ups of her superstructure and fittings. The red warning light was flashing on his control panel, indicating that it was too dark for good exposures, but he continued to press the trigger because he knew that even bad pictures could be immensely valuable to Naval Intelligence. Down on the *Bedford*'s main deck some other, far less sophisticated cameras were also being aimed at the Russian by a few sailors who had ventured out into the snow and spray to obtain proof that they had met the enemy. These would be far worse pictures, but still good enough to strike awe among family and barroom acquaintances.

By the time the two ships were some three hundred yards apart, with the *Bedford* slowing down to cross close astern of the *Novo Sibirsk,* a number of Russian crewmen had swarmed out on deck to line the railings and stare at the big American destroyer. Their faces were pink blobs framed by the darker hoods of their arctics—the same clumsy, heavy arctics used by anybody forced to work in this bitter climate. But, of course, there was also the inevitable sprinkling of rugged individualists who came out bareheaded and wearing nothing but their working fatigues—as in the American or English navies, these seemed to be engine-room or galley personnel with an obsessive need to show themselves off as fresh-air fiends. In fact, these Russian sailors looked remarkably like their American counterparts, clean, neat, well-fed, rosy-cheeked youths. Lieutenant Burger remarked that there were no women among them, pointing out this was unusual for a Soviet research vessel, an observation which Captain Finlander took note of and complimented him for. With a rare flash of humor, Commander Allison added that they also lacked that shaggy, piratical appearance affected by the bona-fide working oceanographic fraternity, hinting that this in itself was highly suspicious! That brought a sly smile to Finlander's lips, then a startled exclamation when he spotted two Russian sailors hurrying toward the stern of their ship, where the ensign of the U.S.S.R. was snapping its red folds in the wind. "Good Lord! Don't tell me they are going so far as to dip their colors to us!"

The executive officer watched them intently through his binoculars, and when they aligned themselves in a formal position by the jackstaff looking back toward their own bridge for a signal, he said: "I suppose we better play along and prepare to acknowledge their salute." He was about to order Ensign Ralston to rush a detail to stand by the colors when the captain intervened, his lighthearted manner completely gone.

"I exchange no courtesies with ships operating under false colors, Buck!" he snapped. "Have you forgotten this is a Soviet wolf in sheep's clothing?"

Allison shrugged. "All right, sir. But if we add insult to injury, that captain is a cinch to lodge a formal protest through diplomatic channels, accusing us of 'buzzing' his ship. . . . We're passing him pretty close," he added with a slight note of reproach.

"Dear me!" Finlander retorted with a sarcastic grimace. "While I don't give a damn about embarrassing our State Department, I certainly don't want to rattle my exec!" While everybody on the bridge but Allison cringed, he bellowed over his shoulder toward the pilothouse: "Pass at legal distance, Mr. Petersen! No more! No less!"

All the binoculars on the *Bedford*'s bridge were trained again on the *Novo Sibirsk* as the faint shrill of a bosun's pipe came drifting across the intervening waves. It was presumably the signal from the Russian OOD to dip their colors to the American warship as age-old naval custom required, and Chief Quartermaster Rickmers anticipated the ceremony by gleefully growling between clenched teeth: "Come on, you Red cruds! Tip your hat to Uncle Sam!"

The two Russian sailors bent down out of sight, but not to untie the halyard of their ensign. When they straightened up they were hefting a garbage can between them which had been hidden behind the railing. Tipping it over the edge, they deliberately dumped the contents into the path of the American ship. A moment later the *Bedford* was forced to churn through the degrading mess staining the white foam of the Russian's wake and one of those sailors swept an imaginary hat off his head and gave her a ceremonious bow. Carried and chilled by the arctic wind, some deep Slavic laughter wafted across the bare hundred yards between ships. On the destroyer's bridge there was a stunned silence, but from one of her amateur photographers somewhere amidships of the main deck there came a defiant, salty bellow:

"Shit on you too, Ivan!"

The silence on the bridge lasted for a few seconds more before Ensign Ralston came out of his shock, gave a fearful glance toward Captain Finlander and wheeled on the chief quartermaster. "Rickmers! Put whoever yelled that obscenity on report!"

The captain had remained hunched over the railing, watching the Russian's slop defile the hull of his ship, without betraying his fury; the upturned collar of his white duffel hid the scar on his throat. But when he heard Ralston's order, he looked up and quietly told him: "Belay that! Let's make allowances for extreme provocation when it's warranted." Then he asked Allison in an equally quiet tone: "Do you still feel like exchanging courtesies with the Commies, Buck?" When his executive officer shook his head and maintained a tight-lipped silence, he gave him a forgiving slap on the shoulder. "All right, then! If it's any consolation to you, I came within a hair of falling for it too. Friendly-enemies deal! Dip the colors regardless, as an expression of the universal brotherhood of all men who pursue their duty on the cruel sea! . . . Well, at least we don't have to analyze that load of garbage to know its significance!"

Ensign Ralston seethed beyond the point of containing himself. "Why don't we steam upwind and give them a good long dose of our dirtiest smoke, sir?" he blurted out.

Finlander gave him a balefully crushing stare from beneath his snow-flecked brows. "I prefer to leave the dirty little acts of defiance to the more amateurish elements among our enemies, Mr. Ralston," he answered coldly, then addressed himself to Allison and the OOD: "Very good. I think we have intimidated this customer in spite of his show of insolence. At least he will suspect we know what he is up to and—*remember*—nothing is more demoralizing than to have the secrecy stripped from one's secret mission. So let's leave him stew about it while we go after his pet pigboat, Moby Dick."

As the *Bedford* pulled away and the *Novo Sibirsk* began to dissolve into the gloomy shroud of another squall, most of the bridge watch retreated into the pilothouse, there to thaw out their numbed faces and ice-crusted clothing. The lookouts remained, once again straining their eyes over a darkening, empty sea; and Captain Finlander remained because this fading gray oblivion was another sunless sunset. Wolfgang Schrepke, also compelled by old habits, moved toward his solitary vigil in the opposite wing of the bridge, but first paused by the captain to say: "I noticed one more thing about that Russian."

"Yes, sir?"

"Those large discharge valves. I recall them to be of the type used for transfer of concentrated hydrogen peroxide."

"Yes?"

"That was the fuel used by our Walther-type U-boat propulsion plants. As a Russian prisoner I was assigned to work on their copy of such a unit. You can look for Moby Dick to be a Chelnikoff Class with a submerged maximum speed of twenty-five knots and a duration of thirty hours without schnorkeling."

"Thank you, Commodore."

Down belowdeck there were two men who were totally oblivious of what had taken place beyond their cabins during the past forty minutes. One was Lieutenant Commander Chester Porter, who had stretched out on his bunk with one of the books he had found in Lieutenant Hirschfeld's collection, Montcalm's *War Psychology in Primitive and Modern Man*. For over two hours he had been absorbed in it, being frequently sidetracked by the profuse marginal notes and the more detailed loose-leaf ones stuck in between pertinent pages. It was these writings by Lieutenant Hirschfeld which he had studied with an increasingly disturbed fascination. Finally he had got up off the bunk and begun to pace back and forth over the narrow confines of his cabin, still reading and muttering disconnected excerpts to himself in agitated whispers: ". . . stresses far exceeding those of any normal peacetime patrol . . . producing hate syndromes . . . war's only natural release, *killing,* is denied

. . . aggravating latent aberrations without recourse to normal checks and balances. . . ."

And one deck lower, Ben Munceford had escaped into his even more isolated cabin (it was actually located below the waterline), determined to avoid any of Finlander's cornball production ideas for the balance of the afternoon. After dark he would venture forth and try to tape some interviews of the crew—*enlisted* crew. In the meanwhile he planned to digest his lunch in peace and maybe doze off a bit. The only thing which prevented this was his shameless desire to refresh the vision of Shebeona in his mind, and that caused him to poke about Lieutenant Packer's locker and drawers. He stopped short of a full scale shakedown search and, when he failed to find her, disgustedly heaved himself up into his bunk, where he lay thinking about Nancy III just to discourage himself on the subject of women. Still Shebeona's picture haunted him. But he soon went to sleep anyway.

# 3.

When the watch changed at 0400 of the following morning, it was pouring with rain. The thermometer indicated a fraction under twenty-nine degrees Fahrenheit, yet it rained a thick, penetrating, all-soaking rain which fell out of a windless, opaque blackness, washing off all the snow which had accumulated on the *Bedford* during the previous day and substituting a sheathing of glass-slick ice. Every raindrop which touched the ship seemed to freeze solid instantly. The decks were like newly surfaced skating rinks, and ice covered even the lifelines, the hand-holds, the vertical surfaces and the antennas, from where it would break loose at intervals, falling and clattering against the superstructure like showers of pebbles. The seas had flattened out as the ship came under the lee of the Greenland coast and her motions were reduced to an occasional easy roll as she drove silently through the night; the wind had completely died out and the only movement in the bitterly saturated air was created by the eighteen-knot forward velocity of the destroyer herself. Both bridge lookouts slipped and fell before they had been on watch for more than a few minutes.

One of the lookouts who promptly fell as soon as he stepped out on the bridge was Fireman Second Class Bertrand W. Meggs, and he would not have been there at all had it not been for Captain Finlander's order to give all of the *Bedford*'s crew a crack at spotting Moby Dick. Meggs had been pleased when Chief MacKay picked him to represent Engineering on the bridge for an hour, but his pleasure had turned into trepidation when he was so rudely acquainted with the appalling topside conditions. It was not so much the fall, although it had been hard enough to leave a throbbing ache in his back and shoulder, but when he finally worked himself out to his post in the port wing by a series of uncertain shuffles and slides, he had blinked his eyes to make sure they were open, then held a hand out in front of his face and been absolutely unable to see it. It was then that the futility of his assignment struck him, the uselessness of his exchanging a warm, bright post at No. 1 boiler for this sodden, freezing, black agony. Moby Dick could have surfaced right alongside without being spotted! Meggs had never in his life seen such a black night, or such a cold, wet one! The quartermaster had made him put on a sou'wester and a slicker over his regular arctics, but a chill was creeping up his bruised backside and an icy little stream of water working its way down his neck, seeping through the collar past two sweaters, shirt and thermal long-johns, to dampen his chest. The rain splattered on the sou'wester pulled down over the closed hood of his parka, making a patter like rain on a tarpaper roof; it was so loud that all other sounds were blotted out, even the hissing of the destroyer's wash.

It crossed Meggs's mind that he was being allowed to take this "eyeball" lookout assignment simply because the sharpest, best-trained eyes on the ship could not see a god-damned thing through this muck anyway—so let some poor nearsighted son of a bitch out of the boiler rooms waste his time trying for the captain's prize! The quartermaster and his regular "eyeballs" were probably sitting on the heaters in the pilothouse, laughing at him. Well—to hell with them! He would try anyway. Maybe a miracle would happen and the god-damned Russian sub would come steaming along the surface with his navigation lights ablaze. Or trailing a bright patch of phosphorescence. Yes! There was sometimes an amazing phosphorescence in these black waters!

Fireman Meggs cautiously felt his way along the railing of the bridge, leaning far out and trying to see if there was any glow in the wash, fifty feet below. But he could see nothing. It was as if the ship were mysteriously flying through the night, supported by nothing but the trillions of raindrops. Then he suddenly bumped up against something like wet leather, soft, yet with a hardness underneath which briefly rippled with a living action. "Jesus! Who's that? Somebody else out here?" he gasped.

"Yes, obviously, sailor."

Meggs's shock subsided and he was happy to find some human company in this stygian blackness, but also irritated because he was not being trusted with the lookout job by himself. "You mean they're wasting *two* of us out here! That's a bunch of crap, by God! Even if they gave us a seeing-eye dog apiece, we wouldn't be worth a fart in the wind!"

The other man took his time before answering, then rather curtly agreed: "It is quite thick."

"Thicker than the inside of an undertaker's drawers, brother! I can't even tell who the hell you are. One of the regular 'eyeballs' around here?"

Again the other man hesitated before answering, but this time he spoke with a somewhat lighter tone. "Yes, I suppose you might call me that."

Fireman Second Class Bert Meggs finally caught the Germanic accent in the voice speaking to him out of the dark and a shock of outright fear shot through his chest. "Christ almighty! You sound like . . . I mean, are you? . . . Yes, Jesus! You are the commodore!" He almost slipped and fell again as he backed off across the icy deck. "Excuse me, sir! It's just so horrible damned black out here I can't see my hand in front of my f . . . face, sir."

"It's all right, sailor," Schrepke told him, sternly, yet somehow also reassuring. "You must not worry about speaking to me or about this very dark night. A good lookout does more than just look. He must *listen*, no? Have you listened yet, sailor?"

"Listened, sir?"

"Yes. Try it now."

Meggs listened and heard only the hard patter of rain against his sou'wester.

"Do you not hear something?" the Germanic voice patiently prodded him out of the black vacuum.

Meggs yanked off the sou'wester and tore open the snaps of his thick woolen hood. When he had bared his head and felt the sting of raindrops on his scalp, he leaned far out over the railing and stared into the void, but straining his ears rather than his eyes. And now he heard it! A weird deep rumbling which seemed to surge faintly above the soft noise of rain falling into the sea. It had an eery, menacing quality which raised the hackles in the back of his neck and set his heart to wildly beating. "Oh, God, sir! What is it?"

"Ah! You hear it too, then. Ice in breakers."

"Ice in breakers?"

"It won't get you your captain's prize, sailor, but I believe he would be grateful if you reported it," Schrepke quietly suggested.

"Ice and breakers! Jesus Christ!" Meggs exclaimed and, wheeling for the pilothouse, began a frantic shuffling, sliding rush for its door. Yanking it open, he electrified the shadowy figures inside by yelling at the top of his voice:

*"Ice and breakers ahead!"*

Three minutes later Captain Finlander came out on the port wing, bareheaded and wearing only his white duffel over white pajamas. He became an almost ghostly figure, shimmering with a pale luminescence as he stood there in the pitch-black night, intently listening. His ship was more silent than ever since her engines had been stopped and she wallowed sluggishly over the oily swells. But the ominous rumbling was so pronounced now that it filled the blackness all around with a tangible threat which could be felt as well as heard. The captain absorbed its vibrations for a moment, then unerringly addressed himself to the invisible Meggs. "Did you sound off about this, lad?"

"Yessir . . . sort of, but . . ." He hesitated, gingerly groped around for Schrepke and was thrown into speechless confusion when he found the German had mysteriously vanished from his side.

The captain had little time to waste and so gave him none to recover and explain what had happened. "Well done, Meggs!" Returning inside the wheelhouse, he joined a badly rattled OOD, Lieutenant Petersen, who was staring at the radar scope with something close akin to hatred. "All right, Mr. Petersen," Finlander mildly admonished him. "There's no use in venting your frustrations on that inanimate object. It has simply been overwhelmed by conditions which—*please note*—can only be coped with by ordinary frail human beings. Well, perhaps I am being unfair. Fireman Meggs seems neither ordinary nor frail, God bless him!"

Behind them a voice crackled out of a speaker on the communications panel:

"CIC to bridge! The MTS is picking up strong ice echoes now, bearing three-one-zero, range two-four-zero-zero."

"Oh, Lord, that's close!" Petersen exclaimed and moved to acknowledge, but Finlander beat him to it.

"Congratulations, CIC!" the captain acidly purred into the microphone. "The eyeball watch appreciates having their reports confirmed by you scientists—even belatedly. Now could we trouble you to keep track of that ice, please? We don't want it closer than a thousand yards or so, if it can be helped. Thank you." Although he was needling them, he spoke without anger and there was something reassuring in the mere fact that he was being flippant about it. Obviously he did not consider the situation dangerous even though they had come close to smashing into the icefields hugging the Greenland coast. He even grinned at Petersen and managed to draw a nervous smile in response. "I suggest you forget radar for the time being and use the master fathometer to help you hold us hove to while I go backstage and cast the navigational bones with Commander Allison."

"Yes, sir. And I'm sorry I messed things up."

"Messed what up? Are we in trouble? No! Just had another close shave which is part of the hazards of arctic operations, that's all. Go to it, boy!"

Commander Allison had also been urgently routed out of his cabin. He was the kind of man who always yanked on his trousers under such circumstances, then rushed for the bridge while still wearing the tops of his pajamas. He and the captain made an odd, un-naval-looking pair as they bent over the chart, carefully studying it in the glow of the red blackout light, each still wearing part of his sleeping garb and part uniform. "The Inertial Navigator and our last reliable radar bearing don't check out, sir," the exec told Finlander. "We should be *here*—about sixty miles southwest of Cape Tupinier and still well off the hundred-fathom curve. But I'm afraid we are in fact badly off our reckoning if surf noises can be heard."

"Not necessarily, Buck. I don't see any reason to question our pampered Inertial Navigational System as long as the CSP room doesn't flood or freeze up. Furthermore, I even doubt if those are shoreside breakers we hear out there. Could very well be a grounded berg left over from last season with a raft of growlers in its backwash to create the uproar. In any case, I'm more concerned about Moby Dick's position than our own—which can't be off more than a mile or two at the very worst. . . . Good Lord, Buck! When will you give up those screaming striped pajamas?"

"I'll buy a nice conservative set of white silks when I make captain. . . . I take it you want to go by the INS position, sir?"

"I see no alternative, do you? With radar haywire and the overcast too thick for any old-fashioned celestial help, that's when we've got to go along with Krindlemeyer and Spitzer's bag of scientific tricks, right?" Finlander's eyebrows cocked suddenly into their most sardonic expression. "And by the way, Buck! You never will make captain if I write in your fitness report that you barge around my bridge in that barber-pole outfit casting aspersions on the navy's pet navigational whizbang. Shocking reactionary attitude, I'd say. Like going around plumping for battlewagons and gunboats." He shook his head and made some disapproving clucking sounds. "Well, I'm going back to bed, but don't hesitate to call me if there's anything I can do."

"Sweet dreams!" Allison threw after him with a stiff, one-sided grin, noticing that the captain was not taking the situation so lightly as to return to the luxury of the double-sized bunk in his stateroom, but retired to the spartan day cabin behind the navigation office. The executive officer still felt worried, but the gnawing apprehension which had flooded his mind when the OOD's panicked call first brought him rushing to the bridge had subsided. Stepping into the wheelhouse, he took his foul-weather gear off its hook on the bulkhead and slipped it on over his pajama tops. He asked the JOOD to send a messenger below for the captain's and his own clothing, then went out into the freezing sleet to check for himself the grim sounds which filled the surrounding night.

During the next hour the *Bedford* remained in the same spot, rolling and heaving lazily while her position was maintained in the absolute darkness by using the fathometer to pick a reference point off the bottom, one hundred and ninety fathoms down. The distant rumble rose and fell without increasing its threat on the average. The downpour slowly moderated and by two bells it was more of a thick, penetrating mist than actual rain. But when the quartermaster of the watch recorded the hourly temperature reading, it had dropped two degrees to twenty-seven Fahrenheit—which meant that the destroyer's unbalancing coating of ice would be freezing more solidly than ever to her superstructure. In thickness it built up only inch by inch, but in aggregate weight, ton by ton. This was why she was getting more sluggish and slower in recovering herself after the low swells passed beneath her keel.

The unnatural cadence of his ship's motions was one of the things which kept Captain Finlander from dozing off as he lay on the bunk in the day cabin, wrapped in the folds of a regulation navy blanket over which he had pulled his white duffel. Raw drafts wafted past the blackout curtains every time somebody opened the wheelhouse doors to the open bridge—which was often as Petersen or Allison stepped out to look and listen, or the lookouts relieved one another at twenty-minute intervals. Ice falling off the halyards and shrouds occasionally rattled against the roof of the pilothouse; the gyro-repeater on the bulkhead went *click-click-click* every time the ship changed heading. Of these things Finlander was conscious as he lay there, and in the back of his mind the old horror of all destroyermen operating in the arctic, capsizing by sheer weight of ice, began haunting him. Back at BUSHIPS, all kinds of geniuses were figuring out how to decontaminate a ship which had been subjected to radiation, but not even the civil service deadheads in the bureau were given the assignment of figuring out how to decontaminate what this filthy night was depositing on the *Bedford*. Well, none too many ships had gone down under the press of ice lately, had they? . . . There was only that Danish corvette two years ago. And a supply ship the year before that. Surely the *Bedford* could never be overwhelmed by such an ignominious fate! Not *his* ship! . . . Maybe the Commie commander of Moby Dick was counting on him nurturing exactly these fears. Counting on it while he himself took advantage of his own craft's natural superiority under such conditions, exposing nothing but the conning tower, periscopes, radar and sensory antennas to the horrible smothering, congealing sleet. If it got too bad, all a submarine had to do was to submerge into the warming bosom of the deep, thaw out for a while, then try again. . . . Finlander pressed his eyes tightly closed, feigning sleep to himself and dreaming of sticking it out until his ship became a nightmare glob of ice. . . .

"Sir! Sir! The Beek just picked up another of those fragmentary signals. Much stronger this time!"

Finlander sat up and found himself staring into the dim faces of Commander Allison and Lieutenant Petersen. "Very good!" he exclaimed with a transparently forced casualness in his voice. "Very good! I'm glad he's so much on the ball. Any bearing?"

"No, sir. But he estimates it's no farther than seventy miles. It pretty well *has* to be seventy miles north or south."

The captain blinked, rubbed his face very hard, driving his knuckles deep into his eyes, then shook his head. "As simple as that, eh? Seventy miles north or seventy miles south. Well, let's see. The ice is probably nearly on the bottom in Scoresby Sound and awfully thick around the entrance. Dangerous stuff for a pigboat of the old type. So let's say seventy miles south. Anything from the *Novo Sibirsk* which might indicate reporting our position?"

"Nothing since last evening's long-winded complaint about us to SOVFLOT, sir. Moby Dick probably monitored that."

Finlander managed a smile. "Very good. Obviously they quickly lost radar contact with us in the sleet and now we are being screened by the Greenland coast. That's perfect. Get under way and start creeping to the southward along the edge of the pack. Keep radar and sonar on low scales. And keep me informed of developments, gentlemen." He lowered himself back into a horizontal position and pulled the blanket over his face, once again closing his eyes. As Lieutenant Petersen tiptoed out of the day cabin behind the executive officer, he whispered: "How the hell does the skipper wake up out of a sound sleep and instantly give a sound evaluation of a tactical situation?"

Allison only grunted.

Finlander's mind was not only awake, but racing as he lay beneath the prickly warmth of the blanket. Seventy miles between him and the detested Moby Dick! The Beek had to be pretty sure of himself to voluntarily make such an optimistic estimate. A pity he could not also have provided a bearing! Seventy miles north or south along this coast could—if he had picked the wrong direction—mean a two-hundred-and-ten-mile error, which meant eleven hours' lost steaming, which meant most certainly a total abort. Stick out your neck, Commanding Officer, and decide! Yes, the ice was very thick to the north and in Scoresby Sound a sub could get itself trapped, yet some submarines were specially built to poke up through the floes, some skippers like Moby Dick's and the *Bedford*'s were unorthodox daredevils. Finlander smiled with his eyes closed, then quickly squelched any glimmer of kinship with his Soviet counterpart. He'd give him coldly professional credit, but that was all. And he was betting he would be operating below Cape Brewster, where the icepack would remain comparatively loose for another two weeks. *Click-click-click-click* chattered the gyro-repeater as the ship turned south; a faint tremor shook the cabin as the turbines picked up revolutions. Three bells were struck and as the melodious sound penetrated through the folds of the blanket it brought him a comforting thought about being able to doze for another hour—maybe really sleep. Instead he found himself standing before Admiral Sorensen, the grizzled little Dane who commanded NATONAV 1 and took sadistic pleasure in dressing down American officers. "You ekted unwisely in turning sou'd, Kep'n," he said with a pronunciation which was exactly like that of a countryman of his own who was a famous comedian in the United

States; but Sorensen was a man devoid of even the slightest sense of comedy. "You should heff turn nor'd, ja? You should heff antizipate de unlikely, ja? Very unwise, Kep'n . . . very unwise. . . ." His angry red face dissolved away with the rising clamor of a GQ alarm.

Captain Finlander shot out of his bunk, kicked himself free of the tangling blanket and, sweeping the duffel over his shoulders, ran for the wheelhouse. But Commander Allison was already coming for him and they met in the navigation office.

"It's really only an air alert, sir," the exec told the captain with a weary irritation.

"Then why the GQ, Buck? I'd like to save our energy for sub-hunting, you know."

"The CIC has been pretty jumpy during the last hour. Spitzer claims he has a UFO on the sky sweeper. Thinks it may be a balloon, but isn't absolutely sure. Range is sixty-two miles, altitude twelve thousand, bearing zero-one-five. I think it's a stray RAOBs from Thule. Shall we secure battle stations, sir?"

Finlander had moved to the chart and stood looking down at it with his brows knitted together in a concentrated bristle. "Not yet, no. Sixty-two miles almost due south of us, is it? And fifteen minutes ago we picked up that mysterious signal. Maybe we are finding some pieces that will fit together, and maybe just a few more will give us a pretty clear picture." He reached for the telephone, dialed Communications Center and asked for Lieutenant Beeker. "Any way you can check out possible Soviet airborne telemetrics?" he inquired.

"If they are close enough, *maybe,* sir," The Beek's tired voice hedged.

"Will sixty-two miles do, Mr. Beeker?"

The Beek's voice lost its weariness. "If that's all, Captain, there's a fair chance. Give me five minutes."

"I'll give you three, then two more to get up here!" Hanging up, he turned to Allison. "I want the meteorological officer to report to me on the double with all his latest synoptics."

Lieutenant Petersen stuck his head through the blackout curtain of the wheelhouse. "The CIC reports the UFO definitely identified as a balloon moving slowly northeast and gaining altitude. Sorry about the false alarm, sir. Shall I secure?"

"Not unless you can satisfactorily explain its presence," Finlander retorted.

Petersen's expression became confused, then startled. "You mean it might have been launched by Moby Dick, sir? Should I order the ADO to stand by to shoot it down?"

"Let's not reveal our position by getting trigger happy, Mr. Petersen. Simply ask CIC to keep accurate track of it." The telephone diverted him with an urgent buzzing. It was The Beek, reporting a little over two minutes after receiving his assignment, to inform the captain that they were recording strong telemetric signals whose range and bearing checked with the CIC's contact. Finlander ordered him to hurry to the bridge, then told Allison: "Piece number one just fell in place, Buck. Now I need another from the met officer. Where is he?"

Even as he asked, Ensign Bascomb came bursting through the blackout curtain and breathlessly announced himself. His clothes looked as if he had dived into them on the fly and he was still fumbling with one hand to hitch up his pants properly; with the other he clutched a roll of weather maps. Finlander reached out and yanked him over to the chart table.

"I've got a fascinating little problem for you, weatherman! Using all available meteorological and target-analyses data, I want you to backtrack a balloon to give me an accurate estimate of the position from where it was launched and when. I'm going into the day cabin to get dressed and when I come back I'll need that information ready."

When he returned four minutes later fully clothed, Lieutenants Beeker and Krindlemeyer had joined the other officers and in a dark corner of the navigation office Finlander glimpsed a shadowy figure with the glint of black leather. The others were clustered around Ensign Bascomb, who was hunched over the chart table, his whole demeanor an agony of concentration, telephone wedged between shoulder and ear, a slide rule in his left hand, the right scribbling figures on the weather chart which he had superimposed over the navigational one.

The captain elbowed his way through the crowd and placed himself next to him. "Well, Bascomb?"

The met officer hung up the phone, made a few quick additional calculations on the margin of his chart, then said: "Assuming it is an average-sized instrument carrier filled with hydrogen, and assuming a rate of ascent of six hundred feet per minute, and assuming wind patterns have been fairly constant, and temperatures *there* are about what they are here, then . . . the launch should have taken place twenty-four minutes ago from *this* position." He laid the parallel ruler along a course drawn from the balloon's known position and drew a rather faint, uncertain circle off a nameless promontory of the Greenland coast. "Of course, sir, this is assuming a hell of a lot of things and, of course, I am aware that this places the launching site in thick ice."

Finlander pulled him away from the chart, took a pair of dividers and pricked off the distance. "Seventy-four miles! It checks! Very good, Mr. Bascomb!" With a pencil he made the circle firmly black. "I have one more question to ask Mr. Beeker. Would you classify those telemetrics as standard RAOB's stuff for weather forecasting?"

The Beek shook his head. "No, sir. More likely microwave analyses."

Finlander nodded. "Then here's the picture as I see it. The Commie pigboat is lying off this point with its conning tower stuck up through the ice as a launching platform for airborne microwave detectors intended to gather information on emissions from our DEW-line system. The fragmentary intercepts we've been picking up are most likely his command to the *Novo Sibirsk* to start monitoring the telemetric data, which they in turn relay on to Moscow disguised as oceanographic observations." He looked around him at their faces and paused to give anybody the chance to add or detract from his evaluation. None spoke. He smiled and suddenly slammed a fist into the palm of his other hand. "Moby Dick has spouted for us, gentlemen! Let's go after him! His radar is probably as fouled as ours, so here is a fine chance to sneak up on him undetected under cover of darkness. We move in blacked out, all high-frequency stuff turned off and under absolute radio silence. This is it! From here on we go all out!"

# 4.

While the *Bedford* drove purposefully but blindly through a morning as black and cold as winter midnight, her bridge lookouts doubled to compensate for the muzzling of her electronic detection gear, a clash took place in the wardroom brought about by tensions beyond those generated by the perilous action at hand. Perhaps heeding the dangers of speeding in complete darkness along the ice-clogged, uncertainly charted Greenland coast, or perhaps only wanting to keep his crew keyed to the chase he had begun, Captain Finlander did not secure his ship from battle stations. Only a few men at a time were permitted to stand down in turns for hot breakfast, and it was because of this that none but Commander Allison and Ensign Ralston were in the wardroom when Ben Munceford came up from his cabin, still rubbing sleep from his eyes. It was natural for him to ask: "What's up? Where is everybody?" It was maybe as natural for the executive officer to contemptuously counter: "You mean you slept all through a GQ? That's what I call being a live-wire reporter!"

"I turned out when the alarm sounded at five-thirty," Munceford replied with a scowl. "But the scuttlebutt had it to be nothing but some balloon, so I went back to bed." When Ralston glanced at the exec with a loud snicker, Munceford's tone became sharp. "So? What's it all about?"

Allison filled his mouth with eggs and concentrated on smearing a heap of jam on a piece of toast. Ralston savored a scalding draft of coffee, gulped it down and casually answered: "Oh, nothing much, Ben. We damned near piled into an icefield at eighteen knots, which isn't too unusual in this kind of operation, of course. And, oh, yes—we're on to Moby Dick and kind of getting set to pounce on him right now. That's all, isn't it, Commander?"

"Yes, Mr. Ralston," Allison agreed, biting off a large chunk of toast and continuing through the mouthful. "I suppose we've been amiss in not providing Mr. Munceford with a printed program. It slipped my mind that these TV correspondents have to work off official handouts."

Ben Munceford's face turned a mottled red beneath the freckles. Yesterday afternoon they had left him oblivious in his cabin while they passed within a hundred yards of a Russian spy ship; now this! He furiously threw his jacket down on a chair and stalked over to the coffee urn on the sideboard. "You guys make a stranger feel right at home, don't you! Christ! If I'd been on deck when we passed that Commie yesterday, I might have jumped over the side just to join the other outcasts." He instantly realized the enormity of what he had said and regretted it, but the hurt kept seething inside him.

Ralston gave him a look of incredulous disgust which became a leer when the executive officer exclaimed: "If we had known that, we certainly would have taken the trouble to notify you, Mr. Munceford."

Munceford burned his lips on the coffee and spluttered. "Damn it, I'm sorry! So I've goofed! But I'm still trying to do a job on this ship."

"Sure you are, Ben." Ralston shrugged with indifference.

Two other ensigns from Engineering came into the wardroom and threw everybody cheery greetings before attacking the platters of food, so Munceford clamped down on his temper and seated himself next to them. Ralston gulped the last of his breakfast, excused himself to Commander Allison and headed for the door; as he passed the chair, he deftly lifted the camouflage jacket off it and took it with him. If the executive officer noticed the action he paid no attention to it and Munceford was sulkily staring into his cup of coffee while dunking a doughnut. He had lost his appetite and it was not until he abruptly got up to escape topside and think things out that he missed his jacket. He stared at the empty chair for a moment, then spun around and faced Allison, who had also risen to leave. "All right! Who took it?" he demanded, his fury now out of control.

"Who took what?" the exec coldly inquired.

"It was your snotty ensign playing smart, right?"

The two engineering ensigns stopped eating and gaped.

"Oh, you're talking about that infantryman's sport coat of yours," Allison said without a glimmer of humor.

"You know god-damned well what I'm talking about!" Munceford shouted. "I want my jacket back. If I don't get it back, I'm going to raise hell with the captain about this childish crap!"

Commander Allison's voice dropped to a snarling whisper. "Complaints to the captain are channeled through the executive officer. Unfortunately he is too busy right now to be worried about a missing item of your wardrobe. Is that clear, Mr. Munceford?"

"Yeah, so I guess I can settle that one for myself with Ralston! But don't think I'm not on to the crazy way this operation is being carried on. That's what I'm going to get to the bottom of, with or without your almighty Captain Finlander. I may be a screwball kind of correspondent, but I'm god-damned curious and don't get scared off from prying in dark corners."

Even before he finished his outburst, Allison was roughly shoving his way past him. But he also had to push past Lieutenant Commander Chester Porter, who was on his way in to breakfast. The surgeon had heard the last exchange and wore an appalled look on his face which turned into consternation when the executive officer whipped back and asked him: "Say, Doc! Where was Steward's Mate Collins this morning when the captain wanted some food shot up to his day cabin?"

"Ah . . . er . . . uh . . . Collins? Oh, well, you see, I'd organized a little litter-carrying drill during the GQ and Collins was the simulated casualty and—"

"What?" Allison exploded. "Do both of you characters foisted on us by the *Tiburon Bay* figure you've joined some kind of picnic? Some company outing? Some sea-scout cruise? Damn it all to hell, get with it!!" With a gesture of utter disgust he turned away and vanished down the passageway.

The surgeon recoiled against the bulkhead and appeared close to slumping to the deck. Uncomprehendingly he blinked at Munceford, who was suddenly strangely sobered by the executive officer's violent outburst. "Yeah, Doc!" he sighed with a low, bitter drawl. "Let's you and me get with it and find out what these cats put in their needles."

A flash of sheer horror came over Lieutenant Commander Porter's expression, but the two engineering ensigns somehow triggered nervous chuckles out of each other and one of them said: "Gosh! I guess these TV types actually do talk like that, don't they!"

By 0940 hours the total darkness had given way to a cold, clammy twilight and the tension on the bridge slackened somewhat as a flat colorless ocean began to gain definition in a widening ring of visibility around the speeding destroyer. Close above her, the overcast pressed down like a sagging ceiling which threatened to collapse at any moment, but the space between clouds and sea was free of sleet and only partially obscured by random patches of fog. Vapor wafted from the faces of the lookouts as they drew sighs of relief and Lieutenant Harwell's tensely alert position in the open doorway of the pilothouse relaxed slightly. But Captain Finlander did not relax or move from his position in the exposed wing; indeed, he quickly brought his men back to their former state of nerves by ordering more speed as the curtain of night drew away; it was as if he were trying to keep up with it and use it as a shield in his approach to Moby Dick. Twenty-one . . . twenty-three . . . then twenty-six knots made the ship tremble from the power of her turbines, and the wake roared as it shot out from beneath the stern in a thrashing maelstrom of foam. Down in the CIC they had to shut down the low-power echo-ranging which had been their dubious insurance against smashing into heavy ice and now, deprived of all their electronic sight and hearing, the men sat idly in the dark, suffering the agonies of the deaf and the blind.

Little by little the twilight lifted and presently the coastal icepack became visible two miles off the starboard beam as a pale white line paralleling their course. Again there were sighs of relief on the bridge, but also gasps of dismay when the improving light revealed their own ship to them. All the familiar lines were subtly distorted by the frozen sheathing deposited by last night's sleet, all the solid battleship gray turned into a translucent and sickly pallor beneath the skin of ice. It covered every part of the *Bedford* above her waterline and had formed clusters of soot-stained icicles snaking like congealed tentacles from the rims of her stacks. Gnarled stalactites hung from the muzzles of the DP guns while others had fused lifelines and shrouds to the deck plates. Most startling of all were the coxcomb shapes curling off the masthead and crow's-nest, and the spiked clusters which had been created by the centrifugal effect on the rims of the radar antennas. As Captain Finlander glanced up at these, the nightmare which had haunted his half-sleep during the night briefly came back and stung him with its reality, but then something else caught his attention. "Buck! What's that flying from our main signal halyard?"

Commander Allison wiped some freezing moisture the wind had stung out of his eyes, peered upward and caught sight of a crazy pennant flashing a mottled conglomeration of colors against the gloomy cloud ceiling. He instantly became filled with rage and embarrassment. "Sir, that is Mr. Munceford's jacket!" he shouted back at the captain in a deeply offended tone.

There came a very fleeting twist of amusement on Finlander's lips before he sternly ordered: "Haul it down!", then dismissed the matter and returned his attention to scanning the seas ahead.

Allison angrily ordered Chief Rickmers to lower the offensive garment from its lofty position above the *Bedford*'s bridge. What bothered him the most was that he would have to discipline Ensign Ralston, humiliating that splendid young officer instead of the horrible Munceford! Then he sickened more when Munceford suddenly appeared on the scene.

The correspondent peered around the ice-crusted bridge, then raised his eyes skyward. Inevitably he spied his jacket and followed it downward until its wild flapping was belayed by Rickmers' gloved fists. Gritting his teeth, Allison placed himself between him and the captain.

But Munceford made no motion until Rickmers came alongside him, gingerly holding the jacket between thumb and forefinger; then he reached out and stopped him. Quickly removing the regulation navy parka he had worn to the bridge, Munceford retrieved his own and squirmed into its shreds, which hung on him with its bright, torn patches of divisional insignia like part of a clown's costume. There was something clownish too about the way the freckles stood out on his livid face, but there was none of that quality in his voice. "Thank you, Chief," he said, handing over the parka. "I won't be needing this one now."

Rickmers mumbled something entirely unintelligible, glanced unhappily toward the fuming executive officer, then fled inside the pilothouse.

"Awful raw morning!" Munceford exclaimed casually to Allison and ambled off to another part of the bridge. Tears burned against his cheek, then froze as he hunched down and fiddled with his camera.

By 1015 hours it was full daylight, although still a depressing and foreboding facsimile of the term. Visibility improved until the barren escarpments of Greenland could be seen as a hazy black wall looming beyond the wide barrier of pack ice, its top blending into the clouds and distance giving it a weird marbled effect caused by snow-clogged crevasses. The overcast clung from the wall, seemed to sag low over the *Bedford*'s masthead, then stretch out over the open wastes of the Denmark Strait, where it grew thin in patches, allowing ghostly halos of sunlight to illuminate parts of the horizon.

After checking their position with the INS, Allison approached Captain Finlander and announced: "We will be abeam Moby Dick's estimated position in eighteen minutes, sir."

"Very good, Buck. Hold this speed and heading for ten more minutes, then stop engines and coast in toward the edge of the pack. Alert CIC to have all detection gear warmed up and ready for instant use. Ask them to put Queffle on the QBH hydrophones. No echo-ranging or radar without orders." He squinted uneasily toward the ragged sun patches bleeding through the gray of the eastern sky. "Pray our nice neutral background doesn't break up on us!"

Ten minutes later the *Bedford*'s speed abruptly slackened, the white water rushing from her stem and stern fell away and gradually abated into a soft murmur. A complete, tense silence enveloped the entire ship as she turned toward the icepack, stealthily approaching it on momentum alone. The JOOD took a visual bearing on the coast through the pelorus and confirmed their position with a low voice. Nobody else on the bridge spoke as all eyes strained through binoculars, sweeping the vast expanse of ice which stretched from the black edge of the sea for four miles to the coast. The individual floes began to stand out as they drew nearer and they could be heard grinding against one another although the sea was so flat that no motion could be seen in the pack. It gave an overwhelming impression of total immobility, desolation and frozen emptiness. Ensign Bascomb could make out the promontory he had picked to mark the Russian sub's probable location, a grim headland looming darker against the dark escarpment and looking as if no living thing had been near it since the beginning of time. Finding himself standing close to the captain, he began to edge away uncomfortably, but stopped when Finlander said either to him or all of them: "Be patient! . . . Keep looking and be patient!"

Even Ben Munceford looked hard after shooting a few feet of film of the bleak panorama, and as he looked, a childishly romantic notion crossed his mind of being the one who actually spotted Moby Dick. Wouldn't that fracture these Annapolis snobs! They would have to give him a prize, of course—but what? Maybe a new camouflage jacket!

"All QBH readouts negative!" the CIC reported over the intercom.

Up in the icicled crow's-nest, Squarehead loosed a stream of profanity at the windows, which were streaked by distorting frozen ripples. He pounded on the switch controlling the wipers, which were still solidly stuck. Then he threw all his weight upward against the hatch in the roof of the aluminum box, and, to his surprise, it finally flew open, throwing a shower of frozen particles to the decks below. With a satisfied grunt he heaved himself through the narrow opening and perched his buttocks on the ten-inch rim, which was pure, slick ice. Seaman Jones sprang up off the top rung in the shaft, clamped his arms around Squarehead's legs and fearfully shouted: "For God's sake, be careful!"

Squarehead did not even glance down at the long freefall to certain death which could be the result of a slip. He only looked up at the frame of the tactical radar antenna, gauging whether it would clear his head in case it started rotating. Then he said: "Pass me up them ten-by-fifties, Jonesy, and quit ruining the press of my pants!" The binoculars were handed up to him, but even as he reached for them, he suddenly exclaimed: "Jesus! We're on fire!"

The Bedford was indeed on fire! The cold fires of billions of ice crystals suddenly energized in a long slanting ray of sunlight which had found an infinitesimal rip in the protecting overcast, shot through it and scored a bull's-eye. For an agonized eternity of five seconds the drab warship blazed and sparkled like a diamond caught in the beam of a burglar's flashlight, exploding out of the hiding gloom with a clarion burst of glory. No marine artist could have captured her fantastic beauty at this moment, nor could any living eye within fifteen miles around have failed to notice her! The clouds quickly swirled in and smothered the sunbeam, but the damage had been done and a chorus of groans rose from the bridge.

"We might as well shoot off some flares and do a good job of announcing ourselves," Commander Allison bitterly exclaimed. "But I suppose turning on the radar will do for a starter."

"No—hold it a few moments more!" Finlander ordered.

Tense silence fell over the bridge again while everybody scanned the ice, but now with less hope than before. The ship had almost stopped and was within a hundred yards of the edge of the icepack, which appeared much looser from close quarters—and the floes bigger and more individually solid. The first little growlers hit the hull with disturbingly loud clangs. It was an unpleasant noise, but had nowhere near the effect of the howl which suddenly came from high up the mast:

"Masthead to bridge! . . . I see something like a big chunk of ice out there that's moving by itself!"

All the faces on the bridge, including the captain's, turned upward and stared in various degrees of shock at the figure far up the mast, precariously perched on the rim of the crow's-nest while excitedly waving one arm toward some objective in the icepack.

Commander Allison gasped, then cupped his gloved hands around his mouth and cut loose his most powerful quarterdeck bellow. "Don't you know how to report a sighting properly, you damned fool? Get back inside there and use the telephone!"

The figure waved and screamed again in wild, oblivious excitement. "Like a piece of moving ice! . . . It's him! . . . Going down! Going down—" He came within a fraction of falling, then suddenly vanished as if somebody had yanked him out of sight from below.

Allison was grabbing for the telephone in the external communication box, but Captain Finlander needed no clarification of the garbled sighting report. "A moving icefloe!" he exclaimed to himself. "Of course! He's got his conning tower painted white!" Raising his binoculars and training them in the general direction indicated by the frantic lookout, he forced every last ounce of effort out of his optic nerves, trying to catch every detail of every pan, chunk and boulder-sized piece of ice among the thousands which came into his view. He tensed for a second when he thought he caught a motion in the congealed conglomeration of shapes out there, then sagged when it seemed only an illusion . . . then jumped a foot into the air when the speaker sang out:

"Bridge from CIC! We have a hard contact on the QBH! Request permission to start echo-ranging!"

"Granted!" Finlander yelled in a spontaneous flash of wild elation which electrified the men around him far more than had the lookout's performance a moment ago. "Boys, we've got him! Got him cold two miles inside Greenland waters!" He shoved his fisherman's cap to the back of his head and laughed. And suddenly all the others were laughing too. Even Allison laughed. Ensign Bascomb swelled up and let out a hoot. The OOD began to jig. The enlisted lookouts, talkers and signalmen grinned and thumped one another on the back. Ben Munceford smiled, but thinly, as he stared out over the icepack in the direction everybody else was pointing—and saw absolutely nothing. He accepted as fact that *something* was out there, evidently Moby Dick, and that it was somehow trapped by the *Bedford,* but he still could not fully understand all the uproar.

"So you've got him!" he exclaimed. "So what are you going to do about it?"

The captain heard the question and took fleeting notice of Munceford's presence on the bridge for the first time this morning; both the question and the sight of the tattered camouflage jacket may have helped sober him, yet he proceeded to ignore the correspondent. The smile was still there, but turned grim, and his voice became fully businesslike as he started issuing orders. "Buck! Tell CIC to lock on and track! Have Fire Control put their ASROCs on stand-by and start feeding target data to the systems! OOD! Keep out of the ice and conn the ship to intercept any attempt to break for open sea! Yeoman! Take down this message for immediate transmission!" He began dictating it within the hearing of Ben Munceford, perhaps purposefully so as to answer his question: "Code Double-A, Most Urgent and Immediate Action to COMAD, NATONAV 1: Have flushed Soviet Russian submarine conducting military reconnaissance inside, *repeat inside,* Greenland-Danish territorial waters, position sixteen miles north Helvigstadt Bay, stop. Request immediate authority to challenge and interdict, stop. Signed Commanding Officer, Coldsnap."

# 5.

In the Communications Center, Lieutenant P. L. M. Packer, R.N., finally snapped out of the brooding lethargy which he had been fighting all morning since being deprived of his normal duties. Radio silence left him with nothing to do and the continued GQ nowhere to go but remain at his battle station—a desk. Yes, he had ambled into the EDA room while Lieutenant Beeker sat in silent communion with his HUFF-DUFF and MESS-PLEX, patiently trying to divine any scraps of radio intelligence out of the ether. He had listened to the low chatter of the idle operators speculating about their chances of catching Moby Dick, but without himself becoming exhilarated by the chase. To the contrary, his depression had deepened and at the bottom of it there was the throbbing hurt of Shebeona. But now, when Finlander's message was given to him for transmittal to NATONAV 1, he at last began to be caught up in the excitement which permeated the ship. It was only a matter of a few minutes to run it through the encoder and have one of the operators flash it on its way. His spirits lifted even more when a familiar voice came in over the PA circuit:

"This is the captain speaking! We sighted Moby Dick a short while ago as he submerged through the icepack and now have him securely locked in our sonar beam. He has no sounding for deep dives, no clear water for high-speed runs under the ice, and we stand between him and the open sea. I have dispatched a message to our Fleet Headquarters with this good news and asking for permission to deal with him. Shortly we shall fire a charge close enough to him that he will fully realize the fatal consequences of not meekly surfacing under our guns! This has been a long, trying stretch at battle stations, but please bear with me for a little longer. The payoff is at hand! Thank you."

"By Jove!" Packer exclaimed. "Looks like we might get cracking, doesn't it!" The Beek gave him a somewhat condescending smile and replaced the one cup of his earphones which he had lifted off an ear in order to hear the captain's short speech; he casually called to Chief Benton:

"Keep tabs on the long-wave frequencies in case that sub starts attempting any underwater transmissions!"

The English officer stepped out on deck for the next few moments, took some invigorating lungfuls of cold air and noticed with satisfaction that the ASROC launcher had been elevated into firing position and trained to starboard, the yellow-green snout of the missile's warhead pointing menacingly toward the icepack. Then Benton called out to him that a NATONAV message was coming in and he rushed back to his decoding machine. When he read the strip it fed into his hands, he gave a quite un-English whoop. The message said:

NATONAV 1 TO COMMANDING OFFICER COLDSNAP—RE YOUR TACREP 11–23–1305Z ACT AT OWN DISCRETION ACCORDING IMMEDIATE TACTICAL REQUIREMENTS OF SITUATION STOP—SIGNED SORENSEN, COMAD.

Lieutenant Packer had barely put down the telephone after enjoying a delighted "Very good!" from Captain Finlander when Chief Benton shouted to him: "Hold it! Here comes one from home plate, sir!" A few minutes later all of his enthusiasm was dampened as he drew the following message out of the decoder.

COMFLANT TO COMMANDING OFFICER COLDSNAP—HAVE INTERCEPTED YOUR TACREP 11–23–1305Z TO COLDSNAP STOP COMMEND EXCELLENT WORK BUT REGRET MUST FORBID ANY ACTION WITHOUT CONFIRMATION THIS HEADQUARTERS DUE CRITICAL RUSSAMERICAN CRISIS BERLIN AND ELSEWHERE STOP SUGGEST PASSIVE SHADOW TACTICS UNTIL FURTHER ORDERS STOP—SIGNED BALDWIN, CINCLANT.

"What a bloody shame!" Packer sighed, reaching for the phone again. "It's going to turn out just another bitched-up inter-Allied raspberry!"

Captain Erik Finlander turned livid and began pacing the navigation office like a caged tiger. His eyes blazed with fury, the scar on his throat pulsed crimson and looked as if it might rupture and start hemorrhaging at any moment. The messenger who had brought him copies of the conflicting messages from NATONAV 1 and COMFLANT cringed as he hurriedly fled. Allison, his face set in a less animated expression of anger, pressed himself against the chart table and braced for what he felt certain would be a blast which would demolish the captain's own standing orders against vile language. Yet when Finlander finally found his speech, it was still controlled beneath the trembling of rage and totally devoid of profanity. It was the vehemence of the delivery which made it so chilling.

"For once we have a chance to act decisively against creeping Soviet aggression! For once we are able to nail a Russian redhanded inside NATO allies' territorial waters and with virtual proof of his subversive intentions! Nice neutral little Sweden with her toy navy has the guts to depth-charge Commie pigboats they catch violating her shores. Even Admiral Sorensen of pipsqueak Denmark is prepared to act decisively in the interest of NATO obligations. But big, tough, armed-to-the-teeth United States of America, winner of every war it ever fought, champion of liberty and rule of law, must hesitate and talk it over! Talk, talk, talk, concede and back up and pussyfoot and procrastinate! That's what they are doing, you know, Buck! My tacrep sent cold chills down the atrophied spines fused to the upholstery of COMFLANT and they got on the hotline to the State Department fags, who have no spines at all! So now they're talk-talk-talking while we sit up here in the arctic on top of that Bolshevik submarine commander who's recovering more of his wits with each second!" He stemmed the torrent for a moment to listen to a voice from the CIC, which had been reporting over the open intercom every other minute since their contact with Moby Dick:

"Positive target echo . . . bearing zero-three-one, steady . . . range two-two-five-zero, steady . . . depth zero-seven-five, steady . . ."

For an instant Finlander looked as though he was about to drive his fist through the speaker. Commander Allison made a half-hearted effort to soothe him: "Maybe the staff at COMFLANT only want a little time to evaluate the situation for themselves, sir."

As he stalked past the chart table, the captain slammed the flat of his hand against it, making pencils, dividers and rulers jump high in the air. "That's what *I* am here for!" he shouted. "Because I *am* here, I know the situation. I'm not asking them to allow me to commit a warlike act. I'm asking they permit me to expose the warlike intentions of a nation who has mesmerized half the world with its eternal blathering about peaceful coexistence! And, above all, I'm asking for this chance to show that the American navy is able and determined to put a stop to this kind of intimidation of our own country!" He slammed the table once more, paced several more turns around the navigation office, then came to an abrupt halt when he found himself face to face with Commodore Wolfgang Schrepke as he stepped in from the wheelhouse.

"Is there anything amiss, Captain?" the German inquired, unzipping his leather jacket and removing his brine-stained cap.

Without a word Finlander thrust the two crumpled messages at him. Schrepke took them, stepped over to the chart table, spread them out under the light, smoothed out their wrinkles and carefully read each in turn. Then he straightened up and said: "I would say your Fleet Headquarters have relieved you of a terrible responsibility which Admiral Sorensen was so quick to conveniently place upon your shoulders."

This stopped Finlander short with a glint of surprise. Another fragment of last night's nightmares flashed through his mind, the part where the sly Admiral Sorensen was dressing him down, snarling: "*You ekted unwisely, Kep'n!*"—but he quickly smothered this vision in his current anger. "Indeed, Commodore Schrepke? Well, unlike some of my European colleagues, I do not shrink from responsibility for my actions!" He buttoned up his white duffel and slapped the long-billed cap on his head, then moved to leave.

"Do we secure from battle stations, sir?" Allison called after him.

"No!" Finlander shouted back and swept out through the blackout curtain.

# 6.

The *Bedford* doggedly weaved along the ragged edge of the ice-pack at a slow six knots to keep prodding the submarine with relentless echo-ranging signals. Moby Dick was moving southward beneath the protective shield of ice, staying between one and two miles offshore and about the same distance from his pursuer, keeping as deep as the shallow, reef-strewn coastal waters would allow, which meant somewhat less than forty fathoms. In the destroyer's CIC they could occasionally hear his sonar pinging in short bursts, obviously ranging ahead to detect rocks and skerries which might fatally block his course through the black deep. "That devil either has better charts than we, or he is a madman!" Lieutenant Spitzer observed with a certain grudging admiration as he checked the submarine's progress on the combat plot.

From time to time Moby Dick would stop to listen on his passive sonar system, in which case the *Bedford* would do the same. Perhaps the Soviet commander was hoping to draw his opponent into the icepack as a rabbit draws a fox into an impenetrable thicket of brambles from where it would be lucky to extricate itself with a whole skin, let alone make a kill! But the sullen Finlander would not allow his turbulent feelings to trick him into any rash action. So the creeping, stalking game resumed after each one of these tense pauses.

An hour dragged by, then another. The overcast which had shown signs of breaking up earlier during the day solidified and turned a bluish leaden color, and presently a fine snow began falling. The harsh rock faces of the distant mountains became softly hazy in the thickening weather and began a play of hide-and-seek with the shifting flurries. As the destroyer moved farther south and came out of the lee of the great northeast bight of Greenland, deep ocean swells regained their power, slowly at first, with gently heaving widely separated crests, then steeper and closer. The icepack came alive in their surge and began to grind and fill the air with a horrible gnashing rumble. This sound filled the deep too and the CIC reported that echo-ranging was becoming disturbed, triggering Captain Finlander to send off another urgent, top-secret plea to both NATONAV 1 and COMFLANT:

. . . TACTICAL SITUATION DETERIORATING IN FAVOR TRANSGRESSOR STOP AGAIN URGENTLY REQUEST PERMISSION CHALLENGE AND INTERDICT BEFORE OPPORTUNITY LOST. . . .

After an interminable delay which actually only lasted for fifteen minutes, NATONAV 1 came through with an uncomforting answer:

. . . AM AMPLIFYING YOUR SITUATION TO COMFLANT WITH POSITIVE RECOMMENDATIONS STOP IF YOU NEED ASSISTANCE WILL ORDER POLAR-BEAR TO YOUR POSITION WHICH CAN MAKE IN EIGHT HOURS STOP—SIGNED SORENSEN, COMAD.

. . . ONLY ASSISTANCE REQUIRED IS AUTHORITY TO TAKE ACTION. . . .

To this came a peremptory one-word signal from COMFLANT:

WAIT

And as they waited, the early afternoon became a melancholy, snow-filled dusk, then suddenly winter night.

After his brief flurry of activity in the Communications Center occasioned by the captain's exchanges with admirals thousands of miles removed from this dismal scene of action, Lieutenant P. L. M. Packer gradually sank back into the depression which had gripped his spirits last night and this morning. Again he was let down by an idleness which aggravated the attrition of his deep personal troubles. Leaning listlessly over his immaculate desk, he stared at the radio-telephone unit attached to the bulkhead a few feet away. As he stared, the wistful thought came to his mind that all he had to do was flip a switch, punch a channel selector, call the Marine Operator at Kirkeness, ask for London—GErrard 2075—and forthwith bridge the horrible void between himself and Shebeona. *"Hello, darling! . . . Didn't you get my telegram?"*

"Here comes a deferred personal over Code C circuit, sir!" one of the radio operators announced and started clacking away on his machine.

Packer came out of his chair and had to check himself from making an undignified rush for the decoder. The Beek was standing in the doorway to the EDA room, munching on a huge sandwich, the wires trailing from his inevitable earphones and connecting him to the MESS-PLEX like an umbilical cord. He was watching the Englishman with a kind of uncomfortable concern as he drew the printed strip through his hands.

PERSONAL SEAMAN 1 THORBJORNSEN, JOHN B., COLDSNAP VIA NATONAV MACKAY—A NEW BOOT REPORTED FOR DUTY THIS DOGWATCH WEIGHING 6 POUNDS 4 OUNCES SOAKING WET AND HOLLERING A LUSTY ALLS WELL STOP CONGRATULATIONS DAD STOP—SIGNED GRANDPOP.

Because he sensed The Beek's eyes on him, Lieutenant Packer hid his bitter disappointment, forced a grin, read the message aloud and filled the austere Communications Center with a bright moment of cheerful laughter.

At 1620 hours Lieutenant Commander Chester Porter finally came to enter a patient in the ship's medical log. A gunner's mate was virtually dragged into the surgery by his section chief with both hands badly frostbitten from clearing ice off an ASROC launcher. The surgeon treated him and noticed how the hands shook from something more than pain, but there was defiance in the man's red-rimmed eyes when he firmly declined being relieved from duty. Porter reluctantly discharged him and returned to the receiving office, where he resumed perusing through the now well-thumbed *War Psychology in Primitive and Modern Man*. All day long he had had little to do but sit there absorbing the text and Lieutenant Hirschfeld's marginal notes. However, after a short while he now closed it and locked it away in his desk, then pulled on his arctics. Leaving Chief Pharmacist McKinley in charge of the sterile inactivity of sick bay, he resolutely set off for the bridge. But on the way up there his resolution wavered slightly and he digressed on a visit into the armored cavern of the CIC. "How are things going? Pretty rough?" he asked Lieutenant Krindlemeyer, who had taken over Central Control while Spitzer was wolfing down an early dinner in the wardroom.

Krindlemeyer peered at the surgeon through his rimless glasses with a blankly owlish expression and answered: "Why, hello, Doc! All systems are go here!"

The surgeon listened to the raucous jumble of sound which was coming in over the sonar audio monitors, winced at the frantic splatters of light in the PPI scopes and watched the chief plotter record the latest tactical data on the big board, then call it up to the bridge in a low, hoarse voice. He noticed the forcibly relaxed attitudes of Lieutenant Aherne and Ensign Ralston at the glowing Fire Control console, the endlessly masticating jaws of the sonar and radar operators, and especially noticed the nervous jiggling of Merlin Queffle's right knee as he sat at the MTS, eyes tightly shut, forehead wrinkled as he pressed the earphones to his ears. Porter took all this in for a minute or two, gained fresh resolve from what he saw, then quietly slipped out through the steel door.

Captain Finlander was seated on the edge of the bunk in his day cabin, his duffel open, cap shoved back, in his hands a bowl of steaming bean soup which he was stirring without much enthusiasm when the surgeon timidly pushed aside the blackout curtain and peered in. "How are things going, sir? Pretty rough?"

Finlander looked up with a scowl which lasted long enough for Lieutenant Commander Porter to take warning, but the following forced grin betrayed him into stepping inside the cabin.

"Hello, Doc!" the captain greeted him with a kind of bitter cordiality. "Somebody once said something about being able to take care of his enemies, but God preserve him from his friends. In this case, *my* friends at Fleet Headquarters!"

Porter laughed politely and dared to perch himself casually on the edge of the desk. "Oh, well—I suppose they've got a lot of things to consider in a situation like this. Things fraught with dangerous consequences if the wrong decisions are made, right?"

Finlander gave him a baleful stare which should have been the final warning, then took a mouthful of soup instead of answering.

The surgeon looked up at the clock on the bulkhead. "Gosh, Captain! We certainly have been at battle stations for an awful long stretch, haven't we?"

"Eleven hours and fourteen minutes," Finlander snapped without looking at the clock. "What about it, Commander Porter? Have there been any intolerable hardships worked on the medical department?"

"Oh, no, sir. I've only had one case of frostbite, but . . ." He stopped himself, suddenly fearfully aware of the captain's dangerous mood.

"But what?" Finlander demanded and in his agitation slopped some of the soup out of the bowl. He glowered down at the greasy red stain spreading over pure white wool, then his eyes snapped back to the surgeon, blazing with a terrible light beneath the black brows.

"B-but I, ah . . . noticed an increasing strain showing in the men, sir, and . . ."

"You think this is news to me?" Finlander shouted, now playing his temper as though it were a discordant percussion instrument. "They know I will never secure from battle stations while we are closed with the enemy. *Never!* But, all right, Doc! So they are strained by this filthy, freezing, frustrating job. Are you giving me a medical opinion that they can't take it any more?"

"Maybe it's more like they're ready to take on too much, sir."

"What the devil do you mean by that, Commander?"

"Well, like . . . this Moby Dick business is all very well—just as long as *you* don't take the part of Ahab too seriously, sir." He gave a nervous laugh, then froze rigid.

The bowl of soup had splattered on the deck as Captain Finlander shot to his feet. He was actually shorter and slighter of build than the bulky surgeon, but he suddenly towered over him and caused him to begin to pitifully shrivel. His voice came forth a full octave lower than before, and with twice the vehemence. "Ahab? Ahab? My name is Erik J. Finlander! I am a captain of the United States Navy and commanding officer of the U.S.S. *Bedford!* That's *who* and *what* I am, sir! Nobody else! Nothing else! And you, sir, will instantly remove yourself from my presence and return to your battle station. Dismissed!!"

Lieutenant Commander Chester Porter quivered before this blast like a jelly suddenly exposed to a violent wind. He slid off the edge of the desk and with a trembling "Y-yes, sir!" slunk out through the curtain. A wet stain was left on a fold where his face had brushed against it.

Moby Dick made his successful break for the open sea sometime between 0150 and 0230 hours of the following morning. The exact minute remained undetermined because the CIC had been thrown into a state of confusion by a very large gam of whales which had run headlong into the scene of creeping battle. They radiated an impossible cacophony of submarine noises, aggravating the already difficult tracking conditions brought about by a now thoroughly activated icepack pounding in breaking seas. To make matters worse, the *Bedford*'s sonar genius, Merlin the Magician, had had to be relieved during the late evening after being on duty for sixteen hours with only a few short breaks. Lieutenant Spitzer had sent him below, secretly happy to be rid of him and wanting to trust the relieving sonarman, who, for over ten fatal minutes, even disputed the fact that it was whales obscuring the tenuous signal they were intermittently receiving off the submarine. Then one of the animals surfaced in the turbulent blackness, unseen but so close to the ship that its vaporous spout swept over the bridge, enveloping Captain Finlander where he stood in swirling snow with an unmistakable fishy halitosis. "Get Queffle back on that MTS immediately!" he yelled over the intercom.

It only took four minutes to return Queffle to the CIC and only a minute more of concentrated, aggrieved listening over the earphone and peering into the PPI scope before he came up with his cocksure diagnosis of the trouble: "Right whales! Fifty or sixty of them! They blanked our hard contact!"

Seething with impotent rage and frustration, Lieutenant Spitzer had no alternative but call to the bridge: "Contact lost! Readouts obscured and blanked by biological and hydrographic interference!"

Finlander heard the baleful voice squawking out of the speaker in the wing and immediately rushed for the wheelhouse. "Don't they understand he's broken out of the pack astern of us? Reverse your course! Make flank speed for ten minutes, then start a maximum-effect sweep!"

The *Bedford* heeled over in a sharp turn and began to pound through the huge swells. Clouds of spray mingled with the snow, and the jarring which shook her from keel to masthead broke loose the remains of yesterday's ice, shedding it in rattling cascades along her flanks. The destroyer drove through the night and ice-clogged black ocean at a perilous thirty-two knots, and when she finally stopped at the end of this wild retracing run to listen for her lost quarry, a final ironic blow was struck at her captain. It came in the form of a message from COMFLANT:

. . . PERMISSION GRANTED TO CHALLENGE AND INTERDICT STOP EXPECT YOU ACT PROMPTLY WITH PRUDENT FORCE AGAINST ANY TRESPASS IN NATO TERRITORIAL WATERS. . . .

Finlander held the scrap of yellow paper which had been delivered to him from the Communications Center at this bitter moment, studying it in the sickly green glow from the navigational radar. Commander Allison read it over his shoulder and shrank away from him, expecting a blast—which did not come. The captain only sucked in his breath and held it for an interminable period before letting go with a prolonged wheeze. Then he stepped over to the intercom and called Spitzer: "What have you got down there now besides interesting wildlife, CIC?" he inquired with fathomless suffering in his voice.

"All readouts negative, sir."

"All right. I'm coming down." He turned to his executive officer. "You take the conn, Buck. I'm going to personally take over the CIC and keep them going until they fall out of their upholstered chairs and have to be carried into sick bay. I'm going to hunt that Commie pigboat until the barnacles grow so thick on this hull we can no longer move. I'm going to catch him, Buck! I'm going to catch him!"

They did catch Moby Dick nine hours later where the blizzard had free reign over mountainous swells running a good twenty miles off the territorial limits of Greenland. But perhaps to use the word *catch* would not be entirely correct—because all that really happened was that the protagonists caught sight of each other through the thick snow and spume for about thirty seconds.

When the watch had changed at 0800 and the *Bedford* was still vainly searching the empty deep, Captain Finlander reluctantly secured the ship from battle stations, yet himself keeping the CIC on full combat alert. He came to regret this action when Moby Dick suddenly materialized with hardly a warning on any of the detection devices. This shocking thing happened simply because the Russian submarine was cautiously poking her snorkel up through the wild seas in order to breathe after the long submerged action and was too close to the heaving surface for the sonar beams to register a return echo. One of those seas almost broached him and for something like thirty seconds the big conning tower thrust clear out of water. A half-smothered "eyeball" lookout in the port wing of the bridge and a bleary-eyed radar operator in the CIC both sang out together. Commodore Schrepke also saw him and was able to get a quick look through his binoculars which confirmed to him it was a Chelnikoff-class submarine.

The GQ alarm went off, propelling two-thirds of the crew out of their bunks almost before they had had time to settle into them.

"Go after him, Buck! Force him down!" Finlander bellowed into the intercom, then started to rush for the bridge. But he quickly realized he would never make it in time and dropped back into his seat at Central Control. Moby Dick was crash-diving—but at least Queffle had a solid contact on the MTS. The hunt was on again!

The Russian submarine had plenty of sounding now that he was well out in the Denmark Strait and he used it well. Pressing down to seven hundred feet, where no trace of the surface turbulence could reach him, he cracked on close to twenty-five knots, taking violent evasive actions along a generally southeasterly course. This made it hard for the *Bedford* to track him accurately, having to fight the huge moving walls of water contesting her pursuit, as well as maintain a speed which made her sonar gear crackle and splatter with ambient noises. Yet she held the contact, mainly because of Merlin Queffle's phenomenal sensitivity and Finlander's skillful tactics of rush-stop-listen-rush. Stubbornly he hung on while more interminable hours dragged by, the horrible bone-wrenching rolls of the destroyer adding a physical pain to the mental agony.

At 1123 hours Lieutenant Packer telephoned Finlander to give him an urgent message from NATONAV 1, asking for amplification of the situation. The captain crisply ordered him to transmit the single cipher which would indicate to both NATONAV 1 and COMFLANT that a critical tactical operation was in progress necessitating radio silence.

Noon passed, cold, gray and engulfed in the swirling folds of a full-fledged blizzard. The watch changed with the ship on battle stations. Commander Allison, showing himself more and more the quiet man of iron determination and endurance, plotted their position in the navigation office and noted that they were close to where the *Tiburon Bay* had refueled them only four days ago. He ignored Ben Munceford, who likewise had not left the bridge since the previous morning and was still wearing his frightful shredded camouflage jacket. "I'm not going to be caught in the sack again with something going on!" he overheard him say to Lieutenant Harwell when the latter told him he was crazy to take the grind with the rest of them.

1530 hours and the grim dusk slipped into an impenetrable darkness. In the log the weather was tersely described: "Heavy snow . . . Temperature 21 F. . . . Wind N. Force 4 . . . Sea-state 5 with NNE swells." The plot in CIC sent up the target information every other minute: ". . . Hard contact . . . bearing zero-zero-five, steady . . . range five-five-zero, steady . . . depth one hundred fifty fathoms, steady . . . target making twenty-four knots, two-four knots . . ." The captain did not make his sunset watch this afternoon; Commodore Schrepke stood it more alone than ever.

When all track of time had ceased to be something sensed by the human mind, 2215 hours came and with it a sudden fading to complete silence on all the sonar receivers in the CIC. Moby Dick had been executing some strangely erratic maneuvers during the past twenty minutes, zigzagging and nearly reversing his course in such a way that Finlander would have suspected he was about to launch a torpedo attack if he had not at the same time pressed down closer to the bottom—*which suddenly seemed to swallow him up!*

The *Bedford* coasted to a stop, heaved to and rolled sickeningly broadside to the seas while making a maximum-effect sonar sweep. Silence! Next she cut a slow, outward spiraling circle, still listening. Silence!

Merlin Queffle looked up from his MTS console with an almost comical perplexity on his pinched, haggard face. "Jeez! It's like he went down a hole or something!" he exclaimed in an outraged falsetto.

His dismay spread through the gloomy CIC like a contagious virus. But Finlander spoke up from the Central Control in a firm, confident voice. "He's got to be there! We're not dealing with the Flying Dutchman, but living men working a rather old type of submarine. They've got only two ways to go: up or down. . . . Cut to a passive sweep on the QBH!"

They listened for five . . . ten . . . fifteen endless minutes. Silence. Then Lieutenant Krindlemeyer's spectacles suddenly flashed over the rim of the hatch to the CSP room and his nasal voice blandly announced: "I'm getting an awfully strong magnetic disturbance down here which suggests there may be a much bigger hunk of iron below us than a submarine."

Lieutenant Spitzer gave a funny squeal and reached across the captain to switch on the magnetometer. Its needle jumped across the scale. Finlander seemed to have caught the implication instantly, although he did nothing but casually call the bridge over the intercom: "Buck! Check our *exact* position, please! Give us any pertinent information on what's on the bottom."

A few minutes later Allison gave their exact position; then he added with a tinge of surprise: "Sir, we happen to be right over the wreck of the H.M.S. *Hood,* the old British battle cruiser!"

For the first time in nearly two days Finlander's face broke into a genuinely spontaneous grin. He leaned back in his chair, stretched his arms over his head, then replied: "Very good! Very good! That's what I thought! . . . All right. Let's thrash around the area a bit, like we were horribly confused. Then rig silent and let's wait for him to get short of breath! . . . I think I ought to let everybody in on this development, Buck. Will you patch in this circuit through ship's PA, please!"

In the Communications Center, Lieutenant P. L. M. Packer was at his desk, guarding this, his useless battle station on the U.S.S. *Bedford.* He only gradually came out of his slumped position as the captain's cheerful voice came over the PA speaker.

"Moby Dick has given us a long, hard chase, gentlemen, but now I think I can safely tell you that he has outsmarted himself. We have lost contact, true! But we know exactly where he is hiding. Fate has it that we are directly above the wreck of a huge English warship—the H.M.S. *Hood*—which was sunk in battle during the last war. Apparently our Commie enemy knew of its location pretty accurately and has probably used it often to shield himself with over forty thousand tons of steel to fox our detection devices. Very smart! But now we are on to that and will be waiting when he has to come up—which should be fairly soon. So hang on, men! The end of our trial is in sight! . . . Thank you."

Packer was rigidly standing up directly under the speaker when the captain finished. He kept on staring at it for over a minute before turning away and dazedly walking past The Beek, who had at last fallen asleep, seated upright in his chair. He passed the row of idle operators, who stared curiously after him, then only shrugged because his behavior had been a bit peculiar lately. Funny ducks, these Limeys!

Lieutenant Packer went through the door leading out on deck without bothering to put on his parka and gantlets. Moving out into the night, he lifted his bare hands to shield his face from the cruel sting of the blizzard, shuffled to the railing and peered over it as if seeking something in the angry black void of the sea. He stood there until a wave bigger than the others rose up and hurled an icy blow at him, and only then did he shy back as if recoiling from the cold grip of death reaching out for him from the deep.

He was drenched to the skin, but he did not hurry down to his cabin to change. He walked slowly, and when he got there and pushed aside the curtain, he found Ben Munceford at the desk, loading tape into his portable recorder.

The correspondent looked at the Englishman with surprise. "My God, Pete, what's happened to you? Did Communications spring a leak?"

Packer merely shook his head and absently began to peel off his sopping clothes.

Munceford resumed loading the recorder while idly drawling away. "Well, it all beats me, anyway. Now that you think you've got that sub pinned down under a wreck or something, what exactly is going to happen next? As far as I can see, all that Russki has to do is come up and tell us to leave him the hell alone now, or he'll file a nasty complaint at the U.N. . . . Say, Pete! What *is* the matter? You not only look wet, but sick too."

"I'm all right, thanks," Packer said, stripping off his shirt.

"Are you still moping over your love life? Still, after two whole days? Is that what's eating you, man?" He laughed, not cruelly but trying to kid him and with an encouraging slap on the shoulder.

"I couldn't care less about love at this moment," the Englishman told him with a flat, unemotional voice.

"Then show me you don't care, Pete! And, most important of all, show *yourself!*" Munceford was still trying to joss him and did not at all expect the reaction he got.

"All right—I will!" Packer retorted. He stepped over to his bunk, bent down and reached up for the under part of the one above it. There was a tearing of tape. Then he was suddenly handing Shebeona's photograph to Munceford, even forcing him to take it. "There you are, Ben! A nice pin-up for you, old man!" His body was racked by a sudden shudder and he whipped a towel around himself to run out to the hot shower.

# PART THREE

# THE BATTLE

# 1.

The time was 0400, the forty-second hour of the chase, the sixth hour since the *Bedford* had started circling over the wreck of the *Hood* like a wolf circling the lair of its trapped prey. The wind had dropped to a bare Force 2, but the snow kept falling and the sea heaved to the cadence of swells which continued marching through the night in endless columns of giants. As she alternately lay hove to or jogging against the drift, the destroyer rolled, pitched and corkscrewed with violent, unpredictable motions which added wrenching aches to the numbing cold plaguing her lookouts and gunners.

Every ten minutes Chief Gunner's Mate Cantrell had to punch the STANDBY-HOLD switch on the panel and crawl out of his armored cubicle to climb precariously up the icy sides of the RAT launcher, clear the missile of snow and freezing slush, then back to his station and return the switch to READY-LAUNCH. In the crow's-nest, where every wild roll of the *Bedford* was multiplied tenfold, Seaman Jones was whipping about through a nightmarish world of absolute darkness; he could not even see the snowflakes brushing against the windshield a few inches beyond his nose. But he kept straining his eyes, trying to judge his relative position to the sea, watching, watching for any telltale swirl of phosphorescence which might betray the fact that Moby Dick was surfacing. He still believed implicitly in his eyes, all the more so since he knew sonar contact had failed. Yet sometimes he could not help losing all sense of direction and, especially during some of the worst rolls, felt as if he was about to be hurled free of the ship. It had happened once—on the *Brinkley*—that the crow's-nest had been completely wrenched from its fastenings to the mast and become the coffin of the drowning lookout. But he did not think about that horrible accident. As his captain had told him to do, he thought about the enemy and kept a smoldering anger going inside him. He thought about those Russian submariners hiding in the placid, motionless deep while he was being slowly beaten to death up here. "I hope you suffocate, you dirty Red bastards!" he snarled.

In the CIC nobody had spoken a word for nearly half an hour. The armor and insulation shut out all sounds of the sea and there was none in here beyond the endlessly repetitive minor-key *ping* of the sonar—which came through crisp and clear, without any fuzz and crackle of a return echo. Captain Finlander was still occupying the chair at Central Control, hunched forward with his arms folded across his chest, his body so rigidly conforming to the *Bedford*'s gyrations that it seemed a part of her. His eyes still watched the PPI scopes, but now they were flicking more often to the men at the consoles. He had become aware of the weariness which was slowly dulling their tense alertness, noticing the fitful contrapuntal actions of their muscles as they failed to synchronize with the rolls and pitches of the ship, perceiving a subtle bloodshot haze glazing their eyes. He studied Queffle with special concentration. The boy's face was damp and shone with a greenish pallor as he hunched over the primary tactical sonar, his eyes too close to the scope to focus effectively, the bony fingers pressing the earphones too hard against his ears to allow perceptive hearing. Suddenly he looked back over his shoulder toward Central Control, a desperate frustrated action in violation of regulations, then visibly flinched when he met his captain's gaze and instantly returned his attention to the fruitless vigil at his instrument. Finlander tried to flash him a reassuring nod, but Queffle had turned away too quickly. Yet not so quickly that the captain had not caught that look of despair. The extraordinary powers of the Breton Kid were failing him. In fact, all the finely tuned fighting pitch of the CIC was draining away, its subdued twilight of glowing tubes and dials turning into a deepening gloom full of frustration and foreboding.

"Number-two ASROC reports iced up and on STANDBY-HOLD," the talker droned with a tired monotone. Ensign Ralston let out a groan.

Finlander knew it was becoming urgent that something happen to bolster the sagging spirits of his men. Nothing he could say would do it. It had to be something more stimulating than a few encouraging words —or taunting ones—from their captain. If only he could flush out Moby Dick with a stick of hedgehogs! What god-damn good was a war without something to go *bang* and jar one out of the deadly rote of it all? How futile this stalking, waiting game! Yet how vital that it be won by refusing to capitulate to its very futility! The *Bedford* or Moby Dick, one or the other, *had* to sneak away or come gasping to the surface with all offensive spirit so thoroughly demolished that they would be henceforth useless as a ship's complement. It *had* to be the Russian. Yet it was the *Bedford*'s men who were wavering now.

Finlander wanted to yell "Get with it or that obsolete submarine will lick us!" but instead he leaned back in the chair, stretched his arms over his head, let out a noisy yawn and exclaimed: "The Commies must have figured out a new secret weapon, men. They're trying to bore us to death."

There was no reaction—not even a chuckle from Ensign Ralston.

"By God!" Finlander loudly exploded. "Under any other conditions I'd dock everybody in here two days' shore leave for failing to react to commanding officer's wisecracks."

"I bet those fucking Russians are splitting their sides . . . *sir.*"

Finlander shot to his feet and wheeled, his body propelled by an electrifying combination of shock and anger. It was Lieutenant Spitzer who had spoken up from the dark corner where he had wedged himself in between a bulkhead and an amplifier rack. His voice had not only a strange high pitch but a belligerent tone which was entirely foreign to him. His balding pate glistened with a sickly pallor beneath the wilting blond strands of hair; his eyes showed the same beady green luminescence as the lights on the control boards. His colorless lips were parted by a leer which appeared entirely toothless in the harsh reflected half-light. As the captain glared at him, sucking in his breath for a withering rebuke, the *Bedford* rolled, steeply canting the deck and causing the usually self-effacing ECM officer to rise up and loom menacingly above him. The blast never came, as Finlander caught his breath in surprise. But there must have been something in his own demeanor which sobered Spitzer because he was as suddenly transformed back to his more normal personality.

"I'm sorry, Captain," he gulped with a miserable whine. "It just slipped out of me, sir. I mean . . . well, I just wonder if the Russians are down there at all, sir."

It took Finlander a few seconds before he got enough of a grip on himself to be nothing but sarcastic. "You confuse us, Lieutenant. Are they there or aren't they? Please make up your mind."

Spitzer looked as though he were trying to push himself through the bulkhead. "Well, sir . . . there's no readout on any of the gear to suggest they are. But maybe Queffle can *feel* them." There was a touch of sarcasm here too.

Out of the corner of his eye, the captain noticed Queffle cringe. He heard the talker by the plot drone out: "Number-one ASROC reports iced up and on STANDBY-HOLD." He looked away from Spitzer to the Weapons Status Board and saw the light of No. 1 ASROC switch from green to amber. No. 2 was likewise amber, which meant that both launchers were inoperative and the *Bedford* was deprived of her most vital anti-submarine weaponry at this critical time. "We certainly must have BUWEAPS develop effective de-icing gear," Finlander growled. "If we had to make a kill we'd be in a horrible jam right now." He turned back to Spitzer, trying to steady the man with a casual tone. "But all your detecting systems are go, aren't they, Jeff?"

"As far as I can tell, sir."

"So sit down at Central Control and make sure, boy!" Finlander motioned him into the chair he had vacated, then stepped over to check the recording graph of the master fathometer. The needle was just tracing another distinctive hump over the flat bottom as, from the bridge above, Commander Allison accurately conned the *Bedford* to pass over the *Hood* for the sixth time in the last hour. Above the contour of the wreck there was not the slightest shadow to suggest that anything as large as Moby Dick was hanging above it. As improbable as it was that the submarine could have sneaked away without being picked up by any of the detecting gear, the situation certainly had become doubtful. On top of all this uncertainty which Finlander knew was permeating the mind of everybody in the CIC, there had been evidence of conflict between their captain and departmental commander. Morale and efficiency were now held together by a very thin thread. Something had to be done—immediately.

Finlander moved along the row of ECM operators and stopped behind Queffle, who kept his eyes staring at his PPI scope and his hands convulsively pressing the earphones to his head. He was aware of the close presence of his captain, and Finlander felt his muscles knotting tight as he touched the boy's shoulder, making him shy away slightly. "All right, Queffle. You're relieved for a while." There was no reaction, and Finlander suddenly pried the fingers open and pulled the earphones from Queffle's head. "Come on, son! Relax!"

Queffle twisted around in his seat and looked up at Finlander with a desperate expression. "I can pick him up, sir. I know I can pick him up. It's just a matter of concentrating on it awhile longer. Don't yank me off now, sir. Please! Please!" He was pleading like a boy begging his coach to give him a last chance to salvage the impending defeat of his team.

"Ease up, Queffle," Finlander said with surprising gentleness. "You're not even sure he's still down there."

"I d-don't know for sure he *isn't,*" Queffle stammered. "I think he might be. He must be. If only I could concentrate enough."

Ensign Ralston suddenly spoke up loudly from his position at Fire Control and there was something of the same pleading in his voice. "Captain, sir, couldn't we drop a shallow charge? If he thought we weren't kidding, he might be bluffed into making a run for it."

One of the stand-by sonar operators let out an approving growl. Finlander realized with a wave of relief that the morale was not as bad as he had suspected. "That's a good idea, Mr. Ralston," he answered, "but I don't think it would work with this character. He's as smart and tough as they come. We've got to face up to that."

"And give up, sir?" Ralston exclaimed, appalled.

"You know me better than that!" Finlander retorted and suddenly found himself addressing everybody in the CIC. "Moby Dick is as smart and tough as they come among submariners. But we are as smart and tough as they come among submarine hunters. So it's going to be a close call like . . . ." He paused for a moment, thinking back. "Like a game I once played with another smart submariner—Stoltz of the U-1020. It took me fifty-two hours to pin him down and kill him. . . . *Fifty-two hours!*" He paused again and his face seemed to harden with the inspiration of fresh determination as he recalled the action. "I didn't win that one by giving up. I won it by making Stoltz *think* I had given up. All right! I'll show you how it happened!" He was suddenly full of a tense suppressed excitement which he sensed was being communicated to his men. He also sensed that he was irrevocably putting at stake their confidence in him by demanding from them a last ounce of perseverance in this nebulous battle. He was betting against all the evidence of the *Bedford*'s electronic gear, against the wavering extrasensory perception of his own pet magician, Merlin Queffle. He was betting that Moby Dick *was* down there, still hiding in the protective shadow of the hulk of the *Hood,* and that he could fox him. Turning to Spitzer, he ordered: "Secure the maximum-effect sweep! Put your department on stand-by GQ. *Relax!* Have the galley send up sandwiches and coffee for all hands. I'm going up on the bridge to brief Commander Allison on the trap we're going to spring." He hooked his hand under Queffle's arm and pulled him out of the chair.

The Breton Kid resisted with a nearly subordinate violence: "You're not yanking me off, sir!" he protested. "You've got to let me see this through!"

Finlander laughed. "Certainly, Queffle! But I'm not going to throw you into the final play with your senses befuddled by fatigue and tension. Come with me." Steadying the skinny little sonarman against a violent gyration of the *Bedford,* the captain led him to the door. After it clanged shut behind them, Lieutenant Spitzer leaned back in his seat at Central Control and announced:

"Okay—so it's all systems guarded for stand-by GQ. Reliefs, take over your stations. All others relax like the skipper said."

The order was obeyed, but with an atmosphere of tense expectancy.

# 2.

In the darkness of the wheelhouse Commander Allison was perched on the captain's chair, which had been moved in front of the recorder of the fathometer. Like a blind man probing his way along with an invisible stick, he was navigating back and forth, back and forth, over the wreck of the *Hood* by watching the trace of the bottom contour on the graph while calling out changes of course to the helmsman. Lieutenant Petersen, the OOD, was standing next to the gyro-compass, checking every move of the wheel. Ensign Whitaker, the JOOD, leaned heavily on the annunciator, listening with unflagging concentration for the frequent engine-room orders. Next to the quartermaster and talker, two bridge lookouts huddled by the heater, thawing themselves out after being relieved from an agonizing twenty-minute watch on the snow-lashed bridge. Only Commander Allison's and the helmsman's faces stood out clearly in the gloom, illuminated by the instruments before them; all others were only vaguely visible as blacker shapes in the surrounding blackness.

Merlin Queffle came up through the shaft, being pushed along by Captain Finlander and securely held by his possessive grip. They stopped by Commander Allison, and the captain exclaimed: "You are doing a terrific job of navigating off the bottom, Buck."

Allison flipped his head away from the fathometer as though he had been awakened out of a trance. "Hello, Captain. Well, sir . . . it's pretty flat down there and the *Hood* stands out like a sore thumb. We've got our drift down pat, so it's only a matter of establishing a fixed pattern of maneuvers." His eyes moved to Queffle, noticing the sonarman's hangdog look. "What's the score in CIC? Still lost contact?"

"He's down there, all right," Finlander answered, sounding absolutely confident. "But we're going to change our tactics. Turn over the conn to your OOD and come into the navigation office, Buck. I'll tell you what we're about to pull."

Finlander had not released his grip on Queffle and he now guided him into the navigation office and through it into his day cabin. There he found Ben Munceford curled up on the bunk, fast asleep. Unceremoniously he shook him awake. "Heave out, Munceford! If you're going to sack out through this action, do it in your own cabin!" As the bunk was vacated by the sleepily startled correspondent, the captain gently shoved the Breton Kid down on it. "Now you lie down and relax your nerves, son," he said. "Just let your mind go blank for a while. I'm going to send to the galley for your favorite drink and sandwich. What would you like?"

"Gee—nothing, I guess, sir," Queffle mumbled. "I think I feel kind of sick."

"Okay. I'll fix you up." Pushing Munceford out of the way, he went to the telephone attached to the bulkhead and dialed the ship's hospital. Lieutenant Commander Porter's weary voice answered the call. "Doc! I want some brandy to the bridge on the double. Bring it yourself and whatever is necessary to put an exhausted man back in shape for another couple of hours." Before the surgeon could ask him for any details, Finlander hung up on him and dialed the galley. "This is the captain speaking. Send a messman up to my day cabin with a peanut-butter-and-jelly sandwich and a thick chocolate malted. On the double." When he turned from the phone, he saw Munceford standing over the bunk, staring down at Queffle, who was lying there with his hands over his face. "Get out of here, Munceford. From now on, make yourself as scarce as possible."

Munceford shrugged and almost fell out of the cabin, propelled by a deep pitch of the destroyer. Finlander sat down on the edge of the bunk and put his hand on Queffle's chest, trying to belay its heaving. "Listen to me, boy," he said in a tone which was gruffly soothing. "I know how you feel. I know you think you've failed us. But that is not true at all. Talents like yours don't just suddenly evaporate. They may become dulled by tension and fatigue, but never simply vanish into nothing. So I want you to know I'm still convinced you're the best sonarman in the whole navy. I'm going to give you a chance to prove it in a little while and have no doubts that you'll come through. Okay, Merlin? Are you with me?"

The hands fell away from the gaunt face and there was a look of wonderment in those bloodshot eyes. "You're the best captain in the navy, sir," the Breton Kid whispered.

Finlander's forehead wrinkled into lines of embarrassment above the thistly brows. "I can be no better than my boys," he answered, gave him a reassuring pat on the shoulder, then quickly left the cabin.

Commander Allison was waiting by the chart table in the navigation office, his eyes watching the gyro-repeater above it, his fingers absently twirling a pair of dividers. When the captain joined him, he turned and looked at him with a calm expectancy. "Something wrong with Queffle, sir?"

"The boy's worn out. But we've got to have him back in shape within an hour. Porter is coming up to nurse him for a while. Here's what I want done. . . ." The captain leaned on the table and began to sub-consciously sketch out the maneuver with a pencil as he spoke. "Belay jogging over the *Hood*. Turn into the seas and leave the area at flank speed. Pick a course so that when we eventually turn around, we will be able to drift back to this exact spot with a minimum of engine ma-neuvers or noise. I want Moby Dick to think we've picked up a false contact and rushed off to investigate it. Or, better still, that we have given up. Let's get at least ten miles away before we sneak back on him. To confuse his sonar even more, have the engine room gradually reduce the revolutions as we draw away. I have ordered CIC to guard on pas-sive so they won't hear our pings. . . . Any comments, Buck?"

Allison looked thoughtfully at the sketch which Finlander had traced on the chart. "Do you think the Russian commander will fall for such a simple old trick, sir?" he asked.

"The simple old tricks sometimes are the undoing of men who have grown too complex in their thinking. I also am sure he's been under terrific pressure for these past forty-two hours. That, combined with oxygen starvation, may well be clouding his judgment."

Allison nodded and said: "Possibly, sir."

"But the main thing I'm counting on is that you'll be able to make our return run so quietly that he won't pick us up. The sea is still pretty rough, so chances are his sonar is bothered by a lot of surface hash. That will screen us to some extent. Yet if we take a real bad sea ourselves, it could give us away. It's up to you and Engineering to make the sneakiest approach ever pulled. Can you do it?"

Commander Allison nodded again, but there was a tinge of doubt in his demeanor which made Finlander ask: "So what's bothering you about the plan, Buck?"

"It's sound as such, sir," the executive officer answered. "But I am wondering whether we should check it with Commodore Schrepke. A mere formality, but—"

"Where is he?" Finlander impatiently interrupted.

"In his usual place on the starboard wing, sir."

Finlander made a face. "Even in this tactical situation? Well, that cinches it as far as I'm concerned. The man is too brooding and withdrawn to be entirely normal. And I know what's eating away at his insides. He's still a U-boatman—a *defeated* U-boatman who knows he should be among the thirty thousand of his colleagues whose bones litter the floor of this ocean. He feels himself a traitor to them, not because he is working with Americans, but because he's working with destroyermen, the mortal enemy of all submariners. Well, I grant you, traitors can be useful, but not when their professional detachment becomes inhibited by remorse and guilt. I have nothing against Schrepke personally, nor do I not respect his rank, but I say let's leave him out there in his own purgatory and go about our business. . . . Do you agree?"

"We can do without him, sir, especially since he hasn't bothered to make any suggestions," Allison answered.

"Very well. So let's pull out of here, Buck."

Both men were startled by a voice behind them which loudly asked: "Do we stand down from General Quarters, Captain?" It was Lieutenant Commander Porter, who had entered the navigation office unnoticed and was standing there with a first-aid kit slung over one shoulder.

Finlander looked sharply at him. "No, Doc. I don't want the whole ship's complement to feel the fight is over. I want them to stay keyed up."

"They're far *too* keyed up, sir," the surgeon warned with an accusing tone. "Sooner or later, some of them are going to start caving in."

The captain's eyes become smoldering slits beneath the shadowing brows. "Then I'll let you patch them up *after* this action is over, Commander Porter. In the meanwhile you will go into my day cabin and work on Queffle. *Medically*—not with any mollycoddling psychiatric mish-mash, sir. I suggest a shot of brandy to begin with."

The surgeon's haggard pallor flushed into a deep shade of mortification. "Has the captain any other medical advice for me?" he asked.

"I advise you to proceed with extreme care, Commander," came the seething retort.

"Thank you, Captain." Porter sullenly turned away and headed for the day cabin.

Commander Allison watched him go with a troubled expression on his face. "Don't misunderstand my mentioning this, sir," he said to Finlander, "but it's going to look bad for us to have serious trouble with *two* surgeons in a row."

"Our only worry is to accomplish our tactical mission, Buck," Finlander answered, "then everything else will take care of itself. Go ahead and execute the maneuver immediately."

Allison said "Aye, aye, sir," and hurried out of the navigation office.

Finlander remained at the table, looking down on the chart with all the lines of his face compressed into a dark scowl. His eyes were on the penciled outline of his plan, but his mind was momentarily festering on the sore subject of surgeons. If it were not for the fact that his executive officer was absolutely right in his fears, he would signal a request to COMFLANT to have Porter relieved. But that would, of course, bring a fleet inspector along with the replacement. The only answer was to either bend the surgeon into the *Bedford* mold or break him so thoroughly that he would come to doubt his own judgment. At least Porter was nothing more dangerous than a confused naval conformist, not a zealot in the cause of humanity, like Hirschfeld. It was definitely not worth the risk of triggering an upheaval at COMFLANT by requesting his replacement. But the man had to be watched. . . .

Finlander was just turning to go into the day cabin when he was alerted by the sound of a familiar *click* which stopped him in his tracks. Looking in the direction of the crisp little noise, he spotted the lanky shape of Ben Munceford in the dark corner by the chart locker.

"Didn't I make it clear you are to make yourself scarce around here, Munceford?" the captain challenged.

"And I did too," Munceford replied with an insolent grin. "At least I thought I was being as unobtrusive as a mouse caught in an alley cats' convention." As he stepped out of his dark corner and up to the chart table, its light revealed the flash of chrome and plastic in his hands.

"As usual, your humor is shallow and out of place," Finlander said, looking down at the tape recorder and fighting back an intense urge to smash it to the deck. "And to tape a discussion between myself and my officers without our permission is a flagrant breach of trust and ethics."

Munceford managed to keep smiling. "Well, Captain, you know I like to get spontaneous off-the-cuff stuff. It has so much more authenticity than faked set-ups. Besides, why get in an uproar when everything's going to be checked by the PRO at COMFLANT before it's released?"

"It's also going to be checked by the commanding officer of this ship before it gets that far," the captain told him icily. "I think you've gotten all the authenticity you need from my bridge. From now on concentrate your efforts on other parts of the *Bedford*."

"Like maybe CIC?"

"You stay out of CIC!" Finlander shouted with such violence that Munceford shied away from him, his face momentarily flustered with the old childish petulance. The captain instantly recovered control of himself. "I want no diversions down there whatever. Besides, *everything* in CIC is classified, so it's of no pertinence to your assignment. Understand? Good. Now get out." He kept his eyes fixed on the correspondent until he passed through the blackout curtain to the wheelhouse, then turned and went into the day cabin, there to check up on the surgeon's treatment of his prized sonarman.

# 3.

In the *Bedford*'s engine-room flats there was neither gloom nor raw chill. Lights illuminating the huge control panel were bright, glinting off polished steel, enamel and jewel-like splashes of bronze. The air sang with the melodious monotone of the turbines and was warm with a faintly pungent odor of dry steam and lube oil. There was a certain weariness here too, but not of the tense kind prevailing on the bridge or in CIC. Engineers are a special breed whose nervous systems are so finely tuned to the machinery in their charge that nothing on or under the wild ocean outside seems to upset their equilibrium, unless it be combined with an erratic flicker of a needle or a strident ambient noise out of a reduction-gear casing. Like Chief Machinist's Mate Lauchlan S. MacKay, who had been almost continuously on duty since the previous morning, as long as Captain Finlander, the Breton Kid, Commander Allison, Chief Quartermaster Rickmers or Lieutenants Spitzer and Krindlemeyer. He was both as fatigued and as enervated as any of them, but the reaction was a capriciousness strange in such an old hand, manifested by his starting to mix a Scottish burr into his Boston flat *a*'s. He was seated at the throttles, leaning back in his chair while fondling a cup of boiler-room coffee, his feet propped up on the control pedestal, his eyes critically appraising a minute nervous twitch in No. 3 boiler's pressure gauge. Into the account of his and Finlander's action against U-1020, he injected a nonsequitur observation that "these automatic fur'rnaces with their thermostatic controls still don't match a detail of flesh-'n'-blood firemen for keeping an even strrrain on the manifolds."

Lieutenant Commander Sanford Franklin jerked himself upright in the chair next to MacKay and pounced on this opportunity to stem the flow of reminiscences from the chief's engagements with U-1020 . . . 784

. . . 866 . . . and other sanguinary but insignificant naval battles of a bygone war, all of which he knew by heart and did not need to sustain him in this prolonged current contest with Moby Dick. "So why don't you have the thermostats calibrated instead of just sitting there bitching about them, Mac?" he demanded.

MacKay lolled his head to port against the roll of the ship and carefully scratched around the navel of his exposed belly. "That I will after things calm doon. But since it takes physicists to nur'rse the pettyfoggin' ailments of this engine room, one must beware of exposing such lubbers to falling into the machinery, causing worse damage than an anemic transistor."

Commander Franklin winced. "Jesus, Mac. You must be flipping, putting on that phony Scottish accent. I'd better have you relieved and sent up to sick bay to get your psychosis reamed out."

MacKay guffawed, blowing a fine black spray of coffee over his chin. "Hoot, mon, Command'rr! If Lieutenant Hirschfeld was there, I'd willingly go, but . . ." He brought himself up short as the telephone suddenly interrupted him with a ring which loudly jarred above the sound of the turbines. With a flippantly insubordinate gesture, he picked up the receiver and tossed it at the engineering officer, who barely managed to catch it in mid-air.

"Engine-room Control. Commander Franklin."

The executive officer was on the other end of the line, and in a few clipped sentences he outlined Finlander's coming maneuver to outwit Moby Dick and the part Engineering was expected to play in it. "Steam out of here like a locomotive," Allison finished by saying, "and come back as silent as driftwood."

"Aye, aye! And it may work at that!" Commander Franklin swiveled around in his chair and threw the phone back at MacKay. "We're about to pull a fake play, Chief. Stand by for flank speed. And you've got about ten minutes to blow tubes and do any other noisy chores needed."

"Chr-rist! It's going to be U-1020 all over!" MacKay exclaimed. Pulling his feet off the console, he threw his cup of coffee into the trash bin, quickly slipped his upper plate out of his mouth and into his shirt pocket and had his hands on the throttles just as the annunciator clanged and switched to ALL AHEAD FLANK. "Hang on, lad! It will be a wild ride!" He shoved the levers smoothly ahead until they touched the emergency gates. From below them the sound of the turbines surged until they reached a frenzied pitch of full power. Franklin looked down there and saw a machinist grab a handhold to keep himself from falling as the propellers bit savagely into the sea and sucked down the stern before thrusting the *Bedford* ahead. Her bow butted solidly into a huge swell which sent a shudder through the ship as she began heeling hard over in a turn. The machinist hung there for dear life, momentarily completely off balance, his face peering up in alarm at the engineering officer. Then he grinned, shook his head and recovered himself.

In the galley the chief cook also grabbed for a handhold, this one on the stove, where he had taken a chance on frying thirty pounds of pork sausage for breakfast. The turbines were three decks down and beyond nine watertight compartments, but he could feel their sudden surge of power through the soles of his shoes. Even as he glanced over his shoulder toward the VIOLENT MANEUVER light, it flashed from amber to red. As the destroyer leaped ahead, smashed through the big swell and heeled steeply, he helplessly watched the hot grease flow off the griddle into the trap, then slosh over it and run onto the tile deck. A hundred sausages rolled and butted against one another like a stampeding herd of little fat pigs; a half-dozen jumped the guard rail and splashed into the spreading puddle of grease. The chief cook swore and yelled: "Belay hot breakfast!" The assistant cook echoed his curse and began pulling himself hand over hand along the steam table to help scoop the sausages into a pan. But as he jumped across to the stove, he slipped in the grease and hit the deck hard.

The chief cook waited for ten seconds until the *Bedford* began straightening up on her keel, then let go of the stove handhold and crouched down by his assistant, who was looking foolishly at his arm. It was broken.

"Lie down flat, Andy, and press it to your chest so it don't hit nothing else," he said, all his anger changed to sympathetic concern. Then he clawed his way over to the opposite bulkhead, reached for the telephone and dialed sick bay. "A corpsman to the galley! We got a casualty!"

In the Communications Center, Lieutenant Peter Packer had just taken a routine HUFF-DUFF bearing on a transmission from the *Tiburon Bay* when he felt the quickening pulse of the *Bedford*'s engines. His hasty calculation plotted the tanker's position as somewhat less than two hundred miles south-southwest of their own, and it was perhaps natural for him to think that Finlander had decided to break off the preposterous cat-and-mouse game with Moby Dick to speed toward a rendezvous. He looked up at the PA speaker, expecting an announcement to stand down from GQ, but no sound came out of it. Instead there came a bass-drum boom as the destroyer hit a heavy sea, followed by the whoosh of spray flying over her entire superstructure. Packer had to brace himself against the plotting table as the *Bedford* lay over in a violently contested accelerating turn. A glance at the gyro-repeater would have told him that she was *not* turning toward the *Tiburon Bay,* rather away from her, pointing her plunging bow northeast toward the desolate blackness of the Denmark Strait. But once he sensed that the endless jogging over the wreck of the *Hood* had definitely come to an end, he suddenly could think of nothing except that the only brief closeness to his father which he had known in his whole life was likewise ending. With each turn of the thundering screws, they were torn farther and farther apart, the schism of death's oblivion once again widening between them—most likely, this time forever!

Lieutenant Packer tore off the earphones and rushed into the radio room, where he grabbed the dozing Lieutenant Beeker and shook him awake. "Look here, Beek! Cover for me a few minutes. I absolutely have to go out on deck."

Beeker blinked at him. "What's the matter, Peterpacker? You going to puke after standing everything this long?"

"No, damn it! I've got to go out for a while, that's all. Do you mind?" He yelled it out with such vehemence that all three radio operators turned from their sets and stared at him.

Beeker shot himself erect in his chair with a startled expression. "Well, okay, Packer. Go ahead!" the communicator exclaimed. But his permission was entirely superfluous, as the British officer was already halfway to the door. He yanked his parka off its hook and, while still struggling into it, vanished through an icy blast and a slam.

A solid wall of snow-filled wind swept down the deck, thrust into Packer's crouched body and propelled it along the heaving, slush-coated plates. Blotches of spume rushed past the *Bedford*'s flanks, flaring a ghostly white before fading back into the absolute night; the diffused blue halos of the battle lights on the main yard performed wild gyrations against the black void of the sky. Particles of ice were wrenched loose from the mast and came clattering down, an occasional larger icicle hitting the deck with a resounding clang. The blower intakes roared angrily as they gulped huge quantities of air for the *Bedford*'s throbbing boiler rooms, and in an eery falsetto accompaniment the halyards and radar antennas began to wail in the slipstream. But Lieutenant Packer noticed none of these things. For a wild moment he was skidding along without moving his feet, miraculously missing the cleats and hose connections which cluttered the deck. Somehow he hooked an arm around a davit of the whaleboat and pivoted around it, changing his course to right angles. A stanchion on the edge of the deck burned his gloveless hands with a searing cold, but kept him from pitching over the side. He hung there, leaning far out, staring into the thirty-knot wash, and beyond it through the calming blackness of the deep into two hundred and ten fathoms of eternity. While the snow lashed his face with squalls of stinging ice needles, he felt a wordless prayer for his unknown father, the *Hood* and all the lost souls calling to him from her algid hulk.

In the starboard wing of the bridge, another man was staring down into the black rushing sea. Commodore Schrepke had been there since leaving the CIC a little after 0300, occasionally fighting the terrible cold by pacing a few steps while slapping his arms across his chest and cracking off the snow freezing to his leather jacket, but mostly crouched by the windscreen and following the battle between the *Bedford* and the Russian submarine without any benefit of fathometers or sonar. In his mind there was a built-in sensory system which not only kept track of the destroyer's seemingly aimless jogging over the black surface, but was also in almost tangible communication with the craft hiding in the blacker deep beneath it. He had done so many times what those submariners were doing now that he could live and feel every moment of every man, bridging the years since he had experienced the same thing as if they had never existed. Perhaps there was a German among the Russians down there. An old U-boatman like himself, and like himself serving in a foreign naval vessel, but a Soviet one because fate had presented no choice and he had finally thrown over any scruples and capitulated to a pitiless destiny. Perhaps it even was one of his own boys, like Raschnau or Manteufel, both of whom had vanished into the faceless maw of Soviet forced labor. Perhaps. Only one thing he knew for certain, and that was that there were no Communists or Nazis or Democrats, Easterners or Westerners or international agnostics hiding down there in the sepulchral sanctuary of the dead British battle cruiser. Only humanoids reduced to the ultimate equality of stark terror, each fighting his own loneliness and desperately binding up his own bowels and backbone with a last thin thread of discipline while listening to the sounds of the hated destroyer's relentless stalking overhead.

When Schrepke felt the *Bedford*'s engines surge with a burst of power and a sudden squall of stinging cold spray whipped over the bridge as she leaped ahead, his heart jumped with relief in his chest, probably in unison with the heart of the Russian commander of Moby Dick. Just as *he* would, he found himself muttering a fervent prayer that the destroyer was breaking off the action and steaming away. But he quickly sensed that there was another, more sinister purpose in the maneuver. The *Bedford* was accelerating and turning, moving on through the range of speed of a normal withdrawal in these sea conditions, failing to pick up the southerly heading which the commodore knew to be her base course, instead coming around until her bow pointed directly into the swells and starting to hurdle them like a greyhound in a steeplechase. Finlander was turning north, and there could be no reason for this except *one*. Schrepke remained where he was for several minutes, staring over the side while enduring the freezing, brine-filled wind, trying to divine whether or not the Russian commander was suspecting the trap being laid for him. Then he turned and rocked toward the wheelhouse.

Lieutenant Commander Porter was genuinely shocked when Commodore Schrepke suddenly appeared in the door of the day cabin, looking in at him, Finlander and Queffle, who was eagerly draining the last of his malted milk. The German was almost solidly caked with frozen slush, his face blotched, his eyes swollen. "My God, sir!" the surgeon exclaimed. "You're badly frostbitten!"

Schrepke stuck the fingers of his right hand in his mouth and pulled off the glove with his teeth, then forced open the stiff folds of his leather jacket. Bits of ice fell from his muffler and made brittle sounds as they hit the deck. "I am all right, Doctor," he said with a smile which looked as though it too should break loose crusts of ice. "But perhaps you will prescribe something warming, no?"

Finlander stared at him with a tinge of shock. "Give him one on the house, Commander," he ordered the surgeon.

"Thank you," Schrepke said. "I will take it in a hot cup of coffee." He remained in the door, bracing himself there against the now bone-rattling pitches of the racing destroyer. His eyes were on the sonarman seated on the bunk, and a look of doubt came to his face, as if seeing Queffle there might make a difference in his evaluation of the situation. "Is your young magician being rewarded for a completed performance, or is he being primed for a grand finale of his black art?" If there was sarcasm in the question, it was not directed at the boy who stared back at him, uncomprehending.

"Queffle is resting," Finlander answered guardedly, "and recuperating after over twenty-four hours of intermittent duty."

"And while he is resting, you are utilizing that time to give the submarine the impression you are departing. Right, Captain?"

"Right, Commodore."

Schrepke nodded, all doubt gone from his face. "Will you please step into the chartroom with me, Captain," he said and abruptly turned from the door, going in there himself without waiting for an answer. He had spoken to Finlander as a superior officer to a subordinate.

Lieutenant Commander Porter was leaning over the small desk, trying to aim a splash of brandy into the sloshing cup of coffee he had poured out of the Thermos jug. He immediately sensed an electrifying tension after the German had spoken, most of it emanating from Captain Finlander, who hesitated for a long moment before following him out of the cabin. Merlin Queffle must have felt it too, because he exclaimed in a nervous whisper: "Geez, Commander! Is he going to chew the skipper over *me?*"

"No, Queffle. Of course not."

"Then what, sir?"

"Nothing that's your business."

For a moment the surgeon wondered whether it was *his* business either, but he was itching to hear the exchange between the captain and the commodore, and, after all, he had an excuse since Schrepke had requested the spiked coffee. So he steeled himself and went after them.

The two men were standing in the pool of red light by the chart table. ". . . and I would appreciate to know exactly what your tactical objective is in continuing the action, Captain," Commodore Schrepke was saying, his guttural English containing a steely Prussian edge.

"I believe you know it perfectly well, sir," Finlander answered him. "To force the Russian to the surface."

"You had him surfaced yesterday, Captain, but forced him down again."

Finlander smiled. "He was not ripe then, Commodore. I am not playing games. My purpose is to so exhaust him and shatter his morale that he will be unable to accomplish the purpose of his trespass on this side of the ocean."

Schrepke noticed the surgeon and reached out for the cup of coffee in his hand, waited a couple of seconds for the *Bedford* to shake herself free of a huge sea, then took a deep gulp of the brew. "In my judgment, these harassment tactics have gone too far and should be terminated immediately," he bluntly told Finlander after recovering from the invigorating pain of the drink.

Finlander shook his head adamantly. "I will break off when it is firmly established in the minds of both my own and the Russian's crew that I'm doing so only on my terms."

Schrepke rolled the cup in his hands, warming his numb fingers with its heat. "How do you know what is in the minds of the Russian crew, Captain? By the electronic phantasmagorias in CIC? Surely not, when they so often short-circuit themselves on their own complexity or are so oversensitive as to become alarmed over a bed of shrimp. Or do you count on the mystic powers of young Queffle? Of course not! You know as well as I do that his only true talent is an accidentally high acuity of hearing. Between those ears there is nothing more formidable than a quite ordinary brain belonging to a confused boy. But if you want to believe in any kind of extrasensory perception, then believe in *mine*. Yes, Captain—*I* have been in that submarine ever since you started chasing it two days ago. I can tell you her captain and crew are now reduced to such a state of desperation that they may no longer act in any way except as animals fighting for survival. I can tell you this because it has happened to me in submarines, so you see there is nothing really mystical about my powers either. I merely remember and put myself in their place."

Finlander had listened with his huge head cocked to one side, his eyes burning behind their network of tired wrinkles, the scar on his throat throbbing. Lieutenant Commander Porter could feel the tremendous pressure building up in the man and wondered whether he was about to finally lose his temper with the one person aboard who was immune to his powers. But the explosion was delayed and something like a smile came to Finlander's lips as he asked: "Is that what you do when you seclude yourself in the wing of my bridge, Commodore? Commune with your old U-boat comrades?"

"In a way, that is my purpose here, Captain, is it not? And I am now giving you the benefit of my findings. Stop this madness before one or the other is driven to precipitate a fatal tragedy."

Finlander appeared to flinch slightly at the word "madness," but his head rocked in one firm negative motion. "I am sorry, sir. I can't break off yet. And for your information, it isn't a question of one or *the other*. Everything is firmly in control aboard *my* ship."

Lieutenant Commander Porter shocked himself by suddenly blurting out: "I respectfully disagree, Captain, sir" and brought upon himself the explosion he had expected to be directed against the German officer.

"Damn you, Porter!" Finlander shouted, his face a livid mask as he wheeled on the surgeon. "Who invited you to partake in this discussion? Get out!"

As if she were echoing her commander's fury, the *Bedford* slammed into a wave and leaped through a hurricane of spray before wildly pitching into the next trough. Porter collided heavily with Schrepke, who had to steady him and then kept a surprisingly hard grip on his arm after the destroyer recovered herself. The surgeon wanted to flee the bridge and Finlander's wrath, but found himself held back by the German.

"Please stay," Schrepke said with a commanding insistence. "I do believe a medical opinion may be in order here."

"What are you insinuating, sir?" Finlander yelled, his voice ringing above the roar of the destroyer's thrusting through the sea. His eyes were no longer slits, but wide and bulging; the wiry eyebrows no longer formed a solid bristle across the bridge of his nose, but had broken adrift among the anguished furrows of his forehead. Lieutenant Commander Porter yanked himself free of Schrepke's grip and recoiled backward. This, then, was the explosion he had feared, but far more horrible than he had ever dreamed. "What sort of medical opinion?" the captain screamed, completely beside himself. "Out with it! You want to throw a bunch of catch-all psychiatric accusations at me you've picked up from Hirschfeld? All right! But spit them out right here and now. Say I've brainwashed my crew and turned them into a bunch of schizos. Then tell *them* and let them laugh you off my ship."

Commodore Schrepke bent away from the blast slightly, but countered in a coolly controlled voice: "I was going to say nothing more than that they are, in their own way, as overwrought as the crew of the submarine, and as liable to make fatal mistakes in this dangerous game." He turned to the stunned surgeon and calmly asked: "Do you not agree with me, Doctor?"

"Go ahead—*Doctor!*" Finlander viciously shouted. "I *dare* you to agree with him!"

Lieutenant Commander Chester Porter suddenly found himself the focal point of the stares of both men, the captain's eyes wild and fearfully threatening, the commodore's gimlets of blue ice which seemed to be penetrating to his soul. He felt a confusion of fear, indecision and bitter frustration welling up inside him, but of the three, fear was predominant. And when he noticed that a fourth man, Commander Allison, had come into the navigation office and was also watching him intently, fear submerged all other feeling. His mouth opened and closed fitfully without a sound coming out of it, the ineffectual silence lasting for a mortifying eternity until the executive officer bailed him out of it.

"Sick bay has just reported a casualty, Commander," he announced. "A broken bone needing your immediate attention."

While the surgeon hesitated a moment longer, Finlander's hand shot out and seized Allison's arm. "I will at least get a straight answer out of you, Buck!" he shouted. "Tell me if this operation has been conducted in an irresponsible, overzealous—in fact, *mad*—fashion."

Allison looked into the face of his captain, then turned his head toward Commodore Schrepke. There came a suggestion of a wrinkling of his beaked nose. There also came one of his rare smiles, but it seemed only to creep up one side of his face, leaving it with an expression of half amused contempt, half sullen truculence. "Maybe so, Captain," he slowly answered, "but only to a frightened submariner."

Finlander let out a single, gleeful "Ha!"

Schrepke shook his head and blinked his eyes as if he disbelieved what he had heard. "I asked a question of Commander Porter," he persisted, "and expect an answer from him."

But the surgeon had been edging away from the chart table and now seized his chance to escape. "Begging your pardon, Commodore," he hastily pleaded, "it seems I'm urgently needed in sick bay." He lunged toward the door, staggering like a whipped drunkard as the *Bedford* violently heaved and shuddered under his feet. His arms flailed at the blackout curtain and in a moment he had clawed his way through it and was gone.

With the surgeon's retreat, all the fury drained out of Captain Finlander and he regained control of himself as suddenly as he had lost it. There was even a gleam of triumph in his eyes as he stared toward the still swirling folds of the curtain. He knew now that he would not have to request the relief of his medical officer. He knew that Bucky Allison was firmly standing by him. Changing his hard grip on his exec's arm to a slap on the shoulder, he told him: "She seems to be working pretty hard, Buck. Have Engineering start easing off the revs before we get any more broken bones aboard. I doubt if our doctor is in shape for a lot of surgery this morning." When he found himself alone with the German officer, he managed a thin smile and said: "I am sorry I lost my temper, sir. It was foolish of me and really quite unnecessary to prove my point."

The malice in the apology did not go unnoticed by Commodore Schrepke, but he was still looking down at the empty spot on the deck where Lieutenant Commander Porter had stood swaying uncertainly a few moments before. He sighed deeply and a shadow of bitter irony briefly animated the inscrutable hardness of his face. "I have at least found out," he said, "that we Germans are not the only ones guilty of breeding submissive militarists."

Having demolished Porter, Finlander had enough resurgence of confidence to press home his advantage over the German officer. "With all due respect, Commodore, I suggest your guilt is rather one of having survived defeat," he answered, deliberately twisting the knife.

Schrepke stiffened almost imperceptibly, then shook his head as if all this had been an unpleasant but irrelevant deviation from the main issue. The unfamiliar commanding tone returned to his voice as he spoke, looking directly into Finlander's eyes. "I must act in this situation according to my responsibilities as senior NATO officer aboard—"

"And I will act upon it according to the prerogatives of the commanding officer of a United States naval vessel," Finlander loudly injected. "In my judgment, it would prejudice the interests of my service to break off the action at this time. That is final, sir!"

"In that case I wish to officially go on record as being opposed to that judgment, Captain."

"That is your privilege, sir. Anything else?"

"Yes—I want you to understand I intend to communicate my opposition to Admiral Sorensen at NATONAV 1."

"That too is your privilege, Commodore," Finlander answered dryly, "but I strongly advise you to await the outcome before putting yourself on record in one way or the other. It would make you look foolish to have tried to stop an action which resulted in thwarting the Soviet navy's most notorious intruder operation."

"Regardless of the outcome, Captain, you have run the most appalling risks for very dubious objectives," Schrepke retorted. He drained his now cold cup of coffee, then began zipping up his leather jacket. "However, since I am unable to make you understand that, let's terminate a useless argument."

As the German moved to leave, Finlander blocked his way, suddenly switching to a manner of patronizing familiarity.

"Look here, Wolfgang. Our relationship has been good on this patrol. Believe me, I do respect you as a man and naval officer. It is very painful to me that this respect is not mutual."

"But it is, Erik," Schrepke replied without a trace of geniality. "You have my respect. But it is the respect of fear. Frankly, your executive officer was right . . . you *frighten* me." He touched the visor of his cap, side-stepped Finlander and walked out of the chartroom.

The captain followed him with a frown containing both satisfaction and perplexity. He stopped a few steps inside the blacked-out wheelhouse, listening to the door of the bridge open and close, feeling the chilling blast of wind which Schrepke had let in from the night as he left. Then he cautiously moved across the heaving deck, checked the compass over the helmsman's rocking shoulders and joined Commander Allison, who was intently studying the dimly illuminated face of the automatic course recorder.

"I see you've sent our frightened U-boat veteran back to his hermit ledge," the exec said without taking his eyes from the instrument.

"Don't kid yourself, Buck," Finlander answered him testily. "Wolfgang Schrepke isn't frightened of anything in this world."

# 4.

The *Bedford*'s captain and executive officer both assumed that the German had returned to his secluded spot on the bridge, there to brood in loneliness over his ineffectual attempt to divert the course of events. But this was a mistaken assumption. He was actually on his way to the Communications Center. Heading there via an exterior companionway and the narrow deck below the bridge, pulling himself along, stanchion to stanchion, through the turbulent blackness. When he had said that he intended to protest the operation to NATONAV 1 and Admiral Sorensen, he had not meant it would be done only in due course after the patrol was completed, although there was some malice aforethought in leaving that impression. He intended to do it *immediately* and in spite of the radio silence imposed by Finlander during the action against Moby Dick. To accomplish this he was counting on two factors: finding Lieutenant Packer, NATO liaison officer for communications, on duty, and by convincing the Englishman of the urgency of transmitting the signal forthwith. Finlander had a right to impose radio silence on his ship, but not at the expense of severing the senior naval officer aboard from contact with his Fleet Headquarters. So there certainly was justification in attempting to circumvent the captain's authority in this matter. And as he pressed on against the lashing wind, Schrepke also thought that he must break Finlander's hegemony over the minds of his crew. He had to find at least one officer—and one with more backbone than the surgeon—to back him up in his attempt to forestall what might become a tragedy; at least find one to give him some moral support so he would not be so damnably much the despised lone German. Of all the men aboard this blighted ship, Lieutenant Peter Packer was his only hope.

Schrepke found the starboard entrance to the Communications Center to be securely dogged, so he had to continue where the deck bent around the forward funnel and turned into nothing more than a catwalk which crossed thwartship to the port side. Whirlwinds whipped around the tall moaning stack and had built a drift of snow which tripped his boots in its cold softness; as the destroyer lurched, he fell and almost rolled between the icicled lifelines to the main deck, invisible in the blackness far below him. But as he lay there for a moment, trying to catch his breath and clear his nostrils of the flying snowflakes, his eyes made out the ominous shape of the ASROC missile poised in its launcher, it dark shadow rising from the void, its green-painted warhead strangely luminous, like a cyclops' eye staring out of a cavern. Dimly he made out a figure clambering on the launcher itself, flailing with what appeared to be an ordinary broom at the frozen spume clogging the steel tracks.

*"Das is doch wahnsinn!"* Schrepke yelled in a sudden outburst of pure anguish. But although the man could not have been more than ten feet below and beyond the catwalk, he did not hear the cry, which was torn away by the wind and drowned in the roar of the sea.

Schrepke staggered to his feet, half slid along the grating where it changed from snow to ice, reached the port deck and turned to fight his way back toward the Communications Center. But as he passed the whaleboat davit, a huge wall of spray erupted out of the wash, and in the instant before it blew away he saw silhouetted against it a man slumped over the wire lifeline. It was only a fleeting glimpse, but it stopped him because he had recognized Lieutenant Packer.

"What in God's name are you doing out here?" the commodore shouted with genuine shock as he pulled himself alongside the Englishman. "Are you sick?"

Packer straightened up with a start, peered into Schrepke's face, then hunched back onto the lifeline. "Yes, I'm sick, Commodore Schrepke," he answered bitterly. "Sick at heart." His eyes returned to the black rush of sea hissing against the hull.

Schrepke felt a sudden surge of hope. Was this young lieutenant suffering from the same forebodings as himself? "Then you should do something about it," he shouted over the wind and put a hand on his shoulder. "Maybe we should *both* do something about it, eh?"

Packer twisted away from his touch and faced him again. Although it was too dark to see the expression on his face, the vehemence in his voice told Schrepke it would not be a friendly one. "I only want one thing from you, sir. Just one thing, that's all. Tell me if you had anything to do with sinking the *Hood.* Did you?"

Schrepke was completely taken aback by the question. "The *Hood?* . . . She was sunk by the *Bismarck,* a battleship. I served in U-boats. What do you—"

"Did your U-boat have any part of the action, sir?" Packer interrupted him with a nearly savage insistence.

Schrepke edged in closer, trying to get an impression of his eyes. "My boat was at sea under orders to intercept British units but . . . I was several hundred miles away when the *Hood* blew up." His tone sharpened as he recovered from his surprise. "Why do you ask me this, Lieutenant? You were nothing but a boy when that happened."

"Nothing but a boy," Packer echoed his words. "An orphan boy. My father died in the *Hood*."

Schrepke suddenly understood why the young officer was out here alone with the sea and raised his gloved hand to touch his shoulder again, but Packer recoiled from him and he was left with his arm raised as if to strike a blow rather than make a gesture of sympathy. He felt the return of the empty loneliness inside him and it seemed to freeze and harden his whole being. "I am sorry," was all he managed to blurt out and he knew how callous it sounded with his harsh German accent. "It does no good to grieve about it now. Not even when we pass over the grave of your father's ship, it does no good."

"It does good to know whom to hate," Packer shouted at him. "I was thinking that maybe I should hate you, sir. Like I hate that god-damned bloody submarine down there, defiling the *Hood* with her filthy presence. I wish Captain Finlander would sink it and to hell with this play-acting. We're all going to try to kill each other soon anyway, so why not now? Why not get down to some serious hating and killing right now?" He turned away and stared off into the night, expecting and getting no answer. But as the silence between them became prolonged, the lieutenant's turbulent feelings slowly abated and deeply ingrained discipline began regaining control. He suddenly became aware of how rudely he had addressed an officer who would have been an admiral in his own navy. With a frantic apology on his lips he wheeled around and was startled to find himself alone. Commodore Schrepke was gone. Even when he lunged away from the lifeline, peering hard through the flying snow, he could see no trace of him. "Oh, God!" he muttered miserably to himself. "I've made a damned fool of myself! I'll have to apologize tomorrow."

# 5.

Ben Munceford had left the bridge and gone out on the main deck to chill his burning anger after the clash with Captain Finlander. He had stood alone in the dark, sheltered from the snow and spume by an ice-coated life raft, hooking one arm through its lashing and hanging on, hating the *Bedford* and her captain. But he had not been there more than a few minutes when the destroyer's wild burst of speed through the swells brought floods of freezing water rushing down the deck. Over the roar of the wake he heard the metallic clang of doors being closed and dogged. He barely managed to splash through a torrent and escape back inside. A seaman slammed the door on his heels without as much as a glance at him, then vanished. Moving with a kind of listless uncertainty, bouncing from bulkhead to bulkhead as the ship pounded from crest to trough, he struggled along the passageway, gravitating toward the wardroom because hunger was gnawing among the other unpleasant feelings in his insides. The wardroom had been converted into an emergency first-aid station during the GQ, but the corpsmen had been returned to mess duties in an effort to get out a hot meal for the rest of the crew. Nobody was there.

Munceford found only some cold dregs in the coffee Thermos, but in a tray there were sandwiches left over from last night's dry chow. Ham and cheese on unbuttered bread, curling and turning stale around the edges. He took one, pushed aside the stacked litters, slumped down at a table and began eating, making a grimace over the crumbly sour taste. On the second bite he gagged and gave up, concentrating his thoughts on the events which were confusing and upsetting his mind so much. Shoving the sandwich aside, he took the tape recorder out of its case, placed it in front of him, switched it on and rewound the tape. Then he pressed the playback button and put his ear down against the tiny speaker.

Out of the plastic box came the voices of Finlander and Allison, thin and weirdly hollow, and sometimes nearly smothered by the rumble of distorted background noises of the *Bedford*'s rolling and heaving. It was a terrible recording, one which no technical director of a broadcasting station would pass as airworthy, yet it was intelligible and to Munceford contained an elusive importance which he could sense but not fully understand. He listened with his eyes closed to the discussion of the plan to lure Moby Dick to the surface, to Finlander's judgment against Commodore Schrepke, to his cutting interchange with Lieutenant Commander Porter. When it was over, he rolled it back and played it through again. This time he found himself no longer thinking of it as show material, but as part of a case to be presented in a court-martial. *As evidence.*

Evidence of what? Were matters aboard the *Bedford* really building toward a court-martial? Was the hounding of Moby Dick finally transgressing the accepted conduct of a cold war? Was the mounting irritation between Finlander and the surgeon building toward a serious clash—like the one he had had with Hirschfeld? There were intimations of these possibilities on the tape, but still nothing concrete or outright damning. It was the tone rather than the words. Somehow all the tense feeling of foredoomed predatory purpose which permeated this ship seeped between the lines transcribed on the acetate ribbon—or was that feeling entirely in his own mind? And if it was, was it an accurate one? While listening to the tape for the third time, he began to toy with the idea of preventing Finlander from confiscating it, of somehow smuggling it off the *Bedford*. He suddenly realized that he needed *more* material like this, either sneaked recordings or comments from somebody aboard whom he could get to really speak out.

Munceford stopped the recorder and sat there staring down at it, his thoughts vacillating from conviction to doubt, from moral principle to crass indifference. Why meddle? Was he supposed to be one of those egghead correspondents who "report in depth"? Finlander himself had made it perfectly clear that he was here because he was nothing but a hack who would not probe too deeply, yet give the illusion that everything was aboveboard in the *Bedford*'s private cold war. All right! Why not play ball? Maybe Finlander would finally and dramatically force Moby Dick to surface in broad daylight and he would be able to get some good shots of the Russian submarine. That would undoubtedly be worth a thousand-dollar bonus from any TV network. No questions would be asked about the circumstances. If the whole story was presented from the point of view of the brave, dedicated American naval officer maintaining a vigil in the cruel arctic, inspiring his valiant crew to endure all the hardships of the patrol, then Captain Finlander would come out of it all smelling like a budding vice-admiral. Ben Munceford would become bona-fide, star-spangled, ass-kissing naval correspondent. His hands fondled the ERASE button on the recorder . . . but he did not press it. For no other clear reason than perhaps sheer contrariness or the fascination of toying with a potentially dangerous course, he pushed the one marked RECORD, palmed the microphone and softly spoke into it:

"As you have heard from the talk on the *Bedford*'s bridge, strange things are going on aboard this ship. Even as the captain and the executive officer lay their plans to trap the Russian submarine they call Moby Dick, there are cross-currents of guilt and conflict. It is a detached world of its own, this world of the *Bedford*. A little lost world at war, detached from the rest of the world at peace."

Munceford stopped the tape, rolled it back and listened to himself. What he said sounded trite and melodramatic, but still he did not erase it. Instead he thought to add to his commentary, but the words would not flow and he found himself sitting there with his mouth open, the tape rolling and nothing but the throb of the turbines being recorded. But in spite of his ineptness, this accidentally became a dramatic pause to emphasize the sudden shrill sound of the bosun's pipe as it blasted through the PA speaker on the bulkhead; instinctively he turned the mike toward it.

"This is the captain speaking!" Finlander's voice crackled through, its tone well modulated, yet with just the right touch of intensity. "I know all hands are weary and disgusted right now, and thinking that the efforts of the last two days have been in vain. Maybe some of you even believe that Moby Dick has been deliberately making fools of us and those Commies are laughing as they hear us retreat with nothing but another petty humiliation to heap on the many endured by our country in this cold war. Personally, I doubt it. They have too little clean air left for a good laugh. But if they believe we're running with our tails between our legs, so much the better because it will make them careless. And if *you* believe it, that's all right too, because then it will make you mad enough to stick this out till hell freezes over—which it looks to me like it's about to do outside right now! In any case, I'm turning this ship around in a few minutes and am going to close in on Moby Dick like a cat stalking a dark alley. When our rat decides it's safe to come out of its hole, we'll be there to pounce. Sounds simple enough, but you all know it will mean more hours of silent stalking, of patient waiting, of uncertainty, of doubt. Well, sit tight and, above all, sit silent. I want every man, whether he is guarding a sonar receiver or watching a steam gauge or sweeping snow off a launcher, to listen, concentrate and keep his whole being so alert that this ship will tingle like a living animal of prey about to attack. If the Russians down there suspect our presence at all, let it be because they sense this, and then let's see if they come up laughing!"

The PA circuit clicked off and Munceford kept staring up at the speaker for a long moment while his recorder ran on. Then he turned the microphone in his palm toward his own mouth and said into it: "Yes . . . a lost little world at war, complete with its own God of War who speaks to us from his Olympian tower of gray steel. Must we believe in him?"

"Do *you* believe in him?" a voice broke in with a jarring sneer.

Munceford jumped around in his chair and felt himself flushing scarlet as he saw Commodore Schrepke standing in the doorway, icy brine running off his skin and black leather. He had obviously been there throughout the captain's speech, perhaps longer, watching and listening. Now he stepped into the wardroom, checked the empty Thermos, then turned on Munceford with a look of contempt tinged with sardonic amusement. "Do you believe in him?" he asked again.

"I . . . I don't know," Munceford stammered.

Schrepke moved in on him and stood swaying with the roll of the ship, pawing at the folds of his jacket to reach the flask in his hip pocket. "You don't know?" he repeated, mimicking his uncertain tone. "Then why do you blather such unmitigated nonsense into your machine? You think it something inspirational to go with your pictures of brave sailors and their sturdy man-of-war, no doubt. Something to fertilize the seeds of patriotism among your grubbing burghers at home, eh? So they pay their taxes more willingly and cheer the parades more loudly and listen more devoutly to the bellicose speeches of their politicians, eh? Ah, yes! Otherwise they might forget our cold war out here and become too preoccupied with the hot business of buying for less and selling for more. . . . But if you don't know whether you believe in it, how can you do a proper job?"

"It's just a story, that's all."

"Oh, just a story, eh?" Schrepke retorted and took a quick pull from his flask. After the alcohol had seared his throat, his voice took on a frightening rasping quality. "I have often noticed how you correspondents treat everything just as a story. Stories to be peopled by your own pet goblins, giants, dwarfs, and frogs who are princes, and rich old kings who trade in fairy princesses. Yes, indeed, these are your stories!" He took another drink, then stuffed the flask back into his pocket. "You terrify or inspire or delude your people with these stories, yet you yourself don't know whether you believe in them or not. Does this not strike you as stupid?"

"Well, all right, Commodore! Now that you've finally decided to talk to me, go ahead and give your version of the truth," Munceford urged, edging the microphone toward him. "I represent a free press, you know. All opinions are welcome."

Schrepke suddenly became aware that the recorder was still running and had taken down everything he had just said. His face twitched with a shock of fury, his fist came up, then swung down, crashing into the table as if it were encased in mail instead of leather. But as quickly as he had reacted, Munceford had been quicker, yanking his precious tape recorder out of the way of the smashing blow. "Thank you, sir!" he exclaimed, pressing the instrument protectively against his chest. "Thank you! That was a very eloquent—and a very *German*—expression of opinion."

Schrepke's fist cocked again, but this time he hesitated, although he could doubtless have knocked the correspondent senseless. Then a violent roll, indicating that the *Bedford* was turning, threw him off balance and he suddenly needed both hands to brace himself against the table. As the ship recovered her equilibrium, so did he his temper. "What do you know of German opinion?" he coldly demanded. "Is your knowledge based on the horror stories fed you in the kindergarten of your trade? Concentration camps, U-boats and goose-stepping legions—these are the things which mean Germany to you, not so?"

Munceford had twisted himself out of the chair and sprung toward the door, where he stopped now, poised to escape if the German officer gave any further signs of violence. "Those things seem more on your own mind than anybody else's," he taunted him.

"Indeed they are!" Schrepke answered with a bitter laugh. "And many more like them. Such as trapped men dying in crushed submarines, cities being incinerated in fire storms and defeated armies herded into the victor's barracoons. I could add many details to your horror stories, my poor little unblooded sanguinary war correspondent! All kinds of personally experienced horrors except one—the ultimate nuclear horror which has become the exclusive province of my former enemies and judges! The irony of this escapes you, I'm sure, but it is nevertheless there. Here am I, a German officer born under Kaiser Wilhelm and weaned by Adolf Hitler, yet so inhibited in a game which you Americans and Russians indulge in with all the cruel juvenile relish of children playing at war. . . . Is your machine still recording all this nicely for you? The sounds of a German pouring ashes on his head sells very well, after all!"

Munceford frowned as he fumbled with his tape recorder, his violent evasive action of a few moments ago having temporarily indisposed it. "If the way things are handled on the *Bedford* has you so upset, Commodore, why don't you do something about it?" he asked testily.

Wolfgang Schrepke snatched a sandwich and slumped into the chair vacated by Munceford. There was suddenly a weary resignation in his demeanor as he shrugged off the question. "If you can't make up your mind whether or not you believe in Captain Finlander, then I suggest you interview Commander Porter instead of me. That should confuse your addled brain even more, my friend!" He chuckled and shook his head. "Finlander and Porter! There is a fascinating study in opposing archetypes of your peculiar American military! . . . One the vainglorious, benevolent martinet who despises weakness, yet feeds his own strength upon it, consuming his subordinates like an inspired cannibal; the other, the plodding officer-intellectual who charts his course by rectitude and platitude, horrified by a colleague as ruthless as Finlander, yet attaching himself to him with the loyalty of a barnacle. Another irony over your head, eh? Ah, well . . . *das macht nichts aus!*" He took a bite out of the sandwich and, abruptly dismissing Munceford's presence from his consciousness, sank into a brooding contemplation.

Not even by Finlander himself had Munceford's intelligence been so insulted, yet the old defensive belligerence did not boil up, which indicated that his mind had also been stimulated. In spite of himself, the taciturn commodore had just bared his breast to him, allowing a revealing glimpse of the seething beneath the disciplined exterior. Munceford at least understood that Schrepke would not have done this had he not been in a state of extreme alarm over something. Over his cloistered isolation on this ship? Not likely, since it was largely self-imposed; anyway, that hard character was sufficient unto itself. Then it had to be over this action against Moby Dick! His mind groped with urgent questions he wanted to ask the German, sincere questions, yet he was defeated by the barrier between them. But there could be no sop for his curiosity now. If this man would not satisfy it, then somebody else! *Commander Porter!* Yes, that had been a good suggestion, perhaps more deliberate than facetious. Because they both knew that Porter was the weakest link in Finlander's chain of command.

It was with a quickening realization that time was running out that Munceford shoved his recorder into its case and left the wardroom. The vibrations of the turbines had dropped to a bare tremor and the motion of the *Bedford* eased with a distinct change of rhythm which indicated she had turned her stern to the seas. The final run on Moby Dick had started! He knew he could not change the course of events, but he ran down the passageway as if he could.

The surgeon had finished setting the cook's broken arm and curtly ordered him into sick bay in spite of his eager protestations about being fit for duty. Chief McKinley escorted the disgruntled man out of surgery as he angrily brandished his splinted arm to show it did not bother him at all. Pharmacist Engstrom laughed and said something about "crazy seacooks" as he started cleaning up the debris of plaster and bandages around the operating table; he looked up with surprise when Ben Munceford came bursting through the blackout curtain. "You're too late if you've come to cover our only casualty in this battle," he greeted him.

"Yeah? Well, it doesn't look like it's over yet," Munceford answered. "Maybe more people will get hurt before we're through."

"It'll be those Commie pigboatmen, in that case," Engstrom scoffed.

Lieutenant Commander Porter gave Munceford a hostile look and retreated into the receiving office, there to escape in the paperwork which the navy appended even to simple operations like the one he had just performed. When he saw that Munceford insisted on following him, he snapped: "So what do you want?"

"Listen, Chester. I know we never hit it off, but I'd like to talk to you."

"About what?" the surgeon asked with complete disinterest.

"Well . . . *things*. The *Bedford*. The way this Moby Dick affair is working out. Frankly, I'm confused as hell and need your help."

"What's the matter, Ben?" Porter asked acidly. "Is the hot-shot TV reporter losing his grip?"

"I'm not so hot. I've found that out on this trip."

The surgeon gave him a curious, surprised look, then sighed. "So don't let it get you. Finlander cuts us all down to size sooner or later."

"Yeah. I heard him cut you to yours a while ago."

Porter stiffened and glared stonily down at the top of his desk, but he said nothing.

"All right, don't get sore," Munceford continued. "He polished me off too. And I'm sure he must have raked Commodore Schrepke worse than either of us, because he just blew his top to me a few minutes ago. Became about as human as his iron-assed kind ever can. The point is, Schrepke not only outranks Finlander, but he's got enough experience in this business to be able to tell whether it's being run right or wrong; you've got to hand him that much, no matter what you think of him. It all adds up to something lousing up this well-oiled war machine. *What?*"

The surgeon continued to stare down at the desk. "The captain and commodore did have a disagreement over whether or not to break off this action," he cautiously admitted.

"You heard it?"

"Yes. I was present." A shudder at the recollection loosened his reserve and he added with feeling: "It was the worst blow-up I've ever been involved in on a navy bridge."

"So you were involved. And I get the idea Schrepke expected you to back him up. But you didn't."

Porter tried to cover a flinch by looking up sharply. "I am an *American* naval officer, damn it!"

Munceford slipped the tape recorder out of its case. "Would you like to hear what Schrepke says you are?" he asked. When he received no answer, he put the recorder on the desk, switched it on, rewound the tape a few feet, then played it back. Porter listened silently, the muscles of his jaws twitching beneath the pale skin as the Germanic English rasped at him out of the plastic box.

"*. . . the plodding officer-intellectual who charts his course by rectitude and platitude . . .*"

When Schrepke's voice faded out, Munceford held out the microphone and switched over to RECORD. "Do you have any comment, Commander?" he pointedly asked.

The surgeon stared at the microphone as if it were the head of a cobra. His lips pressed together and his head shook angrily, but there was something like desperation in his eyes.

"Come on!" Munceford wheedled. "Isn't it the opinion of at least two of the better brains aboard that things are being pushed beyond a very dangerous point? That a hell of a lot more is at stake than the pride of an American and a Commie captain? Aren't you one of the *Bedford*'s officers who believe this?"

Porter's lips remained tightly sealed, but his head was suddenly nodding instead of shaking. His body was beginning to sag, as if caving in under the weight of the truth. Munceford pressed in on him, brandishing the microphone in his face. "You *do* believe it! Then say so, for God's sake! I believe it too, so it won't be only you and the German against everybody else on this crazy ship. But we've got to get together on it. We've got to get it on record—okay?" He was about to grab the surgeon by the shoulder and shake him when he was diverted by a sharp voice behind him.

"Shall I heave this character out, sir?" It was Engstrom, standing in the doorway of the receiving office with an angry, perplexed expression on his face.

Ben Munceford straightened up and felt a cold pang of frustration, but he swung the microphone toward him and announced with a sarcastic tone: "Ah, here is Pharmacist's Mate Engstrom, a man who is not so shy about expressing himself. So what is your opinion about this action, Mr. Pharmacist's Mate? Go ahead and tell us!"

"Sure!" Engstrom hissed belligerently, then cut loose a torrent. "I say it's a tough enough deal out here without having some mealy-mouthed civilian trying to put doubts in our minds about it all and making us think it's wrong what we're doing. We're chasing a god-damned Red spy sub on our side of the ocean, and that's good enough for me and ought to be good enough for you besides being god-damned grateful somebody's doing the job for you so you're free to run around and shoot your mouth off—okay, smart guy?"

Munceford's freckles rippled under a grin which was almost genuine.

"Now, there's a loud and simple opinion if I've ever heard one," he exclaimed and turned back to Porter. "It should inspire the commander to put in his own two cents' worth."

"Shall I heave this character out, sir?" Engstrom again asked his CO, this time stepping into the office with his arms flexing for action. There was something pathetically frightening about the skinny, bespectacled boy's ferociousness, and it seemed to jolt the surgeon out of his daze. He reached out and put his hand over the microphone Munceford was pointing at him and said:

"Never mind, Engstrom. I can handle it. You go back to your station." He waited until the pharmacist's mate had reluctantly backed out of the door, then took his hand off the microphone. His haggard face wrinkled into a pained frown of concentration as his lips soundlessly rehearsed the words he was groping for.

Munceford tensed as he waited for him to speak, wondering whether the man was at last ready to muster the courage of his convictions and openly condemn Finlander's vendetta against Moby Dick. It would come too late to influence the immediate events, but at least it would give some real substance to this story. He would no longer be just a hack. "So come on, Commander. You almost got it off your chest a moment ago. So do it now!"

Lieutenant Commander Porter tore his eyes away from the microphone and looked directly into Munceford's face.

"As a doctor," he began, articulating his words carefully, "my doubts and fears over this action are medical. Psychosomatic, really. The crew of this ship are torn by conflicting emotional stresses which far exceed those of any ordinary peacetime patrol. The necessity to savagely and relentlessly exert their power as fighters creates a hate syndrome; their natural revulsion over having to act contrary to deeply ingrained American permissive instincts creates a guilt complex. This is nothing new for Americans at war, of course, only we are *not* at war. The natural release of war's tremendous pressures—*killing*—is denied. Frustration builds and compounds the pressure until it begins to make men unpredictably aggressive, withdrawn, volatile, lethargic . . . in psychiatric terms, they are aggravating latent aberrations without recourse to normal checks and balances. . . ."

"And perfectly capable of losing control of themselves," Munceford eagerly coaxed.

The surgeon shook his head, but only to protest the interruption. "That is my simple diagnosis of this action as an ordinary medical man," he persisted, "but I am also a *navy* doctor and must accept the risks of any given naval situation. Certain degrees of schizophrenia may be among them, and unfortunately the opportunities for group therapy are extremely limited out here. So instead of therapy, we use a man like Finlander to keep things from falling apart."

Munceford frowned and protested: "But surely the four stripes on his sleeve don't make *him* immune to cracking up!"

Porter squirmed in his chair. "I agreed there are risks," he answered with a rising pitch. "I agreed we are under a severe strain. I will even agree that Captain Finlander is taking terrible chances. But then so is the Russian commander; furthermore, he is still down there continuing to take them. And *that* is the whole point and justification of what we are doing. As a naval officer, I refuse to challenge the judgment of my captain. I actually suspect he is made of the same stuff as John Paul Jones and a lot of other patriotic heroes we have been taught to revere in our history. To doubt him would be the same as to doubt them, to reject all the benefits Americans have derived from the aggressive spirit of men like him." His lips pressed together, cutting off the flow of words, and he leaned back with a somewhat melancholy look of smugness.

Ben Munceford blinked and shook his head, then swiched off the recorder. "Well," he sighed, "that was a beautiful speech and I suppose Finlander will be delighted to hear it if he gets his hands on this tape. But I still wonder whether you believe it deep down. You certainly haven't been acting so god-damned inspired lately."

The surgeon squirmed uncomfortably. "I've been scared and . . . I'm still scared. But when the chips are down, Commodore Schrepke cannot make me disloyal to my ship and my captain. Nor can you. Now, if you will excuse me, I've got to fill out a casualty report."

"Okay, Commander. Thanks a bunch. I'm sorry I disturbed you."

After Ben Munceford left him, Lieutenant Commander Porter sat there staring for a long time at the assistant cook's Form 28 without touching his pen to it. For a moment tears brimmed his eyes, but they quickly dried, leaving a stinging little hurt outside and an emptiness inside, as if everything in him had finally dried up.

Munceford stood in the passageway outside the ship's hospital, hesitating as he realized that he really had nowhere to go now. Nowhere that really mattered. He did not want to return to the wardroom in case

Schrepke was still there, so he headed in the opposite direction and found himself at the hatch leading down to Engineering Control. He lifted it open and felt a waft of oily warmth strike his face and squinted against the bright lights reflecting off polished metal gratings. The noises from the engine room were now no more than a tensely suppressed humming. He eased himself through the hatch and went down the ladder.

Lieutenant Commander Franklin and Lieutenant Brubeck were standing at the main panel, looking like scientists in their spotless white coveralls as they checked the multitude of dials and recorders, making notes on complex charts attached to clipboards. They merely accorded Munceford a quick glance when he stepped off the ladder and walked up to them. "So how's the war going down here?" he asked with his old flippant manner returning.

"All systems are go," Brubeck answered shortly. He did not take his eyes from an oscilloscope whose fiery green line was dancing nervously. "The cycling of number-two WP generator has a flutter, sir," he said to Franklin.

The lieutenant commander watched it for a few seconds. "It's within functional limits, but keep checking it."

Munceford moved over to the master control console and sat down in an empty chair next to Chief MacKay, who was crouched over the throttles as if he expected an order from the bridge at any moment. His leathery face was screwed up into a grimace of intense concentration, his eyes glued to the revolution indicators.

"You bearing up under the strain, Chief?" Munceford asked him.

MacKay's head jerked around. "What? Oh, it's you, Mr. Munceford!" The grimace became a grin. "Sure! No sweat at all."

"What are you feeling right now, Mac? A hate syndrome? A guilt complex? Or both mixed together?"

The chief's face went as blank as a piece of rock. "Uh? What was that?"

"I mean, how do you feel about it all? Good or bad?"

"I feel I'm doing my job, and that's good, ain't it?" He looked at Munceford as if he had asked a very foolish question, then remembered his duty and turned back to the rev counters. But he added with a scowl: "I only wish we could take this son-of-a-bitch all the way—like Finlandei and I did on U-1020. But we can't, and that's bad. Too god-damned bad!"

Lieutenant Commander Franklin came up behind Munceford. "Please don't take Chief MacKay's mind off his work, Mr. Munceford. The bridge has asked for hair-trigger reactions on the throttles. . . . May I trouble you for my seat? Thank you."

Munceford quickly got up and moved to the railing which separated Engineering Control from the engine room below. His eyes followed the white shape of Lieutenant Brubeck as he noiselessly scrambled down the series of ladders and scurried along the gratings between the huge turbine casings, then crouched down to nurse some small part of a generator. A machinist joined him and they both knelt before the machinery, their hands waving and motioning as if they were making incantations before an altar.

Munceford hooked one leg around a stanchion of the railing to brace himself against the long, corkscrewing pitches of the *Bedford,* took out his tape recorder and erased everything on the tape.

# 6.

After addressing the crew over the ship's PA, Captain Finlander seated himself in his chair by the wheelhouse window and stared blankly through the glass at the blackness beyond it. He remained there, isolating himself with his own thoughts, until Commander Allison brought the *Bedford* around and set her on a return course for the wreck of the *Hood,* her power reduced so that she was partly surfing down the swells rolling up on her stern, partly loping along under the slow paddling revolutions of her screws. Then he got up and joined his executive officer to watch with him the difficult work of the helmsman.

"Steer like you've never steered in your life," Allison told the seaman at the wheel. "If you feel her getting away from you, don't wait for orders. Catch her before she makes a noisy splash." He knew it was the trickiest kind of conning any helmsman could take on, this blind running before the seas with bare steerage way. A big wave could broach the ship, its rush of water negating the bite of both rudder and propellers unless the counter-measures were instantaneously accurate. So he had Ensign Whitaker keep an open circuit to the engine room, ready to call for immediate backing on one or the other propeller in case the rudder lost control. There was as much strain on Ensign Whitaker as on the helmsman because a wrong order to Chief MacKay would fatally aggravate an impending broach.

But Finlander knew that the greatest strain of all was falling on Bucky Allison. His calculations and minute corrections had to bring the ship back over an infinitesimal, invisible reference point lying two hundred and ten fathoms below a black void of heaving ocean. The forty-one thousand tons of twisted metal which had been the *Hood* were nothing but a needle in a liquid haystack. Closer to the Iceland coast it might have been possible to take some radar bearings to help him, but it was too far and the hash created by the heavy snowfall too heavy. "How are you going to make it, Buck?" Finlander asked the exec as he checked his stop-watch in the reflected glow of the automatic course recorder.

"By pilotage and—I hope—by some sort of ESP of my own," Allison answered.

"If anybody has a sixth sense for this sort of thing, you do." They both held their breath for a moment as they felt the *Bedford*'s stern begin to slew around under the thrust of a steep sea. The boy at the wheel let out an agonized little grunt, his reflexes reacting with explosive speed as he spun the steel disk. The ship steadied and the sea slid under her, coasting her along on her stealthy way. The captain let out a soundless gasp of relief, then said: "All right. I leave the bridge to you, Buck. I'm going back to sweat it out in the CIC."

On the way there, Finlander stopped in his day cabin and found Merlin Queffle lying on the bunk, staring up at the ceiling. He sat up when the captain came in and exclaimed with a nervous eagerness: "I'm ready, sir!"

The captain studied him for a moment. "You didn't really rest, did you, Queffle?"

"Sure, sir. I'm all right now."

"Now you listen to me, son! If you can't pick up anything on the sound gear, I don't want you to blame yourself. It will simply mean that the Russian has evaded us, that he just isn't around any more. And that is *my* responsibility, not yours. So don't go flying to pieces over it. Understand?"

"He's there, sir," Queffle answered and bared his rabbit teeth in what was supposed to be a confident smile. "I can feel him in my earbones already."

Finlander remembered what Commodore Schrepke had said about this sonarman's talents and shoved him back on the bunk somewhat roughly. "Maybe what you feel is your own blood pounding in your ears," he said. "You can't detect Moby Dick without sonar. So don't try to kid me by saying you hear things you think I want you to hear. We're not playing around with some kind of supernatural séance here, but conducting a tough ASW operation. Stick to factual readouts of our detection systems—okay? All right, so let's get going!" He yanked Queffle to his feet and gave him a shove toward the door.

Lieutenant Spitzer had put the CIC back on full GQ immediately upon the *Bedford*'s turnaround. Krindlemeyer, his alter ego, had come up from the CSP room and was leaning over his shoulder at Central Control, myopically peering at the scopes and dials through his bifocals. Lieutenant Aherne had relieved Ensign Ralston at Fire Control, but the latter hovered close to the console, watching its rows of winking lights with as much eagerness as if he were still in charge. The radar and sonar operators were in silent concentration at their posts and the CPO on the plotting board was poised to process any contact they managed to pick

up. There was still weariness in everybody's face, but it was an under-
current submerged by the nervous tension which hung in the air like a
physically gaseous thing. If anything, it increased when Captain Finlander came through the steel door with Merlin Queffle in tow.

"You stand by as relief on MTS for the time being," he told the
Breton Kid. "I don't want you in harness until we close the range some
more."

Queffle started to protest, but sulkily obeyed and placed himself behind
the operator at the Master Tactical Sonar console. Captain Finlander
walked over to Krindlemeyer and Spitzer. "What's the status, gentlemen?" he asked.

"All systems go, sir," Spitzer reported.

"Sensitivity should be eighty per cent according to input efficiency
from CSP, sir," Krindlemeyer reported, peering balefully at his captain
over the edges of his spectacles. "Layering zero. Sea-return four-point-
five, sir."

"Very good," Finlander said. "We should be able to hear a porpoise
fart at six miles' range with that kind of saturation." As Krindlemeyer
and Spitzer chuckled dutifully, he stepped over to Fire Control. "I see
our weapons all seem accidentally in a state of readiness," he said as he
checked the status board.

Lieutenant Aherne nodded. "Yes, sir. With the seas behind us and this
slow speed, there's not much problem of spray slushing up the launchers."

"Just so those gunners keep on the ball," Ensign Ralston injected
irritably, "and aren't lulled to sleep by the easy going."

"Simmer down, Mr. Ralston," the captain shot at him over his shoulder. "Or I'll send you topside on an inspection just to see how easy the
going is out there."

"I'd be glad to go, sir."

"I said to simmer down! . . . Lieutenant Aherne, have you been
clearing your auxiliary firing circuits periodically?"

"Yes, sir. And local control is standing by on the hedgehog."

"Very good. It seems there's nothing I can criticize here except possibly a bit of overanxiousness on the part of your junior fire-control
officer." He wheeled on Ensign Ralston, who was leaning over the board
and fiddling with a perfectly adjusted rheostat. "If you're so darn
eager to keep busy during your relief period, Ensign Ralston, how about
calling the galley and asking my steward to shoot me up some breakfast?"

"Certainly, sir. Bacon and eggs?"

"My guess is everybody's getting another lot of dry rations this morning. That will have to do for me too."

Ralston hurried to the telephone talker by the plotting board while the
captain moved in behind the sonar operators and inspected their blank
PPI scopes. Because they were listening on passive systems, there were
no pings coming in over the speakers—only a faint hissing sound. The

tactical radar scope, however, was cluttered with hash caused by the snow, and unless Moby Dick suddenly snorted within a few hundred yards of the *Bedford,* it could not possibly pick up any contact. But that did not keep the radarman from studying the blur of pulsating blobs with an intense red-eyed concentration.

When he completed his round of the CIC's complex interlocking functions and found them operating to his complete satisfaction, Finlander returned to the Central Control station and seated himself next to Spitzer. "All right," he exclaimed as he hunched down in his seat and crossed his arms over his chest, "nothing to do now but wait while we close in."

# 7.

A half-hour dragged by. Not a glimmer of a signal penetrated the silence of the deep. Commander Allison reported from the bridge that he estimated the *Bedford* had returned to within six miles of the *Hood,* a range clearly sufficient to pick up Moby Dick's echo-ranging if he started probing toward the surface. But there was not even the *clickety-click* of a single shrimp. It was as if all the myriad beings which inhabit a cubic mile of ocean were holding their breath in suspense along with the protagonists of this stalking conflict. Merlin Queffle stared at the PPI screen from over the shoulder of his relief and strained his ears toward the muted speaker. His hands were entwined over his left knee, which danced an agonized, unceasing beat; at increasingly frequent intervals he shot a pleading glance toward his captain, whose eyes appeared only half open as he sat swaying in his chair at Central Control.

But Finlander's half-open eyes did not mean he was only half awake, although the *Bedford*'s long steep yawing, strangely dampened compared with earlier, was having a nightmarish lullaby effect on her crew. He was aware not only of Queffle's suffering, but of the states of mind of all the men in the CIC, while at the same time his own kept analyzing and evaluating the situation minute by tense, endless minute. Would Moby Dick move out of hiding without an echo-ranging sweep? Possibly. But most probably that sly Russian was doing exactly the same thing he was, listening on passive sonar and refusing to, be drawn into a rash action even though he might suspect the destroyer had long since retired out of range. But could he already have pulled out while the *Bedford* was at the apogee of her deception maneuver? *Was* that possible? Should he have kept Queffle on sonar to guard against such a move? Should he put him in *now?* The temptation was tremendous to order Spitzer to start a maximum-effect sweep and fill the surrounding ocean with its tactile electronic fingers—which, of course, could pick up Moby Dick if he had started to rise and move, but would also send him scurrying back into hiding and return the battle to its previous deadlock. This patient, silent waiting was better, no matter how trying on the nerves.

Steward's Mate Collins came into the CIC with the captain's breakfast tray, which contained some pork sausages and a half-scrambled, half-fried egg, rendered unrecognizable by the pitching griddle of the galley. Finlander was pleased and relieved his tensions in some casual banter with the Negro steward. "Well, well! Hot chow! I feel like a pampered character, Collins. My compliments to the cook! Stay awhile and watch, so you can tell him we too are on the job!" Collins nodded politely, then looked around him, taking in the many luminous scopes and dials, and the men making their trance-like obeisance to them. His face remained inscrutable, an expression which the captain mistook for awe. "All these instruments and technicians are pretty impressive, aren't they, Collins?" he said through a mouthful of egg. "Maybe impressive enough to inspire a bright boy like you to switch his ambitions from medicine to electronics?"

"No, sir," the Negro answered politely but firmly.

Finlander looked at him more carefully and more accurately appraised his demeanor. "Oh? Commander Porter has been brainwashing you, I suppose."

"No, sir, only tutoring me in my studies."

"Yes—all shrouded in the hokus-pokus of medicine's mystical mission to succor suffering humanity," Finlander said with outright derision. "That's old witch-doctor stuff, Collins! Today the electronic scientist has taken over the navy, the world and outer space. You should get out of the dark ages, boy."

"It's still dark enough in here for witchcraft, sir," Collins answered quietly. This brought a peculiar look from Lieutenant Spitzer, who swiveled around in his chair and stared at him for a moment. Finlander frowned too, but then was gracious enough to laugh.

"All right, Collins. I give in! When we get back to Newport, I'm going to recommend you be sent to Pharmacist School. That may help you get into college and pre-med after your hitch is over. The rest is up to you." He turned away from the genuinely grateful "Thank you, Captain!" and redirected his full attention to the tactical situation at hand. He called the bridge and asked Commander Allison for another estimate of the ship's position. Five miles from the *Hood*—closing at the rate of a mile every eight minutes. His eyes swept along the rows of empty PPI scopes, then fixed themselves upon Merlin Queffle's dancing knee. "Queffle! Get in there and see if you can pick up anything!"

The Breton Kid shot to his feet and yanked his relief away from the console. In a moment he was hunched at the set, his hands pressing the earphones over his head, his eyes bulging toward the scope. The knee no longer danced.

Ensign Ralston's nervousness was also abated when, a few minutes later, he relieved Lieutenant Aherne at Fire Control. But there was nothing for him to do there except wait, as everybody else was doing, and as the hands of the clock crept on, his tension began building up again.

Spitzer and Krindlemeyer exchanged positions, the latter vanishing down the hatch to check on things in the CSP room below. The ready light of No. 1 ASROC flashed to amber and the telephone talker reported it was being cleared of slush, but the trouble could not have been serious as the light went back to red within two minutes.

Eight more minutes of empty, inactive, gut-sucking silence. Another mile slipped by. Then one of those freak swells, much bigger than the others, caught up with the *Bedford* and began skidding her sideways down its slope. A tremor vibrated the deck and bulkheads of the CIC as the starboard engine reversed to brake the impending broach, but she heeled over steeper and steeper, and the tremor became a shuddering with a muffled rumble which jarred and shook everybody to the marrow. The ship did not broach completely, but perilously hung on the brink while burying herself in a thundering rush of white water. The sonar speakers and scopes crackled and sparkled with the hash of her own turbulence. Merlin Queffle cringed in his seat, pried up the cups of his earphones as if they were blasting a physical pain into his head and shot a horrified look at his captain. Finlander's knuckles turned white as he gripped the arms of his chair and his eyes bored through the network of conduits and steel plating overhead, penetrating to the struggling helmsman up there. Slowly the *Bedford* recovered herself and stopped laboring, but Lieutenant Krindlemeyer spoke up with an ominous tone.

"That could have been picked up on enemy's passive system."

"For how far?" the captain demanded.

"The needle hit twenty-six. Two miles at least, sir."

Commander Allison's voice came down through the bridge intercom, speaking with a controlled chagrin. "Sorry, gentlemen! She got away from us for a moment there. A very big sea."

Finlander looked as if he were about to shout a furious criticism into the microphone, but instead he calmly said: "All right, Buck! Keep on your toes. They usually come in three's." He was right. Two more big waves caught the *Bedford,* but smaller than the first, and with the helm thoroughly alerted. The splash was not as bad, yet enough to agitate the scopes and needles.

Had they been heard? Was there no reaction only because there was *nothing* down there? The questions tore at Finlander's brain, but he did not yield to impulse as Ensign Ralston did.

"Mightn't we as well shoot the works and start echo-ranging, sir?" the young officer exclaimed in anguish.

"No!" Finlander retorted. "But maybe Moby Dick will be that foolish if he thought he heard us. Queffle! Turn those earbones of yours on to maximum. Krindlemeyer! Patch him into the QBH hydrophone and stream it out. Bridge! Reduce revs and hold her for a QBH sweep."

Lieutenant Krindlemeyer's fingers flew over the switches. Queffle hunched down, knotting himself into an agonized ball of concentration. For two . . . three . . . four minutes everybody in the CIC breathed only enough to keep himself from exploding. The tense silence was broken only when the door opened and Commodore Schrepke stepped inside, allowing it to slam shut with a raucous metallic clang which made everybody jump.

Captain Finlander twisted around and glared at the German. Schrepke glanced about him with a cold glint in his eyes, then retreated into a corner, there to wait and watch with the rest of them.

At 0645 Commander Allison estimated that he had brought the *Bedford* within a half-mile of the *Hood*. It was only a guess, but an educated one backed up by his considerable seaman's instinct for the effects of wind and waves. Twenty minutes earlier he had shut down the master fathometer, depriving himself of his "blind man's stick" in retracing his steps by the bottom contour. That instrument transmitted a strong submarine signal, and although it went straight down in a narrow cone, he was taking no chances that the Russian would hear it. The near broach had shaken him enough. But if he had to navigate the last few miles by guess and by God, then he needed to do it closer to the elements and outside the stifling confines of the blacked-out wheelhouse. The helmsman who so nearly lost control had vomited immediately after saving the situation, permeating the darkness around him with a horrible rancid smell; the relief lookouts, thawing out by the heater during their twenty-minute rests, cooked in their soaking clothes and added a peculiar pungent odor of their own. The executive officer squirmed into his parka and went out on the bridge.

It was even darker out there, of course, but the wind and snow were crisply clean, and he could hear and feel the sea surging along the hull of his ship. It was not blowing hard, less than Force 2 from the northeast; the swells were rolling along as big as ever, but without breaking and with longer periods between them. Snowflakes swirled and danced around his face, invisible, but stinging when they brushed against his skin. As he moved along the edge of the windscreen, he bumped into the port lookout, who jumped as if he had been awakened from being asleep on his feet.

"Watch it, son! Keep moving and keep looking."

A frightened apology came stuttering from the dim shape. Allison moved on to the wing and noticed that Commodore Schrepke was no longer in his usual place, but he did not give that much thought. For two or three minutes he concentrated on sensing the unseen forces of the arctic night which were affecting his ship. He only considered the navigational problem at hand and did not speculate about where Moby Dick was out there, lurking just beneath the black waves or in the blacker deep—or not there at all. That was CIC's problem, Finlander's and that poor skinny kid Merlin Queffle, who was tearing his nerves to shreds over his MTS. All Allison had to worry about was putting the *Bedford* back over the *Hood*—although he realized that only blind luck would put him *exactly* over it without using the fathometer. But they were close, very close now. He crossed the bridge and stepped back inside the wheelhouse, picked up the telephone and called the CIC.

"We are plus or minus a thousand yards."

"Are you sure, Buck?" Finlander's voice asked.

"As sure as I possibly can be, sir."

"Right. Stop engines and let's listen awhile."

Commander Allison passed the order on to Ensign Whitaker and went back out onto the bridge. As she lost steerage way, the *Bedford* slowly swung broadside to the swells and began rolling heavily as she lay dead in the water.

Up in the masthead lookout, Seaman Jones had just spelled Squarehead and he muttered furiously as he felt the motion begin to accelerate from the relatively mild one when the ship was loping along a following sea. "Here we go again, like a god-damned yo-yo!" he shouted down to his partner. Suddenly he smelled the smoke of a cheap cigar come wafting up the shaft, trapping itself in the pitching crow's-nest. "Jesus, Squarehead! If you don't put that thing out, I'm going to puke on your head, so help me!"

Squarehead laughed, tamped out the precious cigar in his glove and tenderly put it back inside his jacket pocket. It was the last one, reserved for himself, of the twenty he had distributed in honor of the birth of his son. Wedging himself into the tube of the mast with one leg hooked through a rung of the ladder, he closed his eyes and thought about the remote joys of buying toys for Christmas.

Down in the CIC, Lieutenant Spitzer confirmed the accuracy of Commander Allison's conning. Switching on the magnetometer, he detected a definite reaction from the needle. "We are in a fairly strong magnetic field, Captain. The wreck of the *Hood,* most likely."

"Or possibly a big fat Russian pigboat?" Finlander asked.

Spitzer shrugged. "Possibly, sir. But at least we know the *Hood* can't go anywhere. *It's* there."

"What do I have to do to give you some faith in your own skills, Spitzer?" the captain wondered wryly. "Very good. Let's remain on passive while we pull a QBH on him. He's got to make a move sometime, even if it's just to ride his tanks up for a snort. He's been going for forty-three hours and forty minutes." In the back of his mind he was wondering how he would debrief these men if it turned out that Moby Dick had managed to sneak away and was long since departed. He forced that dismal problem out of his mind, leaned back in his chair and congealed his body into an attitude of patience. But the strain was beginning to tell on him as it was doing on everybody else. The abysmal silence was getting on his own nerves. He noticed that Queffle's knee was dancing again and he had to suppress an urge to yell at him to control that abominable muscular twitching. However, it was Ralston who gave him a chance to vent his mounting pressures. The ensign swore when it came time for him to give up his position at the firing switches to Lieutenant Aherne.

"Just my damned luck to have to sit on my hands when things may get hot! Hell!"

"If you don't keep yourself under better control, Mr. Ralston," the captain shouted at him, "I'll send you below!" Then he wheeled on his hapless ECM officer. "It's also your job to maintain discipline in this department, Mr. Spitzer. Look up from your instruments just once in a while and see what's going on in here!"

Spitzer peered around with something which passed for severity. "All right! Everybody ease up. It's only an exercise."

Captain Finlander erupted violently for the second time that morning. "It is *not* only an exercise!" he bellowed at Spitzer. "There's a real, live Commie submarine down there and you're letting everybody get sloppy careless about it. Wake them up!"

Spitzer cringed in his chair. "B-but, sir. I thought you were reprimanding Mr. Ralston for being overanxious."

"Are you arguing with me, Mr. Spitzer?"

"N-no, sir . . . no." He turned from the livid Finlander and this time pressed forth a genuine snarling kind of anger. "Get on the ball in here, damn it!" he shouted at everybody in general, then singled out Ensign Ralston in particular. "You, Mr. Ralston! Try to alternate with Mr. Aherne without any hysterical demonstrations, okay? Go into the head and stick your face in cold water or something."

"I'm sorry, sir," Ralston gulped, speaking to the captain, not Spitzer. "I admit I'm overexcited and must control myself. I am sorry." He slumped down unhappily in the chair behind Aherne and stared into the sweating palms of his hands.

Normally Captain Finlander would have accepted the apology and even soothed Ralston with a few encouraging words; the young ensign was one of his favorites. But now he chose to ignore him and instead began to worry about whether he had unduly shaken his vital ECM officer, a man whom he did not understand at all and subconsciously distrusted. As proud as he was of this technological marvel of a ship, the scientific types necessary to run her sometimes baffled and irritated him. There was too much science and too little navy in them and he wondered how they would react when the chips were down, in a real naval battle. But then it struck him that this time it was Ralston, the epitome of the young Annapolis line officer, who was at fault. Later he would have to at least soften his rebuke to Spitzer. But for the time being he continued to seethe, his eyes fixing themselves on Queffle's dancing knee.

"Queffle! You're going to wear a hole through the deck with your jiggling!"

The Breton Kid did not react in the least, being lost in his own world of divining the deep, everything beyond the earphones and PPI scope totally shut out. His relief, sitting behind him, heard the captain and reached out, putting a restraining hand on the offending knee. Queffle's hand left its tense position on the left earphone, swung down and viciously parried the gentle touch. The relief jumped back and stared helplessly toward Captain Finlander.

"Oh, hell! Let him alone!"

For several minutes the captain sat back, watching and listening to the completely inert readouts. As the *Bedford* wallowed in the troughs and topped the crests broadside too, the rolls became extreme and the aches and pains in tired bodies became aggravated by the motion. Through the open hatch to the CSP room came the sound of Krindlemeyer's slide rule falling off the desk and clattering noisily against the deck.

"Can't you keep things properly secured down there?" Finlander shouted.

Spitzer almost simultaneously hit the appropriate intercom button on his communications panel and yelped into the microphone: "For Christ sake's, Krindle! We're suppose to be rigged silent!"

A long, uneasy and sterile silence followed during which Finlander gradually became aware of a prickly feeling in the back of his neck. When he finally turned around and looked behind him, he found himself staring into the impassive face of Commodore Schrepke. The German had not moved from his position against the bulkhead since entering the CIC nearly an hour earlier. The two men locked eyes for a long moment.

"Well, Commodore," Finlander finally exclaimed, managing a nearly pleasant tone, "how do you estimate the situation? Don't you think our Commie friends are nearing the end of their endurance?"

Schrepke nodded. "They are only men just like your own crew. And you can see how near the end of theirs *they* are."

Finlander's face blackened, but he managed to maintain an even tone by a tremendous effort at controlling himself. "Don't let a little family squabbling fool you, Commodore," he answered. "We're a long way from the end of our rope. Anyway, longer than the Russian is from his, I bet."

The black leather rippled under a shrug of the massive shoulders. "The strain is worse in a submarine, no doubt about that."

Finlander nodded and thought for a moment. Then he asked the German officer: "What would you do if you were in the Russian's place right now?"

"I would not lie down there and suffocate," Schrepke retorted.

Finlander nodded again, this time with evident satisfaction. "Then it's only a matter of time," he exclaimed loudly enough for everybody in CIC to hear him.

But time passed and nothing happened. The terrible rolling continued to inflict a ceaseless torture of perpetual motion. Spitzer noticed that the needle of the magnetometer was registering a fading magnetic radiation from the *Hood,* which clearly indicated they were drifting away from it. One dubious encouragement came when the radarman reported his scope was clearing of hash, indicating the snowfall was easing up, and providing at least four miles of effective radar scanning; but no blip was activated by the sweeper.

Up on the bridge, Commander Allison took notice of the lightening snow; it was still pitch black, so he could only feel the lessening sting of the flakes against his numbed face. The wind was freshening and veering uneasily around the compass, upsetting his estimation of their drift. However, there was little doubt in his mind that they had now passed to the southwest of the wreck. Stepping into the wheelhouse, he reported this to the CIC.

In the Communications Center, Lieutenant Packer had cleared his troubled mind and stood behind one of the radio operators as he received a priority signal from NATONAV 1, requesting immediate acknowledgment and a tacrep. When the operator looked at him questioningly, he shook his head, picked up the phone and called Captain Finlander about it.

"Maintain radio silence as ordered!" he was told curtly.

A few minutes later they intercepted an exchange between NATONAV 1 and the *Fritiof Nansen.* When he decoded it, Packer found that the destroyer was being ordered to their position to investigate the *Bedford*'s silence. They were obviously becoming alarmed at NATONAV 1 and he began to wonder if he might not be partially blamed for not keeping them informed. Perhaps they would expect him to protest to Captain Finlander and Commodore Schrepke. As he mulled this over, Lieutenant Beeker came in from the EDA room and announced: "We're picking up some weak radar emissions."

"The *Tiburon Bay?*" Packer asked.

"Negative. Probably the *Novo Sibirsk.*"

"Ouch! The Russian mother ship is coming to look for her lost chick!" Packer exclaimed. "Of course! They have been out of touch too for over forty-three hours!" He grabbed the phone and called the captain again.

After receiving the second report from Communications Center, Finlander's mind became a turmoil of thoughts, all unpleasant. With no signs of a contact, NATONAV 1 getting excited, the *Fritiof Nansen* on the way and the *Novo Sibirsk* probably approaching their position, he was coming to realize that his tactical situation was rapidly deteriorating. It would be at least four hours before the Russian "research ship" could reach the area, but it would be compromising to allow her to find the *Bedford* here. The *Nansen* should be stopped from a useless digression; NATONAV would have to be answered very soon, or his own COMFLANT would start screaming too. It had finally become urgent to consider breaking off this action, of admitting that Moby Dick had outmaneuvered him again, that even an old-fashioned Russian snort boat could evade a super-destroyer like the *Bedford*. What chance would there then be against the atomic units the Russian navy was readying? Finlander fought down a surging feeling of wild frustration and tried to keep his mind professionally objective. For a moment he stared at Queffle's dancing knee, then swiveled around in his seat to face Commodore Schrepke.

"Could you have made a mistake in identity?" he asked the German. "Could Moby Dick be a later class with some advanced kind of oxygen regenerators aboard?"

"I do not think so, Captain."

"Then he *has* to come up?"

"Yes—he has to come up."

Finlander turned away and glanced at the battle clock. Forty-five hours and three minutes. Time was running out, but maybe he could squeeze out just a little more. Perhaps those Russians were gasping out their last minutes of endurance down there right now, the diving officer poised to blow all tanks. Or perhaps they were a hundred miles away, laughing as they approached their rendezvous with the *Novo Sibirsk*. But then why was the *Novo Sibirsk* heading this way with her powerful search radar probing the night? He *had* to still be down there.

"We are completely out of the magnetic field, Captain," Lieutenant Spitzer informed him.

Finlander got up from his chair and staggered against the rolling to place himself behind Merlin Queffle and stare at the empty luminous disk of the PPI scope. It did not contain the faintest spark of activity. Well . . . as a last-ditch resort, they might as well start a maximum-effect active sonar sweep. "Mr. Spitzer! Belay the QBH and—"

His words were cut off by a piercing yell from Merlin Queffle which froze him and everybody else in the CIC: *"Wait! . . . Wait!"*

A couple of seconds passed in an agonized, stunned silence.

Then Queffle screamed again: "I hear him! . . . I hear him! . . . I have a *contact!"*

Finlander spun around and bounded back to Central Control, jumping into the chair and simultaneously yanking the talker set over his head. "Bridge! We have a contact! We will conn from CIC." Then he was momentarily diverted by the shocking sight of Lieutenant Aherne suddenly turning away from his switches and attempting to direct a stream of vomit into a paper cup. Ensign Ralston was staring stupidly at the fire-control officer, apparently paralyzed by the strange sight.

"God damn it to hell, Ralston!" Finlander screamed. "Don't just sit there! Relieve that man!"

Ralston let out a shocked yelp, yanked Aherne out of the chair and took his place. "All weapons arm-safe!" he called out with a trembling voice. "All systems go!"

Queffle had hunched back over his console after his initial outburst and seemed knotted into an attitude of prayer, his eyes closed as he ignored the PPI scope and pressed every last ounce of his nervous energy into the rubber cups of the phones. All eyes were upon him, all minds questioning him.

"Are you *sure*, Queffle?"

The Breton Kid gradually relaxed as if he were coming out of a trance and Finlander had a horrible feeling that he was about to admit to hallucinations. But the sonarman grinned and said: "Definite audio contact growing stronger." As he said it, a faint blob blossomed on the PPI scope, and he added: "Contact now bearing zero-four-zero, range three-two-double-zero closing, depth one-eight-zero."

Captain Finlander let out a long wheezing sigh, shedding all of his agonizing doubts and fears, and cheerfully exclaimed: "Very good! Let him come! Let him come! Stand by for the payoff! . . . Talker! Alert the engine room for maneuvering. Silence throughout ship." He swung around to shoot a triumphant grin at Commodore Schrepke, but it froze on his lips when he saw that Ben Munceford had entered the CIC and was standing next to the German. The correspondent's face wore a churlishly defiant half-smile as he turned his hands palm out toward the captain to show that he was armed with neither camera nor tape recorder. Commodore Schrepke was distastefully edging away from him while otherwise ignoring his presence and locking his gaze on the plotting board. For a second Finlander thought of ordering somebody to throw Munceford out, but there had been enough disruptions in the

CIC, so he shrugged indifferently and turned his full attention to the board—where Moby Dick was at long last appearing again as a white X edged in black.

# 9.

After the initial excitement of regaining contact with the Russian submarine, there followed another period of tense waiting while they tracked his creeping movement up from the deep and along a north-easterly course which gradually put the silently drifting *Bedford* between it and the sheltering wreck of the *Hood*. Moby Dick was rigged for silent running with his screws barely turning, but he created just enough disturbance to energize the destroyer's listening gear, which in turn registered the vibrations upon Queffle's sensitive ears and kindled a pip on the PPI, pinpointing his position. The tension in the CIC remained highly charged, but the overtones of hysteria had gone with the corroding elements of doubt and uncertainty. It was now a cold, calculating, even businesslike tension in which all outward functions were performed with an exaggerated calm.

"Contact . . bearing zero-five-six . . range two-nine-five-zero, closing . . . depth, one-four-zero, rising. . . . Contact . . ."

This droned calling of target information was not really necessary because it was being automatically fed from Queffle's MTS into the computer circuitry of the CSP room, there to be masticated and digested in a millionth-second gulp by Krindlemeyer's and Spitzer's martian robot, thence flashed back through a network of conduits, finally animating the cells of a deadly sort of senseless intelligence in the warheads of the poised ASROC's. If ordered to go by a flick of Ensign Ralston's finger, they knew *where* even before the plotter had finished calling out the target information.

Terrifyingly marvelous, Ben Munceford thought, without really understanding how any of it worked.

Lieutenant Spitzer was more concerned with how *well* the systems were working. A weak transistor, a collapsed diode, a micro-soldered filament vibrated loose—any one could throw the whole thing into a meaningless confusion. There were built-in monitors, auxiliary circuits and fail-safe devices, of course—electronic ganglions watching over electronic ganglions—but he kept a visual check on it all through the rows of winking lights and flicking needles spread out on the console before him. And then, as a final double-check, Ensign Ralston was manually feeding the target information into the weapons by punching matching numbers on a keyboard with his right hand. The left one rested on the firing switches—as yet locked by the red safety bar.

Suddenly the glowing blob on the MTS scope began to fade out. Finlander leaned forward, eyebrows arching, jaw jutting.

"Contact fading on bearing zero-six-four . . . range two-nine-three-zero, steady . . . depth one-double-zero, steady. Target has stopped. Target has stopped."

"He's listening for us," Finlander whispered.

"I have audio contact," Queffle reported. "Target engines are stopped, but I hear his auxiliaries. Sounds like a hot bearing."

Finlander smiled thinly. "Let's hope Commander Franklin keeps ours cool! Do you think he can hear us, Mr. Spitzer?" he asked the ECM officer.

"If they've got a man like Queffle, they might hear our hull break the wave patterns, sir. Otherwise we are a pretty inert target."

"All right. Let him sweat. We'll surprise him at the right moment. . . . Mr. Ralston! Contact Yeoman Pinelli in hedgehog local control and tell him to man his camera. Stand by the magnesium flares for a flash shot. When Moby Dick surfaces we'll make him say cheese and I think I'll send the chief of the Soviet Naval Staff a copy of the picture—compliments of the U.S.S. *Bedford!*"

Ralston grinned, called hedgehog control and transmitted the order.

But Finlander's plan was not to be. As the next swell lifted the *Bedford,* passed under her hull, then sucked her into the following trough, the attendant wrenching motion broke loose a huge chunk of ice which had formed around the housing of the radar antenna motor on the mainmast. Squarehead saw it flash by within inches of his face as he peered through the windshield of the crow's-nest, making him gasp: "Christ! What was that!" It hurtled downward through the blackness, broke into smaller pieces as it glanced off the forward stack, then crashed onto the main deck like an avalanche of rocks. A single hundred-pound piece hit the tarpaulin cover of the whaleboat, was hurled back into the air by the trampoline effect and made a huge splash in the sea, fifty yards away. The bridge lookout gave a yell: "Man or heavy object overboard!" He had been unable to tell which and was thoroughly alarmed. Commander Allison rushed across the bridge and stared out into the darkness.

In the CIC the ice was heard hitting the deck as a muffled rumble, but the chunk which fell in the sea made all the sound gear crackle. The PPI scopes flared like frightened green eyes. Merlin Queffle jumped in his seat and yelled: "Jeeze! Something big fell off the ship!"

"That tears it!" Spitzer exclaimed. "A deaf old woman could hear that without her ear trumpet."

"Shut up!" Finlander snarled, staring intently at the scopes, hoping they would get away with the calamity, but his ECM officer had been right. In the next instant the submarine's active sonar waves rippled against the *Bedford*'s hull and set her sensors to wildly reacting. The captain ground his fist into his palm. "Switch to active echo-ranging!" he ordered Spitzer, then called through the conning circuit: "All ahead standard! Come left to one-two-five degrees!"

A shudder rippled through the hull as the engines burst into life and the propellers bit into the water. The speakers vibrated with a strong return echo and the sonar PPI's registered such a brilliant blip of Moby Dick that it was like having a picture of him poised there, two thousand yards away and one hundred fathoms down.

Commander Allison's voice came over the bridge intercom: "We just shed five hundred pounds of ice off the foretop. Sorry."

"Never mind, Buck!" Finlander snapped back. "We're still giving him one hell of a surprise. Contact is positive."

It was so positive that even Ben Munceford could clearly make out what was happening. The Russian submarine was turning away while still pressing toward the surface and Finlander was conning the *Bedford* so as to catch up and place himself on top of him. If this had been real war, Moby Dick would clearly be finished—*but it wasn't real war*. Munceford glanced at Commodore Schrepke, edged up to him and asked: "So we've got him cold! So what do we do with him now?"

Schrepke's face was an unfathomable mask, but one drained of all color. He shook off Munceford and stepped up behind Finlander, leaning over him. "Let him surface, Captain," he rasped with as much pleading as he was capable of using.

"He's still acting too smart. I'm going to push that red devil's nose into his own bilges. Helm, come five degrees left!"

"He's more desperate than smart at this point, Captain," Schrepke pressed him. "You are going to force him to fight. This is a careful, responsible commander you're dealing with, but he has reached his limits. Let him surface and let him go, or he is going to fight."

If Spitzer heard the ominous prediction, he pretended not to. Finlander looked up at the German for a moment. "You think he's going to shoot at us, do you, Commodore?"

"I know I would in his place," Schrepke answered. "So would you."

Finlander turned and leaned toward Ensign Ralston. "Fire Control! Arm number-one ASROC!"

Ralston looked up from his dials with a startled expression which immediately switched to one of intense anticipation. His hand shook as it flipped the red safety bar and the warning horn cut through the CIC with its short, sibilant blast. "Number-one ASROC armed and ready, sir!"

Finlander looked back into Schrepke's face, his expression challenging, yet icy calm. "All right, Commodore. Let him try anything he wants to."

"Captain, you are a fool!" Schrepke hissed at him, throwing every bit of the fear and anger which he felt into the words. This time Lieutenant Spitzer glanced up from his panel with an incredulous expression.

The scar on Finlander's throat pulsed angrily as he glowered at the German. "I'm not going to shoot first, Commodore. But if he fires a torpedo at me, then . . ." His voice rose up above the pinging of the sonar and the range-calling of the plotter. ". . . then I'll fire one!"

"Fire one!" Ensign Ralston's voice echoed in a high pitch of excitement.

Captain Finlander wheeled in his seat and his body was suddenly racked by a spasm which came together with a passing faint tremor through the *Bedford.*

The stunned silence which ensued was broken by the talker at the plotting board. "Number-one ASROC launched and clear," he announced in a matter-of-fact voice which almost instantly turned into a weird squeal of amazement. "Jesus Christ aw'-mighty! *It really is!*"

His anguished exclamation was immediately followed by Commander Allison's voice through the bridge intercom, and for once it sounded as if he were thoroughly shaken. "CIC! . . . CIC! Number-one ASROC has fired!"

"For God's sake, Ralston!" Finlander gulped hoarsely, rising to his feet in shocked horror and tearing off his headset.

The ensign's taut muscles began turning to jelly and he suddenly sagged down in his seat, trembling violently as he stared at the hand still gripping the firing switch. He yanked it away as if it had burned him. "B-but, sir . . . you said *fire one* . . didn't you?"

"It is done now," Schrepke exclaimed with a clipped finality. "It is all over and done now."

All eyes watched the PPI scope of the Master Tactical Sonar with hypnotic fascination. A second, smaller blip suddenly blossomed on it, close to the bigger one which was Moby Dick. "ASROC has separated from rocket booster and has entered the sea . . . on target . . . all systems go!" the plotter announced with a quavering voice. The small blob wavered around the bigger one, hovered around it for what became an agonized eternity . . .

"Oh God! Miss him! Miss him!"

. . . but then seemed to join it and cause a single bright flare which quickly died and faded out to nothing. Queffle pried up his earphones just as the speaker erupted in a horrible cacophony of grating, tearing, ripping sounds. It gradually diminished to a crackling patter, but then the shock wave of a tremendous underwater explosion hit the *Bedford*'s steel hull, making her tremble and ring with a ghostly boom, like the tolling of a huge bell. Then silence.

"I heard her break up!" Merlin Queffle screamed. "I heard them dying down there!" He tore off his earphones and collapsed over the console, his body racked by sobs.

All eyes remained on the sonarman for only a moment before slowly turning upon the captain. Everybody knew what had happened now and the shattering reality of it was beginning to penetrate home. Forty-five hours, eighteen minutes since it started, and now it had ended in forty fatal seconds. The Russian submarine they had wistfully called Moby Dick had been blown to pieces and the hundred-odd men aboard her scattered to the deep. They all knew it—except possibly Ben Munceford, who could not immediately bring himself to believe this had actually happened before his eyes and stupidly mumbled: "What's the matter? . . . What's going on?" until his words were choked off by the awful realization.

# 10.

Lieutenant Spitzer secured the CIC, giving his orders in a steady voice, but with a peculiar trance-like expression on his face. One by one the men trooped out, some staring with curious awe at the brooding figure of their captain slumped at Central Control, others clumsily avoiding a look at him as they passed. The CPO of plot helped Lieutenant Aherne, who was too sick to fully understand what had happened; two sonarmen supported Merlin Queffle between them, dragging him through the door still blubbering about hearing men die in the black deep. Finally only Commodore Schrepke and Ensign Ralston were left with Finlander in the silent room, now darker than ever since all the dials and scopes had been extinguished. The assistant fire-control officer had remained paralyzed at his console, looking down at the fatal switch with glazed, red-rimmed eyes. But now he got up and stepped over to the captain, braced himself and exclaimed with a pathetic fortitude: "Sir, it was all my fault. I am prepared to take full responsibility for what happened."

Finlander did not appear to hear him.

"Sir, please . . ."

Commodore Schrepke reached out and took Ralston by the arm, gently pulling him away and guiding him toward the door. "Your captain cannot talk to you now," he said. "And no matter what you tell him, he knows where the responsibility lies. He certainly knows that your blame is but an incidental one. So do not waste his time with self-reproaches." He did not say it harshly, perhaps even with a tinge of sympathy, but the ensign suddenly began to shake uncontrollably and tears began streaming down his cheeks. Schrepke steadied him and, reaching under his leather jacket, brought out his tarnished silver flask. "Here, my boy. You need a little medicine."

The tears did not stop as Ralston stared at the flask, but he suddenly struck it away as if it contained poison. "You are going to crucify him for this, aren't you?" he yelled at the German.

"I am neither Judas nor Pontius Pilate," Schrepke answered him evenly, "but a sailor who will give up only to death many secrets as terrible as this."

Ralston fended off his helping hand, straightened himself up and through a tremendous effort suppressed his trembling. But he could not stop crying. Fumbling for the iron door, he yanked it open and fled.

Schrepke went back to Central Control and sat down in the chair next to Finlander. He felt the engines stop and knew that the *Bedford* was coasting in over the spot where Moby Dick had died. Finlander seemed completely oblivious of it and sunk in deep thought, but suddenly he spoke up and asked: "What did you mean, Wolfgang, when you said you would only give up secrets like this to death?"

The German did not answer him immediately and when he did, it was to say: "I was talking to a hysterical boy."

Finlander looked Schrepke straight in the eyes. "Were you suggesting that what I have done can be covered up in some way? Kept a deep, dark secret?"

Schrepke hesitated a moment with a faint nodding of his head. "What would happen if it became general knowledge that we sank a Soviet submarine in the high seas after deliberately tracking him for forty-eight hours?" he asked.

"All hell would break loose," the captain quietly replied.

"A nuclear hell, Erik?"

Finlander's long silence betrayed the fact that he feared such a possibility, but he said: "That would be sheer insanity, to precipitate nuclear war over an incident such as this."

"The incident itself proves how rampant insanity is."

A half-hour ago this reply would have triggered Finlander's temper, but now he took it with an unflinching calm which was, perhaps, far more frightening. He said simply: "Yes."

They were both diverted by the sounds of annunciator signals being transmitted from the bridge to the engine room and looked at the gyro-repeater and rudder indicator above the Control Center. Commander Allison was maneuvering the *Bedford* in a slow, tight circle. "I must go up on the bridge," the captain muttered without making the move. "I must see this thing through to the end and carry the responsibility all the way. I will, of course, log your protests against the action, Wolfgang. You attempted to stop it and you must be absolved."

Schrepke shook his head. "I am not looking for absolution, nor could I ever find it. What do you think the Russian government will do when they find out that a senior officer of the West German navy was aboard the ship which sank their submarine? Would they accept his protestations that he acceded to the orders of the captain? Some of my colleagues were hanged not so long ago with the same kind of excuse on their lips. And they deserved their fate. For my own part, I must accept my responsibility. I cannot do it with pride or honor, but at least I can try for courage."

Finlander leaned forward and tried to see Schrepke's face, which was only a blur in the faint glow of the red blackout lights. He opened his mouth to speak when the bridge intercom crackled to life and Commander Allison's voice interrupted him: "Could the captain please come to the bridge? This is urgent."

"In a few minutes, Buck! You carry on."

Allison became insistent and it was evident that he was still badly rattled. "Captain Finlander! We are circling the area of the sinking. There is oil and wreckage, but no signs of survivors. EDA reports an increasingly strong radar emission on the Soviet frequency. Estimate eighty miles away. Communications has intercepted repeated calls for Moby Dick originating from the same range and bearing as the radar emissions. Communications also reports repeated calls to us from NATONAV 1 and Polar-bear. I recommend immediate action, sir."

Before Finlander could answer him, he felt an iron grip clamp down on his arm. Schrepke's other hand shot out and locked the microphone button in the off position so that Allison could not hear what he was going to say.

"Tell him to reopen communications with NATONAV 1 and report contact lost and action broken off—*no more.*"

"You still think there is a way of covering up this thing?" Finlander asked him with both doubt and hope.

"We cannot risk having the Soviets break the code of an action report. I most emphatically suggest you keep any mention of it off the air, Captain. I speak officially, but also as your friend. Do not make any action report."

A tremendous load seemed to fall suddenly from Finlander's shoulders. "Yes, sir," he agreed, his hands waving before him as if grasping at a solution he had glimpsed in the darkness. "You are right. We will keep the secrecy of this and pass it on as such to our Fleet Headquarters, who then will have no choice but do the same . . . will they? Of course not! Obviously the Commies know nothing about it as yet! They haven't heard from their precious pigboat for over forty-five hours—and now they *never will.* So it can be done!" He pushed Schrepke's hand away from the intercom lever and spoke into the microphone with much of his old vigor and confidence. "Buck! Reopen standard Code C communication channels with NATONAV 1 and report to them contact is lost, action broken off and we are resuming base course."

"No action report, sir?"

"Negative. Negative. The lid is down tight on that. Search the area for five more minutes, then retire away from radar emissions for thirty minutes before resuming base course. Announce a special briefing of all off-watch officers in the wardroom at 0700. I'll be right up . . . so keep an even strain, Buck!" When he switched off and rose up out of the chair, there was a fatalistic kind of cheerfulness about him. "Well, I'm going to leave this electronic chamber of horrors and cleanse myself in the wind and spray of a good, old-fashioned open bridge. It's my guess that I won't be permitted that privilege much longer. . . . Are you coming?"

Commodore Schrepke began to lift himself from his seat, but froze halfway up as Commander Allison's voice came through the intercom again:

"Captain! We have picked up human remains!"

Schrepke slumped back into the chair. "If you don't mind, I will stay here until we are under way again," he rasped.

"I understand, sir," Finlander whispered. "The flotsam of a smashed submarine must bring back terrible memories for you. I understand."

"But we must still be practical about such things. Especially in this case. Remove all the evidence you can. And about the slick of oil—I suggest you pump some of your own into it so that if the *Novo Sibirsk* finds it, it will not be so easily identifiable."

"That is a very good idea," Finlander agreed. He put his hand on Schrepke's shoulder in a hesitant gesture of friendship. "You are a very fine officer, Wolfgang. We may have had our quarrels and old enmities have stood between us, but, no matter what happens to me now, I will tell them you are a fine officer and that I consider you a good friend. Please believe I mean it."

Commodore Schrepke answered with a wistful irony: "What you feel for me now is the kinship of the damned, my poor captain." The hand pulled away from his shoulder, but the dark figure remained by his side for a moment. "Go clean up matters on your bridge, Erik," the German urged him. "You have only little time left."

"All right. Lock the door when you leave."

After Finlander had gone, Schrepke remained in his seat for a couple of minutes to give him plenty of time to climb the shaft to the bridge. Then he got up and went over to Fire Control, leaned down over the console and carefully read the labels along the rows of switches. Finding the one he wanted, he gingerly grasped it between thumb and forefinger, slowly, very slowly pushing it forward. Two red lights winked on. On the Weapons Status Board a sign lighted up, reading NO. 2 ASROC—

LOCAL CONTROL. He stood there for a moment, listening and tensely waiting, as if he expected some kind of drastic reaction to what he had done. But the intercoms remained silent; no alarm sounded, nobody came bursting in. With a deep sigh he left, rammed home the automatic locking bar of the CIC door, climbed down the shaft to the main deck, then on through silent passageways to his own cabin. There he brought out his small leather suitcase, opened it and from beneath the neat packing of socks and underwear brought forth his service pistol. He methodically examined its magazine and chamber, then put it down on the desk. From a drawer he took a shabby wallet, and from it a fading, dog-eared photograph of a smiling woman with a solemn-faced blond young boy. This too he put down on the desk. Before seating himself for a last communion with his dead family, he carefully checked his watch as if to predetermine how much time he could allot to them.

# 11.

Outside of her gloomy interior, the *Bedford* had suddenly erupted in a blaze of lights. From her armored honeycombs of compartments and stations, men had poured out on deck and swarmed to the railing and lifelines, from where they silently stared into the sea. Scattered snowflakes still danced in the brilliant periphery created by the floodlights and they sparkled like floating diamonds when caught in the more powerful beam of the probing searchlight. On the heaving dark swells, a darker blotch of oil, perhaps an acre wide, stained the sea like a pool of black blood, viscous and shimmering weirdly with dull flashes of iridescence; here and there it was coagulating around bobbing lumps of shapeless debris. Two seamen on the foredeck were wielding the same long-handled dip nets they used to pick up garbage for the surgeon's analysis, trying to snare these lumps as Commander Allison slowly maneuvered the ship through the slick. One of them had been put in a bucket, which was being passed from man to man in a fitful journey toward the bridge; some stopped its progress momentarily to look at the contents with morbid shock, others closed their eyes and practically threw it on to the next link in the human chain. One seaman fainted as soon as it left his hands. Chief Quartermaster Rickmers, the last to receive it, put it down under the light by the wheelhouse door, where it arrived just as Captain Finlander was stepping out on the bridge in his white duffel.

A stunned, awe-struck circle formed around the bucket and among the men was Ben Munceford, paralyzed with his camera in his hands as he gaped at what had been a full-grown, living man only an hour ago —now a mangled, oil-soaked glob of gore contained in a two-gallon bucket with plenty of room to spare.

"Th-that . . . that ain't human, in Christ's name?" Munceford gulped.

"No, not any more," a seaman answered and turned away.

Captain Finlander said: "It is the pressure of the deep which did it, not the explosion." It was almost as if he were denying his complicity, but actually this last incontrovertible piece of evidence of what he had done was searing itself upon his mind. He had seen such remains before when nearly twenty years ago he had blown to pieces the ill-starred U-1020. For that action he had received the Navy Cross; for this one he would receive excoriation and infamy. No matter how well the navy would be able to protect the terrible secret, there was no protection possible for him, and, in some small measure, this grisly butcher's scrap which had once been a man would be avenged.

Commander Allison waited for his captain to order that something be done with the remains, but when he continued to stare at them along with the others, Allison took the initiative upon himself. "Mr. Whitaker! Throw something over that and carry it down to Commander Porter for disposition."

This seemed to snap Ben Munceford out of his paralysis. "Wait!" he exclaimed and, raising his camera, snapped on its brilliant Solarpack light.

Without a word Captain Finlander struck out with his gloved fist and exploded the light with a single blow. Everybody jumped back, cringing from the shower of hot glass. Munceford yelped and dropped the camera. When he started to bend down to retrieve it, the captain kicked it beyond his reach. Munceford straightened up and glared at him, white-faced and shaking, but there was no childish petulance in his manner. "That will do you no good," he said. "You can bust up all the cameras you like, tear up all the tapes and do your damnedest to muzzle me, Captain. But it will do you no good. I finally have this story straight in every detail. I'm going to see to it the truth is told."

"The matter will shortly be out of my hands, Mr. Munceford," the captain answered with an icy calm. "In the meanwhile I am having you confined to your cabin. You will remain there until we dock in Reykjavik. If you attempt to move about this ship—even to the wardroom— you will be locked in the brig. Mr. Whitaker! Escort Mr. Munceford below."

Ensign Whitaker picked up the bucket with one hand and took Munceford's arm with the other. The circle of men opened up, allowed them to pass, then scattered to line the windscreen and peer down at the brilliantly illuminated oil slick lapping at the *Bedford*'s hull.

Captain Finlander slowly walked to the part of the bridge where Commodore Schrepke used to spend his lonely vigils and, like him, stared down into the fouled sea. Commander Allison stood silently behind him for a moment, then joined him shoulder to shoulder. "How in God's name did this happen, Erik?" he asked.

"A misunderstood order, I think," Finlander quietly answered. "The details are all a mixed-up nightmare in my own mind, but they don't matter for the moment. There were eleven men in the CIC when it happened and the Investigation Board will pick the pieces out of their brains and fit them together for my court-martial. Right now I must do better what I have been trying to do all along, so help me God, and that is to protect my country. The *Bedford* must be made a more silent ship than she has ever been before."

Allison looked down at the men swarming along the foredeck below the bridge, leaning over lifelines or clambering on the turrets in groups of ten and twenty. There must have been a hundred in view down there, peering and pointing at the stain of Moby Dick's killing, letting it saturate permanently into their consciences. "This is going to be an awfully rough one, Erik," the executive officer whispered. "Awfully rough. I admit I'm badly scared."

"So am I, Buck," the captain replied, then added a bitterly suppressed outburst: "The cold war! How can governments expect their military to guide their actions by such a blatantly sordid euphemism? Is there really such a thing possible as a half-war? Can one half-fight with these deadly weapons? Did those Russian submariners half-threaten us? Are they now only half-dead down there? Should I only have half-feared them when the crews of so many American ships and planes are totally dead as a result of Russian actions? Does it not all naturally culminate in a totality of death and destruction? The answer lies in that bucket they passed up to this bridge a few minutes ago. I'd like to pass it on around among the world's cabinets and make every last politician take a good long look. Look and see what this cold war really is. The same as any war. Death." Finlander shook himself and checked the luminous dial of his watch. "All right, Buck. Let's get out of here before those Soviet radar emissions get strong enough to give them a return echo. I'm going to run home to Uncle Sam, tell him what a terrible thing I have done, accept my beating and hope that he can protect himself and the rest of his children from the consequences."

Without a word Commander Allison turned and walked off toward the wheelhouse. Captain Finlander remained where he was, looking down at the men below him. Then he leaned far over the windscreen, cupped a hand to his mouth and shouted to them: "Take a last look, men! Let the sight and feel of it sink in. Let it burn into your hearts and minds so well that you will never have to ask or speak about it among yourselves in order to recall it. Then, when the lights go out, clear the decks and seal it all up inside of you. From this moment on, learn to live with this secret, because if you become in the least bit careless with it, then an infinitely more terrible thing may strike far beyond this ship. There could be a millionfold more dead than those wretches who have perished here—God rest their souls!" For a moment longer he stared down at the hundred white faces looking up at him, watching that whiteness ripple away as they turned back for a last glance at the oil slick, then he nodded at Rickmers, who was standing by the wheelhouse door. The chief nodded back, vanished inside, and an instant later all the floods and exterior lights went out on the *Bedford* as he pulled the main blackout switch. The ship's decks emptied of life, once again became deserted and lashed by cold spray as she gained speed and retreated into the dark folds of the arctic night.


As the *Bedford* got under way, Lieutenant Beeker drew a sigh of relief and left the EDA room, where he had been anxiously monitoring the Russian radar emissions. "I was wondering if the skipper was going to hang around and let the *Novo Sibirsk* pick us up," he said to Lieutenant Packer. "Their microwaves are getting pretty solid now. Not more than sixty miles away."

Packer had just completed supervising the reopening of communications with NATONAV 1, had coded and transmitted the captain's messages to them and was now standing by the radio operators who were receiving and acknowledging some routine FOX Scheds—a kind of calm before the storm of amplification requests he suspected would soon be crackling out of the ether. His duty here had prevented him from going out on deck to witness the brief salvage operation, but one of the stand-by operators had brought back a crudely lucid eyewitness account. He had been one of the men who had helped pass the bucket up to the bridge. Somewhere in the back of the English officer's weary mind the idea began to crystallize that they were *actually* at war. They *had* to be, since there had been a killing. Sometime during this awful long arctic night it must have started, although they had intercepted no messages about it from NATONAV 1 or any other fleet headquarters or task force. Well, these days war would start in secrecy, of course. Just sudden actions with sudden deaths, as there had just been out here. "Moby Dick tried to slip us a fish!" the relief radio operator had passed on the scuttlebutt, "but the skipper was on his toes and beat the bastard to it!"

And here came the quick promotions which always went hand in hand with war. The operator on Channel 5 received some personals and Lieutenant Packer quickly unscrambled them on the decoding machine:

ERIK J. FINLANDER, CAPTAIN, USN, COLDSNAP VIA NATONAV GENAVRAD
—YOU HAVE MADE ADMIRALS LIST STOP A CINCH FOR CONFIRMATION IF
YOU KEEP UP SPLENDID WORK STOP WELCOME TO THE CLUB AND CON-
GRATULATIONS—SIGNED RIERSEN, BENTLEY, MCLAURIN.

"A cracking day for the skipper," Packer muttered to himself, then
stiffened as he ran the next one through the decoder. The printed strip
it fed into his hand read:

P. L. M. PACKER, LIEUTENANT RN, COLDSNAP VIA NATONAV MACKAY—
FIND I WOULD RATHER HAVE YOU AND LOSE YOU THAN NEVER HAVE
YOU AT ALL STOP SO COME BACK AND LET US LOVE WELL IF NOT
WISELY FOR WHATEVER TIME YOUR NAVY ALLOWS US—SIGNED SHE-
BEONA.

Packer read it through a second, a third and a fourth time. He passed
a trembling hand over his face, his palm rasping against the stubble
sprouting over his jaws, then read it a fifth time. His mind was a complete confusion now, a numbed mixture of thoughts of war, death and
love. Shebeona wanted him back! But wasn't the very thing she feared
happening already? Would she stick if there was war? Would she quickly
become another forgotten Packer widow?

Lieutenant Beeker came up behind him. "Was one of those personals for you, Pete?" he asked, glancing over his shoulder at the strips
of paper in his hand. "Bad news?"

Packer quickly whipped Shebeona's cablegram out of sight. "One was
for me. Nothing serious, really. The other seems to indicate your navy
has a brand-new admiral." He handed him the one about Finlander.

Beeker glanced through it and exclaimed: "God! I wonder if this
will hold good after we dock. Well, better let him enjoy it while he can.
Messenger!" He stuffed it into a yellow envelope and dispatched it to the
bridge, then noticed that the Englishman was still leaning over the decoder
with a drawn, blank expression on his face. "Are you all right, Pete?"

"I don't know," Packer answered. "Everything seems all so god-
awfully mixed up. What is happening? Are we at war? Has the whole
world been plunged into darkness or is it only *us,* Beek?"

Beeker peered carefully into his face for a moment and frowned as if
he wondered about this himself. He turned to the rows of radio operators and called out: "Hey, Swanson! You're guarding GB circuits. Anything unusual happening on the outside?"

Swanson shrugged. "No, Mr. Beeker. Nothing much. The President
has agreed to meet with Khrushchev sometime soon. There's some kind
of scandal in New York City about rats in the schools. The Green Bay
Packers got taken seventeen-nothing. The big news from both sides of
the pond seems to be about Jack Paar lousing up the deal in Berlin."

Beeker sighed with relief, then turned back to Packer and smiled.

"You see, everything's absolutely normal. . . . Look, I'll run the store for a while if you want to take a break, Pete. You seem pretty beat, boy."

Packer was suddenly both eager to accept this offer and strangely exhilarated by a fresh flood of nervous energy. "Thanks a lot, Beek!" he exclaimed. "I'll be back very soon and you can call me immediately if there's an avalanche of top-secret squawks out of NATONAV 1. But I do need to get down to my cabin right away. As a matter of fact . . . I absolutely *have* to!"

He left the Communications Center and as he progressed on his downward journey through the *Bedford*'s pitching decks and passageways, his pace quickened with the full realization that Shebeona wanted him and no war had come between them as yet. At the same time, something near panic gripped him as he remembered that *Munceford* had her picture now. What madness could have driven him to give away Shebeona's photograph to that man! Allowing him to possess even a paper likeness of her suddenly rankled Packer as if Munceford possessed her physically. He began to run. Run with a wild, fearful, elated recklessness. And as he whipped around the corner of the passageway leading to his cabin, he violently collided with Commodore Schrepke.

The two men almost fell over and had to claw at each other to keep their balance. Lieutenant Packer's hand slipped against cold leather and when it clamped down on the man's waist, it was over something hard and butt-shaped beneath the folds. The impression flashed through his brain that it felt like a gun, but, realizing who it was, he knew it had to be Schrepke's famous schnapps flask. With a frantic apology, he disengaged himself from the German officer.

Schrepke kept a grip on his arm and pinned him against the bulkhead beneath the red blackout light. "Ah, it's you, *Leutnant* Packer! Still in a state of agitation, I see. What has happened to the cool, level-headed British navy?"

"I'm awfully sorry, sir," Packer gasped, out of breath and more befuddled than ever. "It's just been a bad night all round for me." He was shocked to find this made Schrepke laugh. He had never before seen the German even smile.

"A bad one for all of us, so never mind," the commodore answered and gave him a comforting pat on the shoulder.

Packer peered into his face and saw that the laughter was not in his eyes, which had a peculiarly restive look of sadness in them. "I have been meaning to also apologize for the way I behaved earlier this morning, Commodore. There was no excuse for it. Especially since I have a feeling you needed me for something. . . . You did, didn't you, sir?"

"Yes, I did. I thought you and I could do something about all this."

"All *what,* sir?"

"It does not matter any more. Fate was against us and it is too late."

The sadness had seeped into his voice now and it sounded so uncharacteristic of him that Packer was completely baffled. "Is there something wrong? Can I help you, sir?"

"No, my boy. The wrong which has been done can only be helped by totally obliterating it. This task I must face alone." The gloved hand crept up Packer's arm, crossed his shoulder and momentarily brushed against his cheek in a gesture which was clumsily tender. "You know, I would have had a son of your age. I never got to know or understand him either. But I love him just the same." He pulled away his hand, turned and quickly vanished down the passageway.

Lieutenant Packer remained pressed against the bulkhead for almost a minute, then he shook himself back to reality and slowly walked the remaining twenty steps to his cabin. When he pulled aside the curtain, he found Ben Munceford sitting on his bunk.

"Well, well, good old Peterpacker!" the American exclaimed with a caustic imitation of an Englishman's English. "Have you come to gloat like Schrepke? To rub my nose in the dirt and tell me what a stupid bastard I am?"

Packer had been glancing back down the passageway, but now he faced Munceford and coldly answered: "No, Ben. I only want you to return Shebeona's picture."

Munceford's head snapped back with a wince. "What? Here we've illegally sunk a Russian sub, brought the world to the brink of atomic war and all you can think of is a pin-up of some broad! Jesus! And they call *me* superficial!"

Packer advanced on him and clenched both fists. "Give her back to me, Munceford. Right now."

Munceford snickered and squirmed away along the edge of the bunk. "Well, okay, okay! Let me see . . . what the hell did I do with her?"

Packer's hands lashed out, grabbed him by his shirt and yanked him to his feet. "Give her back!" he shouted and began to shake him violently. But something clattered to the deck as he did it, and when he caught the flash of tarnished silver, it had an instant sobering effect upon him. It was Commodore Schrepke's flask.

Munceford pulled himself free of the Englishman's grip and dropped all of his sarcastic manner. "All right, Pete! I'll get your picture for you. Just spare me any more fits on this ship. I've just about had a bellyful of them." He went to his locker, opened it up and started rummaging in the tangle of dirty clothes. He found the photograph lying in the bottom corner, picked it up and, without a glance at the beautiful girl on it, held it out toward Packer.

But the lieutenant did not reach for it. He was holding the flask in his hand, staring at it with a perplexed frown. "How did you get this?" he asked.

Munceford snapped it out of his hand and shoved the photograph into it instead. "Here! You keep your girl and I'll keep the booze. Each to his own, okay?"

Packer held the picture as if it no longer mattered in the least. Something like fear was in his eyes as he asked again: "How did you get that flask? It belongs to Commodore Schrepke."

Munceford flopped back down on the bunk and started to unscrew the stopper. "Sure it does. That Dutchman dropped in on me a while ago. I suppose I disturbed his sulking next door when Finlander's strong-arm boy brought me down here after I got kicked off the bridge. I'm kind of under arrest, you know. Anyway, he came in to see why I was cursing a blue streak and, by God, I told him. Like I'm going to tell everybody who comes within shouting distance of me from here on out." He took a deep draft out of the flask and made a terrible grimace. "Christ! What I'd give for a decent shot of real American bourbon whisky! This German rot-gut gags you more with each drink!"

All of Packer's anger had drained out of him, and he leaned over Munceford with a deadly earnest expression on his tired face. "For God's sake, Ben! Have you somehow got yourself raving drunk? If you have, say so. If you haven't, tell me what you know about Schrepke. Why did he give you the flask?"

"He said he gave it to me so I'd anesthetize myself," Munceford answered heatedly, "because, he said, he couldn't stand the screams of cowards. Well, hell! I'm not a coward, I'm only a fool. I wasn't screaming, I was cursing. When I scream, it will only be to make this story heard in spite of anything he thinks he can do to stop it. He can blow up this ship, he can . . . Hey! Where are you going?"

Lieutenant Peter Packer had suddenly straightened up as if a spring had been released in his backbone, whirled around and hurled himself through the curtain into the passageway outside the cabin. Munceford stared at the rippling blue folds of material as they closed behind him, frowned over the fading sound of his running, then shrugged. "He can ply me with all the anesthetic he wants to. All the Schrepkes and Finlanders of the whole damned world combined won't shut me up. Besides, I'm a changed man. I'm getting smart. And . . . I've kicked the habit!" He turned the flask upside down and let the remaining schnapps splatter on the deck. There were only a few drops left.

# 12.

Lieutenant Packer shot up the shaft, stumbled into the wheelhouse and was so winded by his long frantic run up from the cabin deck that he fell across the radar pedestal and hung there, gasping for breath. There was a startled shuffling among the relief lookouts and Chief Quartermaster Rickmers squinted through the dark and rasped: "Who is that?" When nothing but agonized panting answered the challenge, Ensign Whitaker switched on his hooded flashlight and directed its beam toward the sound. "Peterpacker! What's the matter with you, for God's sake?"

"Is . . . is Commodore Schrepke on the bridge?" the Englishman managed to blurt out.

"No—he's not in his usual perch, but—"

"I've got to see the captain immediately!" The tone of his voice caused another uneasy stirring among the men in the wheelhouse. The helmsman dared a quick, startled glance over his shoulder.

Whitaker moved up to the radar pedestal, thrusting the beam of his flashlight into Packer's white face. "The captain is in his day cabin with the exec. But I don't think—"

"I've got to see him!" Packer yelled and pushed the flashlight away. He spun around, almost bowled over Rickmers, ran through the blackout curtain of the navigation office and burst into the day cabin, where he half collapsed against the desk.

Captain Finlander was stretched out on the bunk, talking in a low voice to Commander Allison, who was leaning against the bulkhead next to it. Both men stared in amazement at the intruder.

"Captain, sir! . . . I think Commodore Schrepke has gone mad! He's prowling about the ship with a pistol!"

Allison stared at Packer as if *he* were the one who had gone mad. It took Finlander a moment to react, then he wearily raised himself and swung his legs over the edge of the bunk. The crumpled radiogram announcing his impending promotion to flag rank fell to the deck and he stiffly bent down to pick it up before saying: "Carrying a pistol does not necessarily indicate insanity, Mr. Packer."

Allison shot in: "But to break in unannounced on your commanding officer could, and . . . ." What he saw in the young officer's face suddenly made him stop and sharply ask: "Are you sure there is something wrong with him?"

"Sir, I ran into him . . . only a few minutes ago," Packer insisted, pressing forth his words in painful spurts. "He had . . . an unholstered pistol in his belt . . . said very queer things . . . about totally obliterating a wrong . . . and acted strange with Munceford, and . . ."

"That one's likely to drive anybody nuts!" the exec snorted. "Pull yourself together, man, and make sense!"

But Lieutenant Packer would not be put off. "Spoke of anesthetizing him . . . said something to me about it . . . being too late . . . was on his way up and . . . he *laughed!*" Gulping down a very deep breath, he held it for a second in a tremendous effort to get hold of himself. When he let go, his voice rose to a near scream: "Sir! I'm absolutely positive he's planning to do something awful and it will happen any minute now!"

"Well, son," the captain said as if he were trying to soothe a hysterical child, "he can't very well sink this ship with a pistol."

"Can't he, sir? A pistol . . . and all the live warheads aboard?"

Allison and Finlander exchanged incredulous looks which contained the first glimmers of alarm. Ensign Whitaker had come to the door and was staring at Packer with a stunned expression; behind him, Chief Rickmers strained to see inside the cabin. The captain passed a hand over his eyes and it noticeably shook. "All right. But before we lose control in another uproar, let's make sure the commodore isn't in his usual place out on the bridge."

"He is not, sir," Whitaker positively injected.

Now Finlander got up off the bunk, strode over to the desk, pushed aside the sagging Packer and picked up the telephone. "This is the captain speaking. Immediately page Commodore Schrepke and ask him to come to the bridge. This is urgent. Request him to confirm to me by nearest phone that he is on his way." After hanging up, he checked his watch and looked into the Englishman's face. "If he does not report in exactly one minute, I'll have the JOOD take a detail and search the ship. Does that make you feel any better?"

Lieutenant Packer shook his head and whispered so low that only Finlander could barely hear him: "Fate was against us . . . it is too late. . . ." He was looking down at the crumpled photograph of Shebeona, which he still clutched in his hand.


Commodore Schrepke heard his name called over the PA system speaker inside the control turret of No. 2 ASROC launcher. He had been standing in the lee of it, pressing himself close to its steel side, staring out into the black void of the ocean, feeling the bite of the wind and sting of the snowflakes which were once again racing through the arctic night, allowing himself a few weirdly incongruous thoughts for a man about to die. Why had he spent so much of his life on this cursed sea which seemed eternally shrouded by the icy darkness of death? The same sea which had caressed the lovely shores of Marienstrand with gentle sun-dancing waves when a boy first heard her siren call and launched his toy ship upon her. Now she would get him at last, yet much too late. She had long since bared her heart to him and revealed its cold black abyss, which contained nothing but the ghosts of men who had perished as they fought her and one another. She had turned bright devotion into sullen obsession and pride into ignominious oblivion. This cold, cold sea and her cold, cold war!

Schrepke was brought back to his task when the bosun's pipe shrilled above the sound of wind and his name was called again. He glanced up at the dim mass of the bridge, then peered in through the slit in the control turret's door. He could see the red light burning bright on the panel and knew that nobody had been into the CIC to close the switches he had opened. Taking off his leather jacket, he let it drop to the deck. Then he pushed the pistol more securely into his belt and started climbing up the steel framework of the launcher.

When he reached the rocket booster and felt the smooth curve of it, he pulled off his gloves and fumbled blindly in the dark for the disconnected power cable. His fingers closed on its coils and pulled. With his other hand he reached for the contact to receive it. For what seemed an eternity his fingers searched along the slick, icy metal. Suddenly the ship's bullhorn on the base of the mainmast blared out:

"Commodore Schrepke! Are you on deck? You are urgently needed by the captain." The voice boomed through the darkness with a fearful, detached kind of desperation, and a second later floodlights flared on, one after another. The gray steel ramparts of the *Bedford*'s superstructure emerged out of the gloom into sharply etched lines of brilliant illumination and deep shadow, all a-swirl in whirlwinds of flying snow.

At the same instant Commodore Schrepke found the connector and drove home the fangs of the power cable. The warhead was armed. With methodical haste he resumed his grim climb toward the end where waited eleven hundred pounds of high explosives.

A small searchlight on the signal bridge burst on, probed about the decks, then suddenly caught the black figure crawling out on the launcher and fixed it in a glaring halo. A voice yelled: "There he is! There he is! Oh, God—stop him! Stop him, somebody!" But the *Bedford* dipped and rolled through a wave and seemed to nudge him along his way.

On the bridge Captain Finlander stood hatless in the biting wind, staring with a fatally entranced fascination. "He must have armed the system when I left him," he exclaimed softly to himself.

The entire bridge watch, excepting the helmsman abandoned to his unyielding duty in the empty wheelhouse, were lining the railing alongside their captain, but only Commander Allison heard his words and was struck by their terrible portent. "Fly down to the CIC!" he screamed at

Ensign Whitaker. "Run for our lives and kill the firing circuits! Run! *Run!*"

Whitaker tore himself away with a yell of terror, but Captain Finlander knew that he would never make it in time. Schrepke had almost reached the deadly tip of the missile where the ice-crusted percussion pin waited with a cold gleam in the glare of the searchlight. Out of the corner of his eye he saw Allison lift the microphone of the bullhorn to his mouth and draw in his breath to scream at the German, but he reached out and yanked it away, then brought it to his own mouth instead:

"Why are you doing this, Wolfgang? Why?" His voice rang out from the gray muzzle on the mast, not frantic with pleading, but with a fatalistic resignation which told that he knew the answer to be foregone and was willing to accept it.

Every man on the bridge could clearly see Commodore Schrepke draw the pistol from his belt as he straddled the part of the missile which protruded beyond the structure of the launcher. He turned his face toward them when he heard the captain's question and as he did that, his hat blew off and crazily fluttered away to vanish in the dark beyond the rushing wake. Then his voice came back to them, answering loudly and clearly without benefit of electronic amplification:

"Only when Captain Ahab vanishes from the face of the seas along with his Moby Dick, and not a single trace of either is left to inflame the vengeance of their kin . . . only then can there follow peace!"

Somewhere along the forward part of the superstructure of the *Bedford* there came the sound of iron doors bursting open and the confused clatter of running feet. But they were too far away. The decks below the bridge were still empty as Commander Allison leaned over the railing and yelled: "Shoot him! Shoot him down!" He straightened up and shouted again to the helpless men around him: "Shoot him! . . . My God! Among all the fantastic weaponry of this ship, is there nothing with which to shoot a lone madman?" Then he saw Schrepke aim his pistol at the warhead and, together with all the other men on the bridge, recoiled and threw himself down behind the thin metal shield of the combing. Only Captain Finlander remained upright, facing the end unflinching.

A fiery red rose blossomed out from the *Bedford*'s waist, appeared to hang suspended in a convulsed ball of flaming petals, then burst into an obliterating explosion outward and upward. In the foretop Seamen Thorbjornsen and Jones saw its searing glow rising toward them as they pressed their faces against the glass windshield of the crow's-nest; it protected them from being instantly incinerated as it enveloped the foretop, but they felt the mainmast buckle and start to fall and knew they would be dead in a few seconds. The explosion acted downward too, ripping through decks and bulkheads which bulged and flew apart into splatters of molten metal. Warheads in No. 2 magazine ignited themselves spontaneously from the searing heat and concussion, adding their energy to the holocaust. No. 1 boiler blew up with a deafening roar which Fireman Bert Meggs never heard because he was scalded to death in one thousandth of a second; the other three boilers went in quick succession, bursting their casings and releasing all of the *Bedford*'s eighty thousand horsepower in a cataclysmal storm of fire and superheated steam. It tore through the open watertight doors to the engine room, then collapsed the entire bulkhead. Ruptured fuel lines spewed black oil into the inferno where scorched flesh mingled with molten metal. Up at the Master Control, Lieutenant Commander Franklin's and Chief Mac-Kay's last living sight was of the turbines rising up off their beds and the steel hull breaking apart like cardboard to allow a wall of green water to fall in upon them; they died only a fraction of a second later than Fireman Meggs, only two seconds after Commodore Schrepke had pulled the trigger of his pistol. By the third second the *Bedford*'s amidships was enveloped in a cascade of explosions which broke her in two between the crumbling funnels. The Beek fell screaming through a fiery crevasse which engulfed him and his beloved HUFF-DUFF. The severed after section slewed off sideways and was almost instantly driven under by the still turning screws; nearly one hundred enlisted men lying in their bunks were taken from living to eternal sleep with but the briefest nightmare transition. . . . Only one man among them, Collins, the Negro steward, suffered a little longer. He was awake, having faithfully resumed his medical studies instead of seeking sleep when the action was over, and now looked up from the delicate sketch he was making of the human heart, meeting death in full consciousness as he was probing the mysteries of life.

But even in her death throes the *Bedford*'s intricate automation systems were attempting to function and save her. In the forward part, which remained afloat and still slicing through the waves at nearly twenty knots, fire alarms were clanging with a feeble din compared to the uproar of explosions. Automatic watertight doors were activated by their miraculous mechanisms and started to close, but mostly too late and well behind the columns of fire which were racing through the passageways. In sick bay Merlin Queffle's hypersensitive eardrums were blown in by the shock wave racing ahead of the flames which cremated him an instant later, as they did Ensign Ralston in the next bunk. Lieutenant Commander Chester Porter died in the receiving office with his pen poised over the ensign's Form 28 in which he had just recorded the young officer's nervous breakdown with a certain smug satisfaction. No. 9 fuel-oil tank, only half full of oil and choked with fumes by a clogged vent, ignited and exploded, breaking through the bulkhead to the wardroom, where Lieutenants Krindlemeyer and Spitzer were holding an oblivious and weary post-mortem of the action against Moby Dick; they died trying to think of ways of making their miraculous electronic weaponry safe from human errors. The next explosion, still less than five seconds after the first, took place in a rocket-propellant storage compartment, which in turn burst the armored walls of No. 1 magazine containing two hundred hedgehog depth charges. With a final roar the *Bedford* now broke apart once more, the third piece spewing writhing serpentines of fire after the flaming ball which had shot into the night and turned the snowflakes for miles around into floating rubies. In his cabin Ben Munceford had been gripping the edge of his bunk, his body knotting tighter as each blast which racked through the ship came one upon the other with the sound of an approaching thunderbolt, and now he screamed as he saw the walls buckle around him, then peel away. Ice-cold water rushed in, turned the flickering lights green before extinguishing them, then engulfed everything in a sinking maelstrom of absolute darkness. But Ben Munceford flailed and fought against it as if he could keep up the sinking ship with his own furious will to live.

It so chanced that as the *Bedford* was sucked down into the deep, a part of her disintegrating hull broke loose and driven by the upward force of trapped air shot back to the surface of the roiled sea. Within this wreckage was carried one single man, Ben Munceford, hurled clear before he could burst his lungs in his wild struggle. His ship was gone, but she had left the sea on fire, and for another perilous moment burning oil threatened to break his gasping hold on life. Then the big swells intervened, scattered the flames, extinguishing them and plunging all into merciful darkness. A charred life raft, blown from its lashings but still buoyant, found the floundering man and allowed him to use the last of his strength to claw himself over its still steaming sides. With his body anointed by an insulating slime of oil, he lay upon the raft, his blood fighting the bitter cold with the fortifying effect of the alcohol it had absorbed only a short time before, but with his mind slipping into a limbo as black as the deep which had taken all his shipmates. Thus he floated on a dirge-like main, one hour passing, then another, until a gray dawn finally overtook the night. The unharming Greenland sharks glided by as if with padlocks on their mouths; the savage skua gulls sailed with sheathed beaks. On the fourth hour a ship drew near, nearer, and picked him up at last. It was the devious cruising *Novo Sibirsk,* who, in her retracing search after her missing children, found only another orphan.

# MARK RASCOVICH

*Born in San Francisco, California, Mark Rascovich
lived in Europe from the time he was two years old until he
was twenty-one. He attended schools in Germany, England,
Sweden and Paris, and was graduated from the Sorbonne. His
World War II service included three years as a reconnaissance
pilot in the Alaskan and African theaters and concluded
with transport duty on the North Atlantic. After the war he
engaged in ocean towing and salvage work. He then turned
to writing for radio and films. Mr. Rascovich has traveled
throughout Europe and the Americas, the Near East and
Africa. He holds pilot licenses for land and sea aircraft and for
watercraft. Mr. Rascovich published a previous novel,* Flight
of the Dancing Bear.

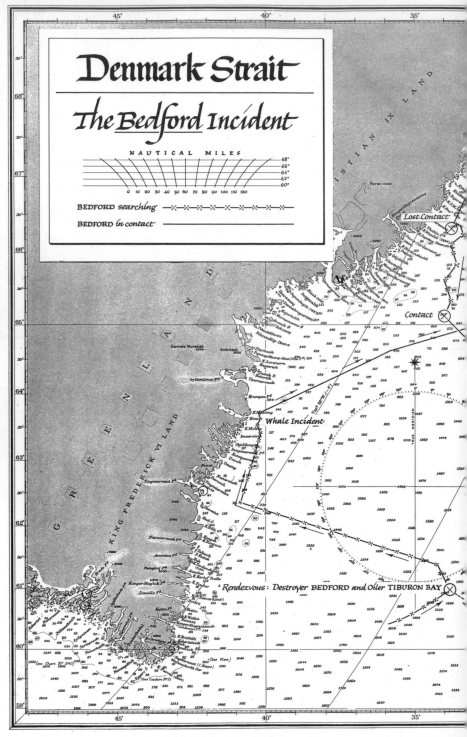

# Denmark Strait

## The Bedford Incident

NAUTICAL MILES

0 10 20 30 40 50 60 70 80 90 100 110 120

68°
66°
64°
62°
60°

BEDFORD *searching* ✕✕✕✕✕✕✕✕✕

BEDFORD *in contact* ━━━━━━━

GREENLAND

CHRISTIAN IX LAND

KING FREDERICK VI LAND

Lost Contact ⊗

Contact ⊗

Whale Incident

² Rendezvous: Destroyer BEDFORD and Oiler TIBURON BAY ⊗

*Adapted from British Admiralty Chart No. 246 with the permission*